THE PLAYBOY INTERVIEWS

OTHER BOOKS IN THE PLAYBOY INTERVIEWS SERIES

THEY PLAYED THE GAME | Henry Aaron • Kareem Abdul-Jabbar • Lance Armstrong • Barry Bonds • Jim Brown • Dale Earnhardt Jr. • Brett Favre • Wayne Gretzky • Allen Iverson • Derek Jeter • Michael Jordan • Billie Jean King • Joe Namath • Shaquille O'Neal • Pete Rose • O.J. Simpson • Mike Tyson

THE DIRECTORS | Robert Altman • Ingmar Bergman • Joel and Ethan Coen • Francis Ford Coppola • Clint Eastwood • Federico Fellini • John Huston • Stanley Kubrick • Spike Lee • David Mamet • Roman Polanski • Martin Scorsese • Oliver Stone • Quentin Tarantino • Orson Welles • Billy Wilder

THE PLAYBOY® INTERVIEWS

LARGER THAN LIFE

EDITED BY STEPHEN RANDALL AND
THE EDITORS OF *PLAYBOY* MAGAZINE

Milwaukie

THE PLAYBOY INTERVIEWS: LARGER THAN LIFE © 2006 Playboy Enterprises International, Inc. From Playboy magazine: copyright © 1963, 1964, 1965, 1966, 1971, 1972, 1973, 1975, 1978, 1979, 1982

No portion of this publication may be reproduced or transmitted, in any form or by any means, without the express written permission of the copyright holders. All rights reserved. Playboy and the Rabbit Head design are trademarks of Playboy.

M Press
10956 SE Main Street
Milwaukie, OR 97222
mpressbooks.com

Portions of this book are reprinted from issues of *Playboy* magazine.
Cover and series design by Tina Alessi & Lia Ribacchi

Library of Congress Cataloging-in-Publication Data

The Playboy interviews : larger than life / edited by Stephen Randall and the editors of Playboy magazine. -- 1st M Press ed.
    p. cm.
 Includes bibliographical references and index.
 ISBN-13: 978-1-59582-045-7
 ISBN-10: 1-59582-045-0
 1. Celebrities--United States--Interviews. 2. United States--Biography. 3. Interviews--United States. I. Randall, Stephen. II. Playboy (Chicago, Ill.) III. Title: Larger than life.
CT220.P58 2005
920.073--dc22
                        2006029399

ISBN-10: 1-59582-045-0
ISBN-13: 978-1-59582-045-7
First M Press Edition: December 2006

10 9 8 7 6 5 4 3 2 1

Printed in U.S.A.
Distributed by Publishers Group West

CONTENTS

vii   **INTRODUCTION** by Stephen Randall

11   **THE BEATLES** | February 1965, interviewed by Jean Shepherd

35   **FRANK SINATRA** | February 1963, interviewed by Joe Hyams

47   **MARLON BRANDO** | January 1979, interviewed by Lawrence Grobel

105   **BETTE DAVIS** | July 1982, interviewed by Bruce Williamson

143   **BOB DYLAN** | March 1966, interviewed by Nat Hentoff | March 1978, interviewed by Ron Rosenbaum

197   **MAE WEST** | January 1971, interviewed by C. Robert Jennings

217   **WALTER CRONKITE** | June 1973, interviewed by Ron Powers

253   **HOWARD COSELL** | May 1972, interviewed by Lawrence Linderman

287   **CASSIUS CLAY / MUHAMMAD ALI** | October 1964, interviewed by Alex Haley | November 1975, interviewed by Lawrence Linderman

339   **BOB HOPE** | December 1973, interviewed by William Murray

361   **JOHN WAYNE** | May 1971, interviewed by Richard Warren Lewis

389   **INDEX**

INTRODUCTION

By Stephen Randall
Deputy Editor, Playboy *magazine*

Those of us who work at *Playboy* often think of the *Playboy Interview* as an exclusive club, open to 12 people per year who have made headlines, influenced the culture or made an impression worth being featured in journalism's premiere Q&A feature.

If that's true, then prepare to meet the VIP section of the club: 14 subjects we think of as larger than life. This collection features people who have moved beyond stardom. You don't have to be a music fan to know the Beatles or Frank Sinatra. Muhammad Ali long ago transcended the sport he redefined. Walter Cronkite has become the paragon to which all other broadcast journalists are compared.

These are men and women whose impact on the culture was so significant they changed the way we viewed ourselves. Before they existed, we were one thing; after them we became another.

That's what makes this group of *Playboy Interviews* so compelling. It is an opportunity to go inside the minds of men and women who changed our world. And unlike so much modern journalism, these aren't short, cursory visits aimed at eliciting a soundbite, but thoughtful, lengthy, intelligent and comprehensive conversations in which these cultural forces are allowed to express themselves in their own words. The result is often more revealing than the best book-length biographies.

That's not to say that everything you'll read will please you. Speaking candidly in less politically correct times—and before the days of media training and spin doctors—some of these subjects share views you'll most likely find reprehensible or, at best, sadly misguided. Not only do the interviews expose the innermost thoughts of these legendary characters during the peak of their importance, but they also shed light on the times in which they lived that shaped their world views.

The interviews in this book are not just the work of 12 great interviewers, but of two talented editors who shaped and guided the *Playboy Interview*. The late Murray Fisher helped create the concept in 1962 and oversaw the interview until 1974. Barry Golson then took over until he left the magazine in 1990. None of these amazing interviews would exist without them.

THE PLAYBOY INTERVIEWS

 February 1965

THE BEATLES

A *candid conversation with England's mop-topped millionaire minstrels*

Our interviewer this month is the inimitable Jean Shepherd, whose nostalgically comic boyhood reminiscences and acerbic social commentary have earned him not only the applause of *Playboy*'s readers, but also a loyal audience of three million for the free-form one-man radio talkathon which he wings weekly over New York's WOR from the stage of The Limelight in Greenwich Village. A nimble-witted and resourceful broadcast reporter who's tilted verbal lances with such formidable subjects as Malcolm X and Harry S. Truman, he debuts herein as an interviewer for the printed page. Shepherd writes of his subjects:

"I joined the Beatles in Edinburgh in the midst of a wild, swinging personal appearance tour they were making throughout the British Isles. The first glimpse I had of them was in a tiny, overheated, totally disorganized dressing room backstage between their first and second shows. I had taken the night flight up from London and suddenly found myself face to face with one, or rather four, of the 20th century's major living legends. All of them looked up suspiciously as I walked in, then went back to eating, drinking and tuning guitars as though I didn't exist. Legends have a way of ignoring mere mortals. I looked hard at them through the cigarette smoke, and they began to come into focus, sprawling half-dressed and self-involved amid the continuous uproar that surrounds their lives.

"They had been playing one-night stands in Glasgow and Dundee, and I went along with them from Edinburgh to Plymouth, Bournemouth and half a dozen other towns. They were all the same: wild, ravening multitudes, hundreds of policemen, mad rushes through the night in a black Austin Princess to a carefully guarded inn or chalet for a few fitful hours of sleep. And then the whole cycle started all over again.

"It became impossible to tell one town from another, since to us they were just a succession of dressing rooms and hotel suites. The screams were the same. The music was the same. It all assumed the ritual quality of a fertility rite. Latter-day Druids, the Beatles sat in their dressing room—a plywood Stonehenge—surrounded by sweaty T-shirts, trays of french fries, steak, pots of tea and the inevitable TV set; while from somewhere off beyond the walls of the theater came the faint, eerie wailing of their worshippers, like the sea or the wind. But the Beatles no more heard it than a New York cop hears traffic. Totally oblivious to the mob—and to the honks and plunks of other Liverpudlian rock 'n' rollers warming up down the hall—they sat sipping scotch from paper cups and watching *Dr. Kildare* on the telly.

"I, meanwhile, sat and watched *them*—and wondered why. In two years they had become a phenomenon that had somehow transcended stardom—or even showbiz. They were mythical beings, inspiring a fanaticism bordering on religious ecstasy among millions all over the world. I began to have the uncomfortable feeling that all this fervor had nothing whatever to do with entertainment, or with talent, or even with the Beatles themselves. I began to feel that they were the catalyst of a sudden world madness that would have burst upon us whether they had come on the scene or not. If the Beatles had never existed, we would have had to invent them. They are not prodigious talents by any yardstick, but like hula hoops and yo-yos, they are at the right place at the right time, and whatever it is that triggers the mass hysteria of fads has made them wailing myths.

"Everywhere we went, people stared in openmouthed astonishment that there were actually flesh-and-blood human beings who looked just like the Beatle dolls they had at home. It was as though Santa Claus had suddenly shown up at a Christmas party. Night after night, phalanxes of journalists would stand grinning, groveling, obsequious, jotting down the Beatles' every word. In city after city the local mayor, countess, duke, earl and prelate would be led in, bowing and scraping, to bask for a few fleeting moments in their ineffable aura. They don't give interviews; they grant audiences, which is the way the world wants its legends to behave.

"All around them, wherever they go, shimmers a strange, filmy, translucent pall of palpable unreality, so thick that you can almost taste it. And at the very center of this vast cloud of fantasy are the four young men themselves, by far the most real and least enchanted of them all. They have managed somehow to remain remarkably human, totally unlike the kewpies created by fandom and the press. In real life, the Beatles don't make Beatle noises. Nor are they precocious teenagers. They are grown-up, scotch-drinking men who know what the world expects of them—which is to be Beatles and to wear long hair, funny clothes and be cute. But all that stops when the curtain falls and the high-heeled shoes come off and the drums are put away.

"Their unimaginable success—which has made them world figures important enough for the Prime Minister and the Queen's consort to discuss in news conferences, and has made them without a doubt the most successful money machine in recent times—has left them faintly bemused, but also extremely guarded in their day-by-day life, almost as though they're afraid that an extraloud sneeze will burst the bubble and they'll be back in reality like the rest of us.

"Of the four, George Harrison seems to be one of the most amused and least unsettled by it all. The truest swinger among them, he is also the most sarcastic, and unquestionably the most egotistical; he fingers his hair a lot, and has a marked tendency to pause meaningfully and frequently before mirrors. Even so, he's a very likeable chap—if he happens to like you. John Lennon, on the other hand, is a rather cool customer, and far less hip than he's been made out to be. He does radiate a kind of on-the-top-of-it confidence, however, and is the unacknowledged leader of the group. Equally poised, but far more articulate and outgoing, Paul McCartney (sometimes known as the 'cute Beatle') reminded me of Ned, the fun-loving Rover Boy: He's bright, open-faced and friendly—the friendliest of the lot; but unlike Ned, he also has a keen eye for a well-turned figure, and he worries a lot about the future. Ringo Starr, the smallest Beatle—even smaller in person than he appears to be on the screen—is a curious contrast with the others. Taciturn, even a bit sullen, he spends a good deal of time sitting in corners staring moodily at the venetian blinds. Still he has a way of growing on you—if he doesn't grow away from you.

"But they all find it difficult to make any real contact with anybody outside of their immediate circle. And vice versa. As they appear unreal to their maniacal fans, so their fans appear to them. And an incessant infestation of interviewers has erected a wall of hackneyed wisecracks and ghostwritten ripostes between them and the press. So getting to know the Beatles, and to draw them out, was a discouraging task at first. I traveled and lived with them for three days before the first crack appeared in the invisible shield that surrounds them. Paul suddenly asked me about my cold—which I had been nursing since my arrival—and I knew that real life had reared its unexpected head.

"We began to become friends. And a week or so and what felt like 10,000 miles and 10 million screams later, we found ourselves ensconced in a hotel room in Torquay in southwest England, on the gray shores of the English Channel. They had just played two shows before a raging throng of subteens in nearby Exeter. Within seconds after the final curtain, like a gang of convicts executing a well-rehearsed and perfectly synchronized prison break, they had eluded a gimlet-eyed army of idolators outside the stage door and careened off in anonymous vehicles, with coat collars up and hats pulled low—four hunted fugitives and one terrified hostage (me)—into the wintry night. Pseudonymously registered and safely padlocked in their suite at the hotel—the identity and whereabouts of which were a more closely guarded secret than SAC's fail-safe recall code—they slipped out of their Beatle suits and into the comfort of sportswear, ordered up a goodly supply of Coke, tea and booze, and began to unwind. We found ourselves talking quietly—and all of a sudden, almost communicating. Somewhere along the line I turned on my tape machine. Here's what I recorded."

PLAYBOY: OK, we're on. Why don't we begin by—
JOHN: Doing *Hamlet*.
RINGO: Yeah, yeah, let's do that.
PLAYBOY: That sounds like fun, but just for laughs, why don't we do an *interview* instead?
GEORGE: Say, that's a fine idea. I wish I'd thought of that.
PAUL: What shall we ask you for a first question?
RINGO: About those Bunny girls—
PLAYBOY: No comment. Let's start over. Ringo, you're the last Beatle to join the group, aren't you?
RINGO: Yes.

PLAYBOY: How long were you fellows working together as a team before Ringo joined up?

JOHN: A few years probably, sort of off and on, really, for three years or so.

PAUL: Yeah, but really amateur.

GEORGE: The local pub, you know. And in each other's uncles' houses.

JOHN: And at George's brother's wedding. Things like that.

PLAYBOY: When you joined the others, Ringo, they weren't quite as big as they are now, were they?

RINGO: They were the biggest thing in Liverpool. In them days that was big enough.

PAUL: This is a point we've made before. Some say that man is made of muscle and blood. . . . No, they don't. They say, "How come you've suddenly been able to adjust to fame, you know, to nationwide fame and things?" It all started quite nicely with us, you see, in our own sphere, where we used to play—in Liverpool. We never used to play outside it, except when we went to Hamburg. Just those two circles. And in each of them, I think we were round the highest paid, and probably at the time the most popular. So in actual fact we had the same feeling of being famous then as we do now.

GEORGE: We were recognized then, too, only people didn't chase us about.

PAUL: But it just grew. The quantity grew, not the *quality* of the feeling.

PLAYBOY: When did you know that you had really hit it big? There must have been one night when you knew it had really begun.

JOHN: Well, we'd been playing round in Liverpool for a bit without getting anywhere, trying to get work, and the other groups kept telling us, "You'll do all right, you'll get work someday." And then we went to Hamburg, and when we came back, suddenly we were a wow. Mind you, 70 percent of the audience thought we were a *German* wow, but we didn't care about that.

PAUL: We were billed in the paper: "From Hamburg—The Beatles."

JOHN: In Liverpool, people didn't even know we were from Liverpool. They thought that we were from Hamburg. They said, "Christ, they speak good English!" Which we did, of course, being English. But that's when we first, you know, stood there being cheered for the first time.

PAUL: That was when we felt we were—

JOHN: On the way up—

PAUL: Gonna make it in Liverpool.

PLAYBOY: How much were you earning then?

JOHN: For that particular night, $20.

PLAYBOY: Apiece?

JOHN: For the *group*! Hell, we used to work for a lot less than that.

PAUL: We used to work for about three or four dollars a night.

RINGO: Plus all the Coke we could drink. And we drank a lot.

PLAYBOY: Do you remember the first journalist who came to see you and said, "I want to write about you"?

RINGO: We went around to *them* at first, didn't we?

JOHN: We went and said, "We're a group and we've got this record out. Will you—"

GEORGE: And then the door would slam.

PLAYBOY: We've heard it said that when you first went to America you were doubtful that you'd make it over there.

JOHN: That's true. We didn't think we were going to make it at all. It was only Brian telling us we were going to make it. And George. Brian Epstein, our manager, and George Harrison.

GEORGE: I knew we had a good chance—because of the record sales over there.

JOHN: The thing is, in America it just seemed ridiculous—I mean, the idea of having a hit record over there. It was just, you know, something you could never do. That's what I thought, anyhow. But then I realized that it's just the same here, that kids everywhere all go for the same stuff. And seeing we'd done it in England and all, there's no reason why we couldn't do it in America, too. But the American disc jockeys didn't know about British records; they didn't play them; nobody promoted them, and so you didn't have hits.

GEORGE: Well, there were one or two doing it as a novelty.

JOHN: But it wasn't until *Time* and *Life* and *Newsweek* came over and wrote articles and created an interest in us that the disc jockeys started playing our records. And Capitol said, "Well, can we have their records?" You know, they had been offered our records years ago, and they didn't want them. But when they heard we were big over here they said, "Can we have them now?" So we said, "As long as you promote them." So Capitol promoted, and with them and all these articles on us, the records just took off.

PLAYBOY: There's been some dispute, among your fans and critics, about whether you're primarily entertainers or musicians—or perhaps neither. What's your own opinion?

JOHN: We're moneymakers first; then we're entertainers.

RINGO: No, we're not.

JOHN: What are we, then?

RINGO: Dunno. Entertainers first.

JOHN: OK.

RINGO: 'Cause we were entertainers before we were moneymakers.

JOHN: That's right, of course. It's just that the press drives it into you, so you say it 'cause they like to hear it, you know?

PAUL: Still, we'd be idiots to say that it isn't a constant inspiration to be making a lot of money. It always is, to anyone. I mean, why do big business tycoons stay big business tycoons? It's not because they're inspired at the greatness of big business; they're in it because they're making money at it. We'd be idiots if we pretended we were in it solely for kicks. In the beginning we were, but at the same time, we were hoping to make a bit of cash. It's a switch around now, though, from what it used to be. We used to be doing it mainly for kicks and not making a lot of money, and now we're making a lot of money without too many kicks—except that we happen to like the money that we're making. But we still enjoy making records, going onstage, making films, and all that business.

JOHN: We *love* every minute of it, Beatle people!

PLAYBOY: As hard-bitten refugees from the Liverpool slums—according to heart-rending fan magazine biographies—do you feel prepared to cope with all this sudden wealth?

PAUL: We've managed to make the adjustment. Contrary to rumor, you see, none of us was brought up in any slums or in great degrees of poverty. We've always had enough; we've never been starving.

JOHN: Yeah, we saw these articles in the American fan mags that "those boys struggled up from the slums—"

GEORGE: We never starved. Even Ringo hasn't.

RINGO: Even I.

PLAYBOY: What kind of families do you come from?

GEORGE: Well, you know, not rich. Just workin' class. They've got jobs. Just work.

PLAYBOY: What does your father do?

GEORGE: Well, he doesn't do anything now. He used to be a bus driver—

JOHN: In the merchant navy.

PLAYBOY: Do you have any sisters or brothers, George?

GEORGE: I've got two brothers.

JOHN: And no sisters to speak of.

PLAYBOY: And how about you, Paul?

PAUL: I've got one brother, and a father who used to be a cotton salesman down in New Orleans, you know. That's probably why I look a bit tanned. But seriously, folks, he occasionally had trouble paying bills—but it was never, you know, never, "Go out and pick blackberries, son; we're a bit short this week."

PLAYBOY: How about you, John?

JOHN: Oh, just the same. I used to have an auntie. And I had a dad whom I couldn't quite find.

RINGO: John lived with the Mounties.

JOHN: Yeah, the Mounties. They fed me well. No starvation.

PLAYBOY: How about *your* family, Ringo?

RINGO: Just workin' class. I was brought up with my mother and me grandparents. And then she married me stepfather when I was 13. All the time she was working. I never starved. I used to get most things.

GEORGE: Never starved?

RINGO: No, I never starved. She always fed me. I was an only child, so it wasn't amazing.

PLAYBOY: It's quite fashionable in some circles in America to hate your parents. But none of you seem to.

RINGO: We're probably just as against the things our parents liked or stood for as they are in America. But we don't hate our parents for it.

PLAYBOY: It's often exactly the opposite in America.

PAUL: Well, you know, a lot of Americans are unbalanced. I don't care what you say. No, really. A lot of them are quite normal, of course, but we've met many unbalanced ones. You know the type of person, like the political Whig.

PLAYBOY: How do you mean?

PAUL: You know—the professional politician type; an authority sort of thing. Some of them are just mad! And I've met some really maniac American girls! Like this girl who walked up to me in a press conference and said, "I'm Lily." I said, "Hello, how do you do?" And she said, "Doesn't my name mean anything to you?" I said, "Ah, no . . ." and I thought, "Oh God, it's one of these people that you've met and you should know." And so Derek, our press agent who happened to be there at the time, hanging over my shoulder, giving me quotes, which happens at every press conference—

GEORGE: You better not say that.

PAUL: Oh yes, that's not true, Beatle people! But he was sort of hanging about and said, "Well, did you ring, or did you write, or something?"

THE PLAYBOY INTERVIEWS

And she said, "No." And he said, "Well, how did you get in touch with Paul? How do you know him?" And she said, "Through God." Well, there was sort of a ghastly silence. I mean, we both sort of gulped and blushed. I said, "Well, that's very nice, Lily. Thanks very much. I must be off now."

PLAYBOY: There wasn't a big lightning bolt from the sky?

PAUL: No there wasn't. But I talked to her afterward, and she said she'd got a vision from God and God had said to her—

JOHN: "It's been a hard day's night." [*Laughter*]

PAUL: No, God had said, "Listen, Lil, Paul is waiting for you; he's in love with you and he wants to marry you, so go down and meet him, and he'll know you right away." It's very funny, you know. I was trying to persuade her that she didn't in actual fact have a vision from God, that it was—

GEORGE: It was probably somebody *disguised* as God.

PAUL: You wouldn't hardly ever meet someone like that in England, but there seemed to me to be a lot like her in America.

JOHN: Well, there are a lot more people in America, so you've got a much bigger group to get nutters from.

PLAYBOY: Speaking of nutters, do you ever wake up in the morning, look in the mirror and say, "My God, I'm a Beatle?"

PAUL: No, not quite. [*Laughter*]

JOHN: Actually, we only do it in each other's company. I know I never do it alone.

RINGO: We used to do it more. We'd get in the car, I'd look over at John and say, "Christ, look at you; you're a bloody phenomenon!" and just laugh—'cause it was only him, you know. And a few old friends of ours done it, from Liverpool. I'd catch them looking at me, and I'd say, "What's the matter with you?" It's just daft, them screaming and laughing, thinking I'm one of them people.

PLAYBOY: A Beatle?

RINGO: Yes.

PAUL: The thing that makes *me* know we've made it is like tonight, when we slipped into a sweetshop. In the old days we could have just walked into a sweetshop and nobody would have noticed us. We would have just got our sweets and gone out. But tonight we just walked in—it took a couple of seconds—and the people just dropped their sweets. Before, you see, there would have been no reaction at all. Except possibly, "Look at the fellow with the long hair. Doesn't he look daft?" But nowadays they're just amazed; they can't believe it. But actually we're no different.

PLAYBOY: The problem is that you don't seem to be like real people. You're Beatles.

PAUL: I know. It's very funny, that.

GEORGE: It's all the publicity.

PAUL: We're taken in by it, too. Because *we* react exactly the same way to stars *we* meet. When we meet people that we've seen on the telly or in films, we still think, "Wow!"

JOHN: It's a good thing, because we still get just as tickled.

PAUL: The thing is that people, when they see you on TV and in magazines and up in a film, and hear you on the radio, they never expect to meet you, you know, even our fans. Their wish is to meet you, but in the back of their mind they never think they're actually gonna meet us, they just don't believe it.

PLAYBOY: You mean you're brave enough to venture out in the streets without a bodyguard?

RINGO: Sure.

GEORGE: We're always on the street. Staggering about.

RINGO: Floggin' our bodies.

GEORGE: You catch John sleeping in the gutter occasionally.

PLAYBOY: When people see you in the street, do you ever have any action?

GEORGE: Well, not really, because when you're walking about, you don't bump into groups of people, as a rule. People don't walk round in gangs, as a rule.

PLAYBOY: Can you even go out shopping without getting mobbed by them, individually or collectively?

JOHN: We avoid that.

PAUL: The mountain comes to Muhammad.

GEORGE: The shop comes to us, as he says. But sometimes we just roll into a store and buy the stuff and leg out again.

PLAYBOY: Isn't that looking for trouble?

PAUL: No, we walk four times faster than the average person.

PLAYBOY: Can you eat safely in restaurants?

GEORGE: Sure we can. I was there the other night.

JOHN: Where?

GEORGE: Restaurants.

PAUL: Of course we're known in the restaurants we go in.

GEORGE: And usually it's only Americans that'll bother you.

PLAYBOY: Really?

GEORGE: Really. If we go to a restaurant in London, there's always going to be a couple of them eating there; you just tell the waiter to hold them off if they try to come over. If they come over anyway, you just sign.

RINGO: But you know, the restaurants I go to, probably if I wasn't famous, I wouldn't go to them. Even if I had the same money and I wasn't famous I wouldn't go to them, because the people that go to them are drags, such snobs, you see, they won't bother to come over to your table. They pretend they don't even know who you are, and you get away with an easy night.

GEORGE: And they think they're laughing at us, but really we're laughing at them. 'Cause we know they know who we are.

RINGO: How's that?

GEORGE: They're not going to be like the rest and ask for autographs.

RINGO: And if they do, we just swear at 'em.

GEORGE: Well, *I* don't, Beatle people. I sign the autograph and thank them profusely for coming over and offer them a piece of my chop.

JOHN: If we're in the middle of a meal, I usually say, "Do you mind waiting till I'm finished?"

GEORGE: And then we keep eating until they give up and leave.

JOHN: That's not true, Beatle people!

PLAYBOY: Apart from these occupational hazards, are you happy in your work? Do you really enjoy getting pelted by jelly beans and being drowned out by thousands of screaming subteenagers?

RINGO: Yes.

GEORGE: We still find it exciting.

JOHN: Well, you know—

PAUL: After a while, actually, you begin to get used to it, you know.

PLAYBOY: Can you really get *used* to this?

PAUL: Well, you still get excited when you go onto a stage and the audience is great, you know. But obviously, you're not as excited as you were when you first heard that one of your records reached number one. I mean, you really do go *wild* with excitement then; you go out drinking and celebrating and things.

RINGO: Now we just go out drinkin' anyway.

PLAYBOY: Do you stick pretty much together offstage?

JOHN: Well, yes and no. Groups like this are normally not friends, you know; they're just four people out there thrown together to make an act. There may be two of them who sort of go off and are friends, you know, but—

GEORGE: Just what do you mean by that?

JOHN: Strictly platonic, of course. But we're all rather good friends, as it happens.

PLAYBOY: Then you do see a good deal of one another when you're not working?

PAUL: Well, you know, it depends. We needn't always go to the same places together. In earlier days, of course, when we didn't know London, and we didn't know anyone in London, then we really did stick together, and it would really be just like four fellows down from the north for a coach trip. But nowadays, you know, we've got our own girlfriends—they're *in* London—so that we each normally go out with our girlfriends on our days off. Except for John, of course, who's married.

PLAYBOY: Do any of the rest of you have plans to settle down?

PAUL: I haven't got any.

GEORGE: Ringo and I are gettin' married.

PLAYBOY: Oh? To whom?

GEORGE: To each other. But that's a thing you better keep a secret.

RINGO: You better not tell anybody.

GEORGE: I mean, if we said something like that, people'd probably think we're queers. After all, that's not something you can put in a reputable magazine like *Playboy*. And anyway, we don't want to start the rumor going.

PLAYBOY: We'd better change the subject, then. Do you remember the other night when this girl came backstage—

GEORGE: Naked—

PLAYBOY: Unfortunately not. And she said—

GEORGE: "It's been a hard day's night."

PLAYBOY: No, she pointed at you, George, and said, "There's a Beatle!" And you others said, "That's George." And she said, "No, it's a Beatle!"

JOHN: And you said, "This way to the bedroom."

PLAYBOY: No, it was, "Would you like us to introduce you to him?"

JOHN: I like my line better.

PLAYBOY: Well, the point is that she didn't believe that there was such a thing as an actual Beatle *person*.

JOHN: She's right, you know.

PLAYBOY: Do you run across many like her?

GEORGE: Is there any other kind?

PLAYBOY: In America, too?

RINGO: Everywhere.

PLAYBOY: With no exceptions?

JOHN: In America, you mean?

PLAYBOY: Yes.

JOHN: A few.

PAUL: Yeah. Some of those American girls have been great.

JOHN: Like Joan Baez.

PAUL: Joan Baez is good, yeah, very good.

JOHN: She's the only one I like.

GEORGE: And Jayne Mansfield. *Playboy* made her.

PAUL: She's a bit different, isn't she? *Different*.

RINGO: She's soft.

GEORGE: Soft and warm.

PAUL: Actually, she's a clot.

RINGO: Says Paul, the god of the Beatles.

PAUL: I didn't mean it, Beatle people! Actually, I haven't even met her. But you won't print that anyway, of course, because *Playboy* is very pro-Mansfield. They think she's a rave. But she really is an old bag.

PLAYBOY: By the way, what are Beatle people?

JOHN: It's something they use in the fan mags in America. They all start out, "Hi there, Beatle people, 'spect you're wondering what the Fab Foursome are doing these days!" Now we use it all the time, too.

PAUL: It's low-level journalese.

JOHN: But I mean, you know, there's nothing wrong with that. It's harmless.

PLAYBOY: Speaking of low-level journalese, there was a comment in one of the London papers the other day that paralleled you guys with Hitler. Seriously! It says that you have the same technique of drawing cheers from the crowd—

PAUL: That power isn't being so much like Hitler; it's that the audiences and the show have got sort of, you know, a Hitler *feel* about them, because the audience will shout when they're told to. That's what the critic was talking about. Actually, that article was one which I really got annoyed about, 'cause she's never even met us.

PLAYBOY: She?

PAUL: The woman who wrote it. She's never met us, but she was dead against us. Like that Hitler bit. And she said we were really boring people. "The Boresome Foursome," she called us. You know, really, this woman was really just shouting her mouth off about us—as people, I mean.

RINGO: Oh, come on.

PAUL: No, *you* come on. I rang up the newspaper, you know, but they wouldn't let me speak to her. In actual fact, they said, "Well, I'll tell you, the reason we don't give her phone number out is because she never likes to speak to people over the phone because she's got a terrible stutter."

So I never did actually follow it up. Felt sorry for her. But I mean, the cheek of her, writing this damn article about us. And telling everybody how we're starting riots, and how we were such bores—and she's never even met us, mind you! I mean, we could turn around and say the same about her! I could go and thump her!

GEORGE: Bastard fascist!

PLAYBOY: Ringo. . . .

RINGO: Yes, *Playboy*, sir?

PLAYBOY: How do *you* feel about the press? Has your attitude changed in the last year or so?

RINGO: Yes.

PLAYBOY: In what way?

RINGO: I hate 'em more now that I did before.

PLAYBOY: Did you hear about the riot in Glasgow on the night of your last show there?

JOHN: We heard about it after.

PLAYBOY: Did you know that the next day there was a letter in one of the Glasgow papers that accused you of directly *inciting* the violence?

RINGO: How can they say that about us? We don't even wiggle. It's not bloody fair.

GEORGE: Bastards!

PAUL: Glasgow is like Belfast. There'll probably be a bit of a skirmish there, too. But it's not because of us. It's because people in certain cities just hate the cops more than in other cities.

GEORGE: Right.

PAUL: There were ridiculous riots last time we were there—but it wasn't riots for us. The crowd was there for us, but the riots after our show—

RINGO: All the drunks come out, out of the pubs.

PAUL: It was just beatin' up coppers.

PLAYBOY: They just used the occasion as a pretext to get at the cops?

GEORGE: Yeah.

PAUL: In Dublin this trip, did you see where the crowd sort of stopped all the traffic? They even pulled a driver out of a bus.

JOHN: They also called out the fire brigade. We had four fire engines this time.

PLAYBOY: People were also overturning cars and breaking shop windows. But all this had nothing to do with your show?

PAUL: Well, it's vaguely related, I suppose. It's got something to do with it, inasmuch as the crowds happen to be there because of our show.

JOHN: But nobody who's got a bit of common sense would seriously think that 15-year-old girls are going around smashing shop windows on account of us.

GEORGE: Certainly not. Those girls are *eight* years old.

PLAYBOY: This talk of violence leads to a related question. Do you guys think there'll be another war soon?

GEORGE: Yeah. Friday.

RINGO: I hope not. Not just after we've got our money through the taxes.

JOHN: The trouble is, if they do start another war, then everybody goes with you.

PLAYBOY: Do you think the Rolling Stones are the first to go?

PAUL: It won't matter, 'cause we'll probably be in London or Liverpool at the time, and when they drop the bomb, it'll be in the middle of the city. So we probably won't even know it when it happens.

PLAYBOY: We brought this up for a reason, fellows. There was an essay not long ago in a very serious commentary magazine, saying that before every major war in this century, there has been a major wave of public hysteria over certain specific entertainers. There was the Irene Castle craze before World War I—

PAUL: Oh, yes.

GEORGE: I remember that well.

PLAYBOY: And then before World War II, there was the swing craze, with Benny Goodman and Artie Shaw, and all the dancing in the aisles. And now you—before—

JOHN: Hold on! It's not our fault!

PLAYBOY: We're not saying you may have anything to do with inciting a war—

PAUL: Thanks.

PLAYBOY: But you don't think you may be a symptom of the times, part of an undercurrent that's building up?

PAUL: That sort of comparison just falls down when you look at it, really. It's just like saying that this morning a fly landed on my bed and that I looked at my watch and it was eight o'clock, and that therefore every morning at eight o'clock flies land on the bed. It doesn't prove anything just 'cause it happens a few times.

PLAYBOY: Let's move on to another observation about you. Did you know that the Duke of Edinburgh was recently quoted as saying that he thought you were on your way out?

JOHN: Good luck, Duke.
GEORGE: No comment. See my manager.
PAUL: He didn't say it, though. There was a retraction, wasn't there?
JOHN: Yeah, we got a telegram. Wonderful news.
PAUL: We sent one back. Addressed to "Liz and Phil."
PLAYBOY: Have you ever met the Queen?
JOHN: No, she's the only one we haven't met. We've met all the others.
PAUL: All the mainstays.
PLAYBOY: Winston Churchill?
RINGO: No, not him.
JOHN: He's a good lad, though.
PLAYBOY: Would you like to meet him?
GEORGE: Not really. Not more than anybody else.
PAUL: I dunno. Somebody like that you wish you could have met when he was really at his peak, you know, and sort of doing things and being great. But there wouldn't be a lot of point now, because he's sort of gone into retirement and doesn't do a lot of things anymore.
PLAYBOY: Is there any celebrity you *would* like to meet?
PAUL: I wouldn't mind meeting Adolf Hitler.
GEORGE: You could have every room in your house papered.
PLAYBOY: Would you like to meet Princess Margaret?
PAUL: We have.
PLAYBOY: How do you like her?
RINGO: OK. And Phillip's OK, too.
PLAYBOY: Even after what he supposedly said about you?
RINGO: I don't care what he said; I still think he's OK. He didn't say nothing about me personally.
PAUL: Even if he *had* said things about us, it doesn't make him worse, you know.
PLAYBOY: Speaking of royalty—
PAUL: Royalty never condemns anything unless it's something that they know everybody else condemns.
RINGO: If I was royal—
PAUL: If I was royal I would crack long jokes and get a mighty laugh. If I was royal.
GEORGE: What would *we* do with Buckingham Palace? Royalty's stupid.
PLAYBOY: You guys seem to be irreverent characters. Are any of you churchgoers?

JOHN: No.

GEORGE: No.

PAUL: Not particularly. But we're not antireligious. We probably seem antireligious because of the fact that none of us believe in God.

JOHN: If you say you don't believe in God, everybody assumes you are antireligious, and you probably think that's what we mean by that. We're not quite sure *what* we are, but I know we're more agnostic than atheistic.

PLAYBOY: Are you speaking for the group or just for yourself?

JOHN: For the group.

GEORGE: John's our official religious spokesman.

PAUL: We all feel roughly the same. We're all agnostics.

JOHN: Most people are, anyway.

RINGO: It's better to admit it than to be a hypocrite.

JOHN: The only thing we've got against religion is the hypocritical side of it, which I can't stand. Like the clergy is always moaning about people being poor, while they themselves are going around with millions of quid worth of robes on. That's the stuff I can't stand.

PAUL: A new bronze door stuck on the Vatican.

RINGO: Must have cost a mighty penny.

PAUL: Believe it or not, we're not anti-Christ.

RINGO: Just anti-Pope and anti-Christian.

PAUL: But you know, in America—

GEORGE: They were more shocked by us saying we were agnostics.

JOHN: They went potty; they couldn't take it. Same as in Australia, where they couldn't stand us not liking sports.

PAUL: In America they're fanatical about God. I know somebody over there who said he was an atheist. The papers nearly refused to print it because it was such shocking news that somebody could actually be an atheist. Yeah, and admit it.

RINGO: He speaks for all of us.

PLAYBOY: To bring up another topic that's shocking to some, how do you feel about the homosexual problem?

GEORGE: Oh yeah, well, we're all homosexuals, too.

GEORGE: Yeah, we're all queer.

PAUL: But don't tell anyone.

PLAYBOY: Seriously, is there more homosexuality in England than elsewhere?

JOHN: Are you saying there is more over here than in America?

PLAYBOY: We're just asking.

GEORGE: It's just that they've got crewcuts in America. You can't spot 'em.

PAUL: There's probably a million more in America than in England. England may have its scandals—like Profumo and all—but at least they're heterosexual.

JOHN: Still, we still have more than our share of queers, don't you think?

PAUL: It seems that way because there's more printed about them over here.

RINGO: If they find out that somebody is a bit bent, the press will always splash it about.

PAUL: Right. Take Profumo, for example. He's just an ordinary—

RINGO: Sex maniac.

PAUL: —just an ordinary fellow who sleeps with women. Yet it's adultery in the eyes of the law, and it's an international incident. But in actual fact, if you check up on the statistics, you find that there are hardly *any* married men who've been completely faithful to their wives.

JOHN: I have! Listen, Beatle people—

PAUL: All right, we all know John's spotless. But when a thing like that gets into the newspapers, everybody goes very, very Puritan, and they pretend that they don't know what sex is about.

GEORGE: They get so bloody virtuous all of a sudden.

PAUL: Yes, and some poor heel has got to take the brunt of the whole thing. But in actual fact, if you ask the average Briton what they think about the Profumo case, they'd probably say, "He was knockin' off some bird. So what?"

PLAYBOY: Incidentally, you've met Mandy Rice-Davies, haven't you?

GEORGE: What are you looking at *me* for?

PLAYBOY: Because we hear that *she* was looking at you.

JOHN: We did meet Christine Keeler.

RINGO: I'll tell you who I met. I met what's-her-name—April Ashley.

JOHN: I met her, too, the other night.

PLAYBOY: Isn't she the one who used to be a man, changed her sex and married into nobility?

JOHN: That's the one.

RINGO: She swears at me, you know. But when she sobers up she apologizes.

JOHN: Actually, I quite like her. Him. It. That.

PAUL: The trouble with saying something like, "Profumo was just a victim of circumstances" or "April Ashley isn't so bad, even though she's changed sex"—saying things like that in print to most people seems so shocking;

whereas in actual fact, if you really think about it, it isn't. Just saying a thing like that sounds so much more shocking than it is.

RINGO: I got up in the Ad Lib the other night and a big handbag hit me in the gut. I thought it was somebody I knew; I didn't have any glasses on. I said, "Hello," and a bloody big worker "Arrgghhh." So I just ran into the bog. Because I'd heard things like that.

PLAYBOY: What are you talking about?

GEORGE: He doesn't know.

PLAYBOY: Do you?

GEORGE: Haven't the slightest.

PLAYBOY: Can you give us a hint, Ringo? What's the Ad Lib, for example?

RINGO: It's a club.

GEORGE: Like your Peppermint Lounge, and the Whisky a GoGo. It's the same thing.

PAUL: No, the English version is a little different.

JOHN: The Whisky a GoGo is exactly the same, isn't it, only they have someone dancing on the roof; and in the Ad Lib they have a colored chap. That's the difference.

PLAYBOY: We heard a rumor that one of you was thinking of opening a club.

JOHN: I wonder who it was, Ringo.

RINGO: I don't know, John. There was a rumor, yes. I heard that one, too.

PLAYBOY: Is there any truth to it?

RINGO: Well, yes. We was going to open one in Hollywood, but it fell through.

JOHN: Dino wouldn't let you take the place over.

RINGO: No.

PAUL: And we decided it's not worth it. So we decided to sit tight for six months and then buy—

GEORGE: America.

PLAYBOY: Have you heard about the Playboy Club that's opening in London?

RINGO: Yes, I've heard about it.

PLAYBOY: What do you think of our Clubs?

RINGO: They're for dirty old men, not for the likes of us—dirty *young* men. They're for businessmen that sneak out without their wives knowing, or if their wives sneak out first, for those who go out openly.

GEORGE: There's no real fun in a Bunny's fluffy tail.

PLAYBOY: Then you don't think a Club will make it here?

GEORGE: Oh yes, 'course it will.

RINGO: There's enough dirty old men.
PLAYBOY: Have you ever read the magazine?
JOHN: Yes.
GEORGE: Yes.
RINGO: I get my copy every month. Tits.
PLAYBOY: Do you read the *Philosophy*, any of you?
PAUL: Some of it. When the journey's really long and you can't last out the pictures, you start reading it. It's OK.
PLAYBOY: How about *Playboy*'s Jazz Poll? Do you read it, too?
JOHN: Occasionally.
PLAYBOY: Do you enjoy jazz, any of you?
GEORGE: What kind?
PLAYBOY: American jazz.
JOHN: Who, for example?
PLAYBOY: You tell us.
PAUL: We only dig those who dig us.
PLAYBOY: Seriously, who? Anyone?
JOHN: Getz. But only because somebody gave me an album of his. With him and somebody called Iguana, or something like that.
PLAYBOY: You mean Joâo Gilberto?
JOHN: I don't know. Some Mexican.
PLAYBOY: He's Brazilian.
JOHN: Oh.
PLAYBOY: Are you guys getting tired of talking?
JOHN: No.
PAUL: No, let's order some drinks. Scotch or Coke?
JOHN: I'll have chocolate.
GEORGE: Scotch for me and Paul and chocolate for the Beatle teenager.
JOHN: Scotch is bad for your kidneys.
PAUL: How about you Ringo? Don't you want something to keep you awake while you're listening to all of this rubbish?
RINGO: I'll have a Coke.
JOHN: How about you *Playboy*, are you man or woman?
PAUL: It's a Beatle people!
GEORGE: Who's your fave rave?
PAUL: I love you!
GEORGE: How gear.
PLAYBOY: Speaking of fave raves, why do you think the rock 'n' roll phenomenon is bigger in England than in America?

JOHN: Is it?

PAUL: Yes. You see, in England, after us, you have thousands of groups coming out everywhere, but in America they've just sort of had the same groups going for ages. Some have made it and some haven't, but there aren't really any *new* ones. If we'd been over there instead of over here, there probably would have been the upsurge over there. Our road manager made an interesting point the other day about this difference in America. In America the people who are the big stars are not our age. There's nobody who's a really big star around our age. Possibly it may seem like a small point, but there's no conscription—no draft—here. In America we used to hear about somebody like Elvis, who was a very big star and then suddenly he was off in the Army.

JOHN: And the Everly Brothers.

PAUL: Yes, the Everly Brothers as well went into the Army at the height of their fame. And the Army seems to do something to singers. It may make them think that what they're playing is stupid and childish. Or it may make them want to change their style, and consequently they may have a harder job getting back on top when they get out. But here, of course, we don't have that problem.

JOHN: Except those who go to prison.

PAUL: It's become so easy to form a group nowadays, and to make a record, that hundreds are doing it—and making a good living at it. Whereas when we started, it took us a couple of years before the record companies would even listen to us, never mind give us a contract. But now, you just walk in and if they think you are OK, you're on.

PLAYBOY: Do you think you had anything to do with bringing all this about?

JOHN: It's a damn fact.

PAUL: Not only us. Us and people who followed us. But we were the first really to get national coverage because of some big shows that we did, and because of a lot of public interest in us.

PLAYBOY: What do you think is the most important element of your success—the personal appearances or the records?

JOHN: Records. Records always have been the main thing. P.A.s follow records. Our first records were made, and then we appeared.

PLAYBOY: Followed closely by Beatle dolls. Have you seen them?

GEORGE: They're actually life-size, you know.

PLAYBOY: The ones we've seen are about five inches high.

PAUL: Well, we're midgets, you see.

PLAYBOY: How does it make you feel to have millions of effigies of yourselves decorating bedsides all over the world? Don't you feel honored to have been immortalized in plastic? After all, there's no such thing as a Frank Sinatra doll or even an Elvis Presley doll.

GEORGE: Who would want an ugly old crap doll like that?

PLAYBOY: Would you prefer a George doll, George?

GEORGE: No, but I've got a Ringo doll at home.

PLAYBOY: Did you know that you're probably the first public figures to have dolls made of them—except maybe Yogi Berra?

JOHN: In Jellystone Park. Do you mean the cartoon?

PLAYBOY: No. Didn't you know that the cartoon character is based on a real person—Yogi Berra, the baseball player?

GEORGE: Oh.

PLAYBOY: Didn't you know that?

JOHN: I didn't know that.

PAUL: Well, they're making *us* into a cartoon, too, in the States. It's a series.

JOHN: The highest achievement we could ever get.

PAUL: We feel proud and humble.

PLAYBOY: Did you know, George, that at the corner of 47th Street and Broadway in New York, there is a giant cutout of you on display?

GEORGE: Of me?

PLAYBOY: Life-size.

RINGO: Nude.

PLAYBOY: No—but the reason we mention it is that this is really a signal honor. For years on that corner, there's been a big store with life-size cutouts of Marilyn Monroe, Anita Ekberg or Jayne Mansfield in the window.

JOHN: And now it's George.

PAUL: The only difference is they've got bigger tits.

RINGO: I suppose that's *one* way of putting it.

GEORGE: The party's getting rough. I'm going to go to bed. You carry on, though; I'll just stop my ears with cotton—so as not to hear the insults and smutty language.

PLAYBOY: We've just about run out of steam anyway.

JOHN: Do you have all you need?

PLAYBOY: Enough. Many thanks, fellows.

JOHN: 'Course a lot of it you won't be able to use—"crap" and "bloody" and "tit" and "bastard" and all.
PLAYBOY: Wait and see.
RINGO: Finish your scotch before you go.
JOHN: You don't mind if I climb into bed, do you? I'm frazzled.
PLAYBOY: Not at all. Goodnight.
RINGO: Goodnight *Playboy*.
GEORGE: It's been a hard day's night.

February 1963

FRANK SINATRA

A candid conversation with the acknowledged king of showbiz

In an age of superstars, Frank Sinatra is generally conceded to be the biggest of them all. One of the box-office giants of the screen, the highest-paid nightclub performer in show business, among the all-time top recording artists of popular or classical music, seven-time winner of *Playboy's* All-Star Jazz Poll—including the 1963 award, announced on page 81—as the favorite male vocalist of both readers and fellow musicians. He is also one of the biggest of the businessman-stars (with a $25 million empire girdling the entertainment world from such lucrative concerns as Reprise Records to Lake Tahoe's Cal-Neva Lodge), first-name friend of presidents, unchallenged title-holder as the most controversial figure in show business and lately—to the surprise of many fans and critics alike—self-effacing philanthropist and goodwill ambassador abroad, giving currency to talk of a "New Sinatra." It was in search of the real Sinatra—new, old or simply mature—that *Playboy* recently approached the press-shy star with a request for an exclusive interview. Rightly refusing to waste his time with predictable small talk, Sinatra agreed to sit down with us only on the condition that we "talk turkey, not trivia," that we attempt to reach the man behind the image, to elicit his deepest feelings and reflections on the things which move and motivate him as a human being. Reassuring him that this very aim is the basic premise and prerequisite of the *Playboy Interview*, we gladly agreed. We then spent an entire week with Sinatra as he ambled easily through the breakneck business schedule that has become his normal routine—answering our questions between takes on the set of *Come Blow Your Horn,* his latest picture for Paramount; in his Dual-Ghia en route home from the studio; during breaks at a Reprise recording session with Count Basie; in corridors heading to and from staff summit meetings on upcoming movie-record-night-club projects; even for an unexpected hour in his Beverly Hills home following the abortive Liston-Patterson fight, which Sinatra had arranged to pipe in on closed-circuit TV for a group of friends (including Dean Martin, Billy Wilder and Los Angeles Mayor Samuel W. Yorty), invited at $100 a seat earmarked for SHARE, a favorite Sinatra charity. The conversation that emerged from these catch-as-catch-can taping sessions is a courageous public declaration of private convictions from a major figure in a business wherein most stars seem concerned less with earning good reviews for their performances than with avoiding offense in their personal lives. Many people will be shocked by what he has to say, but many more, we aver, will feel that the candor of his insights adds a new dimension to their understanding of the complex, articulate and thoughtful man who is the chief executive of his profession.

PLAYBOY: Frank, in the 20 years since you left the Tommy Dorsey band to make your name as a solo singer, you've deepened and diversified your talents with a variety of concurrent careers in related fields. But so far, none of these aptitudes and activities has succeeded in eclipsing your gifts as a popular vocalist. So why don't we begin by examining Sinatra, the singer?

SINATRA: OK, deal.

PLAYBOY: Many explanations have been offered for your unique ability—apart from the subtleties of style and vocal equipment—to communicate the mood of a song to an audience. How would *you* define it?

SINATRA: I think it's because I get an audience involved, personally involved in a song—because I'm involved myself. It's not something I do deliberately; I can't help myself. If the song is a lament at the loss of love, I get an ache in my gut. I feel the loss myself and I cry out the loneliness, the hurt and the pain that I feel.

PLAYBOY: Doesn't any good vocalist "feel" a song? Is there such a difference—

SINATRA: I don't know what other singers feel when they articulate lyrics, but being an 18-karat manic-depressive and having lived a life of violent emotional contradictions, I have an over-acute capacity for sadness as well as elation. I know what the cat who wrote the song is trying to say. I've been there—and back. I guess the audience feels it along with me. They can't help it. Sentimentality, after all, is an emotion common to all humanity.

PLAYBOY: Of the thousands of words which have been written about you on this subject, do you recall any which have accurately described this ability?

SINATRA: Most of what has been written about me is one big blur, but I do remember being described in one simple word that I agree with. It was in a piece that tore me apart for my personal behavior, but the writer said that when the music began and I started to sing, I was "honest." That says it as I feel it. Whatever else has been said about me personally is unimportant. When I sing, I believe. I'm honest. If you want to get an audience with you, there's only one way. You have to reach out to them with total honesty and humility. This isn't a grandstand play on my part. I've discovered—and you can see it in other entertainers—when they don't reach out to the audience, nothing happens. You can be the most artistically perfect performer in the world, but an audience is like a broad—if you're indifferent, endsville. That goes for any kind of human contact: a politician on television, an actor in the movies or a guy and a gal. That's as true in life as it is in art.

PLAYBOY: From what you've said, it seems that we'll have to learn something of what makes you tick as a man in order to understand what motivates you as an entertainer. Would it be all right with you if we attempt to do just that—by exploring a few of the fundamental beliefs which move and shape your life?

SINATRA: Look, pal, is this going to be an ocean cruise or a quick sail around the harbor? Like you, I think, I feel, I wonder. I know some things, I believe in a thousand things and I'm curious about a million more. Be more specific.

PLAYBOY: All right, let's start with the most basic question there is: Are you a religious man? Do you believe in God?

SINATRA: Well, that'll do for openers. I think I can sum up my religious feelings in a couple of paragraphs. First, I believe in you and me. I'm like Albert Schweitzer and Bertrand Russell and Albert Einstein in that I have a respect for life—in any form. I believe in nature, in the birds, the sea, the sky, in everything I can see or that there is *real* evidence for.

If these things are what you mean by God, then I believe in God. But I don't believe in a personal God to whom I look for comfort or for a natural on the next roll of the dice. I'm not unmindful of man's seeming need for faith. I'm for *anything* that gets you through the night, be it prayer, tranquilizers or a bottle of Jack Daniel's. But to me, religion is a deeply personal thing in which man and God go it alone together, without the witch doctor in the middle. The witch doctor tries to convince us that we have to ask God for help, to spell out to him what we need, even to bribe him with prayer or cash on the line. Well, I believe that God *knows* what each of us wants and needs. It's not necessary for us to make it to church on Sunday to reach Him. You can find Him anyplace. And if that sounds heretical, my source is pretty good—Matthew: 5–7, The Sermon on the Mount.

PLAYBOY: You haven't found any answers for yourself in organized religion?

SINATRA: There are things about organized religion which I resent. Christ is revered as the Prince of Peace, but more blood has been shed in His name than any other figure in history. You show me one step forward in the name of religion and I'll show you a hundred retrogressions. Remember, they were men of God who destroyed the educational treasures at Alexandria, who perpetrated the Inquisition in Spain, who burned the witches at Salem. Over 25,000 organized religions flourish on this planet, but the followers of each think all the others are miserably misguided and probably evil as well. In India, they worship white cows, monkeys and a dip in the Ganges. The Moslems accept slavery and prepare for Allah, who promises wine and revirginated women. And witch doctors aren't just in Africa. If you look in the L.A. papers of a Sunday morning, you'll see the local variety advertising their wares like suits with two pairs of pants.

PLAYBOY: Hasn't religious faith just as often served as a civilizing influence?

SINATRA: Remember that leering, cursing lynch mob in Little Rock reviling a meek, innocent little 12-year-old Negro girl as she tried to enroll in public school? Weren't they—or most of them—devout churchgoers? I detest the two-faced who pretend liberality but are practiced bigots in their own mean little spheres. I didn't tell my daughter whom to marry, but I'd have broken her back if she had had big eyes for a bigot. As I see it, man is a product of his conditioning, and the social forces which mold his morality and conduct—including racial prejudice—are influenced more by material things like food and economic necessities than by the fear and awe and bigotry generated by the high priests of commercialized superstition. Now don't get me wrong. I'm for decency—period. I'm for anything and everything that bodes love and consideration for my fellow man. But when lip service to some mysterious deity permits bestiality on Wednesday and absolution on Sunday—cash me out.

PLAYBOY: But aren't such spiritual hypocrites in a minority? Aren't most Americans fairly consistent in their conduct within the precepts of religious doctrine?

SINATRA: I've got no quarrel with men of decency at any level. But I can't believe that decency stems only from religion. And I can't help wondering how many public figures make avowals of religious faith to maintain an aura of respectability. Our civilization, such as it is, was shaped by religion, and the men who aspire to public office anyplace in the free world must make obeisance to God or risk immediate opprobrium. Our press accurately reflects the religious nature of our society, but you'll notice that it also carries the articles and advertisements of astrology and hokey Elmer Gantry revivalists. We, in America, pride ourselves on freedom of the press, but every day I see, and so do you, this kind of dishonesty and distortion not only in this area but in reporting—about guys like me, for instance, which is of minor importance except to me; but also in reporting world news. How can a free people make decisions without facts? If the press reports world news as they report about me, we're in trouble.

PLAYBOY: Are you saying that—

SINATRA: No, wait, let me finish. Have you thought of the chance I'm taking by speaking out this way? Can you imagine the deluge of crank letters, curses, threats and obscenities I'll receive after these remarks gain general circulation? Worse, the boycott of my records, my films, maybe a picket line at my opening at the Sands. Why? Because I've dared to say that love and decency are not necessarily concomitants of religious fervor.

PLAYBOY: If you think you're stepping over the line, offending your public or perhaps risking economic suicide, shall we cut this off now, erase the tape and start over along more antiseptic lines?

SINATRA: No, let's let it run. I've thought this way for years, ached to say these things. Whom have I harmed by what I've said? What moral defection have I suggested? No, I don't want to chicken out now. Come on, pal, the clock's running.

PLAYBOY: All right, then, let's move on to another delicate subject: disarmament. How do you feel about the necessity and possibility of achieving it?

SINATRA: Well, that's like apple pie and mother—how can you be against it? After all, despite the universal and unanimous assumption that both powers—Russia and the United States—already have stockpiled more nuclear weaponry than is necessary to vaporize the entire planet, each power continues to build, improve and enlarge its terrifying arsenal. For the first time in history, man has developed the means with which to expunge all life in one shuddering instant. And, brother, no one gets a pass, no one hides from this one. But the question is not so much whether disarmament is desirable or even whether it can be achieved, but whether—if we *were* able to achieve it—we would be better off, or perhaps infinitely *worse* off.

PLAYBOY: Are you suggesting that disarmament might be *detrimental* to peace?

SINATRA: Yes, in a certain very delicate sense. Look, I'm a realist, or at least I fancy myself one. Just as I believe that religion doesn't always work, so do I feel that disarmament may be completely beyond man's capacity to live with. Let's forget for a moment the complex problems we might face in converting from a cold war to a peace economy. Let's examine disarmament in terms of man's political, social and philosophical conditioning. Let's say that somehow the UN is able to achieve a disarmament program acceptable to all nations. Let's imagine, a few years from now, total global disarmament. But imagine as well the gnawing doubts, suspicions and nerve-wracking tensions which must, inevitably, begin to fill the void: The fear that the other side—or perhaps some third power—is secretly arming or still holding a few bombs with which to surprise and overcome the other. But I firmly believe that nuclear war is absolutely impossible. I don't think anyone in the world wants a nuclear war—not even the Russians. They, and we, and the nth countries—as nuclear strategists refer to future nuclear powers—face the incontrovertible certainty of lethal retaliation for any nuclear strike. I can't believe for a moment that the idiot exists in any nation that will push the first button—not even accidentally.

PLAYBOY: You foresee no possibility of world war *or* of effective disarmament?

SINATRA: I'm not an industrialist or an economist. I know I'm way out of my depth when I attempt even to comprehend the complexity of shifting the production of a country from war to peace. But if somehow all those involved in production of implements of destruction were willing to accept reason as well as reasonable profit, I think that a shift in psychology might be possible. And if this were to happen, I believe that the deep-seated terror in the hearts of most people, due to the constant threat of total destruction, would disappear. The result would be a more positive, less greedy, less selfish and more loving approach to survival. I can tell you this much from personal experience and observation: Hate solves no problems. It only creates them. But listen, you've been asking me a lot of questions, so let me ask you a question I posed to Mike Romanoff the other night. You know, Mike is quite a serious thinker. When we spend an evening together, we play an intellectual chess game touching on all topics, including those we are discussing here. Anyway, I asked Mike what would happen if a summit meeting of all the leaders in every country in the world was called, including Red China, at the UN. Further suppose that each leader brings with him his top aides: Kennedy brings Rusk, Khrushchev brings Gromyko, Mao brings Chou. All these cats are together in one room, then—boom! Somebody blows up the mother building. No more leaders. No more deputies. The question I asked Mike, and the one I ask you, is: What would happen to the world?

PLAYBOY: You tell us.

SINATRA: I told Mike I thought it might be the only chance the world has for survival. But Mike just shook his head and said, "Frank, you're very sick." Maybe so. Until someone lights the fuse, however, I think that continuation of Cold War preparedness might be more effective to maintain the peace than the dewy-eyed notion of total disarmament. I also wonder if "total" disarmament includes chemical and bacteriological weapons—which, as you know, can be just as lethal as nuclear weapons. Card players have a saying: "It's all right to play if you keep your eyes on the deck"—which is another way of saying, "Eternal vigilance is the price of liberty."

PLAYBOY: Do you feel, then, that nuclear testing should be continued?

SINATRA: Absolutely not. I think it's got to stop, and I think it *will* stop—because it has to stop. The name-calling in the UN and the finger pointing at peace conferences is just a lot of diplomatic bull. Both sides have to live on this planet, and leaders in all countries know that their children and grandchildren have to live here, too. I suspect that when the limits of strontium 90 in the atmosphere get really dangerous, scientists in both camps will persuade the politicians to call a final halt to testing—probably at precisely the same time, with no urging from the other side.

PLAYBOY: You spoke a moment ago of the fear and suspicion that might nullify any plan for lasting and effective disarmament. Isn't continuing nuclear preparedness—with or without further testing—likely to engender these emotions on an even more dangerous scale?

SINATRA: Fear is the enemy of logic. There is no more debilitating, crushing, self-defeating, sickening thing in the world—to an individual or to a nation. If we continue to fear the Russians, and if they continue to fear us, then we're both in big trouble. Neither side will be able to make logical, reasoned decisions. I think, however, that their fear and concern over the ideological balance of power in some areas is far from irrational. Our concern over a Sovietized Cuba 90 miles from Key West, for instance, must be equated with Russian concern over our missile bases surrounding them. It is proper that we should be deeply concerned, but we must be able to see their side of the coin—and not let this concern turn into fear on either side.

PLAYBOY: On a practical level, how would you combat communist expansion into areas such as Cuba, Laos and the emerging African nations?

SINATRA: It strikes me as being so ridiculously simple: Stop worrying about communism. Just get rid of the conditions that nurture it. Sidestepping Marxian philosophy and dialectical vagaries, I think that communism can fester only wherever and whenever it is encouraged to breed—not just by the communists themselves, but by depressed social and economic conditions. And we can always count on the communists to exploit those conditions. Poverty is probably the greatest asset the communists have. Wherever it exists, anyplace in the world, you have a potential communist breeding ground. It figures that if a man is frustrated in a material sense, his family hungry, he suffers, he broods and he becomes susceptible to the blandishments of any ideology that promises to take him off the hook.

PLAYBOY: Do you share with the American Right Wing an equal concern about the susceptibility of our *own* country to communist designs?

SINATRA: Well, if you're talking about that poor, beaten, dehumanized, discriminated-against guy in some blighted Tobacco Road down in the South, he's certainly in the market for offers of self-improvement. But you can't make me believe that a machinist in Detroit, ending a 40-hour week, climbing into his '63 Chevy, driving to a steak barbecue behind his $25,000 home in a tree-lined subdivision, about to begin a weekend with his well-fed, well-clothed family, is going to trade what he's got for a Party card. In America—except for tiny pockets of privation which still persist—Khrushchev has as much chance of succeeding as he has of making 100 straight passes at the crap table.

PLAYBOY: In combating communist expansion into underdeveloped areas here and abroad, what can we do except to offer massive material aid and guidance of the kind we've been providing since the end of World War II?

SINATRA: I don't know. I'm no economist. I don't pretend to have much background in political science. But this much I know: Attending rallies sponsored by 110-percent anti-Communist cultists or donning white sheets and riding with the Klan—the one that's spelled with a "K"—isn't the answer. All I know is that a nation with our standard of living, with our Social Security system, TVA, farm parity, health plans and unemployment insurance can afford to address itself to the cancers of starvation, substandard housing, educational voids and second-class citizenship that still exist in many backsliding areas of our own country. When we've cleaned up these blemishes, then we can go out with a clean conscience to see where else in the world we can help. Hunger is inexcusable in a world where grain rots in silos and butter turns rancid while being held for favorable commodity indices.

PLAYBOY: Is American support of the UN one of the ways in which we can uplift global economic conditions?

SINATRA: It seems to me that a lot of us consider the UN a private club—ours, of course—with gentlemen's agreements just like any other exclusive club. Only instead of excluding a person, a race or a religion, the members of the UN have the power to exclude entire nations. I don't happen to think you can kick 800 million Chinese under the rug and simply pretend that they don't exist. Because they do. If the UN is to be truly representative, then it must accept *all* the nations of the world. If it doesn't represent the *united* nations of the world, then what the hell have you got? Not democracy—and certainly not world government. Everybody seems to have forgotten that President Kennedy, before he became president, in his book, *Strategy of Peace*, plainly advocated recognition of Red China. So I'm not too far out on the limb, am I?

PLAYBOY: With or without mainland China in the UN, what do you feel are the prospects for an eventual American rapprochement with Russia?

SINATRA: I'm a singer, not a prophet or a diplomat. Ask the experts or read the Rockefeller brothers' reports. But speaking just as a layman, an ordinary guy who thinks and worries, I think that if we can stay out of war for the next 10 years, we'll never have another war. From all I've read and seen recently, I'm betting that within the next decade the Russians will be on the credit card kick just as we are. They're going to want color TV, their wives are going to want electrified kitchens, and their kids are going to want hot rods. Even Russian girls are getting hip. I've seen photos of them at Russian beach resorts, and it looks just like the Riviera. They're thinning down, and I see they're going the bikini route. When GUM department store in Moscow starts selling bikinis, we've got a fighting chance, because that means the girls are interested in being girls and the boys are going to stop thinking about communes and begin thinking connubially. I've always had a theory that whenever guys and gals start swinging, they begin to lose interest in conquering the world. They just want a comfortable pad and stereo and wheels, and their thoughts turn to the good things of life—not to war. They loosen up, they live and they're more apt to *let* live. Dig?

PLAYBOY: We dig.

SINATRA: You know, I'd love to visit Russia, and sometime later, China, too. I figure the more I know about them and the more they know about me, the better chance we have of living in the same world in peace. I don't intend to go there with a mission, to sell the American way of life: I'm not equipped to get into that kind of discussion about government. But I'd love to go and show them American music. I'd take Count Basie and Ella Fitzgerald with me and we'd do what we do best. We'd wail up a storm with real American jazz so that their kids could see what kind of music our kids go for, because I'm sure that kids are the same all over the world. I'm betting that they'd dig us. And that's *got* to create some kind of good will, and man, a little good will is something we could use right now. All it takes is good will and a smile to breach that language barrier. When the Moiseyev Dancers were in Los Angeles, Eddie and Liz Fisher gave a party for them, and although I couldn't speak a word of Russian, I got along fine. I just said, "Hello, baby" to the dancers and they shouted, "Allo, babee" back at me. We had a ball.

PLAYBOY: Frank, you've expressed some negative views on human nature in the course of this conversation. Yet one gets the impression that—despite the bigotry, hypocrisy, stupidity, cruelty and fear you've talked about—you feel there are still some grounds for hope about the destiny of Homo sapiens. Is that right?

SINATRA: Absolutely. I'm never cynical, never without optimism about the future. The history of mankind proves that at some point the people have their innings, and I think we're about to come up to bat now. I think we can make it if we live and let live. And love one another—I mean *really* love. If you don't know the guy on the other side of the world, love him anyway because he's just like you. He has the same dreams, the same hopes and fears. It's one world, pal. We're all neighbors. But didn't somebody once go up onto a mountain long ago and say the same thing to the world?

January 1979

MARLON BRANDO

A candid—if reluctant—conversation with the country's greatest actor

He is considered by many to be the world's greatest living actor, the man who changed the style of the movies, the most influential and widely imitated actor of his generation. He burst onto our consciousness wearing a torn T-shirt, mumbling, growling, scowling, screaming for "Stel-la!" as Stanley Kowalski in Tennessee Williams's *A Streetcar Named Desire*, first on Broadway, then on film. It marked the beginning of a career that was to be as wild as many of the characters he so expertly portrayed.

An intensely private man, Marlon Brando stirs emotions and elicits reactions that go beyond his status as either actor or political activist. He's been called brilliant, a lout, considerate, arrogant, gentle, selfish, a chauvinist, generous, an egomaniac, selfless. He has passed into myth, become history. The highest paid and most respected actor in America, he is one of the select artists who will doubtless be remembered into the next century.

From the beginning, Brando unleashed a raw power that had never been seen before on the screen. He talked through his body, affecting viewers emotionally each time he got beat up and stood up. What audiences knew of courage they saw enacted by Brando time and time again, from *The Men* to *On the Waterfront* to *Viva Zapata!* And what they thought was evil was reinterpreted and given new dimensions as Brando became a wild punk hoodlum, a Nazi officer, a kidnapper, a bandit, an Ugly American Ambassador, a Mafia chief.

Like a figure in a classical Greek drama, after rising to the top during the 1950s, his career plummeted to disappointing lows in the 1960s. Yet, when people thought he had nothing left to give, he mounted a magnificent and stunning comeback with *The Godfather* and *Last Tango in Paris*, a film so brutally and sexually honest that it was hailed as adding a new dimension to the art.

Born in Omaha, Nebraska, on April 3, 1924, "Bud," as he was called, had lived in three states and five locations by the time he was six years old. His father, whom Brando describes as "a strong, wild man who liked to fight and drink," was a manufacturer of chemical feed products and insecticides. His mother was a semi-professional actress, who once appeared with Henry Fonda in a 1928 production of a Eugene O'Neill play.

After being expelled from military school, he told his parents he would enter the ministry. They talked him out of it. Then he thought he'd become a musician, as he had a passion for playing the bongo drums. When no one hired his five-piece band, he worked for six weeks laying irrigation ditches for a construction company. Eventually, he drifted to New York, following his two older sisters, who had studied acting and painting. It was 1943 and he enrolled in Erwin Piscator's Dramatic Workshop at the New School for Social Research. His teacher was Stella Adler, a disciple of Constantin Stanislavsky, who believed in discovering a role from the inside out.

Under Adler's tutelage, Brando took acting seriously. He demonstrated a love for makeup, wigs and foreign accents, and he began studying philosophy, French, dance, fencing and yoga. What he did mostly, however, was observe people. He had the ability to pick up others' characteristics and translate them into revealing gestures.

He dressed in jeans and T-shirts, lived in numerous cheap apartments and, like most beginning actors, stood in unemployment lines. Occasionally, he worked at odd jobs, such as being a night watchman or an elevator boy at Best's department store. For a while, he roomed with an old school friend, Wally Cox, who eventually moved out because he could no longer tolerate Brando's pet raccoon.

In the summer of 1944, as a member of New York's Dramatic Workshop, he performed in Sayville, Long Island, where casting agent Maynard Morris "discovered" Brando. Morris got him some screen tests and then recommended he audition for the Rodgers and Hammerstein production of *I Remember Mama*, by John Van Druten. With Stella Adler encouraging him, Brando auditioned, got the part and spent the next year earning $75 a week playing the oldest son of immigrant Norwegians.

During that time, another older woman entered his life: agent Edith Van Cleve, who recognized the young actor's raw energy. She got him other auditions, none of them clicking until Mrs. Adler convinced her husband, producer-director Harold Clurman, to cast Brando in Maxwell Anderson's *Truckline Café*. Determined to make him stop mumbling and articulate, Clurman had Brando climbing ropes, screaming, falling, being kicked around the stage during rehearsals. The effort worked, but the play didn't, closing within two weeks. Brando, though, was noticed. A young Pauline Kael remembers feeling embarrassed for him—"I looked up and saw what I thought was an actor having a seizure onstage"—until she realized he was acting.

In 1946, he appeared with Paul Muni in *A Flag Is Born*, about the plight of stateless Jews. It was his first involvement in a political cause and the money raised was sent to the League for a Free Palestine. A year later, when Williams completed *A Streetcar Named Desire*, Brando was ready to make himself known.

There are those who saw him as the ruthless, savage, sexy Kowalski during his year-and-a-half-long run on Broadway who can still describe the way he moved onstage. Critics quickly hailed him as the most gifted actor of his generation. But the role was demanding and led Brando into analysis, which lasted for a decade. It also led him into films, which he openly disdained but which offered him the opportunity to make more money, work fewer hours and reach a wider audience. Brando went to Hollywood and never returned to Broadway.

From 1950 to 1955, Brando starred in eight films, the first six of which, as actor Jon Voight recently said, "were absolutely enormous." Those films were *The Men*, *A Streetcar Named Desire*, *Viva Zapata!*, *Julius Caesar*, *The Wild One* and *On the Waterfront*. Brando had established the Method as the acting force to contend with.

What Muni called Brando's "magnificent, great gift" was recognized in 1955 when he won the Oscar for Best Actor for his role as Terry Malloy in *On the Waterfront*, which he accepted. Eighteen years later, he won his second Oscar, for his role as Don Vito Corleone in *The Godfather*, but by then, Brando's social consciousness had risen dramatically and he disdained awards, refusing to accept it and asking an American Indian woman to stand before the academy and the world to explain why.

Between *On the Waterfront* and *The Godfather,* Brando made 19 pictures (he's made 30 in his 28-year career to date, including *Superman* and the yet-to-be-released *Apocalypse Now*). Some of them have been strong and sensitive, such as *The Young Lions, Reflections in a Golden Eye, Burn!* and *The Nightcomers;* and some have been embarrassing and trite, such as *A Countess from Hong Kong* (written and directed by Charles Chaplin) and *Candy.* But whatever the role, his acting has consistently surprised and often confused his audience with its unpredictability.

Throughout his career, Brando has preferred to speak out on issues of social importance rather than on acting and the movies, involving himself in causes far removed from make-believe. He has actively participated in marches and spoken out on behalf of the Jews, the blacks, the American Indians, the downtrodden and the poor; and against capital punishment, bigotry, awards, most politicians, and policing organizations whenever they seem to infringe upon individual rights and freedoms. For Unesco, he flew to India during a famine; in the state of Washington, he was arrested for participating in an Indian fish-in over river rights; in Gresham, Wisconsin, he ducked bullets along with radical Indians from the Menominee tribe demanding a return of disputed land. Attacking critics who dubbed him insincere, Shana Alexander wrote in a *Newsweek* column, "No American I can think of has taken his own initiative to reduce injustice in this world more often, and been knocked down for it more often, than Marlon Brando."

His relationships with mostly foreign women have been mysterious and often stormy. He has been legally married and divorced twice: in 1957, to British actress Anna Kashfi, who had claimed to be of East Indian origin, and in 1960, to Mexican actress Movita. He had a child with each woman and, for a dozen years, he publicly battled through the courts with his first wife for custody of their son. In Tahiti for *Mutiny on the Bounty* in 1960, he met his co-star, Tarita, with whom he now has two children.

While in Tahiti, he discovered Tetiaroa, an atoll of 13 islands 40 miles north. When it came up for sale, he purchased it and he goes there as often as he can, usually about four months of each year. To find out more about this complex and intriguing man, who has refused until now to sit for any lengthy interview, *Playboy* sent freelancer Lawrence Grobel (who also interviewed Barbra Streisand and Dolly Parton for us) to Tahiti at Brando's invitation. Grobel reports:

"When I got this assignment—17 months ago—I was told that Brando was ready to talk and I should prepare for the interview immediately. Having waited nearly a year to see Barbra Streisand, I should have known better. One had only to do a little research to see that the man disliked talking about acting almost as much as he loathed discussing his private life.

"By October 1977, I was ready to see him, but he was far from ready to see me. Phone conversations with his secretary Alice Marchak, who has been with Brando for 23 years, indicated that she was as much in the dark about when we'd get together as I was. Then one day while I was talking with Alice, Brando picked up the phone. He apologized for the delay, wanted to know how old I was and warned me that the only thing he was interested in talking about was Indians. I told him for an all-encompassing interview, Indians was not enough.

"After two more postponements, he asked if I'd like to do the interview in Tahiti. Naturally, I agreed and a date was set for April.

"By mid-June, I finally boarded a jet for Papeete. I landed at 4:30 A.M. and was met by Dick Johnson, an American who lives in Tahiti and works as Brando's accountant there. On the following day, I flew to Tetiaroa, where Brando, looking like a ragged version of an East Indian holy man, was waiting as I disembarked. For the next 10 days, we ate our meals together, went for walks along the beach, went night sailing, played chess and managed to tape five sessions, lasting anywhere from two to six hours each. It seems only appropriate to begin the interview with a question about Tetiaroa."

PLAYBOY: This island you own is certainly a perfect place to talk—no phones, no unexpected visitors, no interruptions.
BRANDO: It's very elemental here. You have the sky, the sea, trees, the crabs, the fish, the sun . . . the basics. Once, I was the only person here, absolutely alone on this island. I really like being alone. I never run out of things to think about when I'm here.
PLAYBOY: As a kid growing up in Nebraska, did you ever imagine you'd end up as the caretaker of a South Sea island?
BRANDO: I knew that when I was 12. In school, I was flunking four out of five subjects and I'd be sent to study hall, where I'd read back issues

of the *National Geographic*. I always felt an affinity toward these islands. Then, in 1960, I came down here and it just sort of confirmed what I'd always known.

PLAYBOY: For most of your career, you've avoided doing any long interviews. Why?

BRANDO: I've regretted most interviews, because they don't write what you say or they'll get you out of context or they'll juxtapose it in such a way that it's not reflective of what you've said. I've read so many interviews with people who are not qualified to give answers to questions asked—questions on economics, archaeological discoveries in Tuscany, the recent virulent form of gonorrhea. . . . I used to answer those questions and then I'd ask myself, What the fuck am I doing? It's absolutely preposterous I should be asked those questions and, equally preposterous, I found myself answering [*laughs*]. I don't know a fucking thing about economics, mathematics or anything else. And then you can say something in a certain spirit, with a smile, but when it appears in print, there's no smile.

PLAYBOY: We can always indicate that with brackets. But when you do make a rare public appearance, as you did with Dick Cavett a few years ago, you don't do much smiling. With Cavett, you stubbornly insisted on spending 90 minutes on one topic, Indians, which seemed to make him very nervous.

BRANDO: Yeah. He kept asking me questions, kept me uncomfortable. Dick was having trouble with his ratings at the time. He's a good interviewer: bright, witty, intelligent, he buzzes things along. But he blew it in my case, because I was intransigent and intractable and would not answer what I thought were silly questions. Which made his show dull. I had another discouraging experience with the BBC. I went on a show that was something like *Tonight*. I was very nervous. All the host did was ask me questions about *Superman*—how much money I got and stuff like that. He said, "Were you able to get into your costume for *Superman*?" And I would say, "Well, in 1973, Wounded Knee took place." I just didn't want to hold still for any of the crap questions, but I wanted to be courteous at the same time. They edited the thing so I said nothing. I really looked like an idiot.

Then I went downstairs to talk to seven reporters from the *London Times*, from all the papers. I talked for three hours with them about the American Indian. They all ran pictures of me in my *Superman* costume and that's all they wrote about. Then, once in a while, on the back page,

"And . . . blah blah blah blah blah the American Indian." I was appalled. I didn't believe the quality of journalism in England was such that they would have to go for the buck that way. It was revolting.

PLAYBOY: But not very surprising. Getting you to talk about Indians isn't much of a journalistic scoop, is it? Not to denigrate what you have to say about that subject, but the fact is, anyone who interviews you would like to get you to talk about other things as well—acting, for example.

BRANDO: Yeah, but what a paltry ambition. I know if you want to schlock it up a little, the chances are the interview is going to be more successful, because people are going to read it; it's going to be a little more provocative and down the line—get your finger under the *real* Marlon Brando, what he really thinks and all that. But I'm not going to lay myself at the feet of the American public and invite them into my soul. My soul is a private place. And I have some resentment of the fact that I live in a system where you have to do that. I find myself making concessions, because normally I wouldn't talk about any of this, it's just blabber. It's not absorbing or meaningful or significant, it doesn't have much to do with our lives. It's dog-food conversation. I think the issue of the Indian is interesting enough so that we don't have to talk about other things. But I have the vague feeling that you know where the essence of a commercial interview lies, and what would make a good commercial story wouldn't necessarily be one that would mention the American Indian at all. To me, it's the only part that matters.

PLAYBOY: But you just mentioned celebrities who talk about things that aren't relevant to their fields of endeavor. Your passion is with the Indians, but your expertise is as an actor.

BRANDO: I guess I have a burning resentment of the fact that when people meet you, they're meeting some asshole celebrity movie actor, instead of a person, someone who has another view, or another life, or is concerned about other things. This *idiot* part of life has to go in the forefront of things as if it's of major importance.

PLAYBOY: But an entire interview dealing with nothing but the problems of Indians would inevitably become boring.

BRANDO: I'd *like* to be able to bore people with the subject of Indians . . . since I'm beginning to think it's true, that everybody *is* bored by those issues. Nobody wants to think about social issues, social justice. And those are the main issues that confront us. That's one of the dilemmas of my life. People don't give a damn. Ask most kids about details about Auschwitz or about how the American Indians were assassinated as a people and they don't know anything about it. They don't *want* to know anything. Most people just want their beer or their soap opera or their lullaby.

PLAYBOY: Be that as it may, you can be sure that people *will* be interested in what you'll undoubtedly be saying about past and present social injustices. But why not also respond to topics that may not be serious but are just plain interesting—such as the fact that, to take a random example, Marilyn Monroe's one ambition was to play Lady Macbeth to your Macbeth?

BRANDO: Look, you're going to be the arbiter of what is important and what you think the particular *salade niçoise* ingredients of this interview ought to be—it's going to have a little shtick, a little charm, a little of Marlon's eccentricities, we're going to lift the lid here and pull the hem of the gown up there, then we're going to talk about Indians. But there are things that you full well know are *important*. Food is one of them, Unicef is another, human aggression is another, social injustice in our own back yard is another, human injustice anywhere in the world. . . . Those are issues that we have to constantly confront ourselves and others with and deal with. Maybe what I'm going to say about them is meaningless or doesn't have any solutions, but the fact is, if we all start talking about them and look at them, instead of listening to my views on acting, which are totally irrelevant, maybe something can get done.

When I say irrelevant, it's certainly relevant to money. You have to have something as a sort of shill for the reader, so if he gets to page one and he reads about what I think about Marilyn Monroe's thoughts about me, King Lear to her Cordelia or something as absurd as that, or did she have a nice figure and what do you think about women using dumbbells to develop their busts?—I'm exaggerating to make the point—then people are going to read that, and then they may go on a little further and read something about Indians that they didn't know.

PLAYBOY: Well, we're finally coming to some agreement. You're absolutely right. So how do you respond to that little item about Marilyn?

BRANDO: I don't know how to answer the question. [*Mockingly*] "Oh, well, that's nice, my goodness, I didn't know Marilyn cared for me in that respect. . . . Hey, well, she's a remarkable actress, I certainly would have enjoyed—" I can't respond to that. It bores the shit out of me.

PLAYBOY: Can you respond to what happened to her?

BRANDO: No, I don't want to talk about that, that's just prattle, gossip, shitty . . . It's disemboweling a ghost. . . . Marlon Brando's view of Marilyn

Monroe's death. That's horrifying. What she said about me and what I'm to say about her can lead to the consequence of nothing.

PLAYBOY: Not necessarily. What if the point of this were to lead to the subject of suicide? You don't know what directions these questions might take.

BRANDO: Now you're giving me your yeshiva bocher, you know what that is? That's two Jews under the Williamsburg Bridge. It's the equivalent of the Christians arguing about how many angels dance on the head of a pin. I'm not casting aspersions on your efforts. All I'm saying is these are money-oriented questions. Those that have the best return are the most controversial, the most startling, the most arresting. The idea is to get a scintillating view that has not yet been seen by somebody, so that you have something unusual to offer, to sell. I just don't believe in washing my dirty underwear for all to see, and I'm not interested in the confessions of movie stars. Mike Wallace had a program, it was an astounding program, some years ago. He got people to come on and talk about themselves. And in conversation, they'd throw up all over the camera and on him, the desk, in their own laps, and tell us about their problems with B.O. or drinking or their inability to have a proper sexual relation with their pet kangaroo. I was floored. I was fascinated with that program. He was wonderful. He's a damn good investigative reporter. Anyway, what people are willing to do in front of a public is puzzling. I don't understand why they do it. I guess it makes them feel a little less lonely. I always found it distasteful and not something I cared to do. Did you ever read any of Lillian Ross's Hollywood profiles in *The New Yorker*? They were mostly quotes of what celebrities said. They just hung themselves by their own talk.

PLAYBOY: That's what many critics said about you when Truman Capote profiled you in *The New Yorker* during the making of *Sayonara*, 22 years ago. Was that the piece that turned you away from doing interviews?

BRANDO: No. What I was very slow in realizing was that money was the principal motivation in any interview. Not necessarily directly but indirectly. We're money-bound people and everything we do has to do with money, more or less. Our projects and activities have to do with the making of money and the movement of money. I am a commodity sitting here. Our union has to do with money. You're making money, *Playboy*'s making money and, I suppose, in some way, I'm making money. If money were not involved, you wouldn't be sitting here asking me questions, because you wouldn't be getting paid for it. I wouldn't be answering the questions if there weren't some monetary consideration involved. Not that I'm getting it directly, but I'm paying a debt, so to speak. When Hugh Hefner paid the bail for Russell Means [leader of the American Indian Movement] a couple of years ago, I was grateful. But people look for the money questions, the money answers, and they wait for a little flex of gelt in the conversation. You can tell when you're talking, they get very attentive on certain subjects.

PLAYBOY: Why don't we just proceed? You *know* people are interested in you for more complicated reasons than those.

BRANDO: No, they're not. You know you wouldn't interview out-of-work movie stars. I just happen to be lucky and have had a couple of hits and some controversial pictures lately, but I was down the tubes not long ago. I always made a living, but I wasn't . . . I wasn't . . . sought after. I suppose if I hadn't been successful in a couple of movies that I would have been playing different kinds of parts for different kinds of money, and you wouldn't be sitting here today.

PLAYBOY: No one wanted to interview you when your career took a dive?

BRANDO: You could see it on the faces of the air hostesses; you could see it when you rented a car; you could see it when you walked into a restaurant. If you've made a hit movie, then you get the full 32-teeth display in some places; and if you've sort of faded, they say, "Are you still making movies? I remember that picture, blah blah blah." And so it goes. The point of all this is, people are interested in people who are successful.

PLAYBOY: And in people who will be remembered. Which is why we're talking.

BRANDO: I don't know. I think movie stars are . . . about a decade. Ask young kids now who Humphrey Bogart or Clark Gable was. "Didn't he play for the Yankees?" "No, no, he was a tailback at Cincinnati."

PLAYBOY: So you think the fascination with someone like yourself is fleeting?

BRANDO: There's a tendency for people to mythologize everybody, evil or good. While history is happening, it's being mythologized. There are people who believe that Nixon is innocent, that he's a man of refinement, nobility, firmness of purpose, and he should be reinstated as president, he did no wrong. And there are people who can do no right. Bobby Seale, for some people, is a vicious, pernicious symbol of something that is destructive in our society that should be looked to with great caution and wariness, a man from whom no good can emanate. To other people, he's a poet, an aristocratic spirit.

People believe what they will believe, to a large degree. People will like you who never met you, they think you're absolutely wonderful; and then people also will hate you, for reasons that have nothing to do with any real experience with you. People don't want to lose their enemies. We have favorite enemies, people we love to hate and we hate to love. If they do something good, we don't like it. I found myself doing that with Ronald Reagan. He is anathema to me. If he does something that's reasonable, I find my mind trying to find some way to interpret it so that it's not reasonable, so that somewhere it's jingoist extremism.

Most people want those fantasies of those who are worthy of our hate—we get rid of a lot of anger that way; and of those who are worthy of our idolatry. Whether it's Farrah Fawcett or somebody else, it doesn't make a difference. They're easily replaceable units, pick 'em out like a card file. Johnnie Ray enjoyed that kind of hysterical popularity, celebration, and then suddenly he wasn't there anymore. The Beatles are now nobody in particular. Once they set screaming crowds running after them, they ran in fear of their lives, they had special tunnels for them. They can walk almost anyplace now. Because the fantasy is gone. Elvis Presley—bloated, over the hill, adolescent entertainer, suddenly drawing people into Las Vegas—had nothing to do with excellence, just myth. It's convenient for people to believe that something is wonderful, therefore they're wonderful.

Kafka and Kierkegaard are remarkable souls; they visited distant lands of the psyche that no other writers dared before—to some people, *they* were the heroes, not Elvis Presley.

PLAYBOY: Do you think all people have heroes?

BRANDO: They have to have. Even negative heroes. Richard the Third: "Can I do this and cannot get a crown? Were it further off, I'll pluck it down!" In other words, the fact that life was denied to him, then he would do his best at being bad, he would make a career of being bad. The worst kind of bad you could be: memorably bad, frighteningly bad, powerfully bad. Had he had the opportunity, he might have been powerfully creative, powerfully loving, powerfully noble. He didn't have the opportunity, because he was twisted and deformed and embittered by that experience. It's wonderfully stated, Shakespeare: "Now is the winter of our discontent/ Made glorious summer by this sun of York." People's energies—whether negative or positive—are there to be used and they will apply, somehow.

PLAYBOY: Bringing this back to you and your own energies, you once said that for most of your career, you were trying to figure out what you'd really like to do.

BRANDO: "You once said." There ought to be a handbook for interviewers and one of the don'ts should be: Don't say, "You once said," because 98.4 percent of the time, what you were quoted as having said once isn't true. The fact is, I *did* say that. For a long time, I had no idea really what it was that I wanted to do.

PLAYBOY: And you didn't feel that acting was worthwhile or fulfilling enough?

BRANDO: There's a big bugaboo about acting; it doesn't make sense to me. *Everybody* is an actor; you spend your whole day acting. Everybody has suffered through moments where you're thinking one thing and feeling one thing and not showing it. That's acting. Shaw said that thinking was the greatest of all human endeavors, but I would say that feeling was. Allowing yourself to feel things, to feel love or wrath, hatred, rage. . . . It's very difficult for people to have an extended confrontation with themselves. You're hiding what you're thinking, what you're feeling, you don't want to upset somebody or you *do* want to upset somebody; you don't want to show that you hate them; your pride would be injured if they knew you'd been affected by what they said about you. Or you hide a picayune aspect of yourself, the prideful or envious or vulnerable, and you pretend that everything's all right. "Hi, how are you?" People look at your face and it's presentable: "And I shall prepare a face to meet the faces that I meet."

So we all act. The only difference between an actor professionally and an actor in life is the professional knows a little bit more about it—some of them, anyway—and he gets paid for it. But actually, people in real life get paid for acting, too. You have a secretary who has a lot of sex appeal and a great deal of charm and she knows it, she's going to get paid for that, whether she delivers sexual favors or not. A very personable, attractive young man, who reflects what the boss says, is smart enough to know what the boss feels and likes and wants and he knows how to curry favor . . . he's acting. He goes in in the morning and he gives him a lot of chatter, tells him the right kind of jokes and it makes the boss feel good. One day the boss says, "Listen, Jim, why don't you go to Duluth and take over the department there? I think you'd do a bang-up job." And then Jim digs his toe under the rug and says, "Oh, gosh, I never thought, J. B. . . . Gee, I don't know what to say. . . . Sure,

I'll go. When?" And he jumps into the plane and checks off what he's been trying to do for four years—get J. B. to give him the Duluth office. Well, that guy's acting for a living, singing for his supper, and he's getting paid for it.

The same thing is true in governmental promotion or of a member of a presidential advisory committee, if he's playing the power game—'cause a lot of people don't want to get paid in money, they want to get paid in something else, paid in affection or esteem. Or in hard currency.

PLAYBOY: But there does seem to be a difference between the professional actor, who does what he does consciously, and the subconscious behavior of the nonprofessional.

BRANDO: Well, the idiot tome on acting was written by Dale Carnegie, called *How to Win Friends and Influence People*. It's a book on hustling. Acting is just hustling. Some people are hustling money, some power.

Those in government during the Vietnam war were trying to hustle the president all the time so their opinion would be taken over that of others and their recommended course of action would be implemented. That play was running constantly. I can't distinguish between one acting profession and another. They're all acting professions.

PLAYBOY: What about acting as an art form?

BRANDO: In your heart of hearts, you know perfectly well that movie stars aren't artists.

PLAYBOY: But there are times when you can capture moments in a film or a play that are memorable, that have meaning—

BRANDO: A prostitute can capture a moment! A prostitute can give you all kinds of wonderful excitement and inspiration and make you think that nirvana has arrived on the two o'clock plane, and it ain't necessarily so.

PLAYBOY: Do you consider *any* people in your profession artists?

BRANDO: No.

PLAYBOY: None at all?

BRANDO: Not one.

PLAYBOY: Duse? Bernhardt? Olivier?

BRANDO: Shakespeare said. . . . Poor guy, he gets hauled out of the closet every few minutes, but since there're so few people around, you always have to haul somebody out of the closet and say, "So-and-so said." That's like saying, "You once said." [*Laughs*] But we *know* what he said. "There's no art to find the mind's construction in the face." Which very plainly means that being able to discover the subtle qualities of the human mind by the expression of the face is an art, and there should be such an art. I don't think he meant it seriously, that it should be established among the seven lively arts, to become the eighth: the reading of physiognomy. But you can call anything art. You can call a short-order cook an artist, because he really does that—back flips, over and under his legs, around his head, caroms 'em off the wall and catches them. I don't know that you can exclude those things as art, except you know in your bones that they have nothing to do with art.

PLAYBOY: So you have never considered yourself an artist?

BRANDO: No, never, never. No. Kenneth Clark narrated a television program called *Civilization*. It was a remarkable series. It was erudite, communicative, polished, interesting to listen to. There was a man who knew who the artists of the world were. He didn't talk about any paltry people that you and I might mention. He doesn't know those people. He talked about *great* art. He certainly didn't refer to the art of film.

PLAYBOY: But film is reflective of our art and culture. Clark's *Civilization* covered a broad spectrum of history. Maybe in 50 or 100 years, the next Kenneth Clark will include the art of film.

BRANDO: Why don't you do an interview with Kenneth Clark and tell him that I want to know [*laughs*] if he considers Marlon Brando an artist?

PLAYBOY: Assume he would say yes.

BRANDO: If Kenneth Clark said that I was an artist, I would immediately get him to a neurosurgeon.

PLAYBOY: Now you're ignoring the authority you've cited. If actors can't be artists, could films be works of art? Would you consider *Citizen Kane* a work of art?

BRANDO: I don't think any movie is a work of art. I simply do not.

PLAYBOY: Would you go as far as saying that a collaborative effort can't be a work of art?

BRANDO: Well, the cathedral in Rouen or Chartres was a collective work, brought about over perhaps 100 years, where each generation did something. But there was an original plan. Michelangelo's Saint Peter was created by him, but thousands of people were involved in it. Bernini or Michelangelo would conceive a piece of sculpture and then have their students, artisans, knock the big chunks out.

PLAYBOY: Who is the artist in such cases?

BRANDO: The person who conceives it, and also executes it.

PLAYBOY: In *A Streetcar Named Desire* and *Hamlet*, Williams and Shakespeare are artists, right?

BRANDO: Yeah.

PLAYBOY: So couldn't there be artists who interpreted those works?

BRANDO: Sure. Heifetz certainly is an artist, for God's sake. He is a particular kind of artist; he's not a creative artist, he's an interpretive artist.

PLAYBOY: Can singers be artists?

BRANDO: [*Long pause*] No.

PLAYBOY: Lyricists? Cole Porter, Harold Arlen?

BRANDO: Shakespeare's a lyricist, he wrote many songs. Yeah, I suppose any creative writing. But you get so far down on the scale. You're not going to call The Rolling Stones artists. I heard somebody compare them—or The Beatles—to Bach. It was claimed they had created something as memorable and as important as Bach, Haydn, Mozart and Schubert. I *hate* rock 'n' roll. It's ugly. I liked it when the blacks had it in 1927.

PLAYBOY: When it was called jazz?

BRANDO: No, it was called *rock 'n' roll*.

PLAYBOY: We thought Alan Freed coined the term in the 1950s.

BRANDO: That's not a new phrase. Rock 'n' roll is as old as the beard of Moses.

PLAYBOY: What about someone like Bob Dylan, who both writes and performs his own work?

BRANDO: There are people who aspire to being artists, but I don't think they're worthy of the calling. I don't know of any movie actors, or any actors.... There are *no* people.... We can call them artists, give them the generic term if they're comfortable with that, but in terms of great art—magnificent art, art that changes history, art that's overwhelming—where are they? Where are the great artists today? Name one. When you look at Rembrandt or Baudelaire or listen to the *Discourses* of Epictetus, you know the quality of men is not the same. There are no giants today. Mao Tse-tung was the last giant.

PLAYBOY: If we limit the discussion to the world of film, there are plenty of actors today who bow to you as a giant. You may be repelled by that, but people such as Al Pacino, Barbra Streisand, Pauline Kael, Elia Kazan have given you that label.

BRANDO: I don't understand what relevance that has. Chubby Checker was the giant among twisters. I don't know what that illustrates. When you talked earlier about film being reflective of art and culture, the question went *flaming* through my mind: What culture? There's no culture in this country. The last great artist died maybe 100 years ago. In *any* field. "And we petty men peep about between his legs to find ourselves dishonorable graves."

PLAYBOY: Shakespeare?

BRANDO: Shakespeare. So we've somehow substituted craft for art and cleverness for craft. It's revolting! It's *disgusting* that people talk about art and they haven't got the right to use the word. It doesn't belong on anybody's tongue in this century. There are no artists. We are businessmen. We're merchants. There is no art. Picasso was the last one I would call an artist.

PLAYBOY: Picasso, you know, was also a very commercial property. If he signed a check for less than $75, it would be worth more if you sold the signature than if you cashed the check.

BRANDO: I think that's a wonderful joke. It's enormously clever. That he could draw the outlines of an outhouse and give it to somebody and it's worth $20,000. 'Cause it's making a commentary on the obscenity of our standards. He knew it was absolute trash, horseshit, but it's just like a Gucci label. Yeah, it's just a label, a Picasso label.

PLAYBOY: Well, the Brando label is also highly valued. Are you astounded by the money you get for a film?

BRANDO: I don't know how we segued into that.

PLAYBOY: A lot of artists, like Picasso, who received large sums of money also considered themselves worthy.

BRANDO: Are you making an association of worthiness with money? These are hustling questions. It's a disposition to get Brando to talk about these issues. You can always feel when something in the conversation is fertile and it's got a dollar sign on it.

PLAYBOY: What we're getting at is that the L.A. County Museum, for one, considers you enough of an artist to have recently sponsored a Marlon Brando Film Festival.

BRANDO: Oh, gee, I missed that. Shucks.

PLAYBOY: There aren't many film festivals of contemporary actors in museums. Isn't that at least . . . kind of nice?

BRANDO: Kind of nice, I guess that covers it. Better than a poke in the eye with a stick. How come you have to know about acting all the time? What else ya got?

PLAYBOY: All right. We'll work politics into our next question: Didn't the Italian-American Civil Rights Organization say that you defamed their community with your role as Don Corleone in *The Godfather*?

BRANDO: I don't know. If they said that about me, then they must have felt that was true.

PLAYBOY: Is it true that you vetoed Burt Reynolds for James Caan's part in *The Godfather*?

BRANDO: Francis would never hire Burt Reynolds.

PLAYBOY: But do you have that kind of control over who acts with you?

BRANDO: Well, you have to have rapport.

PLAYBOY: Have you been accused of ethnic slurs when you've played other nationalities in your films?

BRANDO: No. I played an Irishman who was a freak psychopath [*The Nightcomers*] and I didn't get any letters from any Irish-American organizations. It would have been difficult to make *The Godfather* with an eighth Chinese, a quarter Russian, a quarter Irish and an eighth Hispanic. Very difficult to take those people to Sicily and call them O'Houlihan.

PLAYBOY: Did you receive $100,000 from Paramount to talk to the press after making *The Godfather*?

BRANDO: I can't remember. When I hear something like that, I always remind myself of the congressman with his hand in the till.

PLAYBOY: Another lapse of memory associated with you is your inability or your refusal to memorize lines. Do you have a bad memory or is it that you feel remembering lines affects the spontaneity of your performance?

BRANDO: If you know what you're going to say, if you watch people's faces when they're talking, they don't know what kind of expressions they're going to have. You can see people search for words, for ideas, reaching for a concept, a feeling, whatever. If the words are there in the actor's mind. . . . *Oh, you got me!* [*Laughing*] *You got me right in the bush.* I'm talking about acting, aren't I?

Actually, it saves you an awful lot of time, because not learning lines . . . it's wonderful to do that.

PLAYBOY: Wonderful not to learn lines?

BRANDO: Yeah, you save all that time not learning the lines. You can't tell the difference. And it improves the spontaneity, because you really don't know. You have an idea of it and you're saying it and you can't remember what the hell it is you want to say. I think it's an aid. Except, of course, Shakespeare. I can quote you two hours of speeches of Shakespeare. Some things you can ad-lib, some things you have to commit to memory, like Shakespeare, Tennessee Williams—where the language has value. You can't ad-lib Tennessee Williams.

PLAYBOY: But how does it affect an actor who is working with you if he's got your lines written out on his forehead or wherever?

BRANDO: It doesn't make any difference. They're not going to see the signs. [*Names a book title.*] I just saw a title on the bookshelf. You didn't see me looking for it, you didn't know that I was even doing that. I can do the same thing if I have. . . . Well, anyway, it's more spontaneous.

PLAYBOY: So it is true that you no longer memorize lines when you act. But you did during the early stages of your career, when you were doing Williams and Shakespeare.

BRANDO: That's quite a different thing, because you cannot. . . . Well, you're getting me. [*Laughs*]

PLAYBOY: But not nearly enough. You can be very interesting when you talk about your profession, but you have an almost psychological reluctance to divulge experiential information that comes naturally to you. Why?

BRANDO: Some politicians will play full ball; that means they'd do anything to get their point across. Some people draw the line at various places.

PLAYBOY: It's interesting that you so easily interchange the words politician and actor. You obviously won't play full ball in an interview, but can't you go at least a few innings? A lot of readers will feel cheated if you simply refuse to discuss the roles you've played as well as your personal background.

BRANDO: That's an odd word to use.

PLAYBOY: Because we're playing, circling. When you said before, "You got me!" we thought you were quoting a line. It's like the minute you click on the word acting, you stop talking about it.

BRANDO: Because I know that your antenna's up.

PLAYBOY: All right, let us ask you about *Superman*, which is opening the same month this interview appears.

BRANDO: I don't want to talk about it.

PLAYBOY: Is there anything at all you can say about it?

BRANDO: I don't want to talk about *Superman*. That's not relevant.

PLAYBOY: For a man who likes to talk, it's a pity that you brake yourself.

BRANDO: I'm fascinated with everything. I'll talk for seven hours about splinters. What kind of splinters, how you get them out, what's the best technique, why you can get an infection. I'm interested in any fucking thing.

PLAYBOY: But will you talk for seven hours about your career?

BRANDO: Of course not. Not two seconds about it.

PLAYBOY: But you have, on occasion, talked with reporters about acting.

BRANDO: I was in error. I made a lot of errors and I don't want to repeat the errors. If we repeat our errors, then it makes this seem forlorn.

There's nothing sadder or more depressing than to see yourself in a series of similar errors.

PLAYBOY: Why do you insist on putting down acting?

BRANDO: I don't put it down. But I resent people putting it up.

PLAYBOY: Where would you put acting, then?

BRANDO: It's a way of making a living. A very good way.

PLAYBOY: Do you *like* acting?

BRANDO: Listen, where can you get paid enough money to buy an island and sit on your ass and talk to you the way I'm doing? You can't *do* anything that's going to pay you money to do that.

PLAYBOY: You do take acting seriously, then?

BRANDO: Yeah; if you aren't good at what you do, you don't eat, you don't have the wherewithal to have liberties. I'm sitting down here on this island, enjoying my family, and I'm here primarily because I was able to make a living so I could afford it. I hate the idea of going nine to five. That would scare me.

PLAYBOY: Is that what bothered you about acting in the theater?

BRANDO: It's hard. You have to show up every day. People who go to the theater will perceive the same thing a different way. You have to be able to *give* something back in order to get something from it. I can give you a perfect example. A movie that I was in, called *On the Waterfront*: there was a scene in a taxicab, where I turn to my brother, who's come to turn me over to the gangsters, and I lament to him that he never looked after me, he never gave me a chance, that I could have been a contender, I coulda been somebody, instead of a bum.... "You should of looked out after me, Charley." It was very moving. And people often spoke about that, "Oh, my God, what a wonderful scene, Marlon, blah blah blah blah blah." It wasn't wonderful at all. The situation was wonderful. *Everybody* feels like he could have been a contender, he could have been somebody, everybody feels as though he's partly bum, some part of him. He is not fulfilled and he could have done better, he could have been better. Everybody feels a sense of loss about something. So *that* was what touched people. It wasn't the scene itself. There are other scenes where you'll find actors being expert, but since the audience can't clearly identify with them, they just pass unnoticed. Wonderful scenes never get mentioned, only those scenes that affect people.

PLAYBOY: Can you give an example?

BRANDO: Judy Garland singing *Over the Rainbow*. "Somewhere over the rainbow bluebirds fly, birds fly over the rainbow, why, oh, why can't I?"

Insipid. But you have people just choking up when they hear her singing it. Everybody's got an over-the-rainbow story, everybody wants to get out from under and wants . . . [*laughing*] . . . wants bluebirds flying around. And that's why it's so touching.

PLAYBOY: Had another person sung that song, it might not have had the same effect. Similarly, if someone else had played that particular *Waterproof* scene with Rod Steiger—a scene considered by some critics among the great moments in the history of film—it could have passed unnoticed.

BRANDO: Yeah, but there are some scenes, some parts that are actor-proof. If you don't get in the way of a part, it plays by itself. And there are other parts you work like a Turk in to be effective.

PLAYBOY: Did you know that *Waterfront* scene was actor-proof when you were doing it?

BRANDO: No, at the time. I didn't know.

PLAYBOY: Was it a well-rehearsed scene or did Kazan just put the two of you there to act spontaneously?

BRANDO: We improvised a lot. Kazan is the best actor's director you could ever want, because he was an actor himself, but a special kind of actor. He understands things that other directors do not. He also inspired me. Most actors are expected to come with their parts in their pockets and their emotions spring-loaded: when the director says, "OK, hit it," they go into a time slip. But Kazan brought a lot of things to the actor and he invited you to argue with him. He's one of the few directors creative and understanding enough to know where the actor's trying to go. He'd let you play a scene almost any way you'd want.

As it was written, you had this guy pulling a gun on his brother. I said, "That's not believable; I don't believe one brother would shoot the other." The script never prepared you for it, it just wasn't believable; it was incredible. So I did it as if he *couldn't* believe it, and that was incorporated into the scene.

PLAYBOY: Many actors cite your performance in *Reflections in a Golden Eye* as an example of superb improvisational acting. Did any of that have to do with the direction of John Huston?

BRANDO: No. He leaves you alone.

PLAYBOY: What about Bernardo Bertolucci's direction of *Last Tango in Paris*? Did you feel it was a "violation," as you once said?

BRANDO: Did I say that once? To whom? [*Laughing*] "As you once said."

PLAYBOY: What you said was that no actor should be asked to give that much.

BRANDO: Who told you that?

PLAYBOY: I read it.

BRANDO: I don't know *what* that film's about. So much of it was improvised. He wanted to do this, to do that. I'd seen his other movie, *The Conformist*, and I thought he was a man of special talent. And he thought of all kinds of improvisations. He let me do anything. He told me the general area of what he wanted and I tried to produce the words or the action.

PLAYBOY: Do you know what it's about now?

BRANDO: Yeah, I think it's all about Bernardo Bertolucci's psychoanalysis. And of his not being able to achieve. . . . I don't know, I'm being facetious. I think he was confused about it; *he* didn't know what it was about, either. He's very sensitive, but he's a little taken with success. He likes being in the front, on the cover. He enjoys that. He loves giving interviews, loves making audacious statements. He's one of the few really talented people around.

PLAYBOY: Pauline Kael made some pretty audacious statements when she reviewed *Last Tango*, saying it had altered the face of an art form. Did such critical reaction to the film surprise you?

BRANDO: An audience will not take something from a film or a book or from poetry if it does not give something to it. People talk about great writers, great painters, great thinkers, great creators, but you cannot fully understand what a great writer is writing about unless you have some corresponding depth, breadth of assimilation. To some people, Bob Dylan is a literary genius, as great as Dylan Thomas was. And Pauline Kael, unconsciously, gave much more to the film than was there. You learn an awful lot about reviewers by their reviews—a good reviewer, that is. From bad reviewers, you can't learn anything, they're just dummies. But Pauline Kael writes with passion, it's an important experience to her. No matter what they like or dislike, talented reviewers reveal themselves, like any artist.

PLAYBOY: For a moment there, we thought you said *artist*. Are there any directors you'd like to work with, such as Bergman, Fellini, Truffaut?

BRANDO: No.

PLAYBOY: What happens when you improvise and the actor you're working with wants to stick to the script?

BRANDO: If an actor can't improvise, then perhaps the producer's wife cast him in that part. You wouldn't be in the film with such a person. Some actors don't like it. Olivier doesn't like to improvise; everything is structured and his roles are all according to an almost architectural plan.

PLAYBOY: Critics often lean toward either you or Olivier as the greatest living actor. Since Olivier's done the classics, do you think that gives him the edge?

BRANDO: That's speculation. Speculation's a waste of time. I don't care what people think.

PLAYBOY: Do you care, though, when people say you don't always give 100 percent when you act?

BRANDO: Stella Adler, who was my teacher, a most remarkable woman, once told me a story about her father, Jacob P. Adler, a great Yiddish actor who brought the European tradition of theater to this country with him. He had said that if you come to the theater and you feel 100 percent inspiration, show 70. If you come to the theater another night and you feel maybe 50 percent, show 30. If you come to the theater feeling 30 percent, turn around and go home. Always show less than you have.

PLAYBOY: Have you ever just walked through a part?

BRANDO: Certainly. Yeah.

PLAYBOY: Often?

BRANDO: No.

PLAYBOY: What about *A Countess from Hong Kong*, directed by Charles Chaplin?

BRANDO: No, I *tried* on that, but I was a puppet, a marionette in that. I wasn't there to be anything else, because Chaplin was a man of sizable talent and I was not going to argue with him about what's funny and not funny. I must say we didn't start off very well. I went to London for the reading of the script and Chaplin read for us. I had jet lag and I went right to sleep during his reading. That was terrible. [*Laughs*] Sometimes sleep is more important than anything else. I was miscast in that. He shouldn't have tried to direct it. He was a mean man, Chaplin. Sadistic. I saw him torture his son.

PLAYBOY: In what way?

BRANDO: Humiliating him, insulting him, making him feel ridiculous, incompetent. He [Sydney Chaplin] played a small part in the movie and the things Chaplin would say to him. . . . I said, "Why do you take that?" His hands were sweating. He said, "Well, the old man is old and nervous, it's all right." That's no excuse. Chaplin reminded me of what Churchill said about the Germans, either at your feet or at your throat.

PLAYBOY: Was he that way with you?

BRANDO: He tried to do some shit with me. I said, "Don't you *ever* speak to me in that tone of voice." God, he really made me mad. I was late one day, he started to make a big to-do about it. I told him he could take his film and stick it up his ass, frame by frame. That was after I realized it was a complete fiasco. He wasn't a man who could direct anybody. He probably could when he was young. With Chaplin's talent, you had to give him the benefit of the doubt. But you always have to separate the man from his talent. A remarkable talent but a monster of a man. I don't even like to think about it.

PLAYBOY: What about when you direct yourself, as you did in *One-Eyed Jacks*? That was a first and last experience for you; did it cure your desire to direct?

BRANDO: I didn't desire to direct that picture. Stanley Kubrick quit just before we were supposed to shoot and I owed $300,000 already on the picture, having paid Karl Malden from the time he started his contract and we weren't through writing the picture. Stanley, Calder Willingham and myself were at my house playing chess, throwing darts, playing poker. We never got around to getting it ready. Then, just before we were to start. Stanley said, "Marlon, I don't know what the picture's about." I said, "I'll tell you what it's about. It's about $300,000 that I've already paid Karl Malden." He said, "Well, if that's what it's about, I'm in the wrong picture." So that was the end of it. I ran around, asked Sidney Lumet. Gadge [Kazan] and, I don't know, four or five people: nobody wanted to direct it. [*Laughs*] There wasn't anything for me to do except to direct it or go to the poorhouse. So I did.

PLAYBOY: Was it a new experience for you?

BRANDO: No, you direct yourself in most films, anyway.

PLAYBOY: Didn't the studio take the film away from you, finally?

BRANDO: I kept fiddling around and fiddling around with it, stalling, so they went and cut the film. Movies are made in the cutting room.

PLAYBOY: Looking back at your body of work, are there any of your films that you aren't at all happy with, that you would like to erase if you could?

BRANDO: No.

PLAYBOY: Would you change many of them if you had a chance to re-edit them now?

BRANDO: No, I wouldn't want to do that. Good God, one of the most awful places in the world to be is the cutting room. You sit all day long in a dark place filled with cigarette smoke.

PLAYBOY: Do you always see the final results of what you do?

BRANDO: Sometimes you see it in the dubbing room. I've been in the screening room sometimes. Some films I haven't seen. You're bound to run into them on television someplace. One film I liked a lot—the only time I ever *really* enjoyed myself—it was called *Bedtime Story*, with David Niven. God, he made me laugh so hard. We got the giggles like two girls at a boarding school. He finally had to ask me to go to my trailer, I couldn't stop laughing. [*Laughing*] We both thought it was such a funny script, a funny story.

PLAYBOY: Would you have liked to do more comedy?

BRANDO: No, I can't do comedy.

PLAYBOY: Are there any recent films that have made you laugh?

BRANDO: I haven't gone to that many movies. I liked *High Anxiety*. Mel Brooks makes me laugh. They had a Laurel and Hardy festival on television; boy, I laughed at that. It went on all night long; I was up half the night laughing.

PLAYBOY: Was it anything special Laurel and Hardy did that cracked you up?

BRANDO: I suppose Hardy's exasperation with Laurel and doing dead takes into the camera and shaking his head. Exasperatedly patient. [*Laughing*] That's ridiculous.

PLAYBOY: What about Marx Brothers films?

BRANDO: No. When I was young, they were funny, but I look at them now and it's embarrassing.

PLAYBOY: How about *The Honeymooners*?

BRANDO: Art Carney is a marvelous actor. And Jackie Gleason is a really wonderful entertainer. I love to watch *The Honeymooners*. Sid Caesar and Carl Reiner had some wonderful routines in *Your Show of Shows*. God, they made me laugh. They bent me out of shape. They were all funny guys.

PLAYBOY: Do you ever watch *Saturday Night Live*?

BRANDO: That's a funny program. Barbara Wawa. [*Laughs*] What is that girl's name?

PLAYBOY: Gilda Radner.

BRANDO: [*Laughing*] They were giving a newscast and somebody gave an opinion about something and she went arrgghhhhh [*sticks finger into mouth, fakes throwing up*]. They're sometimes outrageous.

PLAYBOY: Have you ever seen John Belushi do his imitation of you?

BRANDO: I don't know his name, but I probably have seen him.

PLAYBOY: Let's get back to movies you've seen. What are some of the more important films made in the past decade?

BRANDO: What do you mean *important*?

PLAYBOY: In whatever sense you think films might be important—significant, meaningful, of social value.

BRANDO: I don't know that films are important.

PLAYBOY: What about a film like *The Battle of Algiers*?

BRANDO: It was a good film, but whether it was important or not, I don't know.

PLAYBOY: What about foreign films?

BRANDO: There's a Japanese film called *Ikiru* that was very touching. Most of the Japanese films—*Woman in the Dunes, Gate of Hell, Ugetsu*.

PLAYBOY: Ugetsu'd if you're rich and famous.

BRANDO: Jesus Christ! God! [*Laughing*] I *love* those jokes! I don't know why I always laugh at that dumb shtick. [*Laughing more*] I have a heart attack on that stuff. It's so *silly*. You don't find many silly comics anymore. Comedians who stand up there and do flatfoot gapes like Willie Howard. Oh, God, he was so funny. What a funny man. The faces he made. I can't think of anybody who made me laugh more.

PLAYBOY: Who was he?

BRANDO: Willie Howard was a Jewish comedian in New York. I was a kid doing plays there and I'd go see him between the matinee and evening show. Good God, did he ever make me laugh. He had this guy who worked with him who did a double-talk routine—the guy would talk to him in double talk and he would share the bewilderment of it with the audience and the frustration of trying to get this guy to say something simple. [*Laughs*] Then his partner died and he worked solo. He made funny faces. He was ridiculous. The most ridiculous person I ever saw in my life. I was hanging on the orchestra pit, just roaring with laughter, and nobody else got the jokes. He was playing to me, just because somebody appreciated him so much. There are very few people who are truly silly and have a sense of the ridiculous. He was one such man. I never got to meet the guy. It's always better if you don't know them . . . comics are famously tragic people.

PLAYBOY: Have you ever seen Lily Tomlin?

BRANDO: Yeah. Good God, is she angry. Whew! She gives me the impression of somebody incandescent with rage that comes out in this crinkle-eyed smiling face. Acid. She's funny, but all of her humor comes from anguish, rage and pain. Don Rickles, too. Most humor does.

PLAYBOY: Even Bob Hope's?

BRANDO: Bob Hope will go to the opening of a phone booth in a gas station in Anaheim, provided they have a camera and three people there. He'll go to the opening of a market and receive an award. Get an award from Thom McAn for wearing their shoes. It's pathetic. It's a bottomless pit. A barrel that has no floor. He must be a man who has an ever-crumbling estimation of himself. He's constantly filling himself up. He's like a junkie—an applause junkie, like Sammy Davis Jr. Sammy desperately longs to be loved, approved of. He's very talented. What happens to those people when they can't get up and do their shtick, God only knows. Bob Hope, Christ, instead of growing old gracefully or doing something with his money, be helpful, all he does is he has an anniversary with the president looking on. It's sad. He gets on an airplane every two minutes, always going someplace. It didn't bother him at all to work the Vietnam war. Oh, he took that in his stride. He did his World War II and Korean War act. "Our boys" and all that. He's a pathetic guy.

PLAYBOY: What about Woody Allen?

BRANDO: I don't know Woody Allen, but I like him very much. I saw *Annie Hall*—enjoyed it enormously. He's an important man. Wally Cox was important. Wally Cox was a lifelong friend of mine. I don't know why I put them together. They're similar to me. Woody Allen can't make any sense out of this world and he really tells wonderful jokes about it. Don't you think it was remarkable that his time came to get his door prize at the Academy Awards and he stayed home and played his clarinet? That was as witty and funny a thing as you could do.

PLAYBOY: Wit certainly wasn't your intention when you had an Indian woman turn down *your* Academy door prize for *The Godfather*, or was it?

BRANDO: No. I think it was important for an American Indian to address the people who sit by and do *nothing* while the Indians are expunged from the earth. It was the first time in history that an American Indian ever spoke to 60 million people. It was a tremendous opportunity and I certainly didn't want to usurp that time. It wasn't appropriate that I should. It belonged much better in the mouth of an Indian. I thought an Indian woman would generate less hostility. But those people considered it an interference with their sanctified ritual of self-congratulations.

PLAYBOY: Do you feel all awards are ridiculous?

BRANDO: Of course they are. They're ridiculous. The optometrists are going to have awards for creating inventive, arresting, admirable, manufactured eyeglass frames—things that hook onto the nose, ones that go way around under the armpit for evening wear. Why shouldn't they? We have newscasters' awards, Globe awards . . . they should have an award for the fastest left-handed standby painter who's painted the sets with his left hand and who has dropped appreciably less paint on the floor while doing it. And then the carpenter's union should have an award for somebody who can take a three-pound hammer and nail two-by-fours together.

PLAYBOY: When you were given the NAACP's Humanitarian Award in 1976, you turned that down.

BRANDO: Yeah, I did. I don't believe in awards of any kind. I don't believe in the Nobel Peace Prize.

PLAYBOY: You did, however, accept the Academy Award in 1955.

BRANDO: I've done a lot of silly things in my day. That was one of them. At the time, I was confused about it and I made a judgment in error. An error in judgment.

PLAYBOY: Do you have a sense of guilt that perhaps—

BRANDO: No, I don't. [*Laughs*] I know some people do, but I've been fortunate in escaping that, I don't know why.

PLAYBOY: Not once in your life did it strike you—

BRANDO: No, and I've been amazed that most people are struck down with that. It hasn't *fazed* me!

PLAYBOY: Would you like to finish the question yourself?

BRANDO: Do I have guilt about . . . [*thinks, long pause, yawns*] . . . no, I cannot. OK, finish it.

PLAYBOY: Do you have any guilt about—

BRANDO: No, I don't. [*Laughing*] I answered that before; why do you keep asking me?

PLAYBOY: Well, you've effectively answered, so let's move on. There's a certain quote having to do with women that has been following you around for some time now.

BRANDO: That's a much better way of saying "You once said." You been rehearsing that?

PLAYBOY: It has to do with your saying, "With women, I've got a long bamboo pole with a leather loop on the end of it. I slip the loop around their necks so that they can't get away or come too close. Like catching snakes." Do you know that quote?

BRANDO: I don't know that quote. That's: When did you stop beating your wife? It's odious. It's unfair. And it's unimaginative to refer to quotes, because you know as well as I do, the press being what it is, it's going to write anything that sounds sensational. To take that as a frame of reference for a potentially volatile question or one that has color in it, it's not proper.

PLAYBOY: Why not think of it as clearing the record, especially if you didn't say it, or if you said it in sarcasm, in jest, and it came out in seriousness?

BRANDO: Who in the world cares? Who would want to dignify that claptrap and crap? We'd be all day doing that. It's a hopeless and useless task. I don't care what people write or what they think. Good Lord, I gave up caring about 20 years ago. Those are mostly conversational scavengers who sit around and wait for some slop to fall off the table. If there isn't any, then they invent some. It's of no consequence at all. Just like all questions about acting.

[*Later, lying on the beach late at night, Brando pointed at the sky.*]

BRANDO: That star next to the moon is always there. I remember I was in Marrakesh on a sparkling, crystalline desert night and I saw the same star. I'd been talking to this girl a long time—it was four in the morning—and the muezzin came out in his minaret and started chanting. It was an enchanted moment. It made me feel like I was in Baghdad in the 12th Century.

PLAYBOY: Was she a Moslem girl?

BRANDO: Nah. Airline hostess.

PLAYBOY: All right, let's stay with women but move away from your personal affairs. Have you had any involvement with the women's movement or with the passage of the ERA?

BRANDO: No.

PLAYBOY: Any feeling about it?

BRANDO: Yeah, it's something that has to pass inevitably and I'm absolutely astounded that the business community has not seen the ERA as an advantage to it, because the intellectual force women can bring to production standards would be very much to its interests. When you consider something like 75 percent of the doctors in Russia are women and 30 percent of the judges in Germany are women, we rank perhaps second only to Switzerland with an antiquated view that women belong in the kitchen doing menial chores.

PLAYBOY: Why do you think certain states won't ratify the amendment?

BRANDO: Why do people hate blacks? Why do people discriminate against Indians? Why is AIM referred to as Assholes in Moccasins in South Dakota rather than the American Indian Movement? People have unconscious fears and floating anxieties, maybe guilt, and they will attach themselves like a raindrop to a speck of matter. People have built-in prejudice, they've got hatred piled up in a very neat place and they don't want to have it scattered by logic.

PLAYBOY: What is it that men hate about women?

BRANDO: I think, essentially, men fear women. It comes from a sense of dependence on women. Because men are brought up by women, they're dependent on them. In all societies, they have organizations that exclude women; warrior societies are famous the world over for that. It comes from fear of women. History is full of references to women and how bad they are, how dangerous. There are deprecating references to women all through the Bible. The mere fact that a woman was made out of a man's rib, as a sort of afterthought. Men's egos are frightened by women. We all have made mistakes in that respect. We've all been guilty, most men, of viewing women through prejudice. I always thought of myself not as a prejudiced person, but I find, as I look over it, that I was.

PLAYBOY: So you *do* feel guilty about your feelings about women in your past?

BRANDO: Not at all. I don't feel the slightest bit of guilt. Guilt's a useless emotion; it doesn't do anybody any good. A healthy sense of conscience is useful.

PLAYBOY: What about gay rights?

BRANDO: The lack of rights that apply to *children* are the ones that appall me. That's head and shoulders above any other rights group. Down here in Tahiti, and in many places, children are treated with respect, like small adults without much of a frame of reference. But for some reason, we feel superior to children, and we also feel a sense of ownership. Mothers feel about their children the way husbands feel about women. It's *my* kid. Women who are in the women's movement, some of them say they are *not* their husband's possession, but then they'll unconsciously refer to their child as a possession. They use the same kind of language about their children as they would hate for their husbands to use about them.

PLAYBOY: A part of your life that's not widely known is your long involvement with Unicef. How long has it been?

BRANDO: About 20 years.

PLAYBOY: What kind of work do you do for them?

BRANDO: We've put on shows in Paris, London, Japan, the United States, traveled around the world, done promos. This has been the Year of the Child. Mainly, my task has been trying to communicate what Unicef has done, how much the world needs Unicef, and what a valuable investment children are, and what an enormous deficit they can be if they're not raised properly. Bring a half-sick child into the world and it costs you a great deal more, because the child will never become independent, the child will constantly be needing attention. You can't bring him up educationally deprived, physically and morally deprived. By the 1980s, there will be some 700 million children without enough to eat, with no jobs and no education. It will hit Southeast Asia first. The most rapidly increasing birth rate is in Mexico. But Bangladesh now has a runaway population growth.

PLAYBOY: Have you done any commercials for them?

BRANDO: We do TV spots, film spots, radio. Last year, I did six spots for Unicef.

PLAYBOY: How do you get people to give?

BRANDO: The best way to get people is to hire the guys who work for the United Jewish Appeal. They know how to get the dough. They're really terrific at separating people from their money.

PLAYBOY: Weren't you once involved in a film made in India that had some connection with Unicef?

BRANDO: I was in the state of Behar during the emergency feeding program. I was with Satyajit Ray, the Indian director. We were walking along, seeing the nadir of human experience. These children kept coming around and, oh, God, the horror. . . . And he was just walking along like he was walking through fields of wheat, pushing the children aside. It's a human obscenity. He said to me, "You don't pay attention to it, you ignore it or you'll go mad. There's nothing you can do." I wanted to film it and show it to people in the United States. I made an entire film, about 45 minutes. It showed children in the last stages of life, of starvation; little crooked, whimpering things, covered with sores, scabrous from head to foot, lining up to get their food that was brought by Unicef.

PLAYBOY: Did you ever show the film?

BRANDO: I showed it to a number of people in my home, including Jack Valenti [president of the Motion Picture Association of America], who was a good friend of President Johnson. It showed children dying right on the camera. One woman offering me a child who was dying, died right on the camera. Children were staggering, falling down. I showed it to somebody at NBC. They said that their news department would cover that and I felt that they didn't want any outside contribution.

PLAYBOY: Which brings us to the subject of the news media and another one of those "You once saids." This time, the quote of yours is that media are "oppressively resistant to feeding the truth to the American people, simply because it doesn't sell." Do you still believe—after the Pentagon papers and Watergate—that we never get the truth?

BRANDO: It's all the news that's print to fit. When I say fit, I mean the market. Because there is a market for news, we see that on television: fierce competition between one news program and another that turns into Jolly Jack and the Fijian dancers. They're entertainment shows. They have teasers all the way along, telling you to tune in at 11, a massacre in Wisconsin. The editor picked *that* out as a teaser. Or, if they haven't got anything going, they'll put a tank-car explosion in there. It's tailored violence; they have what they call the tasteful frontier of violence.

PLAYBOY: Do you think the media encourage violence or react to it?

BRANDO: It's a subtle question. Especially now with terrorism the way it is. Look, we've had more than 100 derailing incidents, and almost always it's a tank car with flammable substances in it. We had about five major grain-elevator disasters in one year. That's put down to coincidence. We're not told they're acts of sabotage. I would assume that the government has gotten together with the news people and said, "Listen, don't broadcast alarming stories about terrorists in the United States." But there are plans afoot to counteract terrorism in the U.S.

PLAYBOY: On the subject of alarming stories, do you think that the oil crisis we suffered a few years ago was a conspiracy rather than a crisis?

BRANDO: I don't know whether or not it was a conspiracy, but there are enough industrial executives who have gone to jail over the past 20 years for price fixing that you wouldn't be going wide off the mark if you said they were manipulating us. For example, if the power companies would quit fighting solar energy and quit leaning on the legislatures and get behind it, it could happen. But the oil and steel companies' interests are allied, manufacturers of cars, plastics—which means oil companies—steel companies, metal, rubber companies, don't want to alter, to retool, it will cost them too much. They say it's going to hurt them, wreck the economy, they're not making enough in profit. The way they piss and moan about their profit ratings, it makes you think over the years they'd have gone out of business long ago. *The Godfather* said that a man with a briefcase can steal more money than a man with a pistol.

PLAYBOY: Do you think big business is out of control?

BRANDO: Corporations have no sense of social responsibilities. They tell lies from morning till night. You see advertisements of the petroleum outfits, everybody wants to take care of the environment, so they show you a doe taking a sip of water in a marsh and in the background we see an oil derrick, and Exxon wants us to know that even the doe is being looked after. They give you all this claptrap that Madison Avenue cranks out. *There's* an art form: advertising. Making people do what you want them to do, that's what Americans are good at. They can manipulate anybody at any moment. And it makes precious little difference whether we're manipulated by the state, as in Russia, or by big business, as we are through advertising.

PLAYBOY: What about our being manipulated by organized crime?

BRANDO: Sure, organized crime exists, no question. Whether or not it has infiltrated every aspect of our lives, I don't know. It's going to give the military-industrial complex a run for its money. But it doesn't consider it organized crime. It thinks it's just business. The other businesses—Big Business—start wars in the name of right, liberty and all that. The Mafia says, "That's just a front; what they really want and what they're after is the goods. It's just money, and they're no different than we are. We have the same objectives, we take better care of our people than they do." I think, quite possibly, that's true.

PLAYBOY: Isn't there something other than money that both kinds of businesses are after? Such as power?

BRANDO: Money *is* power. Money translates into guns, in the name of defense, of course. If you have enough money, you can do anything. You can even get a president shot. All you have to do is hire Sam Giancana, Sirhan Sirhan. You can get anybody killed for a can of beer. Hire some dumbo hit man, pay him $50,000. You can hire a 17-year-old kid, he'll be out in the streets in two or three years.

PLAYBOY: Let's talk about the assassinations of the Kennedys and Martin Luther King Jr. Do you think it's possible that it was a lone assassin in each case?

BRANDO: It's possible but by no means probable. And certainly, if they had not been killed, there were plans afoot to kill them. For political reasons. No different from Diem or Allende. If the CIA had known that Castro was a Communist, it would have assassinated him long before the Bay of Pigs. It would have had troops fighting on the side of Batista.

PLAYBOY: Do you suspect the FBI and/or the CIA as having anything to do with the assassinations in the 1960s?

BRANDO: They had to have been involved in them. It's safe to assume that the FBI or the CIA is capable of committing murder. The assassination, for instance, of Fred Hampton in Chicago was FBI-coordinated. When the FBI started out, there was never a force in the world more efficient and better at what it did. But gradually it became politicized, it was reflective of Hoover's jingoistic concepts of the world: life as it should be in the United States according to Saint Hoover. Hoover very cleverly had information on *everybody*.

PLAYBOY: Getting back to the Kennedys, did you ever meet John Kennedy?

BRANDO: Yeah, it was at a fundraising affair at the Beverly Hills Hotel while he was President. He was table-hopping, as he had to, and he said, "Hello, how are you, nice to meet you"—he didn't say that, but he had his shtick. I said to him, "Aren't you bored to death?" He looked at me and said, "No, I'm not bored." I said, "You've got to be bored." He thought I was being hostile. Then he realized that he was bored having to do that, going around, people gawking at him. Then a Secret Service man came to the table and said, "Kennedy would like to see you after dinner." So we went to his room there and the evening consisted of everybody getting drunk, including Kennedy. Then he told me that I was overweight and I said that he was getting fat and jolly and I could hardly recognize him. We all stormed into the bathroom and weighed ourselves. Afterward, he said, "I know what you've been doing with the Indians, I know what you've been doing." And that was that. A kind of strange interlude.

PLAYBOY: What did you think of Robert Kennedy?

BRANDO: I think Bobby Kennedy really, finally, cared; he realized that all of the rhetoric had to be put down into some form of action. That's perhaps the reason they killed him. They don't care what you say, you can say as much as you want to, provided you don't *do* anything. If you start to do something and your shuffling raises too much dust, they will disestablish you. That's what happened to Martin Luther King. J. Edgar Hoover hated black people, hated Martin Luther King. If he stayed in the civil rights area, fine, that's just what they wanted him to do: let the Civil Rights bill pass so we can deal with the Africans and get their raw materials. So Martin Luther King was in service to what the government wanted, anyway. But when he got on the issue of the Vietnam war, he was talking to 23 million people who were pretty willing to go down the road he told them to go down. That was too heavy. He upped the ante and they didn't want to go that high.

PLAYBOY: Is that also why Malcolm X was killed, in your opinion?

BRANDO: He was a dynamic person, a very special human being, who might have caused a revolution. He had to be done away with. The American government couldn't let him live. If the 23 million blacks found a charismatic leader like he was, they would follow him. The powers that be could not accept that.

PLAYBOY: Did you ever meet him?

BRANDO: No, I'm sorry I didn't; he was a great man. We won't see the likes of Malcolm X again in our lifetime. He was a man of extraordinary talents, capacities, abilities. If he had lived, America would have been far better off. Our consciousness, who we are, what we do, what we intend . . . instead of believing the claptrap that we read about ourselves, and listening to *The Marines' Hymn* and all the romantic jingoistic jargon that we're shook to death with every day.

I'm often amused when I read American history and I read what great things America was going to be, what great things we were going to produce, the magnificent life we were going to have. We were determined to be an impressive and strong nation that needed a lot of people and a lot of land. And all those people who came: "Give us your great unwashed." Well, we got all the great unwashed there were. From every prison we certainly got a lot of scum and dummies. We didn't get the cream of the crop. We got people from the lowest echelons of society who couldn't make it or weren't happy where they were. Or who were taken from Africa, brought to America in chains and turned into animals.

PLAYBOY: How do you feel about President Carter's stand on human rights?

BRANDO: Carter has done something that no other president has done: He has brought into the sharpest contrast the hypocrisy of the United States in respect to human rights. He's done a great favor to the Indians, because you couldn't find a president who'd given them the opportunity to point out the disparity between what Carter says and what actually happens. He's taken up the issue of human rights like the Holy Grail—put the rhetoric in Mondale's mouth and sent him off to do Sir Galahad's work. I don't know whether it was oversight or political stupidity, I can't imagine what it was that made him think that he was going to get away with it; that somehow the world was not going to know that we don't have any human rights for Indians, we don't want to reinstate them. The only time I've ever heard him refer to Indians was when someone asked him a question about the infiltration of people from Mexico into the U.S. and called them immigrants, and he said, "Well, outside of a few Indians, we're all immigrants." So I would take that to mean that he dispensed with the Indians because they were few in number and therefore entirely irrelevant. But the fact is that there are about 40 million Indians in North and South America. People tend to forget that there are one million Indians in Canada. And Mexico is primarily an Indian nation. They were possessors of great civilizations. Of the five races in the world, they're the only ones who are not represented in the UN.

PLAYBOY: Have you ever tried to meet with Carter, perhaps with a delegation of Indian leaders?

BRANDO: My guess is it wouldn't do any good. Carter would give you a mint julep and a tap dance, but that's all it's going to amount to.

PLAYBOY: Sounds like you won't be endorsing Carter in 1980.

BRANDO: If Jerry Brown runs against him, I'll vote for Jerry Brown. I think he's a terrific fellow and would make a hell of a president.

PLAYBOY: Are there other politicians you trust?

BRANDO: Jim Abourezk [senator from South Dakota] has done something without equal as far as I know. In his own state, he's come out very strongly in support of AIM. He's taken some rather strong clouts, been beaten about the head and shoulders politically for supporting the Indians. But what's right to him is right.

PLAYBOY: Well, we've come this far without really getting into the issue of the Indians as much as you hoped for, so let's begin with—

BRANDO: Let me ask you why you *want* to talk about the Indians.

PLAYBOY: Well, as you know, it's a hell of a lot more interesting than discussing our views on sex or show business or—

BRANDO: [*Cracking up, strong laughter.*]: It's funny, I was laughing, seeing the words in the interview, and then your line. [*More laughter*] That's funny. I love those kinds of outrageous retorts.

PLAYBOY: Do Indians have the kind of sense of humor you do?

BRANDO: People never think of Indians' having a sense of humor, but they are the most hilarious people I ever met. They'll laugh at anything. They'll laugh at themselves. They're sarcastic, sardonic, they're funny on every single level. They simply could not have survived without their superb sense of humor.

PLAYBOY: How did you first become conscious of the Indians?

BRANDO: I read a book by D'Arcy McNickle, a Flathead Indian who had a degree in anthropology from the London School of Anthropology or something, and another book by John Collier, who was then head of the Bureau of Indian Affairs. Then I went to see D'Arcy McNickle in Tucson. I discussed with him Indian affairs and history. He recommended that I see a group called the National Indian Youth Council. So I attended many of its meetings and, through that, I became absorbed in American Indian affairs.

PLAYBOY: And through your absorption, what is it that is most shocking to you?

BRANDO: What is shocking to me is that we can consistently try to expunge an entire people from this planet and not have known to the world the silent execution that has taken place over a period of 200 years. And that this government that we live under—which we all say is wonderful and fall to our knees and worship—has systematically deprived the Indian of life, liberty, the pursuit of happiness and, at the same time, has screamed around the world, like a whistling skank with rabies, that we believe in life, liberty and the pursuit of happiness. How in the world can we do that at the same time that we're strangling the life out of the only native culture that existed on this land? The American government has shot them, murdered them, starved them, tried to break their spirit, stolen from them, kidnapped their children and reduced them to rubble. That is what shocks and angers me.

I am *ashamed* to be an American and to see fellow human beings who, if human rights mean anything at all, have every right to the land they live on, and more land than they have. There were 10 million Indians, according to the *Encyclopaedia Britannica*, at the time of Columbus. There are now about one million. They owned all of the United States; they have precious little to call their own now. They were independent; they have nothing now. Any time a white man wanted a piece of land from an Indian, he was able to get it. So they took all the river valleys, they took all the fertile land, they took almost all the forests, they took everything and left the Indian *nothing*. Nothing but memories, and bitter ones at that.

When the government didn't do it militarily, it did it with documents and promises. We lied, we chiseled, we swindled; swindle, swindle, swindle, nothing less than swindle. Swindled the Indian. And we now will say we did not swindle. We *did* swindle. We *did* kill. We *did* maim. We *did* starve. We *did* torture. We did the most heinous things that could be done to a people. We will not admit it, we do not recognize it, it is not contained in our history books, and I want to pull my hair out when I read high school textbooks that deal with the destruction of a people in two paragraphs.

Our relationship with the American Indian is unprecedented in history. There's no country in the world that has made as many solemn documents, agreements, treaties, statements of intention as the United States has and broken every one of them, and had every intention of breaking them when it made them. No group of people has ever so consistently and cruelly suppressed another group of people as the Americans have the Indians. There were some 400 treaties written—*not one* was kept. That's a terrific record. Not one treaty! It is outrageous, it's shocking and unfair and a *lot* more important than whether or not I like to get up in the morning, put my Equity card in my pocket, go to the studio and put on my makeup and do my tap dance, going through a day of let's pretend. There's something obscene about that.

PLAYBOY: With all that has been done to them, what is it the Indians now want from the government?

BRANDO: What the Indians want is very plain: They want their own laws to apply in Indian land; they want an increase in the land base that was stolen from them; they want their treaties recognized. They want sovereignty, hunting and fishing rights, no taxation. They want to pursue their lives as they see fit. They want their economy reinstated.

They want nothing more and nothing less than what the Jews have in Israel. We have long, loud and often said people have a right to self-determination, and we stand behind any country in the world that so determines that it is going to be an entity unto itself. We went to Vietnam and killed millions of Vietnamese and thousands of Americans to prove that what we've said was true; we backed it up with force. But we are not willing to offer reinstatement to the American Indian, because there's no future in it. We reinstated the Japanese and the Germans because we wanted to be a presence in Asia and Germany. And a lot of Nazis got back into power so that the organization could be created to resist the Russians. But the American government just hopes that the Indian will fade away into history and disappear.

PLAYBOY: Do you really think the American government would willingly carve up American land and give it to the Indians, establishing a separate country within the United States?

BRANDO: Of course; why not? Drive through the Southwest and you're impressed with how little of the country is used. We probably have the fewest people per square mile in the United States than almost anyplace in the world. There's ample room for the Indian to be given back enough land to live on; future populations could be accommodated in that area. There are enough riches in this country so that the Indian could be properly re-established as a viable community. France gave all of its colonies back; for the most part, so have the Dutch, the Belgians, the British. Some of them gave up their colonies screaming, kicking, scratching, fighting; some did it because they read the handwriting on the wall. No Indian has the hope that the *Niña*, the *Santa Maria* and the *Pinta* are going to sail up the Hudson one day and we're all gonna get on them and go back to jails in England. But it's a very reasonable and logical expectation to assume that America is going to do what every other colonial power has done.

PLAYBOY: What do you think was the biggest mistake the Indians made?

BRANDO: If Indians had joined together and made a concerted effort to keep the white man from stealing their land and decimating their people, they could have wiped the people off the face of the earth as soon as they hit Plymouth Rock. But the Indians don't get along with one another. They never thought of themselves as a unified people.

But I'm on the horns of a dilemma, because I am not the spokesman for the American Indian. They have orators, poets, people who are giants, people who are able to talk better than most poets we know who write. Wonderfully articulate people. But they're never asked for an interview in *Playboy*, they're never asked to go on *60 Minutes*. When there's an occasion, newsmen always stick the microphone in my face. I don't know how many times I've said, "Listen, there are perfectly eloquent gentlemen standing to my left and to my right, please ask them, they are Indians, I am not; they know far better than I do why they're here; don't ask me why I'm here." But their editors say, "Go out and get a recording of the fire coming out of Marlon's nose." It's so distasteful to me that nobody gives a *shit*. I've called up I don't know how many magazines, spoken to writers of international renown, to senators who head the investigating committees—everybody's out to lunch.

PLAYBOY: Would you say that Indians have been more discriminated against than blacks were before the Civil Rights Act?

BRANDO: It's not an ouch contest.

PLAYBOY: What about missionaries? Have they done any good for the Indians?

BRANDO: The church has a tremendous debt that it owes to the Indian. The church was borrowed by the government as a force to so-call civilize the Indian. It was simply designed to disenfranchise the Indian, which it did. The church was in control; they sat in a room and they divided Indian reservations up like pies: Catholics here, Protestants here, you take this, we'll take that, go get 'em, boys. And they went in there in force and threw the Bible around with a will.

PLAYBOY: Had you been born an Indian, do you think, knowing what you know, that you'd be militant?

BRANDO: That's like saying if your aunt had balls, she'd be your uncle. I don't know what it's like to be an Indian. I can only imagine. And what I imagine is it's pretty horrible to be an Indian who cares about being an Indian, cares about maintaining himself as an Indian, cares about trying to establish an image of himself in front of his children. I suppose it would make me pretty goddamn mad.

PLAYBOY: Let's talk about some of your personal involvements. In 1964, you were arrested at a fish-in for Indian river rights in Washington, weren't you?

BRANDO: It was a priest from San Francisco, myself and an Indian from the Puyallup reservation. They wanted to test whether or not we would be willing to be arrested. We were arrested, but they didn't book us. We went to the jail and then they just dismissed us. They got a call from the governor's office or something. Soon after that first fish-in, we went to northern Washington and fished there, but it was the wrong place. We just froze to death. I almost got pneumonia. I was dying. Oh God, I was sick. That was my last fish-in.

PLAYBOY: Then, in 1975, you joined a group of Menominee Indians who had taken over a monk's abbey in Gresham, Wisconsin, in their attempt to get back the deed for land that had once been theirs. Didn't that turn into violence?

BRANDO: They were shooting bullets twice a day, in the afternoon and at night. Dog soldiers came and they were fighting it out for over a month. One guy was shot, a white guy. I was in there for about a week, with Father Groppi and some other priests. It was unbelievable, people going out with guns and ammunition, lying in the snow and firing at 2:30 in the morning; everybody sleeping, huddled, trying to get warm, bullets flying around. I was up on the roof one time and bullets started sizzling by me, *whheew, whheew*—sounds very funny. The bullets come by before you hear the gun.

PLAYBOY: Were you scared?

BRANDO: No. The Indians were determined that they should get that deed to the land. It was previously Indian land that had just been grabbed. The church wasn't using it, it was just sitting around in a Catholic bank book. There were contingent plans to go in with percussion bombs and gas. That would have killed a lot of people, because the Indians wouldn't have surrendered; the expression they had on their arm bands was Deed or Death. They finally got the deed. And then those goddamn Alexian Brothers, the group of priests who owned the property, took it back after everything died down. Those lying bastards! I was right there in the room when they were negotiating. They gave their word that the [abbey] should go to the Indians for a hospital and that the land should be returned to the Menominee reservation. They subsequently, arbitrarily, took it back, broke their word. After the Indians were arrested, they said, "We didn't mean that." There was no noise about it then. And some Indians are still sitting in jail.

PLAYBOY: Dennis Banks is the Indian activist who was recently granted political asylum in California by Governor Brown. Banks had fled South Dakota, where he faced sentencing on riot and assault convictions, and he was involved in a shooting with the Oregon highway patrol some time ago. His trailer was shot up and when the police traced the ownership, it was found that it belonged to you. Could you have been charged with aiding and abetting a fugitive?

BRANDO: I am not now nor have I ever been a Communist. [*Laughs*] Let me put it this way: I would certainly aid and abet any Indian if he came to me at this time. I had Dennis down here in Tahiti. I invited him to come down, because they were after him.

PLAYBOY: How long did he stay?

BRANDO: About two months.

PLAYBOY: Did the government know Banks was here?

BRANDO: Yeah. Dennis Banks is a remarkable man, he's a man who's got finely honed instincts; lives by his wits, which are considerable. He's the kind of man young Indians can look to to be inspired by. Russell [Means] is the same.

PLAYBOY: Why didn't the FBI go after you?

BRANDO: The Justice Department didn't see a practical way of indicting me, because it would have inflamed the issues and gotten a lot of coverage. For Russell Means to be thrown in jail is one thing, but for me to be put under indictment for aiding and abetting an American Indian who was forced to go underground due to political pressure—the entire thing was fraught with a very special kind of concern that it did not get too large.

Had the people in Wounded Knee been black or white, they would have had them dead within 20 minutes. You would have seen something that would have made the S.L.A. shoot-out look like a strawberry festival. But they couldn't do it. The only reason they didn't do it was not for any humanitarian reason but because the silhouette of the American Indian around the world is so famous, thanks to Hollywood.

PLAYBOY: When did you come to feel that, second only to the government, Hollywood has done more harm to the American Indian than any other institution?

BRANDO: I can't give you a date when the lightbulb went off in my head. I became increasingly aware just recently of the power of film to influence people. I always enjoyed watching John Wayne, but it never occurred to me until I spoke with Indians how corrosive and damaging and destructive his movies were—most Hollywood movies were.

PLAYBOY: Have you ever discussed this with Wayne?

BRANDO: I saw John Wayne only once. He was at a restaurant. He came over, very pleasant, wished us all a good evening and a happy meal and walked away. First and last time I saw him.

PLAYBOY: In 1971, in his *Playboy Interview*, John Wayne said that he didn't feel we did wrong in taking America away from the Indians. He thought the Indians were "selfishly trying to keep it for themselves" and that what had happened in the past was so far back that he didn't feel we owed them anything. Care to comment?

BRANDO: That doesn't need a reply, it's self-evident. You can't even get mad at it; it's so insane that there's just nothing to say about it. He would be, according to his point of view, someone not disposed to returning any of the colonial possessions in Africa or Asia to their rightful owners. He would be sharing a perspective with Vorster if he were in South Africa. He would be on the side of Ian Smith. He would have shot down Gandhi, called him a rabble-rouser. The only freedom fighters he would recognize would be those who were fighting Communists; if they were fighting to get out from under colonial rule, he'd call them terrorists. The Indians today he'd call agitators, terrorists, who knows? If John Wayne ran for president, he would get a great following.

PLAYBOY: Do you think his views are prevalent in Hollywood?

BRANDO: Oh, sure, I think he's been enormously instrumental in perpetuating this view of the Indian as a savage, ferocious, destructive force. He's made us believe things about the Indian that were never true and perpetuated the myth about how wonderful the frontiersmen were and how decent and honorable we all were.

PLAYBOY: Besides Wayne, you've been outspoken about the insensitivity of many of the Jewish heads of studios, who were in power during the heyday of the cowboy-and-Indian pictures. What made you so angry?

BRANDO: I was mad at the Jews in the business because they largely founded the industry. The non-Jewish executives you take for granted are going to exploit *any* race for a buck. But you'd think that the Jews would be so sensitized to that that they wouldn't have done it or allowed it. You've always seen the wily Filipino, the treacherous Chinese, the devilish Jap, the destructive, fierce, savage, blood-lusting, killing buck, and the squaw who loves the American marshal or soldier. You've seen every single race besmirched, but you never saw an image of the kike. Because the Jews were ever watchful for that—and rightly so. They never allowed it to be shown onscreen. The Jews have done so much for the world that, I suppose, you get extra disappointed because they didn't pay attention to that.

PLAYBOY: Has there been any Jewish reaction to what you've said about the Jews in the movie industry?

BRANDO: No. You have to be very careful about that issue, because the blacks are concerned about the blacks, the Indians are concerned about the Indians, the Jews are concerned about the Jews. In the United States, people are trying to look out for their own. The Puerto Ricans are not going to take up the Indian cause. The Indian cause is not going to be concerned about the injustice to the Japanese. Everybody looks to whatever's close at hand.

PLAYBOY: You once mentioned two films—*Broken Arrow*, with Jeff Chandler, and John Ford's *Cheyenne Autumn*—as *not* having treated Indians negatively. Are there any others you can add?

BRANDO: Not *Cheyenne Autumn*. That was worse than any other film, because it didn't tell the truth. Superduper patriots like John Ford could never say that the American government was at fault. He made the evil cavalry captain a foreigner. John Ford had him speak with a thick accent, you didn't know what he was, but you knew he didn't represent Mom's apple pie.

PLAYBOY: Do you approve of *any* of the films Hollywood has made about the Indians?

BRANDO: I can't think of any offhand.

PLAYBOY: What about one called *Soldier Blue*?

BRANDO: Oh, yeah, with Candice Bergen. That film left a lot to be desired; it dealt more with blood and guts than with the philosophy, which is important. It was certainly horrifying—the attack at Sand Creek, when they slaughtered the Indians. In many ways, that was representative of what happened. There were also parts of *Little Big Man* that I thought were useful. It had a lot of good, fair things in it.

PLAYBOY: I imagine you expect to have a lot of good, fair things in *The First American*, the TV project you've agreed to do for ABC. It's your first venture into television; can you talk about it?

BRANDO: We've been given a chunk of money to do as many programs as we can on that. Hopefully, we're going to get four programs out of it. If they like them, they will do more. We're certainly going to work as hard as we can to make them interesting, provocative and truthful. These issues are going to be clearly drawn, so that people can't duck them anymore. The Indian view will be heard, and it will be heard round the world. I'll take it to every country, I'll get arrested, I'll give them a show, I'll entertain them. People will say, "Where's Marlon been arrested this time?" I'm totally committing myself to getting this issue across.

PLAYBOY: How long will each show be?

BRANDO: An hour and a half. Hopefully, there's gonna be 13 or 14 made. We shouldn't have to go around, hat in hand, scratching and tapping on doors, climbing transoms, to get money to do a historical survey of the American Indian and how we reduced him to rubble. Jesus Christ!

PLAYBOY: Will you act in every show?

BRANDO: I will be in a number of them. So far, I see myself in one of the four, and I'll probably be in another.

PLAYBOY: Is it your intention to play figures like Kit Carson and Custer?

BRANDO: I'm too old to play Kit Carson and Custer. Kit Carson was a relatively young man, most of those guys were. You can cheat 20 years . . . but there are a lot of people I could play.

PLAYBOY: Well, if they could turn Dustin Hoffman into a 120-year-old Indian in *Little Big Man*—

BRANDO: Oh, I've played a 70-year-old man—you can go older, but it's very hard to go younger. Loretta Young finished her days in a blaze of ectoplasm, along with the number of silk screens that they had to put on the lights to soften them so her wrinkles wouldn't interfere with the fun.

PLAYBOY: Will *The First American* be commercialized, as *Holocaust* was, or will you have some control over the way it's presented?

BRANDO: *Holocaust* was as obscene as anything I've seen on television. I was infuriated by that. It made me gag. I was embarrassed for the people who did it; it was horrifying! Elie Wiesel, who was a man who survived Auschwitz, came out and broadsided the program. It should be treated sanctimoniously as an event in history, it should not be sandwiched between some dog-food ads. How can you go from a concentration-camp scene to a smiling woman selling dog food? God! It was appalling. Finally, it's better that they put that on than nothing.

PLAYBOY: Aren't you also going to play the part of American Nazi leader George Lincoln Rockwell in the upcoming second half of *Roots*? What made you want to portray him?

BRANDO: Everybody ought not to turn his back on the phenomenon of hatred in whatever form it takes. We have to find out what the anatomy of hatred is before we can understand it. We have to make some attempt to put it into some understandable form. Any kind of group hatred is extremely dangerous and much more volatile than individual hatred. Heinous crimes are committed by groups and it's all done, of course, in the name of right, justice. It's John Wayne. It's the way he thinks. All the crimes committed against Indians are not considered crimes by John Wayne.

PLAYBOY: Will you play Rockwell as an evil character?

BRANDO: I don't see anybody as evil. When you start seeing people as evil, you're in trouble. The thing that's going to save us is understanding. The inspection of the mind of Eichmann or Himmler. . . . Just to dispense with them as evil is not enough, because it doesn't bring you understanding. You have to see them for what they are. You have to examine John Wayne. He's not a bad person. Who among us is going to say he's a bad man? He feels justified for what he does. The damage that he does he doesn't consider damage, he thinks it's an honest presentation of the facts.

PLAYBOY: So your motivation is to understand prejudice, shed light on the darker parts of souls such as Rockwell's?

BRANDO: Understanding prejudice is much more helpful than just condemning it out of hand. There is a point, however, where you can understand so much and then you've got to take a gun out and say, "I'm not gonna let you do this to me anymore; if you do that, I'm gonna kill you." If somebody came to my house, I'd do damage. I'd kill somebody. I wouldn't hesitate.

PLAYBOY: You say that, but the act of doing it is something else.

BRANDO: I've pointed guns at people. Loaded guns.

PLAYBOY: Did you have your finger on the trigger?

BRANDO: Damn right I did. I've told people to get down, lie on the floor, frisked them, got their identification.

PLAYBOY: Burglars?

BRANDO: You betchya.

PLAYBOY: Did any intruder ever *not* lie down immediately?

BRANDO: No. Three or four times, I've pulled a gun on somebody. I had a problem after Charles Manson, deciding to get a gun. But I didn't want somebody coming in my house and committing mayhem. The Hillside Strangler victims—one of the girls was found in back of my Los Angeles house. My next-door neighbor was murdered, strangled in the bathroom. Mulholland Drive is full of crazy people. We have nuts coming up and down all the time.

PLAYBOY: Do you get a lot of hate mail?

BRANDO: Not a lot. I've gotten some threatening letters.

PLAYBOY: Do you give them to the FBI or are you under surveillance by them for other reasons?

BRANDO: Jack Anderson got some stuff from the Secret Service that had me on the list of those who had to be put under surveillance every time the president came to town. Back in the 1960s, there was a truck from the electric company parked in front of my house, around 11 at night. I said to them, "What's going on?" "Oh, just fixing the lines." I happen to know something about electricity, so I asked some questions and the guy in charge didn't know and gave me dumb answers. I've had the FBI visit me on five occasions, asking me a lot of questions.

PLAYBOY: Which probably gave you some good material for that movie you've wanted to do about Wounded Knee. What's happened to that project?

BRANDO: I have a very specific notion to make a film out of Wounded Knee to show the FBI and the Justice Department how what happens to Indians happens, and the way the minds of the politicians work in respect to the Indian. I think it would make a very good movie. It would start with the trial of Banks and Means and keep flashing back to how it happened.

PLAYBOY: Didn't Abby Mann, who wrote *Judgment at Nuremberg*, do a script for you?

BRANDO: He did three scripts.

PLAYBOY: Were any of them close to what you wanted?

BRANDO: Hardly. Really bad scripts.

PLAYBOY: Did you have anyone in mind to direct it?

BRANDO: I tried to get a guy I did a movie with before, Gillo Pontecorvo. He did *The Battle of Algiers*. I thought he'd be perfect for this movie. I was in another movie with him, almost fucking killed him, and he almost killed me. Good God, what a battle that was.

PLAYBOY: That was *Queimada*, or *Burn!*

BRANDO: Yeah, *Queimada*, which I thought was a wonderful movie. Jesus, they couldn't flush it away fast enough. I couldn't believe it, about an interesting time well told.

PLAYBOY: Why was it flushed away so fast?

BRANDO: I don't know. They let it die, it never appeared anyplace, as though it got the plague or something. Very mysterious. Anyway, Gillo met with the Indians and they scared him to death. Bunch of guys met him at the airport, with about half a bag on, scared the shit out of him. He came back, didn't know what was going on. I told him, he won't understand for a long time what the Indians are—they're very strange folks. And he was going along with it. And then he wanted Franco Solinas, a full-fledged Marxist, to write the script. And it was then the Indians backed off and said, "Nothing doing, we're not going to have a goddamn Communist writing our story." So that was the end of that.

PLAYBOY: What really happened when you worked with Pontecorvo? What it just a conflict between director and actor?

BRANDO: No, the guy was a complete sadist. He did an awful thing: He paid the black extras a different salary than he paid the whites on location in Colombia. Then he gave the blacks different food because he thought they'd like it.

PLAYBOY: So what did you do?

BRANDO: I started out saying, "Jesus Christ, Gillo, you can't pay the blacks different money, you've got to give them the same food, what the fuck, black journalists are coming down here, you think they're gonna hang around here 10 minutes without talking to the blacks and finding out what the fuck's going on?" I said, "I'm not gonna take the fall for that, goddamn it; you can't do that, that's what this picture's about." I went raving on.

PLAYBOY: Did you finally have it out with him?

BRANDO: One day, he had me do so many takes on one scene, I just blew fucking up. *Screamed* at the top of my lungs, "You are eating me like ants!" [*Laughs at the memory*] He jumped off the floor about four feet. I could have broken glasses if there'd been any around. I didn't know I was going to do it, it just happened.

There were *so* many horror stories with that film. I came to the set one day, on location on this mountain road, and the wardrobe woman was sitting near the camera and she had a kid. I said, "What's the matter with the kid?" She said he was sick. I said, "What's the matter?" "Well, he vomited a worm at lunch." I said, "He vomited a worm?" She said, "Yeah, he's got a fever." I said, "Where's the doctor?" She said, "We're going to take him to the doctor after the next shot." I said, "Take him now!" She said, "Gillo wants to finish the scene first, then that will kill the location." So I called out and had the chauffeur come up and I said, "Take the kid to the fucking hospital right now." I really got steamed. If Gillo had been taller, I would have fucking fought with him. I really would have punched the guy out. I just looked at him. He said something and I got in the car and went home.

PLAYBOY: After all that happened, how was Pontecorvo to work with?

BRANDO: He started carrying a gun. Finally sent word to me that he was going to use it if I didn't do what he said. He laughed, but he actually had a gun on his belt. He was very superstitious, hysterically superstitious. He had two pocketsful of lucky charms. On Thursdays, you could not ask him any questions. He could not stand purple. If there was *anything* purple on the set, he would get rid of it—including wine at lunch. And I found out that the prop man has to play the first part in every picture. And that the prop man has to wear certain tennis shoes in all his pictures. And that he has to print a certain take.

I went after his superstitions. I walked under ladders. I had him fainting, staggering, just hanging on the ropes. I would spill salt all over the place, throw it around, on the ground. I'd open a door, take a mirror and say, "Hey, Gillo!" Then I'd take a hammer and go, "*Whoom, whoom*" [*laughs*]. He was trying to bullshit with me, he treated me like one would treat Burt Reynolds—I don't know why I've got it in for *that* poor apple.

But, as I said, you have to separate people from their talent. And, even at the time, I did not want to blow the picture, because it was an important picture. I really felt that it could have been a wonderful movie. But I had to give the very strong impression that I didn't give a fuck and I was willing to blow it all.

PLAYBOY: Wasn't it during the making of that picture that you were thrown off a plane because they thought you were a hijacker?

BRANDO: Yeah. One time I was coming back from a three-day vacation, dragging my poor ass to the plane in Los Angeles. It was National Airlines, the only connecting flight to Colombia for three days. As I got on the plane, I said, "Are you sure this is the flight to Havana?" The hostess was tired. She didn't say anything, she just went to the pilot and said, "We've got a wisenheimer on board who wants to know if this is the flight to Havana." And the pilot said, "Get him off the flight." [*Laughs*] I couldn't believe my ears. I said, "I'm awfully sorry." She said, "You get off this flight or I'm going to have the FBI man here in a minute." I had a beard, so she didn't know who the fuck I was. I got off and ran past the counter and the guy said, "Mr. Brando, wait, what happened? Mr. Brando?" I was running like a son of a bitch, because I knew that he was going to tell the hostess, who would tell the captain, who would call the tower; the tower would call the desk and they were going to stop me and say, "Oh, it's all a big error." I was streaking down that thing like Jesse Owens in the old days. Then, of course, it appeared in the papers and all that shit. But I got three extra days out of it that I never would have gotten. Oh, I was never so glad. That was just wonderful.

PLAYBOY: Was *Burn!* the most frustrating of all your films?

BRANDO: I never had any trouble like that. Never.

PLAYBOY: What about *Mutiny on the Bounty*?

BRANDO: Oh, no, that's just all horseshit. Carol Reed wasn't doing the picture that they wanted and he was taking too much time. They also didn't have a script. And Reed quit. The stockholders' meeting was coming up and the next thing I know, it appeared in the paper, some magazine article blaming me for the whole fucking thing. They did that to Elizabeth Taylor on *Cleopatra*.

PLAYBOY: Was that the magazine you sued for $4 million?

BRANDO: *The Saturday Evening Post*. I just couldn't believe that they would do that. They dumped it all on me—its costs, its delays—and then the publicity mills just kept grinding it out. They were making up all these stories and they paid some fella to do a job on me in *The Saturday Evening Post*. So I hired a publicist for the first and only time in my life and said to him, "Listen, I'm not going to hold still for this; find out what's going on." He was Sam Spiegel's public-relations man, Bill Something, who later got hit by a taxi—serves him right.

PLAYBOY: Died?

BRANDO: Yeah. As it turned out, MGM was paying him off. They were paying him a salary and he was telling the head of the studio everything I told him. He wasn't representing me at all.

PLAYBOY: Did you ever follow through with *your* suit?

BRANDO: Yeah. I can't remember what happened; I think the *Post* settled, gave me some money.

PLAYBOY: Was that the only time you've ever sued a magazine?

BRANDO: Yeah; I wouldn't do it again. It's not worth the effort. Magazines want you to sue them. They'll write anything that's scurrilous, that sells a few hamburgers. What they get out of publicity is far in excess of what they pay in lawyers' fees. So Evel Knievel got a baseball bat and broke that guy's arms. I don't think that's such a bad idea.

PLAYBOY: Especially since you've broken at least one photographer's jaw yourself, when you punched Ron Galella in the mouth when he was taking pictures while you were going to dinner with Dick Cavett in Chinatown. Was that the only time you've lost your temper like that?

BRANDO: Oh, I've punched photographers out. Any time it has to do with the kids, I just go berserk. I can't stand any kind of invasion of privacy like that. I can't go to Italy anymore, because I'll be in jail. Last time I was there, a bunch of paparazzi were out there. I was saying good night to some guests. I had my son in my arms and I was outside and they started taking pictures. I put the kid down and ran after this guy. [*Laughs*] I took a terrific fucking swing at this guy. I couldn't see, they had lights on me, hell. I missed him and fell on my ass. Then I ran in and got a bottle of champagne and came running out the front door looking for anybody I could get hold of. One guy jumped on the hood of a car and then on the sidewalk. I followed him, chased him two fucking blocks. He was more scared than I was mad. I reached out to catch him and he jumped onto this streetcar and took off. I went back, two o'clock in the morning, and there's this tough guy banging on the door. My kids are in there, my wife. So I got a knife and I was just going to have it out with him. Tarita was wrestling and fighting me for the knife. Then I got myself together and realized, What the fuck am I doing? Go out and stab somebody in Italy and it's goodbye, Rachel.

So I called the American Embassy and said, "Let me speak to the ambassador." They said he was asleep. I said, "I don't care what the fuck he's doing, I didn't ask you that, I told you to get him on the phone!" I was just pissing mad. Poor guy was intimidated. He got the ambassador out of bed. "Mr. Ambassador," I said, "I'm being intimidated here and I'm not going to stand for much more of this. You're going to have to make some arrangements." I went on and on.

The next morning, two *carabinieri* are out in front of my house in their fucking uniforms. And a photographer was out there, too. I had to go to work and the guy pointed his camera at me and the *carabinieri* put his hand right over the lens. He had no business doing that at all, it's completely against the law. But he did that, pushed the guy into a car, took him down to headquarters, said, "What have you got here, dope in this camera? Heroin? What is this stuff?" Opened the camera. "Oh, film. Sorry." They never bothered me after that.

PLAYBOY: What about Galella?

BRANDO: With Ron Galella, I really had to sit down and talk about that. I broke the guy's jaw. Sure, he was annoying me, but then, if it's so annoying to me, I should be in the lumber business. But the guy *wanted* to get hit. He was looking for some kind of incident like that. This guy was following me all day long. Taking pictures while I was on [Cavett's] show. And afterward, Dick and I went to Chinatown to get something to eat and the fucking guy comes around to take pictures. Finally, I started to get exasperated. I went over to the guy and said, "Would you please just take a few more pictures? You've had enough for today; give us a break." He was drawing crowds around us. So he said, "Well, if you'll give me some decent poses, take off your glasses, maybe I'll think about it." I didn't think. Just the attitude was overbearing. And that was it. He sued me. Cost me $40,000. No, it cost me $20,000; the rest was taken off in taxes. The last time I saw him, he was wearing a football helmet with a feather coming out of the top.

PLAYBOY: You're known to have kept friends since childhood. Do any of them talk about you?

BRANDO: None of my friends, if they're my friends, talk.

PLAYBOY: What happens to friends who write books about you?

BRANDO: They're not friends to begin with. Friends don't write books, acquaintances do.

PLAYBOY: Have you ever read any of those books?

BRANDO: No. Life is not about that. Surely, life is about something other than sitting and reading books about yourself.

PLAYBOY: Are there many people in your profession for whom you have a lot of respect?

BRANDO: There are not many people in anybody's *life* that one can have a lot of respect for. No. How many people in your life do you have a lot of respect for?

PLAYBOY: A handful.

BRANDO: A handful? Well, same here.

PLAYBOY: What about Jane Fonda, Robert Redford?

BRANDO: I think Jane Fonda has done something. I could see her doing most anything. Redford's certainly been effective in pursuing his interests. Who always sings "I Left My Heart in San Francisco"?

PLAYBOY: Tony Bennett.

BRANDO: Yeah, Tony Bennett. He's been extremely helpful all the way along. He's a very decent guy, a very kind man. But I've never met a movie actor yet who made me fall to my knees in awe and wonder.

PLAYBOY: What about Tennessee Williams?

BRANDO: He's an enormously sensitive and cruelly honest person. If there are men who have a clean soul, he's one of them. He's an important and very brave man.

PLAYBOY: Any others?

BRANDO: Stella Adler and Elia Kazan were extremely important to me. I don't think I would have been able to ply my trade as well had I not been with them.

PLAYBOY: What distinguished Stella Adler from other acting teachers? What was she able to show you?

BRANDO: She was a very kind woman full of insights and she guided and helped me in my early days. I was certainly confused and restless. Outside of her phenomenal talent to communicate ideas, to bring forth hidden sensitivity in people, she was very helpful in a troubled time in my life. She is a teacher not only of acting but of life itself. She teaches people about themselves. I wouldn't want to say that it's psychotherapy, but it has very clear psychotherapeutic results. People learn about the mechanism of feeling. Whether they ever go on to being actors or not, it's irrelevant, they've learned a lot from her.

PLAYBOY: She once said, though, that she never taught you anything; she just opened doors for you and you kicked them down.

BRANDO: I would like to ask you, Vas ya dere, Charley? [*Laughs*] That's the great phrase that sustains me from one problem to another. It's so simple: Finally it comes down to saying, Vas ya dere, Charley?

PLAYBOY: One man with whom you were impressed was Justice William O. Douglas. Didn't you once go to see him about something?

BRANDO: Yes, I did. I was absolutely tongue-tied. I didn't know what in the world to say. I met him twice. Once in his chamber, he was gracious enough to admit me. I had a briefcase full of notes and wanted to talk about the American Indian. I couldn't put a sentence together. He sat there, "Yes?" He listened attentively. I suppose that intimidated me more than anything, that he was listening. I stuttered around, stammered. He said, "I have to go to the bench now." I said, "Oh, yes, yes, of course, quite so. Goodbye, Mr. Justice, Mr. Dougal, uh. . . ."

PLAYBOY: Was that the only time that's ever happened to you?

BRANDO: Yeah.

PLAYBOY: That doesn't seem to happen to people like Bob Hope, John Wayne or Sammy Davis Jr. when they meet with politicians like Nixon and Ford. How effective are such people in influencing others to support someone like Nixon?

BRANDO: Well, we ate the pudding, so. . . . I think it's just window dressing. Politicians go and get a few movie stars to put behind their ears like political flowers. It's parsley. They're just attention-getting devices, like those flags in the used-car lots that wave in the wind, multicolored iridescent things, drive along and they attract your attention for two seconds and that's the end of the show.

PLAYBOY: But when celebrities lend their names to $1000-a-plate dinners, it does seem to bring in the money.

BRANDO: They're shills. Political shills.

PLAYBOY: Do you think that was Carter's intention when he named Paul Newman to be a delegate to the United Nations special session concerning disarmament?

BRANDO: [*Laughs*]

PLAYBOY: Why are you laughing?

BRANDO: [*Laughing*] I wasn't laughing, I was coughing. Something in my drink.

PLAYBOY: You're not drinking anything. Anyway, would *you* get involved if Carter asked you?

BRANDO: I would not be involved in any formal or informal way with the government. If I can be helpful, it will not be because I'm an officeholder. I think Paul would be very effective as a politician. He's an intelligent, personable, fair-minded guy.

PLAYBOY: Since we've got you talking about one actor, you'll understand it if we segue into opinions on other actors. Wasn't there a rivalry between you and Montgomery Clift in the old days?

BRANDO: I think that's beneath me. It's too silly.

PLAYBOY: We had to ask.

BRANDO: I know you had to ask me, but then I had to say it's too silly when you did ask me.

PLAYBOY: Another such rivalry, according to the press, is between you and Frank Sinatra, stemming from the fact that you got the better role—and better songs—in *Guys and Dolls*. Sinatra has apparently called you the most overrated actor in the world.

BRANDO: I don't think that's true. You didn't hear him say that. Vas ya dere, Charley? And you weren't. So, unless he says that to my face, it's not going to have any great significance. And even if he did say it, I don't know if it's going to break my stride.

PLAYBOY: The press does play up rivalries, obviously.

BRANDO: Of course they do. That's how they make their bread and butter. What else are they going to do, write serious stories about people?

PLAYBOY: What magazines do you read?

BRANDO: *Scientific American, Science Digest, The New York Review of Books, The CoEvolution Quarterly.*

PLAYBOY: Serious stuff. Do you ever lighten it with something like the *Reader's Digest*, to keep in touch with the common man?

BRANDO: The *Reader's Digest* is the most popular publication in America, outside of the Bible, as far as I know. It is also the worst piece of trash I've ever seen in my life. I shouldn't say that—maybe they'll do an article about Indians. [*Laughs*] But I think they know it is not *The New York Times Book Review*; it's not *Esquire*; it's not *Playboy*; it's not *Scientific American*.

PLAYBOY: What about books?

BRANDO: I used to read an awful lot. Then I found that I had a lot of information and very little knowledge. I couldn't learn from reading. I was doing something else by reading, just filling up this hopper full of information, but it was undigested information. I used to think the more intelligence you had, the more knowledge you had, but it's not true. Look at Bill Buckley; he uses his intelligence to further his own prejudices.

Why one reads is important. If it's just for escape, that's all right, it's like taking junk, it's meaningless. It's kind of an insult to yourself. Like modern conversation—it's used to keep people away from one another, because people don't feel assaulted by conversation so much as silence. People have to make conversation in order to fill up this void. Void is terrifying to most people. We can't have a direct confrontation with somebody in silence—because what you're really having is a full and more meaningful confrontation.

PLAYBOY: It's a good thing you didn't express that in the beginning of this interview or it would have been a very short interview, indeed. Before we began taping, you told us of a recurrent nightmare you have about being sick, in the Korean War—

BRANDO: I didn't say the Korean War. I said that it just would be horrible . . . to be someplace in a war where you're freezing and sick, you have diarrhea, no way of getting back . . . it would be awful.

I always wondered why people went off to war, get themselves blown apart. The Korean War, the Vietnam War, why would they do it? Why not say, Christ, I'll go to jail for five years and that will be worth it, but I'm not going to get my head blown off, that's absurd, I'm not going. A lot of them did it. But the number who did not go was not so impressive as the number who went.

PLAYBOY: When you were of draft age, how did you avoid the army?

BRANDO: I beat the army by being declared psychoneurotic. They thought I was crazy. When I filled in their forms, under "Race," I wrote, "Human"; under "Color," I wrote, "It varies." Also, I got thrown out of military school, which helped.

PLAYBOY: You must have made your parents proud.

BRANDO: When I was kicked out of military school, my father thought I was a nogoodnik, I wasn't going to amount to anything. When I went into acting, that was the worst thing. When I started making money at it, he couldn't believe the kind of money I was making. It kind of blew his mind. He didn't know how to handle it.

PLAYBOY: How about yourself? How did you respond to the pressure? Did you ever become dependent on drugs or drink?

BRANDO: How individuals or society responds to pressure is the determination of their general state of mental health. There isn't a society in the world that has not invented some artificial means to change their minds, their mood, whether it's cacao or kola nut or alcohol. There are five million or 10 million alcoholics in the United States.

But all kinds of drugs have been with man forever and a day. If they're used as a means of escaping from problems, then the problems are only going to increase. Confrontation of problems is the only manner of solution of problems. Problems don't go away. Drugs are not a solution, they're a temporary relief.

PLAYBOY: A lot of people who can afford it go into analysis to get help with their problems, but those who can't often resort to drugs or alcohol.

BRANDO: It would be nice to say that poor people aren't happy, but rich people are snorting cocaine, that's the rich people's drug. When *all* the kids are smoking, dropping acid, taking cocaine, then you have to say there must be something wrong. In the main cities, when you can't walk out in the streets without getting mugged or being in fear of your life, something's wrong. All the rich people do is move farther and farther away from the areas of trouble.

PLAYBOY: Until you finally come to an island?

BRANDO: Until you finally come to an island.

PLAYBOY: Do you think the rich take cocaine as a means of escape or for pleasure, to enhance sexual activity, as a stimulation, whatever?

BRANDO: If it's a pleasure not to be yourself, not to have doubts about yourself, or to have an exaggerated sense of your own importance, then perhaps it is a pleasure. But it's a questionable one, because you're dealing with an unreal world and eventually you're going to have a rendezvous with a brick wall, and you'll have to return to whatever you are.

PLAYBOY: Well, we all know who you are, at least as an actor and an activist, but who would you have liked to be if you could choose any period in history in which to have lived?

BRANDO: I think I would have liked to be a caveman, a neolithic person. It would have been nice to see what the common denominator of human existence was before it started to be fiddled with.

PLAYBOY: Would you have wanted to be an extraordinary caveman?

BRANDO: I would have been Ralph Kramden. Just your average cave dweller.

PLAYBOY: We think we just spotted another segue—at least it makes us think of the mumbling caveman you portrayed in *Streetcar*, which made Method acting a household word. Does being labeled a Method actor mean anything to you?

BRANDO: No.

PLAYBOY: Does it bother you?

BRANDO: B-O-R-E. Bore.

PLAYBOY: Is that what a Method actor does—to bore through to the core of a character's being?

BRANDO: It bores through and goes beyond the frontiers of endurable anguish of interviews.

PLAYBOY: Well, this painful interview is almost over.

BRANDO: Oh, listen, it hasn't been painful at all. It's been delightful. Although I feel like I got in a rummage sale: Would you want this dress? No, that *shmatte*. How about this corset? Well, we could take the rubber out and make a slingshot out of it. I'm dizzy. We've gone from the shores of Marrakesh to the halls of William O. Douglas.

PLAYBOY: A couple of final questions: Do you believe in God?

BRANDO: I believe there must be some order in the universe. So far as there is order, there is some force in the universe. It's hard for me to conceive it's just happenstance or a confluence of disorder that makes the universe what it is.

PLAYBOY: And are you optimistic or pessimistic about the future of life on this planet?

BRANDO: You can't live a life saying, Well, this is the end, so we might as well get out the banjo and the rowboat and get it on, just go laughing and scratching along until Gabriel blows his horn. Whatever the circumstances are, one has to keep trying to find solutions. Even if it seems impossible. They have never invented a system that worked: Religion didn't do it, philosophy didn't do it, ethics didn't do it, economic systems won't do it. None of the systems that deal with man's problems have ever worked. But to live a life of hopelessness, it's not possible.

PLAYBOY: Are you afraid of death? Do you think about it?

BRANDO: "Of all the wonders I yet have heard, it seems to me most strange that men should fear; seeing that death, a necessary end, will come when it will come." Another wonderful speech on death.

PLAYBOY: Do you remember more of Shakespeare than of any other author?

BRANDO: He's *worth* remembering. "For God's sake, let us sit upon the ground / And tell sad stories of the death of kings." I can't remember it all. [*Thinks*] "That rounds the mortal temples of a king / Keeps Death his court and there the antic sits, / Scoffing his state, and grinning at his pomp, . . . and with a little pin / Bores through his castle wall, and farewell, king!"

PLAYBOY: It was announced in the papers that you had consented to play King Lear on Broadway and that Elia Kazan would direct. Yes or no?

BRANDO: No.

PLAYBOY: Here's an offbeat question for you: What are things that repulse you?

BRANDO: The most repulsive thing that you could *ever* imagine is the inside of a camel's mouth. It's so awful! That and watching a girl eat small octopus or squid. I mean, I'm not squeamish about anything, I could make an ocarina out of a petrified turd with no problem, but that. . . . There's a certain frog that carries its eggs on its back and after they are fertilized, these froglings burst forth from the skin. . . . It just makes me sick. I don't like to look at somebody's sticky saliva. These people who laugh—ha, ha, ha—and there's a stringer of saliva from their upper tooth to the bottom lip and it bends every time they go *ha*, *ha*, it pulsates. Jesus, with one girl, you could take her saliva and walk across the street with it and lay it down on the sidewalk and still be connected. The viscosity of some people's saliva is remarkable.

PLAYBOY: What else offends you?

BRANDO: Bullfighting. I'd like to be the bull but have my brain. First, I'd get the picador. Then I'd chase the matador. No, I'd walk at him until he was shitting in his pants. Then I'd get a horn right up his ass and parade him around the ring. The Spaniards don't think anything more of picking an animal to pieces than the Tahitians do of cutting up a fish.

PLAYBOY: Which brings us, full circle, back to Tahiti. This island of yours is an unbelievably beautiful setting.

BRANDO: Yeah. I could open this up for tourism and make a million dollars, but why spoil it?

PLAYBOY: Do you find it impossible to leave this place once you're here?

BRANDO: It's very hard. But . . . "miles to go before I sleep, and miles to go before I sleep."

PLAYBOY: Didn't Marilyn Monroe write that?

BRANDO: I think Marilyn did, yeah. It was either her or Fatty Arbuckle, I can't remember.

July 1982

BETTE DAVIS

A candid conversation with—fasten your seat belts, everyone—Hollywood's unsinkable dowager empress about her loves and her battles, on (and off) screen

As far back as 1935, an observer suggested, "Bette Davis would probably be burned as a witch if she had lived 200 or 300 years ago. She gives the curious feeling of being charged with power that can find no ordinary outlet." More than a legend, Davis today is the indestructible first lady in that select company of all-time-great movie stars once described by a French critic as "the sacred monsters" of cinema. There's nothing halfway about her, never has been, but the unmistakable Davis imprint on a role—achieved by her head-on collision with more than 80 films—has won her two best-actress Oscars and a total of 10 nominations, an awesome record. In 1977, she received the American Film Institute's Life Achievement Award (she is, so far, the only actress thus honored), which seemed to certify her standing as the dowager empress of screen drama—with Katharine Hepburn the only possible challenger to her throne.

Davis arrived in Hollywood as a promising Broadway ingénue more than half a century ago, in 1930, and was so controversial from the very start that an entire history of American movies might be written around her triumphs, defeats, fierce battles and occasional Pyrrhic victories. At first, it was young Bette who felt the barbs for being unbeautiful, atypical and altogether out of step with what movie moguls believed a star ought to look like. A couple of decades—and a couple of Academy Awards—later, she would become the unlikely synthesis of radiant Hollywood glamor and cynical Broadway chic in her definitive role, as Margo Channing in *All About Eve*. Her campy, mannered, flamboyant, egomaniacal Margo is a superb performance, often (wrongly) thought to be a self-portrait—bits and pieces of Bette Davis with sly Tallulah Bankhead undertones.

Ruth Elizabeth Davis was born of solid Yankee stock in Lowell, Massachusetts, on April 5, 1908, during a mighty thunderstorm that seemed in retrospect to have been an apt piece of celestial stage managing. As a young girl, she impulsively gave herself a new first name, borrowing from Balzac's novel *La Cousine Bette*, and stubbornly retained the spelling after her father mocked it as just a whim. Her parents separated when she was seven, and the abrupt departure of her father—a patent lawyer named Harlow Morrell Davis—left Bette with a younger sister, Bobby, and her beloved mother, Ruthie, who became a roving photographer to support her daughters.

Once she decided to become an actress, while still in her teens, Bette was unstoppable. Eva Le Gallienne rejected her as too "frivolous" for Madam's prestigious repertory theater, so she went to drama school instead; got hired for her first professional job with George Cukor's winter-stock company in Rochester, New York (Cukor subsequently fired her); ushered and acted in summer stock at Cape Cod; finally made her New York debut in 1929, at the Provincetown Playhouse in Greenwich Village, in a play called *The Earth Between*. Brooks Atkinson of *The New York Times* called her "an entrancing creature." A year or so later, Bette Davis was summoned to Hollywood.

Dismayed by wretched roles in six bottom-drawer movies during 1931–1932, Bette was packed to go back to New York in defeat when England's venerable George Arliss phoned to say he needed a fresh young leading lady for his new production, *The Man Who Played God*, at Warner Bros. Davis unpacked, destined for her first big hit, and stayed to make 14 more films until 1934, when Warner's reluctantly lent her to a rival studio to play the slatternly Mildred opposite Leslie Howard in W. Somerset Maugham's *Of Human Bondage*. With that, the misunderstood and frequently miscast starlet became a major star.

Davis didn't win her first Oscar until *Dangerous*, the following year, but found a friendlier climate for a time at Warner's. Meanwhile, she had married "Ham" Nelson, her high school sweetheart, in August 1932—still a virgin on her wedding day, at the age of 24. The marriage was destined to be as stormy as her career, for Nelson by then had his own nightclub orchestra but nothing to match his wife's fierce ambition and earning power. Inevitably, the strains increased, and Davis became the ex-Mrs. Nelson while shooting *Juarez* with Paul Muni in 1938.

Two years earlier, she had staged a revolution against the peonage of the studio-contract system when she walked out on her Warner Bros. contract. The studio sought an injunction to stop her from making two films abroad, and the subsequent trial, in London, cost Davis more than $30,000. She lost. Nevertheless, her firm convictions persuaded Jack L. Warner to pick up her court costs and give her better roles—propelling her into her golden era, highlighted by *Jezebel* (for which she won her second Oscar, in 1938), *Juarez, Dark Victory, The Old Maid, The Private Lives of Elizabeth and Essex* (all released in 1939), *The Letter* (1940, with director William Wyler), *The Little Foxes* (1941, again with Wyler) and her classic "woman's picture," *Now, Voyager* (1942). During that peak period, she was sometimes referred to as the fourth Warner brother.

Her offscreen life was far less satisfactory. Married for the second time, on New Year's Eve, 1940, to aircraft engineer Arthur "Farney" Farnsworth, who was night manager at a New England inn when she met him, Davis found domestic bliss elusive and brief. In August 1943, Farnsworth collapsed on Hollywood Boulevard and died the next day from a previously undiagnosed cranial injury. In November 1945, Bette married artist William Grant Sherry after a month's acquaintance. Their daughter, B.D., was born in May 1947, during a period otherwise characterized by Bette's steady professional decline in a series of pictures that fortified the public's image of her as a chain-smoking, hip-swinging, saucer-eyed caricature. It was in *Beyond the Forest* (1949) that Bette said "What a dump!" and collected the worst reviews of her career. She dumped Sherry shortly after, their divorce becoming final on July 4, 1950. Three weeks later, she married actor Gary Merrill, her virile co-star in *All About Eve*, a comeback and a triumph on all counts.

During a lively but "black" decade with Merrill, Bette settled in Maine, in a house they called Witch Way, and the couple adopted two children: Margot, in 1951, and Michael, in 1952. In the wake of *Eve*, sickness and tragedy dogged Bette. Young Margot was found to be brain-damaged and ultimately had to be institutionalized.

Davis's own health slumped during her return to Broadway in a sold-out but critically unsung 1952 musical revue, *Two's Company*, which she had to leave to undergo jaw surgery for osteomyelitis. She would go back to the stage in full sail several more times—notably in Tennessee Williams' *The Night of the Iguana*, in 1961. Since 1973, when she made the first of her appearances as a legendary lady of movies, she has toured regularly in a sight-and-sound *Bette Davis in Person* show, consisting of film clips and fast answers from the podium.

Her marriage to Merrill came to an end in 1960, followed by fractious years of thrashing through a custody fight over Michael. By then, she was past 50, a seemingly fading star in the Margo Channing image she had immortalized a decade earlier. Then came *What Ever Happened to Baby Jane?* in 1962, in which Davis's baby–Grand Guignol put her right back in the game with her 10th Oscar nomination (but brought little joy to co-star Joan Crawford).

No snob about TV, as far back as the 1950s Davis had begun to shift gears and ensure her durability. Since 1970, she has been one of the upstart medium's hardest-working actresses, doing everything from movies of the week to Westerns, working always with the same indefatigable, compulsive energy that often drives her frazzled colleagues up the wall.

Davis currently resides in West Hollywood, presumably pondering new challenges, munching on her laurels and eating journalists for breakfast. We sent *Playboy* Contributing Editor and movie critic Bruce Williamson to face the formidable lady in her lair. He reports:

"She is shorter than you expect, with Bette Davis eyes, hair, voice, hands—Bette Davis everything—wearing a shirt and a flowered-print skirt. Greeting me at the door with a firm Yankee handshake, she led me into her warm, woody top-floor apartment, which, except for its wide-screen view of smoggy Hollywood, might be a cottage in Maine.

"In my line of work, I find few celebrities who still have the power to strike me with awe. This was the day—genuine movie-fan excitement on my part, and the first interview session passed nervously. But on the second day, she wore little or no makeup, had her hair tucked under a visored baseball cap and said, 'I curled my hair for you yesterday because it was the first time we'd met.'

"Now she obviously meant business, and although she rarely permits herself to be interviewed at home, she had decided to give me a tour of her apartment, 'which is really rather a museum. I think you'll find it interesting.' Indeed, I did. Framed Davis memorabilia everywhere—an Edith Head costume sketch for *All About Eve*; a sketch of her Carlota costume from *Juarez* above an authentic sketch of Carlota signed by the empress herself; a photo collection of Bette with her political heroes—FDR, Al Smith, several Kennedys, Anwar Sadat. Framed on the wall near the door is a *New Yorker* cartoon depicting two matronly matineegoers outside a theater, one saying: 'I like Bette Davis and I like Joan Crawford. But I don't know if I like Bette Davis and Joan Crawford.'

"She calls the small bright alcove off her terrace 'my blood, sweat and tears room,' because it's the resting place of her Oscars—the first so tarnished and aged that it looks greenish-gray rather than gold—and of innumerable awards, citations and plaques. In her living room, there's a chaise with an afghan draped over it, done in a ladybug design for the good luck they bring. There's also a small needlework pillow bearing the words No Guts No Glory, which speaks for itself.

"Whenever we settled down to talk, Davis smoked steadily, striking large kitchen matches on the underside of an end table if she didn't find a lighter handy. No booze was served while the tape machine ran—a house rule, she informed me with a knowing smile to indicate she's learned a few tricks of the trade through the years.

"By the beginning of the fourth day, she was becoming rather tired of talking about herself and greeted me plaintively with: 'Before you came to Los Angeles, I had a life beyond *Playboy*.' She readily acknowledged, however, that she had agreed to do this and, by God, she would see it through.

"One memorable evening, after we had finished taping, we were joined by Marilyn Grabowski, *Playboy*'s West Coast Photo Editor. We had drinks in the trophy room off the terrace. Bette put on an LP titled *Miss Bette Davis*, an EMI record made in England some five years ago but never released in the U.S. It's a collection of movie theme songs, including such standards as "Until It's Time for You to Go" and "I Wish You Love." 'I'm going to have that last one sung at my funeral . . . it's all arranged,' said Davis, who gave us a private singalong performance of virtually the entire album with frequent asides, really acting in a hushed, hoarse whisper a number called *Loneliness*, campily croaking "I've Written a Letter to Daddy", from *Baby Jane*. Still into it, she sat there with a glorious sunset behind her while Hollywood itself slowly faded into a backdrop of distant twinkling lights in the darkness. Bette, in close-up, had an enthralled audience of two. Such a great Bette Davis finale, I wondered later whether she had planned it that way. Now we flash back to the beginning."

DAVIS: Is this going to be one of those lovely, long, old-fashioned interviews like they used to do years ago?

PLAYBOY: Maybe even lovelier and longer. But, to begin, do you have any idea how intimidating Bette Davis is supposed to be?

DAVIS: Oh, I'm supposed to be *frightening*. But *until* you're thought of that way, *I* think you haven't made it! This involves, of course, making many enemies. And if you don't dare to be hated, you're never going to get there. *Never!* I think that unless you provoke great pros and cons about your work, you are really not a very important performer. To be an uncontroversial actor is nothing to aim for.

PLAYBOY: But you didn't start out aiming to be controversial, surely. Or did you?

DAVIS: No, of course not. I just worked very hard and, well [*points to her couch*], like that little pillow says, No Guts No Glory. I had a lot of guts to fight for what I believed in, and that makes enemies. It wasn't easy, and today I am very grateful that I did what I did, since all these films of mine are displayed year after year after year. . . . How could I know that would happen? Yet I thank God that I really put forth an effort to make them *good*.

PLAYBOY: And that was often an uphill fight?

DAVIS: Very often, yes. Yet, you see, there's a great misconception about the terms temper and temperament. Because anyone without temperament is *never* going to make it in the arts, in any art. But temper is a totally different thing. People who scream and yell and carry on . . . that's not *temperament*, that's just bad behavior.

PLAYBOY: You're saying you raised hell only over important issues rather than indulged in ego trips over another actor's close-ups.

DAVIS: Exactly. I never did that. I always wanted everybody around me to be the best, because you're only as good as the people you work with. I was always strong in my beliefs, and my kind of person is difficult to cope with, but I have never had a jealous moment in my life. I just prayed to God I got good people.

PLAYBOY: You certainly worked with a *lot* of people. At the beginning, wasn't it at Universal Studios that you were subjected to an infamous day of screen tests with 15 men?

DAVIS: Yes, but it was just one of the things they made me do. First, the Universal man in New York wanted to change my name to Bettina

Dawes. Then, when I got to Hollywood, I was the test girl, with all these men flopping on top of me, one after another, with the cameras over to the right. Oh, it was terrible! And I wasn't some little . . . nobody, you know. I'd been in the theater for three years and I'd been very successful, too. It was insulting, just *torture*.

PLAYBOY: Who were the men? Anybody we know?

DAVIS: All actors, and I don't remember any of them except that beautiful Mexican Gilbert Roland—terrific, a gorgeous guy—whom I worked with at Warner's years later. He was the only one who sort of knew I was in agony; he was just darling to me and whispered: "Don't worry, it won't always be like this."

PLAYBOY: Did you raise any hell at the time?

DAVIS: Heavens, no. They had me under contract. That was my day's work.

PLAYBOY: Coming from Broadway, did you find it difficult to adapt to acting for the screen? Did you have to learn to be more low-key?

DAVIS: [*Flaring visibly*] *Low-key?* Never! I did not buy it! Never, never! I fought that battle from the beginning. I think acting *should* be larger than life. The writing, the scripts should be larger than life. It should *all* be larger than life.

PLAYBOY: Did anyone ever suggest you play down a bit for the camera?

DAVIS: Oh, over and over. You still run into directors today who tell you that, but I never bought that theory at all: "Do less in a close-up than you do in a long shot. Don't, for God's sake, give any suggestion that you're *acting*. Just be natural. . . ." No, no, no, no, no, no, no!

PLAYBOY: The message is coming through: You like things larger than life.

DAVIS: Personally, no; not in *private*. Those are two different things. I'm talking about *acting* now. I've been very fortunate with reviews, number one. But the biggest over-all criticism through the years has been that I'm *too much*. That's usually when I'm acting with people who don't do *anything*, so of course I look like I'm doing too much. That has never depressed me, because that's the way I do things, and that's the critic's taste; if he doesn't like what I do, I'm sorry. But I believed my way would work, and I *proved* it.

PLAYBOY: How did you feel at the American Film Institute tribute four years ago, hearing your praises sung, watching all those film clips of the characters you've played?

DAVIS: Well, it was impressive but torture. You think about yourself as a young girl who started out in the New York theater back in 1928, 1929, whatever, and then, suddenly, there you are that evening. It was awesome . . . just *fracturing*.

PLAYBOY: Was there a particular moment when you knew you had become a movie star?

DAVIS: The big moment for me, I suppose, was the day I walked up Broadway and saw my name blazing in lights on the marquee of the Warner theater. That's a thrill for any performer. My mother and I stood there, just *seeing* it, and I said, "Well—progress." You know, it's terrific to reach that point, but it never affected how I feel about *me*.

PLAYBOY: Which you attribute to your Yankee common sense?

DAVIS: Yes. And my father gave me a very good brain, so that helps you hang on. There's a beautiful book—I think it's *My Grandmother Called It Carnal*—all about the rigidity of a Yankee upbringing. No catering, no sloppiness, no softness. No comfortable chairs in the house, no really soft beds.

PLAYBOY: Comfort was carnal?

DAVIS: Oh, yes. And even now, I don't really enjoy a thing if it's too easy. I'm very strange. That's one reason Joe Mankiewicz suggested what should be my epitaph: Here Lies Bette Davis—She Did It the Hard Way.

PLAYBOY: Do you still see yourself as a solid Yankee with a passion for order?

DAVIS: Definitely. I can't bear disorganization, in the kitchen or anywhere. A place for everything, everything in its place. I feel sorry for people who waste their time hunting for things. This is hereditary, too. I got it from my father. He could go through a pitch-dark room and find handkerchiefs, socks, whatever....

PLAYBOY: You make yourself sound like some kind of Yankee-Doodle Dandy. One would think you were born on the Fourth of July.

DAVIS: [*Hoot of laughter*] Strangely enough, I was *conceived* on the Fourth of July, on Squirrel Island, in Maine, in circumstances that probably affected my whole life; who knows? My parents were on their honeymoon, married July first, and due to a water shortage, my mother could not properly take care of herself to keep from becoming pregnant. Which put my father into an absolute *rage*, screaming at everybody in the hotel, raising hell. He was just *wild*, but . . . well, nobody could get rid of me. My mother had many, many friends in Lowell, Massachusetts, but I arrived exactly nine months later, so they weren't able to say she was pregnant when she was married. Her reputation came out clean.

PLAYBOY: And you were born during—

DAVIS: A thunderstorm, in my grandmother's house in Lowell. Very tumultuous beginnings, you see. My father was never meant to be a father, in any case. He despised little babies—thought children should be seen and not heard—so we almost never saw him. He was never meant to marry, either, really. Mother and Daddy were divorced when I was seven years old.

PLAYBOY: Do you feel that strengthened you, in a way?

DAVIS: Oh, I was *born* with strength, *born* liberated, the whole thing. There's no question about it. I never really had a father, in my opinion, and I was glad he and my mother separated, because they didn't get along. He was a brilliant, cruel, sarcastic man. He came to see my first play in New York and was really very proud, though it was he who'd said, "This theater is just nonsense. . . . Send her to secretarial school; she'll make money quicker."

PLAYBOY: During your teens, didn't you once have a date with Henry Fonda? In his December 1981 *Playboy Interview*, he said he kissed you and received a follow-up letter from you accepting his proposal, which scared hell out of him.

DAVIS: I don't remember that much, honest to God. I only know we went to Princeton and ended up in the stadium, a beautiful moonlit night. I met him through a beau of my sister's. He *may* have kissed me. He was very shy, Hank, very shy. This was long before the Cape Playhouse, where I saw him again. . . . Aahh. [*Deep sigh*]

PLAYBOY: What's that for? Do you still have a crush on him?

DAVIS: No, though he was very beautiful. He just never took to me. We were making *Jezebel* together when his daughter Jane was born.

PLAYBOY: One of the earliest show-business stories about you is your being fired from a Rochester stock company by George Cukor. You've never explained why.

DAVIS: Really, I didn't live up to what was expected in those days of a stock-company ingénue, who had *other* duties . . . you know what I'm talking about. Socializing. Socializing very seriously, let us say, with people in the company. That was just not my cup of tea.

PLAYBOY: Was that a clearly stated prerequisite for holding your job?

DAVIS: Clearly stated, no. But I understood it.

PLAYBOY: That sounds like just a minor early skirmish. Let's go through the Bette Davis wars later on, starting with your famous case against Warner Bros.

DAVIS: That was fighting for good scripts and directors. Decent parts, great directors. I wasn't getting them; that was my particular beef when I walked out on Warner Bros. and went to England. Because I knew I'd have no career the way things were going. Making movies like *Parachute Jumper, Bureau of Missing Persons, The Big Shakedown.* Oh, it was terrible!

PLAYBOY: After they took you to court in London, you lost your case but more or less won your point, didn't you?

DAVIS: Well, they respected me more when I came back. They didn't fool around so much. And the first role I was given was in *Marked Woman*, a very good picture, with Bogey.

PLAYBOY: Didn't you miss out on an even better part, however—Scarlett O'Hara?

DAVIS: That was bought for me by Jack Warner and his people before I left for England. Warner sent for me and said, "Please don't leave—I just bought a wonderful book for you." And I said, "I'll bet it's a *pip!*" and walked out of his office. Well, much later, David Selznick acquired *Gone with the Wind* from Warner and wanted me to do it with Errol Flynn, but I *wouldn't* have done it with Flynn, so that was really no great disappointment.

Everything worked out, because, meanwhile, I had the pleasure of doing *Jezebel* and winning the Oscar for it. And if I may be privileged to say so, I really think that [director] Willie Wyler's feeling of the South, in *Jezebel*, was more truly Southern, even, than *Gone with the Wind's*. My favorite story about *Gone with the Wind*, of course, is about the college president who said, "If the South had had *that* many soldiers, they'd have won the war."

PLAYBOY: Wasn't *The African Queen* also meant to be a Bette Davis movie during your years at Warner's?

DAVIS: I wouldn't put it that way, but they bought it for me and then I left Warner's for good in 1948. I always wanted to do it with John Mills, the English actor, who would have been absolutely perfect for it at the time. This was not my *largest* disappointment, but I was let down. Such a marvelous part.

PLAYBOY: Once you began to get the great parts and had the power to do so, you were known for being rough on directors. At what point would you decide that you might have to take over some of the director's job?

DAVIS: You would find that out pretty soon. There were different varieties. First, the chauvinistic director who *had* to win, as a man—while you, as a woman, could have the best ideas in the world and his male ego could not *allow* you to be right. Then there was the director who simply wasn't competent, as you soon learned by how he directed you and the rest of the cast. Then, if the script wasn't right . . . oh, my scripts were some mess of rewriting in those days! When you had a good script, as in *All About Eve*, you wouldn't touch it. But on *Now, Voyager*, my script was scratched to pieces. I'd sit up nights and restore scenes from Olive Higgins Prouty's novel; they were *right* just the way she had written them. Such situations didn't make you popular, though; nope.

PLAYBOY: Didn't you order two sets of costumes for one of your Elizabethan movies?

DAVIS: Yes. Michael Curtiz, who directed *The Private Lives of Elizabeth and Essex*, never should have directed it at all, because it just was *not* his type of film. He was great for the very flamboyant kind of thing Flynn did. And he said, "No, no, you can't have the skirts so big, so many ruffs," etc. The designer and I had copied the Holbein paintings of the era. So we just went and made up a *totally different* wardrobe and got it tested and approved by Curtiz. Then, when we started shooting and wore the original clothes, nobody ever knew the difference. I had very definite ideas about costumes, hair, all those details. As the star, you're the one who gets the blame or the praise in the end, when a film comes out. And *that* is something you must never, *never* forget. Wyler—and he was a very tough man to work for—said one day, "I don't care what goes on while we make this picture; I care only about what the audience sees when they pay for it." Well, *that* was the basis of any difficulties I perpetrated. Definitely. I was going to get it right, one way or another. When I had differences with incompetent directors, it was really self-preservation. And that's why, when I see my films today, those scripts don't embarrass me, the performances don't embarrass me, the clothes don't embarrass me. . . .

PLAYBOY: And you fought for all of it?

DAVIS: Oh, yes, I fought . . . always. Now, of course, you and I know that movies are a director's and a cameraman's medium, totally. But I still believe audiences don't go to see directors; they go to see *people*.

PLAYBOY: Tell us about the time you were president of the motion picture academy. Didn't you resign just a few days after you took the job?

DAVIS: Oh, it was longer than that. But I definitely resigned. [Darryl] Zanuck put me in there, for whatever reason—as just a figurehead, I suspect. As with everything I've ever done, I took the job seriously and had excellent ideas, all of which were pooh-poohed. I was the first to suggest that they abolish votes by extras, which they all thought was the wildest thing they'd ever heard. Well, three quarters of the Hollywood extras at that time couldn't even speak English, and to have extras voting for the Oscars was absolutely absurd. *Thousands* of them. If you were up for an Oscar and you bought them ice cream every Saturday afternoon, you'd get it. Absolutely ridiculous. When Jean Hersholt came in as president after me, he got this rule changed. But I threatened to quit, and Zanuck finally said: "If you resign, you'll never work again in this town." Some years later, he *begged* me to come play Margo Channing. That was kind of fun.

PLAYBOY: While we're on the subject, will you tell how you personally started the tradition of calling the Academy Award the "Oscar"?

DAVIS: Well, the rear end of it looked like my first husband's, Ham Nelson's, bare behind. And Ham's middle name was Oscar, which I didn't even know for years. He had never told me, he hated the name so.

PLAYBOY: How did the rest of the world learn about this?

DAVIS: I really can't remember. It's all so far back, and the academy resents enormously the fact that I've gotten credit for the name. I don't believe it was called the Oscar until after I got one and really *looked* at it, which was . . . oh, God, 1000 years ago! It was my consolation prize for *Dangerous*. But whether or not I named it officially isn't going to make a bit of difference in my life. At this point, they may *have* the honor; I return it to them!

PLAYBOY: You mentioned a consolation prize. Do you still feel that the Oscars you received are not those you wanted and most deserved?

DAVIS: Yeah, I should have gotten one for *Baby Jane*. Definitely. I hadn't thought there was a doubt in the world, and that was a huge disappointment.

PLAYBOY: Who won instead?

DAVIS: Anne Bancroft, for *The Miracle Worker*. But I have always felt that an actor who's played a part onstage for two or three years should be in a different category. Playing a part you've never played before is a much bigger test. They make this kind of distinction in other categories; with writers, for instance. Anyway, that year, 1962, I felt I *should* have had it, no matter who else was up.

PLAYBOY: What about the other Oscars?

DAVIS: I'd say I won honestly for *Jezebel*. But *Dangerous* . . . You know, there was just no comparison between that and *Of Human Bondage*. Well, the entire town thought I would win for *Bondage*, but *It Happened One Night* swept everything that year, and everyone said it was a cheat. That's what used to happen. The Price Waterhouse accounting came in the following year, because of it. The academy received hundreds of letters saying what a gyp it was, so they hired Price Waterhouse. All the studios used to divide the prizes up, really. They're much fairer today than they were.

PLAYBOY: Anything else?

DAVIS: I should have had it for *All About Eve*, and that was another case of the stage thing—Judy Holliday's winning for redoing her Broadway role in *Born Yesterday*. Now, [Gloria] Swanson was up for an award that same year, for *Sunset Boulevard*, and if she'd won, I'd have shouted hooray. She was sensational, just fantastic, and she had never won. But who knows; she may still. I think they decide to give you one just before you die. Of course, someone like Garbo never won—and should have for *Camille*, no question about it. She was brilliant. But people resented her. She made all her money here and she hadn't become a citizen, and everyone resented that *very much*. It was the same with Chaplin.

PLAYBOY: Did you ever receive a nomination as best supporting actress?

DAVIS: No, and I don't want one. I would refuse it. I'm not going to be in that position, because my name is *always* billed above the title. My role in *Death on the Nile* was small, yet I had star billing. I will never be below the title, so I will never be in a supporting category.

PLAYBOY: Isn't it true that some of your best roles tended to be the definitive film versions of plays other actresses had done on Broadway?

DAVIS: Mmmm. I was disappointed myself, I must say, when I played *The Night of the Iguana* on Broadway and did not get to do it on the screen, because I was never asked. Ava Gardner got the part. But motion-picture producers always say, "Pooh—we don't want *her*; she's not box office." That's why Julie Andrews didn't get *My Fair Lady*. Angela Lansbury absolutely should have done the movie of *Mame*; Ethel Merman should have done *Gypsy*. It's terrible, terrible.

PLAYBOY: But we were referring to *your* being on the other end of this unfair tradeoff. Weren't *Jezebel*, *Dark Victory* and *The Little Foxes* all Tallulah Bankhead stage vehicles originally?

DAVIS: Yes, though I believe Miriam Hopkins wound up playing in *Jezebel*. And *Dark Victory* was not enormously successful on the stage.

PLAYBOY: Bankhead rather resented you, didn't she?

DAVIS: She wasn't madly in love with me. We met at a Warner's party, where she said, "You've played all the parts I've played on the stage, and I was so much better." And I said, "Miss Bankhead, I agree with you." As a matter of fact, I tried to get [Sam] Goldwyn to let her do *The Little Foxes*, another of those situations where they wouldn't take the stage star. Sinful. Then it became a very complicated story with Wyler, because he wanted me to play the movie totally differently and I said, "I'm sorry, but the way Miss Bankhead played it is the way [Lillian] Hellman wrote it," so it became a kind of permanent argument, in a way. Yet now I think it's a wonderful picture.

PLAYBOY: Was there any truth in the story that you were doing a bit of Bankhead shtick in *All About Eve*?

DAVIS: No truth at all. She claimed that, and we've always had a certain resemblance, with that long bob she had, but no . . . we never even *thought* of her. Bankhead was *far* more eccentric than Margo Channing.

PLAYBOY: There was no genuine feud between you?

DAVIS: She had a certain thing about me, no question, partly because I was successful in films. She did a radio show for years on which she used to take me to the cleaners all the time, but . . . well, she wasn't terribly good on the screen, which I think was a big disappointment to her. She did *Lifeboat* and a role as Catherine of Russia; that's about it. She always played Tallulah Bankhead, and she was a fascinating woman—when she behaved herself. She usually gave a great opening-night performance, and that was *it*.

PLAYBOY: Were there any authentic feuds between you and fellow performers?

DAVIS: Never, really. I don't *have* feuds. Professionally, there's no way I could work if I were having a feud. It's just not my nature. It's true there was an unspoken war between Miriam Hopkins and me, because she fought me every foot of the way. Miriam was a wonderful actress but a bitch, the most thoroughgoing bitch I've ever worked with. She used to drive me *mad*, but I never blew up at her, because if you let her get to you, you'd be the loser. So I coped with her, but I'd go home and just scream my head off afterward . . . really *scream*.

PLAYBOY: What about your alleged feud with Joan Crawford?

DAVIS: I never feuded with Crawford in my life. [*Slowly*] *Never any problem at all*, I repeat for the record. During *Baby Jane*, the whole world hoped we would fight but we did not. We were both pros. With three weeks to make the picture, can you imagine we'd spend time *feuding*?

PLAYBOY: You weren't exactly friends, though, were you?

DAVIS: Socially, we never knew each other, no. But that doesn't mean anything.

PLAYBOY: Earlier, before *Baby Jane* but after *Eve*, you had made another film about an actress. . . .

DAVIS: *The Star.* That was one of the best scripts ever written about an untalented, movie-mad actress. Well, of course, you know whom it was written about, don't you?

PLAYBOY: That was going to be the next question.

DAVIS: Crawford. It was written by the Eunsons, Katherine Albert and Dale Eunson, two of the biggest writers in the business. She, in particular, was a fan-magazine writer who'd done most of the stories about Crawford. Oh, and I kept saying "Bless you" to the crew, all that sort of thing she did. Oh, yes, that *was* Crawford. I often wondered if she ever realized it, but I never, never knew. I wasn't imitating her, of course. It was just that whole approach of hers to the business as regards the importance of glamor and all the offstage things. Yet, believe me, these women were responsible for the public's fascination with Hollywood, much more so than people like me. *Much* more.

PLAYBOY: You mean the American dream of what a movie star is supposed to be?

DAVIS: Absolutely. And Joan was the epitome of this. I got another Oscar nomination for *The Star,* an independent picture . . . Fox never spent a *dime* publicizing it.

PLAYBOY: While we're on the subject of Crawford, did you read *Mommie Dearest?*

DAVIS: Yes, and I don't blame the daughter, don't blame her at all. She was left without a cent, living in a motor home in Tarzana, and I doubt she could have written this if it weren't true. One area of life Joan should never have gone into was *children.* She bought them . . . paid thousands for them, and here was a role she was not right for. No, I don't blame Christina Crawford; I don't think anyone would *invent* her book. You couldn't just make it up.

PLAYBOY: You believe Crawford's mother role was just another publicity gimmick?

DAVIS: But *of course!* Christina's very honest about that. Joan was the perfect mother in front of the public but not behind the front door. She wanted this image that just wasn't meant for her. I've never behaved like . . . well, I doubt that *my* children will write a book.

PLAYBOY: Then you feel as if you have succeeded pretty well in your mother role.

DAVIS: I love my children, love them and actually brought them up by myself. They were still very young when Gary and I were divorced. B.D. was the oldest, but Mike and Margot were fairly young, and one being a boy child—not easy. Of course, I didn't have any children until my career was basically made. I was 39 years old when I had B.D. So I've always spent a great deal of time with them, and I'm terribly grateful I didn't have children when I was much younger.

PLAYBOY: You mean because you'd have had to turn them over to boarding schools and babysitters?

DAVIS: But I *wouldn't* have. I never would have done that. I think I'd have chosen the children and had an entirely different sort of life.

PLAYBOY: You'd have given up your career?

DAVIS: Oh, definitely. As dedicated as I was, with the kind of drive I had, I soon realized my career was an all-consuming affair.

PLAYBOY: You've talked about having had an abortion—

DAVIS: I had two—during my first marriage, to Ham Nelson. I don't want to talk about my marriages. But . . . well, that's what he wanted. Being the dutiful wife, that's what I did. And I guess I will thank him all my life. Because if I'd had those two children . . . I see myself at 50, with the children all grown up, wondering whether or not I ever would have made it. I think there's nothing sadder, and I'm sure I'd have given it all up if I'd had children earlier.

PLAYBOY: We seem to have backed into an answer as to where you stand politically on abortion.

DAVIS: I believe abortion is *better* than having 10 million children you can't support! Of course, there are many people against it, the Catholic Church's big argument being that you're killing a human being. Perfect nonsense! Ridiculous, this murder thing! There is no child involved if you get an abortion at one month. I've seen an awful lot of this famous-parent business with children . . . *oh, boy*, have I! There's one great thing happening today. When I was a child, born in 1908, education taught you that your destiny was to marry and have children. Just because you're a woman—but that is *not* your destiny. There are many great women who were just never meant to be mothers, that's all. We are improving this way enormously.

PLAYBOY: Yet you're an extremely ambitious woman, who has children and no regrets—

DAVIS: Oh, *today*, if I didn't have my children and my grandchildren, I'd be the most bored human being who ever lived! They're my top priority in life.

PLAYBOY: Are your grandchildren aware of you as Bette Davis, with any notion of what that means?

DAVIS: Well, of course. B.D.'s son Ashley is *13*; what are you talking about? He played a very big part with me in *Family Reunion*, a recent film on TV. We don't know how far his aspirations go, but he loved doing it.

PLAYBOY: Does he know your films?

DAVIS: Oh, certainly, up to a point.

PLAYBOY: Let's go back to those movies. What are your personal all-time favorites?

DAVIS: Well, the basic thrill occurs when a film comes out the way you'd dreamed about it when you began—and that means the total film, the script, everything; not just my own part. By this standard, *Dark Victory* was a favorite. *Jezebel* was one and *Now, Voyager*.

PLAYBOY: Sounds as if those you liked best were also your biggest successes.

DAVIS: No; well, they all succeeded from that point on. *Elizabeth* succeeded; *The Letter* succeeded; but they weren't necessarily my favorites. Playing Elizabeth was a thrill, but I have to admit I wasn't mad about having Errol Flynn in it. I would have loved to have had Laurence Olivier, thank you very much.

PLAYBOY: Did you ask for Olivier?

DAVIS: No, I didn't honestly think of it at the time, and Warner's wanted Errol. Soon after *All About Eve*, I gave what I consider one of my best performances, in *Payment on Demand*, among the best bloody films ever done about this driving kind of American woman . . . oh, that was *written* for me! I was a great part of that story, which was originally called *The Story of a Divorce*—which is what it *should* have been called, because that's what it was all about.

PLAYBOY: Why was the title changed?

DAVIS: Howard Hughes was the producer, and he messed around with the ending. We had the perfect ending, where she's got her husband back and starts all over again telling him what he should do about his career, and so forth, and he gets up and walks out. Marvelous. But Hughes wouldn't let us do that. He also insisted we call it *Payment on Demand*, a very cheap title, and made us end with a touching reunion at the front door. I begged him not to redo the ending, but I remember Hughes saying, "Doesn't every woman still want a roll in the hay?" And I said, "No—this is *not* her big drive after 35 years." I lost the argument, but it was still a terrific picture, excellently directed, just great.

PLAYBOY: What about *Eve*?

DAVIS: That was such a great, huge box-office success, which is why I've always told Mankiewicz, "You know you resurrected me from the dead."

And, of course, I was never supposed to play that part. I was a replacement for Claudette Colbert . . . and, oh, what a happy replacement. She had something wrong with her back. Since then, the few times I've seen her, I've always said, "Thank you, dear, for your bad back."

PLAYBOY: Did you ever see *Applause*, the musical version of *Eve* that Lauren Bacall did on Broadway?

DAVIS: Yes, but long years before she ever did it, I tried to buy the rights to *All About Eve* for a musical. And Fox wouldn't sell them. I always felt it was a natural, and I would have *done* that musical. I always imagined singing that song called *Fasten Your Seat Belts*—that would've been incredible. Then, when I first saw it, Bacall didn't even get a *laugh* on that line in the show, just banged a guitar and finished. I couldn't believe my ears—one of the most famous lines!

PLAYBOY: So you feel they blew it?

DAVIS: Oh, no, no, please don't ever imply I said that. I don't say that at all. But what she played was more like a Hollywood star than a theater star, and Margo was *of* the theater. There's a vast difference. I also saw Anne Baxter do *Applause*—the original Eve herself, who's a very dear friend, and she was marvelous; she emphasized the age thing of Margo somewhat more than Bacall did.

PLAYBOY: Except for "Fasten your seat belts," probably the most famous Bette Davis line is "What a dump!" Do you ever use it these days?

DAVIS: [*Cackling wickedly*] Ooohh, *yes*. I start every *Bette Davis in Person* show with this. A marvelous suggestion from my stage manager, because when we began, they were never sure whether to present me as a tragedy queen of cinema or a real human being. So we now open with film clips, ending with the "Fasten your seat belts" line from *Eve*. Then I come onstage, light a cigarette, look all around the auditorium and say, "What a *dump!*" Sometimes the theaters *are* dumps and sometimes they're gorgeous, but it's a marvelous idea either way. Really breaks the ice—people laugh and know they can sit back to relax with the show instead of having to *revere* me. I have a ball doing the show. I'll be doing it all my life, every now and then. I love it and I'm good at it, because I'm very quick.

PLAYBOY: While you missed a chance to do the musical version of *All About Eve*, weren't you one of the first big movie stars to go back to Broadway in a musical, years before Rex Harrison started talk-singing in *My Fair Lady*?

DAVIS: That was *Two's Company*, in the 1950s. Then I did *Miss Moffat* a few years ago, which I had to leave because of illness. I just love the whole field of music. During the war, Frank Loesser wrote *They're Either Too Young or Too Old* for me, as a jitterbug number in . . . oh, I have a hard time remembering these things.

PLAYBOY: Wasn't that *Thank Your Lucky Stars*, in 1943?

DAVIS: Thanks, yes. When I made my record album in England, I recorded the Loesser song; also the title song from *Hush . . . Hush, Sweet Charlotte*, because [Robert] Aldrich wouldn't let me record that for the film—which was stupid of him, I thought, because it's marvelous. Anyway, the original idea of *Two's Company* was to make fun of myself, you know, after 21 years of fame and being who I was. It was a fun idea, but some of the critics were furious with me, thinking I'd ducked my own field, I suppose, by not doing a drama.

PLAYBOY: Do you expect to do any more stage work aside from your *In Person* show?

DAVIS: I wouldn't do Broadway theater again for anything in the world. Never. I prefer films; I think theater is a dog's life, grueling. And I'm too selfish; I find eight shows a week absolutely inhuman, plus I cannot be replaced. Someone like me, from motion pictures, cannot have an understudy, because the box office for picture people is astronomical. Astronomical. If you don't appear, customers just get up and turn in their tickets. Therefore, you have a monkey on your back and aren't allowed even a small case of *flu*! It's frightening. So you sit around between shows and worry about your health—I find that a very stupid way to live. Anyway, acting in motion pictures is much more believable, in my opinion; you can do much more in a performance.

PLAYBOY: Besides those we've mentioned, are there any other important roles you wanted to do and didn't, for whatever reason?

DAVIS: There are three or four. One was *The Visit*, [Friedrich] Düerrenmatt's play, which I did everything in the world to get and would have been right for. They were making that in Italy with Ingrid Bergman while I was there on another film, and I have no comment on her performance—except that Miss Bergman was simply *much* too young and much too beautiful. I also wanted to do *Who's Afraid of Virginia Woolf?* That, of course, is where [Edward] Albee made the "What a dump!" line famous . . . when the heroine does an imitation of me. When I did the line originally, in *Beyond the Forest*, I just threw it away . . . absolutely nothing. Let me see . . . then I wanted to do the movie of *Mame*. I wrote Zanuck a letter saying I'd pay for my own test, I'd buy my own wardrobe if he'd let me test for *Mame*. . . .

PLAYBOY: You wanted to play Mame in the movie musical?

DAVIS: Yes, but Lucille Ball had already been signed. Then I was offered the wonderful part that Bea Arthur played, Mame's friend. But I don't think Miss Ball wanted me.

PLAYBOY: You'd have played second fiddle to Lucy?

DAVIS: Certainly! That's a great part.

PLAYBOY: On the other hand, are there any big Bette Davis films that you actively dislike or wish you hadn't done?

DAVIS: The big ones, no. We're not talking about *Parachute Jumper* again, I hope. Well, *In This Our Life* was a bomb, dreadful, with Olivia de Havilland and me, directed by John Huston. From a great book. I was all wrong, too old for it. As a matter of fact, I had a great suggestion for Warner's publicity department. When *In This Our Life* was finished and turned out *so* bad, I suggested they take out big ads and quote Bette Davis as saying this was the *worst* film she ever made . . . that would've been brilliant perverse publicity. But it was hard to get people to try new ideas.

PLAYBOY: During all those ups and downs, were there any gurus or mentors who influenced your professional life?

DAVIS: George Arliss was the first one, because he gave me my first decent part; William Wyler, who directed three of my best films; and Hal Wallis—my boss for 10 years at Warner Bros. Those were my three great good-luck people.

PLAYBOY: Considering the love-hate nature of your relationship with Warner Bros., exactly what did Wallis do for you?

DAVIS: Well, he *ran* Warner Bros. He bought me all those books and New York plays—*The Corn Is Green, The Old Maid, Old Acquaintance*. All of them. *Now, Voyager*. Hal was interesting, because he didn't really like my work very much. He liked slapstick much more than drama. He told me eventually, after many years, that he'd never been able to *stand* my films. He just didn't like tragedy, but he said, "As long as you can sell it, I'll buy it." And we're still great friends.

PLAYBOY: Before that, you had never suspected that Wallis secretly hated Bette Davis movies?

DAVIS: No, I was *very* shocked. I couldn't believe it, really.

PLAYBOY: How did you feel about your leading men in movies? It seems pretty clear that Errol Flynn was not a favorite.

DAVIS: Because he was not a very good actor. He said so himself. He was enormously beautiful, but it didn't mean anything to him to be known as a great actor, so he didn't really work very hard. He was kind of lazy, with a so-what attitude, which was not my attitude. Never, never, never! I didn't have a *favorite* leading man, because Warner's was not like Metro, where they'd put teams together. We all carried films on our own. [Charles] Boyer was beautiful to work with. I was very fortunate to work with Leslie Howard. I always wanted to do a really important film with Bogey and once had a script called *The Prizefighter and the Lady*, which would have been ideal for us, though we didn't get to do it. George Brent was beautiful. Paul Henreid was beautiful. I made two films I enjoyed very much with Hank Fonda. Claude Rains was not exactly in the leading-man category, but what a wonderful actor. I made four films with him and he was one of my great, great friends. But my favorite actor, I suppose, was [Spencer] Tracy. Always will be. We worked together only once, when I did a tiny part in *20,000 Years in Sing Sing*.

PLAYBOY: What about Alec Guinness? After you had worked with Guinness on *The Scapegoat*, you were quoted as saying he performed by himself and for himself.

DAVIS: Mmm-hmm. He was probably the *most* difficult. But I also think he was very uncomfortable in that film as a leading man. That was never his type of role. He played two parts, as twins, and you could never tell which was which. But any remarks I've made about male actors don't come from actual *conflicts*. They're mostly based on general observation. It's just true that men are more vain. They spend more time on their hair and on everything else than women do. They always say women keep them waiting, but many husbands take longer than their wives getting ready to go out. I mean, if there's one bathroom in the house, God help you, God help you—you sure line up and wait for the male, absolutely.

PLAYBOY: This seems as good a place as any to ask, if we may, why there's a small brass plate on the door identifying your bathroom as The Zsa Zsa?

DAVIS: Well, I'll tell you why. I had a duplex suite in a New York hotel last year, with a powder room that was very . . . oh, satin walls, elegant fixtures; you know, nothing like my plain Yankee enamel-type bathroom. So one day I said, "This looks as if it ought to be in Zsa Zsa Gabor's house." Some time later, a friend had the sign made for me. . . .

PLAYBOY: So the john became the Zsa Zsa?

DAVIS: That's right.

PLAYBOY: Let's talk about men and women a bit, shall we?

DAVIS: Well, I just don't want to talk about my marriages, because I'm bored with the subject. I have been a single woman for more than 20 years now and have vowed never to discuss them again. However, I *believe* in marriage. To be a woman all by yourself is absurd. If you're lucky, I think marriage is the only answer. But some women are unlucky. You need a great deal of luck in marriage, I think—plus wisdom in your choice. But you don't know until after you've made the choice, do you?

It's true, really, that God's biggest joke on human beings is sex, which is totally blinding. Totally. We all have a tendency to give attributes to people that we *want* them to have—this is a very human failing prior to marriage. But, truthfully, when the physical attraction goes—and how suddenly it *can* go!—you find yourself looking at somebody and saying. "I *don't* believe it! *What* did I ever see in this person?" The one thing I never did was pretend to be someone I wasn't before marriage, something men do as much as women—put on a great, big, beautiful act, then go right back to being the way they were after they get you.

PLAYBOY: Could it be argued that you're something of a man-hater?

DAVIS: Not at all. I deny that. I've *always* liked men better than women. A woman can't go floating through life, going to restaurants by herself, living on her own as easily as a man can. Yet I do believe that men, more than women, will not face issues, particularly in a marriage. Will do *anything* to get away from trouble. But life can get pretty desperate at times without a man; as the old song says, "It's nice to have a man around the house." Which reminds me of another line—a brilliant one by Ogden Nash, which was censored from one of my plays: [*Hoarsely hums, torch style*] "The day he went away he left the seat up.... And I was too lonely to put it down."

PLAYBOY: But still, haven't men sometimes seen you as a man-hater?

DAVIS: Oh, no, no, no, I am *not*. Though I do believe there's a tendency in some males to feel that we can't possibly *exist* in this world without them. That's one thing we're finding out today—that women can. And it's a great deal up to us to change the attitude of the males. She's right, Germaine Greer. I believe *wildly* in Greer's book *The Female Eunuch*. I try to get every woman I know to read her book, because *women* have to change before men will change their attitude toward women. As long as women marry for security, however long all that goes on, men will not change. Greer is attractive, remember, and has great regard for men.

PLAYBOY: Can you describe the kind of man who might have been Mr. Right for Bette Davis?

DAVIS: I always used to say, only someone like J. Paul Getty or John F. Kennedy when he was President of the United States. You know, I'm really saying somebody with strength, who's identifiable to himself. Yet that kind of man would not want to take on a famous woman—wouldn't dream of marrying a big Hollywood star. In other words, I basically had no chance of getting a man who might have been right for me.

PLAYBOY: Is the real problem simply that of being Mr. Bette Davis?

DAVIS: Of course—a terrific problem and understandably so. And you feel very bad because, with all the care and sensitivity in the world, you can't solve the problem outside your own home. I mean, I never went around inside the house insisting I be called Bette Davis! I was always called by my married name in private everywhere . . . if I were asked my name.

PLAYBOY: You once said that the trouble in your marriages always lay in the scripts and the castings—do you want to expand on that?

DAVIS: Well, strong women marry only weak men, I've decided. If a man allows his life to be run by a woman, it's his own fault. That's an old home truth about the henpecked husband. I don't think any woman really wants it to be that way, but a great many men abdicate their responsibilities, then beef and say they are put upon. Fortunately, I think men and women are communicating much more today, taking equal roles.

PLAYBOY: Quoting you: "I've lived in a permanent state of rapture and I was never able to share it with a male; it exhausted them." Is that your romantic history in a nutshell?

DAVIS: Well, this enthusiasm, drive, having a real go at everything, is a trait I inherited from my mother and her whole family. It is just *exhausting*, and men aren't as apt to be this way. Although I said that half in fun, in a way it's true.

PLAYBOY: You were in your mid-20s when you entered what you describe in your 1962 biography as "a nice antiseptic marriage" to Ham Nelson. You write that "the deflowering of New England was unthinkable to this passionate pilgrim." Were you simply trying to avoid becoming Hollywood's oldest living virgin?

DAVIS: That had nothing to do with Hollywood. It was a question of how I'd been brought up. On *The Dick Cavett Show*, Cavett asked me when I gave up my virginity. So I counted to 10 and said, "When I was married—and it was *hell* waiting." It was true, but I don't think anyone believed me.

PLAYBOY: If you were young and single today, would you have different moral standards?

DAVIS: Oh, yes; if I'd been brought up in this era, I think I'd have had affairs. I might never have married. I didn't bring up my children to think as I was taught to think. I didn't bring up my daughter [B.D.] this way.

PLAYBOY: You mean preserving her virtue at all cost?

DAVIS: I never taught her that; therefore, I knew she wouldn't marry just for sex. That's what was wrong in my time. Well, I had known Ham since I was 16, in prep school. And there's no question, it's clear now, that my biggest romance, my all-consuming love affair, was with my work. And if you paid the price....

PLAYBOY: You've said that your husbands actually beat you....

DAVIS: Oh, I was beaten many, many times. I didn't seem to bring out the best in men. I've often said that, too. My third husband, Sherry, was basically the biggest offender.

PLAYBOY: You wrote that he threw you out of the car on your honeymoon "for some forgotten reason." Can't you remember what provoked such hostility?

DAVIS: I don't know; who knows? He would just *beat* me. It's hard to imagine that I took it.

PLAYBOY: From the Bette Davis we've seen, it's hard to imagine you wouldn't shoot the guy dead.

DAVIS: But as a person, quite apart from my professional attitudes, I can be a big patsy. I'm an Aries, and we under the Aries sign are always patsies about our own problems. We take a lot. Of course, I shouldn't have taken it. And that's why I had to go.

PLAYBOY: What do you think of palimony?

DAVIS: What's that? [*Brief break while it's explained to her*] Well, I wouldn't know what to say, because I've always earned my own living and never asked a dime in any divorce from anybody. Any woman that does this I don't understand—aside from child support. I mean, why saddle a man for the rest of his life? For what reason? The fact is, I have *paid* alimony.

PLAYBOY: You have?

DAVIS: Oh, sure. I paid alimony for about three years. It just seemed the sensible thing to do under the circumstances. I don't quite understand a man who accepts it, except there are all kinds of people, all kinds of circumstances. Every divorce is different, you know, and a big thing in life is to learn not to judge others. Please, God, don't judge. I'll say no more.

PLAYBOY: With which of your husbands do you feel you came closest to having marriage work?

DAVIS: Gary Merrill, maybe. Gary and I might possibly have made it work.

PLAYBOY: And you still believe, on principle, in the desirability of being "a downright, upright, four-square married lady"?

DAVIS: Oh, that's a marvelous line from *Eve*. That's when the characters finally decide to marry, yes. Gary and I fell in love while doing that picture.

PLAYBOY: On the subject of love, there's a great and former secret love whom you have spoken about, even written about in your bio, describing him as a titan, "a man who would have run my life from sunrise to sunset." Are you ready to identify him now?

DAVIS: [*Deliberately, eyes popped*] I'm not gonna say *anything*!

PLAYBOY: Since his death last year, there's been evidence brought forth and widely circulated that the man we're talking about must have been director William Wyler. Do you have any comment?

DAVIS: [*Long, stony pause*] I will *not* discuss Wyler in this way as long as I live, out of respect for his family.

PLAYBOY: Well, it is no secret, is it, that George Brent—your leading man in *Dark Victory* and in numerous other films—was one of the big romances of your life?

DAVIS: Yes, that's right. I adored him, *adored* him.

PLAYBOY: There's yet another mystery man in your past, whom you once described provocatively in print as your partner in a "catastrophic relationship with the prototype of the Hollywood male . . . extremely attractive and one of the wealthiest men in the West—or East, for that matter." Do we get three guesses?

DAVIS: I have no idea who that was. At one point, I was sort of chased by several who might fit the description.

PLAYBOY: You're putting us on. Charles Higham's unauthorized biography [*Bette*] says Howard Hughes was this powerful man, and in his version, it involved a love triangle, tape recordings and blackmail. Don't you at least want to comment on it for the record?

DAVIS: This book does not *exist*, as far as I'm concerned! I do not intend to read it, but it is a pack of lies, based on excerpts I have seen. I will not talk about the book or anything in it, now or ever. To *hell* with the book! That's my comment.

PLAYBOY: All right, let's move on to other people's peccadilloes you've mentioned publicly. You were quoted as saying that Errol Flynn would "co-star with anyone on the lot." What was *your* experience while working with him?

DAVIS: Errol did once say to me, "If I made a pass at you, Bette, you'd laugh in my face, wouldn't you?" And I said, "Yes—I certainly would." No, I was never very interested in boys with blackboards and chalk—and there were plenty of them, you know; they'd make chalk marks, vying with one another to see how many famous women they could get into the hay.

PLAYBOY: And Flynn led the pack?

DAVIS: Errol? Oh, yes, heavens . . . though he really liked young girls.

PLAYBOY: Who were the others?

DAVIS: Well, I tend to be kind of nice about things like this. But Leslie Howard was *definitely* a great ladies' man. He was something. His wife used to say that the only leading lady he hadn't gone to bed with was Bette Davis. That remark became famous in Hollywood. I had a little pride about things like that. I really didn't have time, and I wasn't personally that crazy about *actors*, anyway. Never was.

PLAYBOY: So you never attended any of those orgiastic Hollywood parties we've heard so much about?

DAVIS: No, no. Those of us who worked very hard were hardly part of the social scene out here at all. You never saw Tracy and such people at parties. Anyway, you couldn't go out and get high and enjoy yourself, because then everyone would say, "Well, *she's* a real drunk." If you wanted to have a ball, you'd stay at home with very good friends. That's the truth.

PLAYBOY: Were you aware of the prevalence of drinking and drug use in Hollywood?

DAVIS: Back then, no. Not drugs. You heard very little about drugs. Now, good heavens, you see examples of it all the time, which I think is terrible for the individuals, taking them nowhere fast. As for me, I have never in my life had a drink while I was working. Some people did, and that's their business, but it's certainly not good for the work. Though, you know, people out here just get written about a lot. There's much more immorality in high society or in small towns in New England. Oh, my dear, those little Yankee towns are *appalling*. The only thing the Puritans ever worried about was getting caught. In my part of the world, it wasn't a sin if nobody knew.

PLAYBOY: You once described yourself as "hopelessly Puritan, helplessly passionate." Do you feel you overcame that conflict?

DAVIS: Well, I didn't intend to become one of those prim New England women who are afraid of sex, didn't want to reach my present age and not have experienced everything, had a full life. Now I'm a virgin again, but I guess I did all right for a little Yankee girl.

PLAYBOY: If you were not Bette Davis but some great historical figure, who would you choose to be?

DAVIS: God, that's an easy one; I wouldn't have to think about it for a second. Elizabeth the First. She was a fantastic woman. I mean, the respect you have for her as a *monarch*, and she was also a very, very vain, tricky flirt. No man ever got to her. Essex tried. He was the one who tried hardest.

PLAYBOY: Speaking of other women you admire, is there any actress whose achievements you have envied?

DAVIS: No, I have never *envied* anybody. Yet I have always wanted to look like Katharine Hepburn, always found her face fascinating and preferred it to my ordinary little round face. Just the *look* is marvelous.

PLAYBOY: Do you know Hepburn?

DAVIS: I've never known her, no. I telephoned her once, after Garson Kanin wrote that dreadful book *Tracy and Hepburn* about her and Spence. I just wanted to express how awful I felt it was, but she didn't seem terribly concerned, really.

PLAYBOY: The late Anna Magnani was a great fan of yours, wasn't she?

DAVIS: Well, *she* was the actress I admired most in the whole world! We were great friends, met many times, and I went and saw her in Italy. God, she's given such great performances . . . terrific stuff. We're terribly alike as actors. I had a photograph of her in my book, with the caption "There's One in Every Country."

PLAYBOY: Which contemporary actresses do you see as having star quality or charisma or whatever you call it?

DAVIS: I think certainly Jane has it. Jane Fonda. I think Streisand. Oh, God, I *know* so—she's something else. I saw her opening night of *Funny Girl* in New York. The minute she walked on the stage, we all knew. You saw a star born. She's just—an individual, who had brains enough to stay looking the way she looks. What happened so often when lots of us came up in Hollywood, the studio tried to change you over . . . fix noses, hair, everything. A few of us had brains enough not to let them. Talk about people today—I think Marsha Mason is damned good. Jill Clayburgh; she's terrific. If she were working all the time, picture after picture, she'd have a different career. You wait so long between films nowadays.

PLAYBOY: With all its faults, do you think the old studio system was advantageous for actors?

DAVIS: Oh, God, yes, because I don't think there's any continuity to careers anymore. There aren't that many films. You had people behind you, they publicized you, bought properties for you, had scripts written for you. They don't write scripts *for* people anymore; they just *cast* them. We became part of the public's lives. Now, pick up a Sunday *New York Times*, you see huge ads for 15 films you never heard of, starring players you have heard even less of—you just don't know *who* they are.

PLAYBOY: Who are your favorite leading men in this generation, if you have any?

DAVIS: Burt Reynolds. He is one really *sexy* male. You know, there's a whole new breed of leading man today. A different kind.

PLAYBOY: And Reynolds represents the new breed?

DAVIS: No, no; he's the only one *left* who's like Gable and Cooper and all the hot, gorgeous, terrific guys of that era. The new breed—well, many of them are Italian—they're just different types, though some are certainly talented. [Jack] Nicholson is very talented, but that's a different kind of male star. Burt knows what I think of him, because they did a big testimonial dinner for him at the Waldorf, which I couldn't attend, so I sent a message saying he's enormously attractive, sexy and a very, very good actor. I would be happy, however, if Reynolds would get out of his motor-car syndrome and start making films about real people.

PLAYBOY: How about Robert Redford?

DAVIS: Redford is absolutely great. I'm glad you mentioned him. But I would lament terribly if he completely gave up acting for directing. He's marvelous. Paul Newman, too. Both very attractive men. Yet I still happen to think that Reynolds is in a different category. I had an absolute passion, of course, for Steve McQueen. He was also terrific.

PLAYBOY: You've expressed skepticism about so-called Method actors of Brando's school, haven't you, even though you admire Brando himself?

DAVIS: I just think he's a very talented guy, and if the Method worked for him—as it obviously did—everybody to his own thing. It's not for me. *Ugh*, no.

PLAYBOY: What's your method?

DAVIS: I go along with Claude Rains, who once said, "I learn the lines and pray to God." I think Tracy said that, too. Trust your intuition. I just go in and *do* it. Yet I believe in voice and dance training. There's no training anymore. Today you can't hear half the actors across the set.

PLAYBOY: In his *Playboy Interview*, Brando said he didn't consider any movie a work of art or any movie actor an artist. Would you comment on that?

DAVIS: Yes, it's perfectly absurd. How he can feel that way, with the work he himself has done as an example, is totally beyond me. Think of *On the*

Waterfront, one of the greatest performances he ever gave. We don't any of us know what happened to Marlon Brando. Of course it's an art form, judged entirely from the standpoint of *his* career without mentioning anybody else's.

PLAYBOY: What do you think about actors these days—and not only Brando—who are paid $2 million or $3 million for doing even a small role in a big film?

DAVIS: If the men in charge are willing to pay, I don't blame the actors. I think the people paying it are just lily guts and absurd, but be it on their heads. They're bankrupting the business. I mean, I would be totally embarrassed. On the other hand, I don't think there's enough money in the world to pay *any* of us for the *hell* we go through trying to give a performance. An actor today is up against worse odds than ever before.

PLAYBOY: Why do you say that?

DAVIS: Well, everything now is being shot on location, and location shooting is miserable, miserable, *miserable*! We used to all live in our own homes and work on those lovely sound stages where we didn't have to worry about wind, rain, heat, cold. There was more control and it was physically so much more pleasant. They call it realism, but that has *nothing* whatsoever to do with acting. For *The Petrified Forest*, we had the gas station *and* the petrified forest on two huge sound stages. We had a whole Welsh village there for *The Corn Is Green*. When I went to Mexico City and saw the Chapultepec Palace, I swore to God the one reproduced on our sound stage for *Juarez* looked just as real.

PLAYBOY: Still, don't you agree that the quality of movies has been improved by such background authenticity, avoiding the "studio look" of many of those early films?

DAVIS: No, I do not. They claim it's cheaper to shoot on location. I claim that we're all stunt people today; we're not actors anymore. When we shot *Family Reunion*, we were outdoors, with the temperature 22 below, trying to *act*, of all things! Hah! It's gotten so *real* today, honest to God, you can stand on a street corner and see the same thing. A lot of actors, the whole Sinatra kind of group—they love going to Paris and all these places. They can have 'em! For me, when anything's utterly naturalistic, so untheatrical, no makeup . . . well, it's a bore.

PLAYBOY: Are you saying that you believe the golden age of cinema is long gone?

DAVIS: Well, those golden years are very romanticized today. Mostly, they were just very hard work, but they had their advantages. Maybe the difference is that the world is less golden. We're in a mess, and our scripts reflect it. Everything gets bigger and more vicious: terror in the streets; dismembered hands floating around. I am truthfully horrified by all the violence and the blood on the screen.

PLAYBOY: But didn't you yourself make a series of gory horror films, beginning with *Baby Jane*?

DAVIS: But ours *weren't* bloody! And those were the only good parts they were writing for mature actresses. I myself can't *look* at all that bloody stuff, I just can't take it. *Baby Jane* had no blood; it was spooky. *The Nanny* had no blood. *Sweet Charlotte* had a shot of a head falling down the stairs, which I thoroughly disagreed with. I tried to get Aldrich to skip that, because I thought it totally unnecessary. I was in one really bloody film, which turned out much bloodier than indicated in the script; that was *Burnt Offerings*, and if you haven't seen it, congratulations.

PLAYBOY: Seen any movies you *have* liked lately?

DAVIS: I see very few. I was mad about *Julia* and *The Turning Point*. Two of the best I've seen in years. They were about real people, with well-written scripts. Those big [Francis] Coppola–[Steven] Spielberg–type films are not to my taste, and that's my privilege. I know many people disagree and find them smashing. My God, did you ever see *The Shining*? Give me a half hour, my dear, and I'll tell you what I thought of *that*. I thought it was monstrous, the most awful picture I had ever seen. Well, I have never liked [Stanley] Kubrick. His kind of movies are simply not for me.

PLAYBOY: OK. But don't you admit there's a kind of psychological violence and sick humor in *Baby Jane* that some people might find just as repellent?

DAVIS: But those characters were *characters*, and *Baby Jane* was actually pretty funny. I suppose the dead birds with mayonnaise *were* kind of unattractive. And the rat. You know, not long after *Baby Jane* opened, I gave a cocktail party in New York and had the head chef at the Plaza Hotel make pâté for me in the shape of a rat. Everyone got a big laugh out of it—this *awful* rat made of pâté served on a huge silver platter, looking a lot like the one in the film. Oh, I tell you, it was *heaven* when I lifted the top off.

PLAYBOY: Are you a card-carrying practical joker, as rumored?

DAVIS: Yes, I'm terrible. Sometimes I go too far. I've always loved dribble glasses. You wait for a very formal dinner party and then give the glass to the person who will be the most embarrassed. Lovely. I had another marvelous gag going once. Under my dinner table, I kept that gorgeous cowbell that's still there in my dining room. When I was ready to ring for the butler or somebody, I'd clang my *huge* cowbell. Well, conversation would stop. Everybody would try to pretend this was a perfectly normal thing to do, not looking me in the eye; then they'd all start talking like mad, wondering, of course, if I didn't know any better. About the fourth time I clanged it, they'd just stare . . . It was hysterical.

PLAYBOY: You pulled another small prank, didn't you, around the time of *Baby Jane*, by placing an ad in one of the trade papers?

DAVIS: That wasn't a serious ad, of course. I was making *Baby Jane* at the time, in 1962, and I placed this help-wanted ad on a full page in *The Hollywood Reporter*—just exactly like any other ad for employment. It said: "Mother of three, divorceé. . . . 30 years' experience. Mobile still and more affable than rumor would have it. Wants steady employment in Hollywood, etc. . . . References on request." Although Rupert Allen, one of the great publicity men out here, advised me against doing it, he ended up congratulating me. That ad rocked the town, finally. Everybody expired with laughter and realized it was a rib. Of course, I was kidding the bankers. The bankers had a list of the bankable people who would be OK'd when the studios went to the banks to finance a film. If you weren't on the list, you didn't get work. For example, Aldrich had had a terrible time getting money for *Baby Jane*, because of Joan and me. The bank people said, "Those two old bags? Recast this film and we'll give you any amount of money you want." That's why we had to shoot the whole thing in three weeks, because we had so little money. Joan and I didn't get big salaries, so we took a huge percentage and made a fortune on it.

PLAYBOY: So you had the last laugh. But was everyone convinced it was a joke?

DAVIS: No. Everywhere I went with *Bette Davis in Person*—Australia or you name it—they'd bring this up and ask, "Were you *advertising* for work?" Well, I *was* working. I'd never stopped working. My God, I would never be so cheap as to take out an employment ad otherwise. It was a riot, a way to say I was sick of the whole system out here, just sick of it.

PLAYBOY: You expressed your view on the violence in today's films. What do you think of sex and censorship?

DAVIS: Well, we could still use about *half* the censorship we had all those years. Though I didn't believe in the Hays Office's brand of censorship. It was all very blue stocking, and I think they actually got big kicks out of the things they censored in films. Now it's all gone way, way over in the other direction. I mean, they haul in nude scenes just for the sake of being sensational. It really boils down to a question of taste, and I don't believe movies were any *less* sexy when they weren't so explicit. We had to duck the issue sometimes. In *Now, Voyager*, you definitely knew they had had an affair up in the mountains, but it was done in a tasteful way; it was the whole point of the story.

PLAYBOY: If you were starting your career now, do you think you could be persuaded to do a nude scene?

DAVIS: No, never. This is one of the tragedies of girls today. Girls lose roles because they *won't* do them, and I see no need for it.

PLAYBOY: Still, there are substantial actresses you respect, such as Fonda and Clayburgh—

DAVIS: Oh, but I think they use doubles for nude scenes. And what's-her-name, Brooke Shields; she has a double, absolutely.

PLAYBOY: Largely because she is underage. No, highly respected actresses *have* done nude scenes.

DAVIS: Well, I just don't believe the totally naked body is really all that interesting. When I saw *Oh! Calcutta!* in San Francisco years ago—I mean, I was a pretty sophisticated woman by then, and I sat way in the back, hoping nobody in the theater knew I was there, frankly—I was shocked most by the audience. Mostly middle-aged or older people. I couldn't decide if they were getting their kicks in their seats in the theater, or were getting themselves ready to go home and get their kicks. That was what fascinated me; but either way, I thought it was an abomination.

PLAYBOY: Yet isn't there a story about your having posed nude for a statue in Boston?

DAVIS: Oh, this was after high school, when I was a very young person. I took all sorts of jobs to earn money; we needed money. I was asked to pose for a statue of *Spring*, for a fountain. I've heard it's still up there in a park someplace, though I've never seen it since.

PLAYBOY: How did this ever come about, given your natural reticence about nudity?

DAVIS: I was hired by a woman sculptress. I don't remember her name now; she never became very well known. She was a rather elderly woman, with a male assistant to help her. She had a little dressing room at the top of the stairs and told me to just go up and strip, please. Well, 15 minutes or more later, I was still *up* there when she called out, "Miss Davis, we're ready." I was absolutely panicked. I didn't dare come out. Why she didn't give me some sort of robe to put on, I never knew, but

I took my clothes off and there I *was*. So I finally had to go down, stark naked in front of her and the male assistant. I tell you, I was *mortified*. It took me years to get over it, as a matter of fact.

PLAYBOY: But you went on with the sessions?

DAVIS: You get used to it, in a way. I was only 18. It does present a picture of a sad little girl, earning money for the family. I was *so* modest. If I had realized I was going to have to be starkers—

PLAYBOY: So the only Bette Davis nude extant is presumably somewhere in Boston, if not banned. Does *Spring* resemble you?

DAVIS: Yes, of course. It was lovely, beautiful. I had the perfect figure for it.

PLAYBOY: Should we send out a search party?

DAVIS: [*Laughs*] Maybe you'll inspire me to locate it.

PLAYBOY: So much for your views on nudity. You've probably had as busy a career in television as any other actress of your generation. How many shows have you done?

DAVIS: I have no idea. I did them all, really—*General Electric Theater, Alfred Hitchcock, Perry Mason, Gunsmoke*. I did *Wagon Train* three times.

PLAYBOY: How do you feel about making TV films as compared with regular movies?

DAVIS: I don't call them TV films. I'm sick of this horrid little snobbery—the same snobbery that the New York theater had for movies—about "real" films versus films for television. You see at least 10 a year on TV just as well acted, just as well done in every way; they're *films*. Unfortunately, we can't have them without the commercials. But I used to tell my children, "Don't beef—if you want to sit at home and see the Sadler's Wells Ballet direct from London, you've got to pay for it somehow."

PLAYBOY: Do you watch old Bette Davis movies on television?

DAVIS: Oh, sure, every now and then. Of course, the cuts they've made just break your heart. Though they are doing less cutting lately, I've noticed. There should have been a clause about that from the beginning. Of course, that was when *all* the old Warner Bros. films were sold to television. A group of 65 films, many of them mine, was sold for only $7 million. This is why I've had more television coverage through the years than almost any other actress.

PLAYBOY: So you credit TV for building up your following with young people?

DAVIS: Oh, of course. At least 80 percent of my fan mail is from young people. My audience anywhere is a good mixture, but always a lot of young people.

PLAYBOY: What about the gay audience? It seems obvious that you and other female stars with a certain flamboyant style have a huge gay following.

DAVIS: I really don't want to discuss that, not at all. Let us face facts. Homosexuals are probably the most artistic and appreciative human beings, who worship films and theater. Certainly, I've been one of the artists they admire very much. It was always said that Judy Garland and I had the biggest following, but I don't think it's fair to say it's because I'm flamboyant. I'm *not* flamboyant. In my personal life, I've never been known as flamboyant. Joan Crawford was flamboyant. Generally, homosexuals are very appreciative of serious work in the arts, so it's highly complimentary to be someone they choose.

PLAYBOY: You have been very popular as a guest on the talk shows, too, haven't you?

DAVIS: Yes, but now I never do a talk show with more than two other guests on it. I think they usually have far too many people. I feel—probably very conceitedly—that I've got plenty to say. So I don't see why I should go to the trouble of getting made up to go wherever I have to go, then do five minutes and have to sit there keeping my mouth shut. It just irritates me to death. Very unpleasant. So I'll go only if they have no more than two other guests—usually a singer and a comedian. I have grown to enjoy it since my first talk show, with Jack Paar, which was terrifying. I'd never been so scared in my life of any performance. Because in these situations, you know, you're sitting there completely exposed—as *yourself*. I learned to get comfortable with it, but it's not easy in the beginning. When you spend your life being somebody else and that's what you enjoy most—being somebody else—well, that's not exactly like everybody else, is it? [*Laughs*] Am I making myself clear?

PLAYBOY: Perfectly. Doesn't it mean you weren't sure how to play Bette Davis?

DAVIS: Well, I never *played* Bette Davis. I suppose that peculiar thing an actor has of wanting to be somebody else shows a certain *not* liking of yourself. I think it's true of me and of anyone else who aspires to be in this profession: You're basically not very mad about yourself.

PLAYBOY: Were you ever in analysis?

DAVIS: No. Almost went three times—almost. When I was puzzled by things happening in my life. Then I decided that was no good, because what was peculiar about me was probably what had made me successful. Because I've seen some very talented actors go into analysis and really lose it. Among my friends, I think I'm one of the few who haven't gone. I've often thought I'd have loved *being* a psychoanalyst if I weren't an actress. Either that or a trial lawyer. You know, a great trial lawyer has got to be a good actor. I played a lawyer once on *Perry Mason*, while Raymond Burr was on vacation. I adored that show.

PLAYBOY: Let's move from law into politics. You were quite active politically during the Roosevelt years, weren't you?

DAVIS: No, no. I campaigned once at Madison Square Garden for FDR's third term. I would have campaigned for Robert Kennedy, definitely. I had great admiration for Teddy [Kennedy] this last time and endorsed him . . . with funds. But I don't *know* anymore. I was always very careful about this. I think we, as actors, have a dangerous position, because we *can* influence millions of people, no question. So we'd better know what we're talking about, and I find it very hard today to know what anyone's talking about or even to know what's going on.

PLAYBOY: Among your supporting cast in *Dark Victory*, many movies ago, was Ronald Reagan. Do you now support Reagan, who once supported you?

DAVIS: I am not for Reagan; that is, I didn't vote for him. We always called him "little Ronnie Reagan," you know, and to all of us who grew up with him, it's kind of *awesome* that he's President [*big chuckle*]. But Reagan has an enormous advantage, because he comes through on television, and a lot of screen actors are not good on live TV. It's a very strange, personal medium. Yet I think it was wonderful that Reagan appointed a woman to the Supreme Court. That's to his credit, very intelligent of him and long past due. I'm not going to say anything against Reagan. He's probably doing very well; let's hope so, because the country needs a kind of resurrection. Let's keep our fingers crossed.

PLAYBOY: OK. Are you a superstitious person, as someone once suggested?

DAVIS: Oh, wildly superstitious. In every way. About hats on beds, walking under ladders, ladybugs for good luck. String . . . if there's ever a piece of string on my clothing, don't take it off me.

PLAYBOY: That's bad luck?

DAVIS: No, *good luck* to leave it on. I have thousands of them, thousands. A bird in the house. I'm just petrified of having a bird inside the house. That's a very old sign of a death. And the day before Farney—my second husband—died, a bird flew up and cracked against the window of our house at Riverbottom. The next day, Farney was dead. That's one that really scares me. Oh, God, I have them all, the works: black cats, broken mirrors. Don't walk with a post between you and a friend. If your nose itches, you'll kiss a fool. Well, I have kissed a *lot* of fools. . . .

PLAYBOY: Do you consider yourself in any way religious?

DAVIS: Yes, I don't think we do it all by ourselves. I believe that God helps those who help themselves. I believe in doing unto others as you would have them do unto you, inasmuch as any of us is humanly able. If you believe in those two things, I say you're religious. But I am not religious in the sense of being a wild churchgoer. I have worked since I was in my teens, and Sunday was my one day off—I was not about to give it up to get dressed and go to church. I was brought up going to Sunday school every Sunday in the world, and I was *surfeited* with church. In my generation, that happened to many of us. Plus, I was a very practical child. I used to confront my Sunday-school teachers with many of the miracles in the Bible and just say, "Now, *this* is impossible—walking on water. *How?*" They didn't like it too much.

PLAYBOY: This sounds familiar. Doesn't it smack of the way you behaved much later, when you got onto a movie set and saw holes in the script?

DAVIS: *Exactly.* Even as a young girl, with the Bible, I could not *believe* the script! It all sounded absolutely wildly illogical—you had *one* fish and fed the multitudes? I didn't mean any of it sacrilegiously; that's just the kind of child I was, and my Sunday-school teachers were not enamored of me *at all.*

PLAYBOY: Was there any point in your career when you experienced real fear of becoming a has-been?

DAVIS: That's hard to know. I've had some rough times. Everybody has hiatuses, and I had some good, thorough ones. I think there was one year when I truly thought it was over. I sat out here for a solid year without one job offer—that must have been the late 1950s, around 1960. I don't recall the chronology, but Gary had been working and was gone so much that I finally brought all the children to Los Angeles and rented a house. Not *one* offer! I wasn't scared, I was desperate. I couldn't believe it, really couldn't understand *why.* But those things happen. And those things change, as they did for me.

PLAYBOY: How do you look at the problem of aging? How do you deal with it?

DAVIS: I'll tell you: I do *not* believe that life begins at 40. I'm so bored with this statement I could scream. Mentally—for a woman, but I think for everybody—life begins at 30. But the thing I hate most about getting older is the physical change, the fact that you're just not as attractive physically.

I think every woman has that, while men get by with much, much more. Men become much *more* attractive when they start looking older. Look at stills of Bogey, for instance—far more attractive as an older man than he was at 30. Look at Robert Wagner—at 19 or 20 he looked ridiculous; now he's a damned attractive guy. Weathering improves men, that's all; but it doesn't do much for women, though we do have an advantage.

PLAYBOY: What's that?

DAVIS: Makeup, which can certainly help. But, you know, you just have to face facts, that's all. You do not *look* as attractive. I do not wish anymore to get into a bikini and go lie on the beach, thank you very, very much. And I never will again. Of course, you cannot be afraid of *being* your age. As an actress, I have a bigger incentive for staying in shape, and I think weight is what makes people look old the quickest—male or female. I don't think a man looks older, for instance, when he starts losing hair. There's nothing wrong with that. I'm sick of toupees. Men look very attractive with half-bald or even bald heads. I think this hair fetish among men today is ridiculous. B.D.'s father, Sherry, was practically bald, and a very attractive looking man, very. Another thing is—yes, I believe the thing I lament most about getting older is the way time melts; years sort of melt together. You eventually live day to day. You really and truly begin to take your days one at a time—with no great excitement about what will happen in six months or a year.

PLAYBOY: Is this a way of dealing with it or a depressing side effect?

DAVIS: I think it's just the way things *are* when you're no longer building a career, raising a family. My life is all in the archives of Boston University's library, where I've sent everything: scripts, reviews and a famous little book in which I've collected dance programs, poems that boys wrote to me, notes. Oh, I kept everything. On the outside, it says: All My Secrets Are Hidden Herein.

PLAYBOY: Any of them shockers?

DAVIS: Not really. But it's as if I always knew something out of the ordinary was going to happen to me. It's really spooky, in a way. I started collecting it all at 13 and drove everybody crazy even then. I always had to have the top jobs, even as a very young person, all through school, being head of the religious society or the debating society or getting the leads in senior plays.

PLAYBOY: You don't seem to have any regrets, do you?

DAVIS: Well, I couldn't stop myself; that's the way I was. You know, I said I don't envy people, but I sometimes envy people who are *not* that ambitious, who don't have this drive to be first in whatever they do, this terrible perfectionism. It's a terrific responsibility and pretty exhausting. I've never wanted to be anybody else, always felt I was lucky to be what I was. Definitely. I'd often change the *exterior*, perhaps. My daughter [B.D.] is beautiful at 5' 11", and I'm kind of a runt at 5' 3" or 5' 3½". While I'm small, I've always been too much; that's the best description of me.

PLAYBOY: Another description of you was in that Kim Carnes song that was so popular last year, *Bette Davis Eyes*. Do you know all the words?

DAVIS: [*Sings*] "She's ferocious. . . . She throws you. . . ." No, I haven't learned the lyrics, really, but I think the writers are damned clever. I wrote to them and said, "How did you know me so well?"

PLAYBOY: Getting back to your own description of yourself—

DAVIS: Let's just say it's going to be a great world when I pass on.

PLAYBOY: Why do you say that?

DAVIS: Because I think I've been a difficult, difficult woman. I've been difficult for lots of people.

PLAYBOY: That's pretty negative thinking. There are probably a lot more people you've made happy than unhappy.

DAVIS: Thank you for that. I will live on that all day. Let's hope that is true. I know in a sense that *is* true, so I'm not going to be silly about it. No question I've inspired some people. I've taught a lot of people to cook, inspired other people to work harder or do something better, though I still say my kind of person is. . . . [*thoughtful pause*]

PLAYBOY: Too much? But isn't too much better than too little?

DAVIS: Probably. I think so. I hope so.

PLAYBOY: What is your all-time favorite movie you weren't in?

DAVIS: *The Best Years of Our Lives*, by Willie Wyler. Now, *that* was one of the greatest films ever made.

PLAYBOY: Guess what? That was our last question.

DAVIS: It *was*? Chrrrist—let's have a *drink*.

March 1966

BOB DYLAN

A candid conversation with the iconoclastic idol of the folk-rock set

As a versatile musicologist and trenchant social commentator, Nat Hentoff brings uniquely pertinent credentials to his role as interviewer of this month's controversial subject, about whom he writes:

"Less than five years ago, Bob Dylan was scuffling in New York—sleeping in friends' apartments on the Lower East Side and getting very occasional singing work at Gerde's Folk City, an unprepossessing bar for citybillies in the Village. With his leather cap, blue jeans and battered desert boots—his unvarying costume in those days—Dylan looked like an updated, undernourished Huck Finn. And like Huck, he had come out of the Midwest; he would have said 'escaped.' The son of Abraham Zimmerman, an appliance dealer, he was raised in Hibbing, Minnesota, a bleak mining town near the Canadian border. Though he ran away from home regularly, young Zimmerman did manage to finish high school, and went on to spend about six months at the University of Minnesota in 1960. By then, he called himself Bob Dylan—in tribute to Dylan Thomas, according to legend; but actually after a gambling uncle whose last name was similar to Dylan.

"In the fall of that year, he came East to visit his idol, Woody Guthrie, in the New Jersey hospital where the Okie folk-singing bard was wasting away with a progressive disease of the nervous system. Dylan stayed and tried to scrape together a singing career. According to those who knew him then, he was shy and stubborn but basically friendly and, beneath the hipster stance, uncommonly gentle. But they argued about his voice. Some found its flat Midwestern tones gratingly mesmeric; others agreed with a Missouri folk singer who had likened the Dylan sound to that of 'a dog with his leg caught in barbed wire.' All agreed, however, that his songs were strangely personal and often disturbing, a pungent mixture of loneliness and defiance laced with traces of Guthrie, echoes of the Negro blues singers and more than a suggestion of country-and-western; but essentially Dylan was developing his own penetratingly distinctive style. Yet the voice was so harsh and the songs so bitterly scornful of conformity, race prejudice and the mythology of the Cold War that most of his friends couldn't conceive of Dylan making it big even though folk music was already on the rise.

"They were wrong. In September of 1961, a music critic for *The New York Times* caught his act at Gerde's and hailed the scruffy 19-year-old Minnesotan as a significant new voice on the folk horizon. Around the same time, he was signed by Columbia Records, and his first album was released early the next year. Though it was far from a smash hit, concerts and club engagements gradually multiplied; and then Dylan scored his storied triumph at the Newport Folk Festival in 1962. His next LP began to move, and in the spring of 1963 came his first big single: "Blowin' in the Wind." That same spring he turned down a lucrative guest shot on *The Ed Sullivan Show* because CBS wouldn't permit him to sing a mordant parody he'd written about the John Birch Society. For the nation's young, the Dylan image began to form: kind of a singing James Dean with overtones of Holden Caulfield; he was making it, but he wasn't selling out. His concerts began to attract overflow crowds, and his songs—in performances by him and other folk singers—were rushing onto the hit charts. One of them, "The Times They Are A-Changin'," became an anthem for the rebellious young, who savored its message that adults don't know where it's at and can't tell their children what to do.

"By 1965 he had become a major phenomenon on the music scene. More and more folk performers, from Joan Baez to the Byrds, considered it mandatory to have an ample supply of Dylan songs in their repertoires; in one frantically appreciative month—last August—48 different recordings of Dylan ballads were pressed by singers other than the composer himself. More and more aspiring folk singers—and folk-song writers—have begun to sound like Dylan. The current surge of 'protest' songs by such long-haired, post-beat rock-'n'-rollers as Barry McGuire and Sonny and Cher is credited to Dylan. And the newest commercial boom, 'folk-rock,' a fusion of folk-like lyrics with a rock beat and background, is an outgrowth, in large part, of Dylan's recent decision—decried as a 'sellout' by folknik purists—to perform with a rock 'n' roll combo rather than continue to accompany himself alone on the guitar. Backed by the big beat of the new group, Dylan tours England with as much tumultuous success as he does America, and the airplay for his single records in both countries is rivaled only by that of the Beatles, Herman's Hermits and the Rolling Stones on the Top 40 deejay shows. In the next 18 months, his income—from personal appearances, records and composer's royalties—is expected to exceed $1 million.

"But there are other changes. Dylan has become elusive. He is no longer seen in his old haunts in the Village and on the Lower East Side. With few exceptions, he avoids interviewers, and in public, he is usually seen from afar at the epicenter of a protective coterie of tousle-topped young men dressed like him, and lissome, straight-haired young ladies who also seem to be dressed like him. His home base, if it can be called that, is a house his manager owns near Woodstock, a fashionable artists' colony in New York State, and he also enjoys the run of his manager's apartment on dignified Gramercy Park in New York City. There are tales told of Dylan the motorcyclist, the novelist, the maker of high-camp home movies; but except among his small circle of intimates, the 24-year-old folk hero is inscrutably aloof.

"It was only after a long period of evasion and hesitation that Dylan finally agreed to grant this *Playboy Interview*—the longest he's ever given. We met him on the 10th floor of the new CBS and Columbia Records building in mid-Manhattan. The room was antiseptic: white walls with black trim, contemporary furniture with severe lines, avant-garde art chosen by committee, everything in order, neat desks, neat personnel. In this sterile setting, slouched in a chair across from us, Dylan struck a refreshingly discordant note—with his untamed brownish-blond mane brushing the collar of his tieless blue plaid shirt, in his black jacket, gray vaudevillian-striped pipestem pants and well-worn blue-suede shoes. Sitting nearby—also long-haired, tieless and black-jacketed, but wearing faded jeans—was a stringy young man whom the singer identified only as Taco Pronto. As Dylan spoke—in a soft drawl, smiling only rarely and fleetingly, sipping tea and chain-smoking cigarettes—his unspeaking friend chuckled and nodded appreciatively from the sidelines. Tense and guarded at first, Dylan gradually began to loosen up, then to open up, as he tried to tell us—albeit a bit surrealistically—just where he's been and where he's going. Under the circumstances, we chose to play straight man in our questions, believing that to have done otherwise would have stemmed the freewheeling flow of Dylan's responses."

PLAYBOY: "Popular songs," you told a reporter last year, "are the only art form that describes the temper of the times. The only place where it's happening is on the radio and records. That's where the people hang out. It's not in books; it's not on the stage; it's not in the galleries. All this art they've been talking about, it just remains on the shelf. It doesn't make anyone happier." In view of the fact that more people than ever before are reading books and going to plays and art galleries, do you think that statement is borne out by the facts?

DYLAN: Statistics measure quantity, not quality. The people in the statistics are people who are very bored. Art, if there is such a thing, is in the bathrooms; everybody knows that. To go to an art-gallery thing where you get free milk and doughnuts and where there is a rock 'n' roll band playing: That's just a status affair. I'm not putting it down, mind you; but I spend a lot of time in the bathroom. I think museums are vulgar. They're all against sex. Anyhow, I didn't say that people "hang out" on the radio, I said they get "hung up" on the radio.

PLAYBOY: Why do you think rock 'n' roll has become such an international phenomenon?

DYLAN: I can't really think that there is any rock 'n' roll. Actually, when you think about it, anything that has no real existence is bound to become an international phenomenon. Anyway, what does it mean, rock 'n' roll? Does it mean Beatles, does it mean John Lee Hooker, Bobby Vinton, Jerry Lewis's kid? What about Lawrence Welk? He must play a few rock-'n'-roll songs. Are all these people the same? Is Ricky Nelson like Otis Redding? Is Mick Jagger really Ma Rainey? I can tell by the way people hold their cigarettes if they like Ricky Nelson. I think it's fine to like Ricky Nelson; I couldn't care less if somebody likes Ricky Nelson. But I think we're getting off the track here. There isn't any Ricky Nelson. There isn't any Beatles; oh, I take that back; there are a lot of beetles. But there isn't any Bobby Vinton. Anyway, the word is not "international phenomenon"; the word is "parental nightmare."

PLAYBOY: In recent years, according to some critics, jazz has lost much of its appeal to the younger generation. Do you agree?

DYLAN: I don't think jazz has ever appealed to the younger generation. Anyway, I don't really know who this younger generation is. I don't think they could get into a jazz club anyway. But jazz is hard to follow; I mean you actually have to like jazz to follow it; and my motto is, never follow anything. I don't know what the motto of the younger generation is, but I would think they'd have to follow their parents. I mean, what would some parent say to his kid if the kid came home with a glass eye, a Charlie Mingus record and a pocketful of feathers? He'd say, "Who are you following?" And the poor kid would have to stand there with water in his shoes, a bow tie on his ear and soot pouring out of his belly button and say, "Jazz, Father, I've been following jazz." And his father would probably say, "Get a broom and clean up all that soot before you go to sleep." Then the kid's mother would tell her friends, "Oh yes, our little Donald, he's part of the younger generation, you know."

PLAYBOY: You used to say that you wanted to perform as little as possible, that you wanted to keep most of your time to yourself. Yet you're doing more concerts and cutting more records every year. Why? Is it the money?

DYLAN: Everything is changed now from before. Last spring, I guess I was going to quit singing. I was very drained, and the way things were going, it was a very draggy situation—I mean, when you do "Everybody Loves You for Your Black Eye," and meanwhile the back of your head is caving in. Anyway, I was playing a lot of songs I didn't want to play. I was singing words I didn't really want to sing. I don't mean words like "God" and "mother" and "president" and "suicide" and "meat cleaver." I mean simple little words like "if" and "hope" and "you." But "Like a Rolling Stone" changed it all; I didn't care anymore after that about writing books or poems or whatever. I mean it was something that I myself could dig. It's very tiring having other people tell you how much they dig you if you yourself don't dig you. It's also very deadly entertainmentwise. Contrary to what some scary people think, I don't play with a band now for any kind of propaganda-type or commercial-type reasons. It's just that my songs are pictures and the band makes the sound of the pictures.

PLAYBOY: Do you feel that acquiring a combo and switching from folk to folk-rock has improved you as a performer?

DYLAN: I'm not interested in myself as a performer. Performers are people who perform for other people. Unlike actors, I know what I'm saying. It's very simple in my mind. It doesn't matter what kind of audience reaction this whole thing gets. What happens on the stage is straight. It doesn't expect any rewards or fines from any kind of outside agitators. It's ultrasimple, and would exist whether anybody was looking or not.

As far as folk and folk-rock are concerned, it doesn't matter what kind of nasty names people invent for the music. It could be called arsenic music, or perhaps Phaedra music. I don't think that such a word as folk-rock has anything to do with it. And folk music is a word I can't use. Folk music is a bunch of fat people. I have to think of all this as traditional music. Traditional music is based on hexagrams. It comes about from legends, Bibles, plagues, and it revolves around vegetables and death. There's nobody that's going to kill traditional music. All these songs about roses growing out of people's brains and lovers who are really geese and swans that turn into angels—they're not going to die. It's all those paranoid people who think that someone's going to come and take away their toilet paper—they're going to die. Songs like "Which Side Are You On?" and "I Love You, Porgy"—they're not folk-music songs; they're political songs. They're already dead. Obviously, death is not very universally accepted. I mean, you'd think that the traditional-music people could gather from their songs that mystery—just plain simple mystery—is a fact, a traditional fact. I listen to the old ballads; but I wouldn't go to a party and listen to the old ballads. I could give you descriptive detail of what they do to me, but some people would probably think my imagination had gone mad. It strikes me funny that people actually have the gall to think that I have some kind of fantastic imagination. It gets very lonesome. But anyway, traditional music is too unreal to die. It doesn't need to be protected. Nobody's going to hurt it. In that music is the only true, valid death you can feel today off a record player. But like anything else in great demand, people try to own it. It has to do with a purity thing. I think its meaninglessness is holy. Everybody knows that I'm not a folk singer.

PLAYBOY: Some of your old fans would agree with you—and not in a complimentary vein—since your debut with the rock-'n'-roll combo at last year's Newport Folk Festival, where many of them booed you loudly for "selling out" to commercial pop tastes. The early Bob Dylan, they felt, was the "pure" Bob Dylan. How do you feel about it?

DYLAN: I was kind of stunned. But I can't put anybody down for coming and booing; after all, they paid to get in. They could have been maybe a little quieter and not so persistent, though. There were a lot of old people there, too; lots of whole families had driven down from Vermont, lots of nurses and their parents, and well, like they just came to hear some relaxing hoedowns, you know, maybe an Indian polka or two. And just when everything's going all right, here I come on, and the whole place turns into a beer factory. There were a lot of people there who were very pleased that I got booed. I saw them afterward. I do resent somewhat, though, that everybody that booed said they did it because they were old fans.

PLAYBOY: What about their charge that you vulgarized your natural gifts?

DYLAN: What can I say? I'd like to *see* one of these so-called fans. I'd like to have him blindfolded and brought to me. It's like going out to the desert and screaming, and then having little kids throw their sandbox at you. I'm only 24. These people that said this—were they Americans?

PLAYBOY: Americans or not, there were a lot of people who didn't like your new sound. In view of this widespread negative reaction, do you think you may have made a mistake in changing your style?

DYLAN: A mistake is to commit a misunderstanding. There could be no such thing, anyway, as this action. Either people understand or they *pretend* to understand—or else they really don't understand. What you're speaking of here is doing wrong things for selfish reasons. I don't know the word for that, unless it's suicide. In any case, it has nothing to do with my music.

PLAYBOY: Mistake or not, what made you decide to go the rock-'n'-roll route?

DYLAN: Carelessness. I lost my one true love. I started drinking. The first thing I know, I'm in a card game. Then I'm in a crap game. I wake up in a pool hall. Then this big Mexican lady drags me off the table, takes me to Philadelphia. She leaves me alone in her house, and it burns down. I wind up in Phoenix. I get a job as a Chinaman. I start working in a dime store, and move in with a 13-year-old girl. Then this big Mexican lady from Philadelphia comes in and burns the house down. I go down to Dallas. I get a job as a "before" in a Charles Atlas "before and after" ad. I move in with a delivery boy who can cook fantastic chili and hot dogs. Then this 13-year-old girl from Phoenix comes and burns the house down. The delivery boy—he ain't so mild: He gives her the knife, and the next thing I know I'm in Omaha. It's so cold there, by this time I'm robbing my own bicycles and frying my own fish. I stumble onto some luck and get a job as a carburetor out at the hot-rod races every Thursday night. I move in with a high school teacher who also does a little plumbing on the side, who ain't much to look at, but who's built a special kind of refrigerator that can turn newspaper into lettuce. Everything's going good until that delivery boy shows up and tries to knife me. Needless to say, he burned the house down, and I hit the road. The first guy that picked me up asked me if I wanted to be a star. What could I say?

PLAYBOY: And that's how you became a rock-'n'-roll singer?

DYLAN: No, that's how I got tuberculosis.

PLAYBOY: Let's turn the question around: Why have you stopped composing and singing protest songs?

DYLAN: I've stopped composing and singing anything that has either a reason to be written or a motive to be sung. Don't get me wrong, now. "Protest" is not my word. I've never thought of myself as such. The word "protest," I think, was made up for people undergoing surgery. It's an amusement-park word. A normal person in his righteous mind would have to have the hiccups to pronounce it honestly. The word "message" strikes me as having a hernia-like sound. It's just like the word "delicious." Also the word "marvelous." You know, the English can say "marvelous" pretty good. They can't say "raunchy" so good, though. Well, we each have our thing. Anyway, message songs, as everybody knows, are a drag. It's only college newspaper editors and single girls under 14 that could possibly have time for them.

PLAYBOY: You've said you think message songs are vulgar. Why?

DYLAN: Well, first of all, anybody that's got a message is going to learn from experience that they can't put it into a song. I mean it's just not going to come out the same message. After one or two of these unsuccessful attempts, one realizes that his resultant message, which is not even the same message he thought up and began with, he's now got to stick by it; because, after all, a song leaves your mouth just as soon as it leaves your hands. Are you following me?

PLAYBOY: Oh, perfectly.

DYLAN: Well, anyway, second of all, you've got to respect other people's right to also have a message themselves. Myself, what I'm going to do is rent Town Hall and put about 30 Western Union boys on the bill. I mean, then there'll *really* be some messages. People will be able to come and hear more messages than they've ever heard before in their life.

PLAYBOY: But your early ballads have been called "songs of passionate protest." Wouldn't that make them "message" music?

DYLAN: This is unimportant. Don't you understand? I've been writing since I was eight years old. I've been playing the guitar since I was 10. I was raised playing and writing whatever it was I had to play and write.

PLAYBOY: Would it be unfair to say, then, as some have, that you were motivated commercially rather than creatively in writing the kind of songs that made you popular?

DYLAN: All right, now, look. It's not all that deep. It's not a complicated thing. My motives, or whatever they are, were never commercial in the money sense of the word. It was more in the don't-die-by-the-hacksaw sense of the word. I never did it for money. It happened, and I let it happen to me. There was no reason *not* to let it happen to me. I couldn't have written before what I write now, anyway. The songs used to be about what I felt and saw. Nothing of my own rhythmic vomit ever entered into it. Vomit is not romantic. I used to think songs are supposed to be romantic. And I didn't want to sing anything that was unspecific. Unspecific things have no sense of time. All of us people have no sense of time; it's a dimensional hang-up. Anybody can be specific and obvious. That's always been the easy way. The leaders of the world take the easy way. It's not that it's so difficult to be unspecific and less obvious; it's just that there's nothing, absolutely nothing, to be specific and obvious *about*. My older songs, to say the least, were about nothing. The newer ones are about the same nothing—only as seen inside a bigger thing, perhaps called the nowhere. But this is all very constipated. I *do* know what my songs are about.

PLAYBOY: And what's that?

DYLAN: Oh, some are about four minutes; some are about five, and some, believe it or not, are about 11 or 12.

PLAYBOY: Can't you be a bit more informative?

DYLAN: Nope.

PLAYBOY: All right. Let's change the subject. As you know, it's the age group from about 16 to 25 that listens to your songs. Why, in your opinion?

DYLAN: I don't see what's so strange about an age group like that listening to my songs. I'm hip enough to know that it ain't going to be the 85-to-90-year-olds. If the 85-to-90-year-olds *were* listening to me, they'd know that I can't tell them anything. The 16-to-25-year-olds, they probably know that I can't tell *them* anything either—and they know that *I* know it. It's a funny business. Obviously, I'm not an IBM computer any more than I'm an ashtray. I mean it's obvious to anyone who's ever slept in the backseat of a car that I'm just not a schoolteacher.

PLAYBOY: Even though you're not a schoolteacher, wouldn't you like to help the young people who dig you from turning into what some of their parents have become?

DYLAN: Well, I must say that I really don't know their parents. I really don't know if *anybody's* parents are so bad. Now, I hate to come on like a weakling or a coward, and I realize it might seem kind of irreligious, but I'm really not the right person to tramp around the country saving souls. I wouldn't run over anybody that was laying in the street, and I certainly wouldn't become a hangman. I wouldn't think twice about giving a starving man a cigarette. But I'm not a shepherd. And I'm not about to save anybody from fate, which I know nothing about. "Parents" is not the key word here. The key word is "destiny." I can't save them from that.

PLAYBOY: Still, thousands of young people look up to you as a kind of folk hero. Do you feel some sense of responsibility toward them?

DYLAN: I don't feel I have any responsibility, no. Whoever it is that listens to my songs owes *me* nothing. How could I possibly have any responsibility to any kind of thousands? What could possibly make me think that I owe anybody anything who just happens to be there? I've never written any song that begins with the words "I've gathered you here tonight. . . . " I'm not about to tell anybody to be a good boy or a good girl and they'll go to heaven. I really don't know what the people who are on the receiving end of these songs think of me, anyway. It's horrible. I'll bet Tony Bennett doesn't have to go through this kind of thing. I wonder what Billy the Kid would have answered to such a question.

PLAYBOY: In their admiration for you, many young people have begun to imitate the way you dress—which one adult commentator has called "self-consciously oddball and defiantly sloppy." What's your reaction to that kind of putdown?

DYLAN: Bullshit. Oh, such bullshit. I know the fellow that said that. He used to come around here and get beat up all the time. He better watch it; some people are after him. They're going to strip him naked and stick him in Times Square. They're going to tie him up, and also put a thermometer in his mouth. Those kind of morbid ideas and remarks are so petty—I mean there's a *war* going on. People got rickets; everybody wants to start a riot; 40-year-old women are eating spinach by the carload; the doctors haven't got a cure for cancer—and here's some hillbilly talking about how he doesn't like somebody's clothes. Worse than that, it gets printed and innocent people have to read it. This is a terrible thing. And he's a terrible man. Obviously, he's just living off the fat of himself, and he's expecting his kids to take care of him. His kids probably listen to my records. Just because my clothes are too long, does that mean I'm unqualified for what I do?

PLAYBOY: No, but there are those who think it does—and many of them seem to feel the same way about your long hair. But compared with the shoulder-length coiffures worn by some of the male singing groups these days, your tonsorial tastes are on the conservative side. How do you feel about these far-out hairstyles?

DYLAN: The thing that most people don't realize is that it's *warmer* to have long hair. Everybody wants to be warm. People with short hair freeze easily. Then they try to hide their coldness, and they get jealous of everybody that's warm. Then they become either barbers or congressmen. A lot of prison wardens have short hair. Have you ever noticed that Abraham Lincoln's hair was much longer than John Wilkes Booth's?

PLAYBOY: Do you think Lincoln wore his hair long to keep his head warm?

DYLAN: Actually, I think it was for medical reasons, which are none of my business. But I guess if you figure it out, you realize that all of one's hair surrounds and lays on the brain inside your head. Mathematically speaking, the more of it you can get out of your head, the better. People who want free minds sometimes overlook the fact that you have to have an uncluttered brain. Obviously, if you get your hair on the outside of your head, your brain will be a little more freer. But all this talk about long hair is just a trick. It's been thought up by men and women who look like cigars—the anti-happiness committee. They're all freeloaders and cops. You can tell who they are: They're always carrying calendars, guns or scissors. They're all trying to get into your quicksand. They think you've got something. I don't know why Abe Lincoln had long hair.

PLAYBOY: Until your abandonment of "message" songs, you were considered not only a major voice in the student protest movement but a militant champion of the civil rights struggle. According to friends, you seemed to feel a special bond of kinship with the Student Nonviolent Coordinating Committee, which you actively supported both as a performer and as a worker. Why have you withdrawn from participation in all these causes? Have you lost interest in protest as well as in protest songs?

DYLAN: As far as SNCC is concerned, I knew some of the people in it, but I only knew them as people, not as of any part of something that was bigger or better than themselves. I didn't even know what civil rights *was* before I met some of them. I mean, I knew there were Negroes, and I knew there were a lot of people who don't *like* Negroes. But I got to admit that if I didn't know some of the SNCC people, I would have gone on thinking that Martin Luther King was really nothing more than some underprivileged war hero. I haven't lost any interest in protest since then. I just didn't have any interest in protest to begin with—any more than I did in war heroes. You can't lose what you've never had. Anyway, when you don't like your situation, you either leave it or else you overthrow it. You can't just stand around and whine about it. People just get aware of your noise; they really don't get aware of *you*. Even if they give you what you want, it's only because you're making too much noise. First thing you know, you want something else, and then you want something else, and then you want something else, until finally it isn't a joke anymore, and whoever you're protesting against finally gets all fed up and stomps on everybody. Sure, you can go around trying to bring up people who are lesser than you, but then don't forget, you're messing around with gravity. I don't fight gravity. I do believe in equality, but I also believe in distance.

PLAYBOY: Do you mean people keeping their racial distance?

DYLAN: I believe in people keeping everything they've got.

PLAYBOY: Some people might feel that you're trying to cop out of fighting for the things you believe in.

DYLAN: Those would be people who think I have some sort of responsibility toward *them*. They probably want me to help them make friends. I don't know. They probably either want to set me in their house and have me come out every hour and tell them what time it is, or else they just want to stick me in between the mattress. How could they possibly understand what I believe in?

PLAYBOY: Well, what *do* you believe in?

DYLAN: I already told you.

PLAYBOY: All right. Many of your folk-singing colleagues remain actively involved in the fight for civil rights, free speech and withdrawal from Vietnam. Do you think they're wrong?

DYLAN: I don't think they're wrong, if that's what they see themselves doing. But don't think that what you've got out there is a bunch of little Buddhas all parading up and down. People that use God as a weapon should be amputated upon. You see it around here all the time: "Be good or God won't like you, and you'll go to hell." Things like that. People that march with slogans and things tend to take themselves a little too holy. It would be a drag if they, too, started using God as a weapon.

PLAYBOY: Do you think it's pointless to dedicate yourself to the cause of peace and racial equality?

DYLAN: Not pointless to dedicate yourself to peace and racial equality, but rather, it's pointless to dedicate yourself to the *cause*; that's *really* pointless.

That's very unknowing. To say "cause of peace" is just like saying "hunk of butter." I mean, how can you listen to anybody who wants you to believe he's dedicated to the hunk and not to the butter? People who can't conceive of how others hurt, they're trying to change the world. They're all afraid to admit that they don't really know each other. They'll all probably be here long after we've gone, and we'll give birth to new ones. But they themselves—I don't think *they'll* give birth to anything.

PLAYBOY: You sound a bit fatalistic.

DYLAN: I'm not fatalistic. Bank tellers are fatalistic; clerks are fatalistic. I'm a farmer. Who ever heard of a fatalistic farmer? I'm not fatalistic. I smoke a lot of cigarettes, but that doesn't make me fatalistic.

PLAYBOY: You were quoted recently as saying that "songs can't save the world. I've gone through all that." We take it you don't share Pete Seeger's belief that songs can change people, that they can help build international understanding.

DYLAN: On the international understanding part, that's OK. But you have a translation problem there. Anybody with this kind of a level of thinking has to also think about this translation thing. But I don't believe songs can change people anyway. I'm not Pinocchio. I consider that an insult. I'm not part of that. I don't blame anybody for thinking that way. But I just don't donate any money to them. I don't consider them anything like unhip; they're more in the rubber-band category.

PLAYBOY: How do you feel about those who have risked imprisonment by burning their draft cards to signify their opposition to U.S. involvement in Vietnam, and by refusing—as your friend Joan Baez has done—to pay their income taxes as a protest against the government's expenditures on war and weaponry? Do you think they're wasting their time?

DYLAN: Burning draft cards isn't going to end any war. It's not even going to save any lives. If someone can feel more honest with himself by burning his draft card, then that's great; but if he's just going to feel more important because he does it, then that's a drag. I really don't know too much about Joan Baez and her income-tax problems. The only thing I can tell you about Joan Baez is that she's not Belle Starr.

PLAYBOY: Writing about "beard-wearing draft-card burners and pacifist income-tax evaders," one columnist called such protesters "no less outside society than the junkie, the homosexual or the mass murderer." What's your reaction?

DYLAN: I don't believe in those terms. They're too hysterical. They don't describe anything. Most people think that homosexual, gay, queer, queen, faggot are all the same words. Everybody thinks that a junkie is a dope freak. As far as I'm concerned, I don't consider myself outside of anything. I just consider myself *not around.*

PLAYBOY: Joan Baez recently opened a school in northern California for training civil rights workers in the philosophy and techniques of nonviolence. Are you in sympathy with that concept?

DYLAN: If you mean do I agree with it or not, I really don't see anything to be in agreement *with.* If you mean has it got my approval, I guess it does, but my approval really isn't going to do it any good. I don't know about other people's sympathy, but my sympathy runs to the lame and crippled and beautiful things. I have a feeling of loss of power—something like a reincarnation feeling; I don't feel that for mechanical things like cars or schools. I'm sure it's a nice school, but if you're asking me would I go to it, I would have to say no.

PLAYBOY: As a college dropout in your freshman year, you seem to take a dim view of schooling in general, whatever the subject.

DYLAN: I really don't think about it.

PLAYBOY: Well, have you ever had any regrets about not completing college?

DYLAN: That would be ridiculous. Colleges are like old-age homes; except for the fact that more people die in colleges than in old-age homes, there's really no difference. People have one great blessing—obscurity—and not really too many people are thankful for it. Everybody is always taught to be thankful for their food and clothes and things like that, but not to be thankful for their obscurity. Schools don't teach that; they teach people to be rebels and lawyers. I'm not going to put down the teaching system; that would be too silly. It's just that it really doesn't have too much to teach. Colleges are part of the American institution; everybody respects them. They're very rich and influential, but they have nothing to do with survival. Everybody knows that.

PLAYBOY: Would you advise young people to skip college, then?

DYLAN: I wouldn't advise anybody to do anything. I certainly wouldn't advise somebody not to go to college; I just wouldn't pay his *way* through college.

PLAYBOY: Don't you think the things one learns in college can help enrich one's life?

DYLAN: I don't think anything like that is going to enrich my life, no—not *my* life, anyway. Things are going to happen whether I know why they happen or not. It just gets more complicated when you stick *yourself* into it. You don't find out why things move. You *let* them move; you *watch* them move; you *stop* them from moving; you *start* them moving. But you don't sit around and try to figure out *why* there's movement—unless, of course, you're just an innocent moron, or some wise old Japanese man. Out of all the people who just lay around and ask "Why?" how many do you figure really want to know?

PLAYBOY: Can you suggest a better use for the four years that would otherwise be spent in college?

DYLAN: Well, you could hang around in Italy; you could go to Mexico; you could become a dishwasher; you could even go to Arkansas. I don't know; there are thousands of things to do and places to go. Everybody thinks that you have to bang your head against the wall, but it's silly when you really think about it. I mean, here you have fantastic scientists working on ways to prolong human living, and then you have other people who take it for granted that you have to beat your head against the wall in order to be happy. You can't take everything you don't like as a personal insult. I guess you should go where your wants are bare, where you're invisible and not needed.

PLAYBOY: Would you classify sex among your wants, wherever you go?

DYLAN: Sex is a temporary thing; sex isn't love. You can get sex anywhere. If you're looking for someone to *love* you, now that's different. I guess you have to stay in college for that.

PLAYBOY: Since you didn't stay in college, does that mean you haven't found someone to love you?

DYLAN: Let's go on to the next question.

PLAYBOY: Do you have any difficulty relating to people—or vice versa?

DYLAN: Well, sometimes I have the feeling that other people want my *soul*. If I say to them, "I don't *have* a soul," they say, "I know that. You don't have to tell me that. Not me. How dumb do you think I am? I'm your *friend*." What can I say except that I'm sorry and I feel bad? I guess maybe feeling bad and paranoia are the same thing.

PLAYBOY: Paranoia is said to be one of the mental states sometimes induced by such hallucinogenic drugs as peyote and LSD. Considering the risks involved, do you think that experimentation with such drugs should be part of the growing-up experience for a young person?

DYLAN: I wouldn't advise anybody to use drugs—certainly not the hard drugs; drugs are medicine. But opium and hash and pot—now, those things aren't drugs; they just bend your mind a little. I think *everybody's* mind should be bent once in a while. Not by LSD, though. LSD is medicine—a different kind of medicine. It makes you aware of the universe, so to speak; you realize how foolish *objects* are. But LSD is not for groovy people; it's for mad, hateful people who want revenge. It's for people who usually have heart attacks. They ought to use it at the Geneva Convention.

PLAYBOY: Are you concerned, as you approach 30, that you may begin to "go square," lose some of your openness to experience, become leery of change and new experiment?

DYLAN: No. But if it happens, then it happens. What can I say? There doesn't seem to *be* any tomorrow. Every time I wake up, no matter in what position, it's always been today. To look ahead and start worrying about trivial little things I can't really say has any more importance than looking back and *remembering* trivial little things. I'm not going to become any poetry instructor at any girls' school; I know *that* for sure. But that's about *all* I know for sure. I'll just keep doing these different things, I guess.

PLAYBOY: Such as?

DYLAN: Waking up in different positions.

PLAYBOY: What else?

DYLAN: I'm just like anybody else; I'll try anything once.

PLAYBOY: Including theft and murder?

DYLAN: I can't really say I *wouldn't* commit theft or murder and expect anybody to really believe me. I wouldn't believe anybody if they told *me* that.

PLAYBOY: By their mid-20s, most people have begun to settle into their niche, to find a place in society. But you've managed to remain innerdirected and uncommitted. What was it that spurred you to run away from home six times between the ages of 10 and 18 and finally to leave for good?

DYLAN: It was nothing; it was just an accident of geography. Like if I was born and raised in New York or Kansas City, I'm sure everything would have turned out different. But Hibbing, Minnesota, was just not the right place for me to stay and live. There really was nothing there. The only thing you could do there was be a miner, and even that kind of thing was getting less and less. The people that lived there—they're nice people; I've been all over the world since I left there, and they still stand out as being the least hung-up. The mines were just dying, that's all; but that's not their fault. *Everybody* about my age left there. It was no great romantic thing. It didn't take any great amount of thinking or individual genius, and there certainly wasn't any pride in it. I didn't run away from it; I just turned my back on it. It couldn't give me anything. It was very void-like. So leaving wasn't hard at all; it would have been much harder to stay. I didn't want to die there. As I think about it now, though, it wouldn't be such a bad place to go back to and die in. There's no place I feel closer to now, or get the feeling that I'm part of, except maybe New York; but I'm *not* a New Yorker. I'm North Dakota–Minnesota–Midwestern. I'm *that* color. I speak that way. I'm from someplace called Iron Range. My brains and feeling have come from there. I wouldn't amputate on a drowning man; *nobody* from out there would.

PLAYBOY: Today, you're on your way to becoming a millionaire. Do you feel in any danger of being trapped by all this affluence—by the things it can buy?

DYLAN: No, my world is very small. Money can't really improve it any; money can just keep it from being smothered.

PLAYBOY: Most big stars find it difficult to avoid getting involved, and sometimes entangled, in managing the business end of their careers. As a man with three thriving careers—as a concert performer, recording star and songwriter—do you ever feel boxed in by such noncreative responsibilities?

DYLAN: No, I've got other people to do that for me. They watch my money; they guard it. They keep their eyes on it at all times; they're supposed to be very smart when it comes to money. They know just what to do with my money. I pay them a lot of it. I don't really speak to them much, and they don't really speak to me at all, so I guess everything is all right.

PLAYBOY: If fortune hasn't trapped you, how about fame? Do you find that your celebrity makes it difficult to keep your private life intact?

DYLAN: My private life has been dangerous from the beginning. All this does is add a little atmosphere.

PLAYBOY: You used to enjoy wandering across the country—taking off on open-end trips, roughing it from town to town, with no particular destination in mind. But you seem to be doing much less of that these days. Why? Is it because you're too well-known?

DYLAN: It's mainly because I have to be in Cincinnati Friday night, and the next night I got to be in Atlanta, and then the next night after that, I have to be in Buffalo. Then I have to write some more songs for a record album.

PLAYBOY: Do you get the chance to ride your motorcycle much anymore?

DYLAN: I'm still very patriotic to the highway, but I don't ride my motorcycle too much anymore, no.

PLAYBOY: How do you get your kicks these days, then?

DYLAN: I hire people to look into my eyes, and then I have them kick me.

PLAYBOY: And that's the way you get your kicks?

DYLAN: No. Then I *forgive* them; that's where my kicks come in.

PLAYBOY: You told an interviewer last year, "I've done everything I ever wanted to." If that's true, what do you have to look forward to?

DYLAN: Salvation. Just plain salvation.

PLAYBOY: Anything else?

DYLAN: Praying. I'd also like to start a cookbook magazine. And I've always wanted to be a boxing referee. I want to referee a heavyweight championship fight. Can you imagine that? Can you imagine any fighter in his right mind recognizing me?

PLAYBOY: If your popularity were to wane, would you welcome being anonymous again?

DYLAN: You mean welcome it, like I'd welcome some poor pilgrim coming in from the rain? No, I wouldn't welcome it; I'd accept it, though. Someday, obviously, I'm going to *have* to accept it.

PLAYBOY: Do you ever think about marrying, settling down, having a home, maybe living abroad? Are there any luxuries you'd like to have, say, a yacht or a Rolls-Royce?

DYLAN: No, I don't think about those things. If I felt like buying anything, I'd buy it. What you're asking me about is the future, *my* future. I'm the last person in the world to ask about my future.

PLAYBOY: Are you saying you're going to be passive and just let things happen to you?

DYLAN: Well, that's being very philosophical about it, but I guess it's true.

PLAYBOY: You once planned to write a novel. Do you still?

DYLAN: I don't think so. All my writing goes into the songs now. Other forms don't interest me anymore.

PLAYBOY: Do you have any unfulfilled ambitions?

DYLAN: Well, I guess I've always wanted to be Anthony Quinn in *La Strada*. Not always—only for about six years now; it's not one of those childhood-dream things. Oh, and come to think of it, I guess I've always wanted to be Brigitte Bardot, too; but I don't really want to think about *that* too much.

PLAYBOY: Did you ever have the standard boyhood dream of growing up to be president?

DYLAN: No. When I was a boy, Harry Truman was president; who'd want to be Harry Truman?

PLAYBOY: Well, let's suppose that you were the president. What would you accomplish during your first thousand days?

DYLAN: Well, just for laughs, so long as you insist, the first thing I'd do is probably move the White House. Instead of being in Texas, it'd be on the East Side in New York. McGeorge Bundy would definitely have to change his name, and General McNamara would be forced to wear a coonskin cap and shades. I would immediately rewrite "The Star-Spangled Banner," and little schoolchildren, instead of memorizing "America the Beautiful," would have to memorize "Desolation Row" [one of Dylan's latest songs]. And I would immediately call for a showdown with Mao Tse-tung; I would fight him *personally*—and I'd get somebody to film it.

PLAYBOY: One final question: Even though you've more or less retired from political and social protest, can you conceive of any circumstance that might persuade you to reinvolve yourself?

DYLAN: No, not unless all the people in the world disappeared.

March 1978

A candid conversation with the visionary whose songs changed the times

It was in March 1966 that *Playboy* published the first full-length interview with Bob Dylan. In the intervening years, he has talked to journalists only rarely, and, shortly before completing his first feature film, he agreed to talk with us. We asked writer Ron Rosenbaum, who grew up listening to Dylan songs, to check in with the elusive artist. His report:

"Call it a simple twist of fate, to use a Dylan line, but perhaps psychic twist of fate is more accurate. Because there was something of a turning point in our 10-day series of conversations when we exchanged confidences about psychics.

"Until that point, things had not been proceeding easily. Dylan has seldom been forthcoming with any answers, particularly in interview situations and has long been notorious for questioning the questions rather than answering them, replying with put-ons and tall tales and surrounding his real feelings with mystery and circumlocution. We would go round in circles, sometimes fascinating metaphysical circles, and I'd got a sense of his intellect but little of his heart. He hadn't given anyone a major interview for many years, but after my initial excitement at being chosen to do this one, I began to wonder whether Dylan really wanted to do it.

"It's probably unnecessary to explain why getting answers from Bob Dylan has come to mean so much to many people. One has only to recall how Dylan, born Robert Zimmerman in 1941 in Duluth, Minnesota, burst upon the early-1960s folk-music scene with an abrasive voice and an explosive intensity, how he created songs such as "Blowin' in the Wind" and "The Times They Are A-Changin'" that became anthems of the civil rights and antiwar movements. How he and his music raced through the 1960s at breakneck speed, leaving his folk followers behind and the politicos mystified with his electrifying, elliptical explorations of uncharted states of mind. How, in songs such as "Mr. Tambourine Man," "Desolation Row," "Like a Rolling Stone" and "Just Like a Woman," he created emotional road maps for an entire generation. How, in the midst of increasingly frenzied rock-and-roll touring, Dylan continued to surround the details of his personal life with mystery and wise-guy obfuscation, mystery that deepened ominously after his near-fatal motorcycle accident in 1966. And how, after a long period of bucolic retreat devoted to fatherhood, family and country music, he suddenly returned to the stage with big nationwide tours in 1974 and, most recently, in 1976 with the all-star rock-and-roll ensemble known as The Rolling Thunder Revue. How his latest songs, particularly on the *Blood on the Tracks* and *Desire* albums, take us into new and often painful investigations of love and lust, and pain and loss, that suggest the emotional predicaments of the 1970s in a way few others can approach.

"The anthologies that chronicle all of that are littered with the bodies of interviewers he's put on, put down or put off. I was wondering if I were on my way to becoming another statistic when we hit upon the psychic connection.

"Late one afternoon, Dylan began telling me about Tamara Rand, an L.A. psychic reader he'd been seeing, because when the world falls on your head, he said, 'you need someone who can tell you how to crawl out, which way to take.' I presumed he was referring obliquely to the collapse of his 12-year marriage to Sara Dylan. (Since the child-custody battle was in progress as we talked, Dylan's lawyer refused to permit him to address that subject directly.) Dylan seemed concerned that I understand that Tamara was no con artist, that she had genuine psychic abilities. I assured him I could believe it because my sister, in addition to being a talented writer, has some remarkable psychic abilities and is in great demand in New York for her prescient readings. Dylan asked her name (it's Ruth) and when I told him, he looked impressed. 'I've heard of her.' he said. I think that made the difference, because after that exchange, Dylan became far more forthcoming with me. Some of the early difficulties of the interview might also be explained by the fact that Dylan was physically and mentally drained from an intense three-month sprint to finish editing and dubbing *Renaldo & Clara*, the movie he'd been writing, directing and co-editing for a full two years. He looked pale, smoked a lot of cigarettes and seemed fidgety. The final step in the moviemaking process—the sound mix—was moving slowly, largely because of his own nervous perfectionism.

"Most of our talks took place in a little shack of a dressing room outside the dubbing stage live at the Burbank Studios. Frequently, we'd be interrupted as Dylan would have to run onto the dubbing stage and watch the hundredth run-through of one of the film's two dozen reels to see if his detailed instructions had been carried out. I particularly remember one occasion when I accompanied him onto the dubbing stage. On screen, Renaldo, played by Bob Dylan, and Clara, played by Sara Dylan (the movie was shot before the divorce—though not long before), are interrupted in the midst of connubial foolery by a knock at the door. In walks Joan Baez, dressed in white from head to toe, carrying a red rose. She says she's come for Renaldo. When Dylan, as Renaldo, sees who it is, his jaw drops. At the dubbing console, one of the sound men stopped the film at the jaw-drop frame and asked, 'You want me to get rid of that footstep noise in the background, Bob?' 'What footstep noise?' Dylan asked. 'When Joan comes in and we go to Renaldo, there's some kind of footstep noise in the background, maybe from outside the door.' 'Those aren't footsteps,' said Dylan. 'That's the beating of Renaldo's heart.' 'What makes you so sure?' the sound man asked teasingly. 'I know him pretty well,' Dylan said, 'I know him by heart.' 'You want it kept there, then?' 'I want it louder,' Dylan said. He turned to me. 'You ever read that thing by Poe, *The Tell-Tale Heart?*' I was surprised at how willing Dylan was to explain the details of his film; he'd never done that with his songs. But he's put two years and more than a piece of his heart into this five-hour epic and it seems clear that he wants to be taken seriously as a filmmaker with serious artistic ambitions.

"In the *Proverbs of Hell*, William Blake (one of Dylan's favorite poets) wrote: 'The road of excess leads to the palace of wisdom.' Eleven years ago, Dylan's motorcycle skidded off that road and almost killed him. But unlike most Dionysian 1960s figures, Dylan survived. He may not have reached the palace of wisdom (and, indeed, the strange palace of marble and stone he has been building at Malibu seems, according to some reports, to be sliding into the sea). But despite his various sorrows, he does seem to be bursting with exhilaration and confidence that he can still create explosive art without having to die in the explosion."

PLAYBOY: Exactly 12 years ago, we published a long interview with you in this magazine, and there's a lot to catch up on. But we'd like at least to try to start at the beginning. Besides being a singer, a poet and now a filmmaker, you've also been called a visionary. Do you recall any visionary experiences while you were growing up?

DYLAN: I had some amazing projections when I was a kid, but not since then. And those visions have been strong enough to keep me going through today.

PLAYBOY: What were those visions like?

DYLAN: They were a feeling of wonder. I projected myself toward what I might personally, humanly do in terms of creating any kinds of reality. I was born in, grew up in a place so foreign that you had to be there to picture it.

PLAYBOY: Are you talking about Hibbing, Minnesota?

DYLAN: It was all in upper Minnesota.

PLAYBOY: What was the quality of those visionary experiences?

DYLAN: Well, in the winter, everything was still, nothing moved. Eight months of that. You can put it together. You can have some amazing hallucinogenic experiences doing nothing but looking out your window. There is also the summer, when it gets hot and sticky and the air is very metallic. There is a lot of Indian spirit. The earth there is unusual, filled with ore. So there is something happening that is hard to define. There is a magnetic attraction there. Maybe thousands and thousands of years ago, some planet bumped into the land there. There is a great spiritual quality throughout the Midwest. Very subtle, very strong, and that is where I grew up. New York was a dream.

PLAYBOY: Why did you leave Minnesota?

DYLAN: Well, there comes a time for all things to pass.

PLAYBOY: More specifically, why the dream of New York?

DYLAN: It was a dream of the cosmopolitan riches of the mind.

PLAYBOY: Did you find them there?

DYLAN: It was a great place for me to learn and to meet others who were on similar journeys.

PLAYBOY: People like Allen Ginsberg, for instance?

DYLAN: Not necessarily him. He was pretty established by the time I got there. But it was Ginsberg and Jack Kerouac who inspired me at first—and where I came from, there wasn't the sophisticated transportation you have now. To get to New York, you'd have to go by thumb. Anyway, those were the old days when John Denver used to play sideman. Many people came out of that period of time. Actors, dancers, politicians, a lot of people were involved with that period of time.

PLAYBOY: What period are you talking about?

DYLAN: Real early 1960s.

PLAYBOY: What made that time so special?

DYLAN: I think it was the last go-round for people to gravitate to New York. People had gone to New York since the 1800s, I think. For me, it was pretty fantastic. I mean, it was like, there was a café—what was it called?—I forgot the name, but it was Aaron Burr's old livery stable. You know, just being in that area, that part of the world was enlightening.

PLAYBOY: Why do you say it was the last go-round?

DYLAN: I don't think it happened after that. I think it finished, New York died after that, late to middle 1960s.

PLAYBOY: What killed it?

DYLAN: Mass communication killed it. It turned into one big carnival side show. That is what I sensed and I got out of there when it was just starting to happen. The atmosphere changed from one of creativity and isolation to one where the attention would be turned more to the show. People were reading about themselves and believing it. I don't know when it happened. Sometime around Peter, Paul and Mary, when they got pretty big. It happened around the same time. For a long time, I was famous only in certain circles in New York, Philadelphia and Boston, and that was fine enough for me. I am an eyewitness to that time. I am one of the survivors of that period. You know as well as I do that a lot of people didn't make it. They didn't live to tell about it, anyway.

PLAYBOY: Why do you think they didn't survive?

DYLAN: People were still dealing with illusion and delusion at that time. The times really change and they don't change. There were different characters back then and there were things that were undeveloped that are fully developed now. But back then, there was space, space—well, there wasn't any pressure. There was all the time in the world to get it done. There wasn't any pressure, because nobody knew about it. You know, I mean, music people were like a bunch of cotton pickers. They see you on the side of the road picking cotton, but nobody stops to give a shit. I mean, it wasn't that important. So Washington Square was a place where people you knew or met congregated every Sunday and it was like a world of music. You know the way New York is; I mean, there could be 20 different things happening in the same kitchen or in the same park; there could be 200 bands in one park in New York; there could be 15 jug bands, five bluegrass bands and an old crummy string band, 20 Irish confederate groups, a Southern mountain band, folk singers of all kinds and colors, singing John Henry work songs. There was bodies piled sky-high doing whatever they felt like doing. Bongo drums, conga drums, saxophone players, xylophone players, drummers of all nations and nationalities. Poets who would rant and rave from the statues. You know, those things don't happen anymore. But then that was what was happening. It was all street, cafés would be open all night. It was a European thing that never really took off. It has never really been a part of this country. That is what New York was like when I got there.

PLAYBOY: And do you think that mass communication, such as *Time* magazine putting Joan Baez on the cover—

DYLAN: Mass communication killed it all. Oversimplification. I don't know whose idea it was to do that, but soon after, the people moved away.

PLAYBOY: Just to stay on the track, what first turned you on to folk singing? You actually started out in Minnesota playing the electric guitar with a rock group, didn't you?

DYLAN: Yeah. The first thing that turned me on to folk singing was Odetta. I heard a record of hers in a record store, back when you could listen to records right there in the store. That was in '58 or something like that. Right then and there. I went out and traded my electric guitar and amplifier for an acoustical guitar, a flat-top Gibson.

PLAYBOY: What was so special to you about that Odetta record?

DYLAN: Just something vital and personal. I learned all the songs on that record. It was her first and the songs were "Mule Skinner," "Jack of Diamonds," "Water Boy," " 'Buked and Scorned."

PLAYBOY: When did you learn to play the guitar?

DYLAN: I saved the money I had made working on my daddy's truck and bought a Silvertone guitar from Sears Roebuck. I was 12. I just bought a book of chords and began to play.

PLAYBOY: What was the first song you wrote?

DYLAN: The first song I wrote was a song to Brigitte Bardot.

PLAYBOY: Do you remember how it went?

DYLAN: I don't recall too much of it. It had only one chord. Well, it is all in the heart. Anyway, from Odetta, I went to Harry Belafonte, the Kingston Trio, little by little uncovering more as I went along. Finally, I was doing nothing but Carter Family and Jesse Fuller songs. Then later I got to Woody Guthrie, which opened up a whole new world at that time. I was still only 19 or 20.

I was pretty fanatical about what I wanted to do, so after learning about 200 of Woody's songs. I went to see him and I waited for the right moment to visit him in a hospital in Morristown, New Jersey. I took a bus from New York, sat with him and sang his songs. I kept visiting him a lot and got on friendly terms with him. From that point on, it gets a little foggy.

PLAYBOY: Folk singing was considered pretty weird in those days, wasn't it?

DYLAN: It definitely was. *Sing Out* was the only magazine you could read about those people. They were special people and you kept your distance from them.

PLAYBOY: What do you mean?

DYLAN: Well, they were the type of people you just observed and learned from, but you would never approach them. *I never would,* anyway. I remember being too shy. But it took me a long time to realize the New York crowd wasn't that different from the singers I'd seen in my own hometown. They were right there, on the backroad circuit, people like the Stanley Brothers, playing for a few nights. If I had known then what I do now, I probably would have taken off when I was 12 and followed Bill Monroe. 'Cause I could have gotten to the same place.

PLAYBOY: Would you have gotten there sooner?

DYLAN: Probably would have saved me a lot of time and hassles.

PLAYBOY: This comes under the category of setting the record straight: By the time you arrived in New York, you'd changed your name from Robert Zimmerman to Bob Dylan. Was it because of Dylan Thomas?

DYLAN: No. I haven't read that much of Dylan Thomas. It's a common thing to change your name. It isn't that incredible. Many people do it. People change their town, change their country. New appearance, new mannerisms. Some people have many names. I wouldn't pick a name unless I thought I was that person. Sometimes you are held back by your name. Sometimes there are advantages to having a certain name. Names are labels so we can refer to one another. But deep inside us we don't have a name. We have no name. I just chose that name and it stuck.

PLAYBOY: Do you know what Zimmerman means in German?

DYLAN: My forebears were Russian. I don't know how they got a German name coming from Russia. Maybe they got their name coming off the boat or something. To make a big deal over somebody's name, you're liable to make a big deal about any little thing. But getting back to Dylan Thomas, it wasn't that I was inspired by reading some of his poetry and going "Aha!" and changing my name to Dylan. If I thought he was that great, I would have sung his poems, and could just as easily have changed my name to Thomas.

PLAYBOY: Bob Thomas? It would have been a mistake.

DYLAN: Well, that name changed me. I didn't sit around and think about it too much. That is who I felt I was.

PLAYBOY: Do you deny being the *enfant terrible* in those days—do you deny the craziness of it all that has been portrayed?

DYLAN: No, it's true. That's the way it was. But . . . can't stay in one place forever.

PLAYBOY: Did the motorcycle accident you had in 1966 have anything to do with cooling you off, getting you to relax?

DYLAN: Well, now you're jumping way ahead to another period of time . . . What was I doing? I don't know. It came time. Was it when I had the motorcycle accident? Well, I was straining pretty hard and couldn't have gone on living that way much longer. The fact that I made it through what I did is pretty miraculous. But, you know, sometimes you get too close to something and you got to get away from it to be able to see it. And something like that happened to me at the time.

PLAYBOY: In a book you published during that period, *Tarantula*, you wrote an epitaph for yourself that begins: "Here lies Bob Dylan / murdered / from behind / by trembling flesh. . . ."

DYLAN: Those were in my wild, unnatural moments. I'm glad those feelings passed.

PLAYBOY: What were those days like?

DYLAN: [*Pause*] I don't remember. [*Long pause*]

PLAYBOY: There was a report in the press recently that you turned the Beatles on to grass for the first time. According to the story, you gave Ringo Starr a toke at JFK Airport and it was the first time for any of them. True?

DYLAN: I'm surprised if Ringo said that. It don't sound like Ringo. I don't recall meeting him at JFK Airport.

PLAYBOY: OK. Who turned *you* on?

DYLAN: Grass was everywhere in the clubs. It was always there in the jazz clubs and in the folk-music clubs. There was just grass and it was available to musicians in those days. And in coffeehouses way back in Minneapolis. That's where I first came into contact with it, I'm sure. I forget when or where, really.

PLAYBOY: Why did the musicians like grass so much?

DYLAN: Being a musician means—depending on how far you go—getting to the depths of where you are at. And most any musician would try anything to get to those depths, because playing music is an immediate thing—as opposed to putting paint on a canvas, which is a calculated thing. Your spirit flies when you are playing music. So, with music, you tend to look deeper and deeper inside yourself to find the music. That's why, I guess, grass was around those clubs. I know the whole scene has changed now: I mean, pot is almost a legal thing. But in the old days, it was just for a few people.

PLAYBOY: Did psychedelics have a similar effect on you?

DYLAN: No. Psychedelics never influenced me. I don't know, I think Timothy Leary had a lot to do with driving the last nails into the coffin of that New York scene we were talking about. When psychedelics happened, everything became irrelevant. Because that had nothing to do with making music or writing poems or trying to really find yourself in that day and age.

PLAYBOY: But people thought they were doing just that—finding themselves.

DYLAN: People were deluded into thinking they were something that they weren't: birds, airplanes, fire hydrants, whatever. People were walking around thinking they were stars.

PLAYBOY: As far as your music was concerned, was there a moment when you made a conscious decision to work with an electric band?

DYLAN: Well, it had to get there. It had to go that way for me. Because that's where I started and eventually it just got back to that. I couldn't go on being the lone folkie out there, you know, strumming "Blowin' in the Wind" for three hours every night. I hear my songs as part of the music, the musical background.

PLAYBOY: When you hear your songs in your mind, it's not just you strumming alone, you mean?

DYLAN: Well, no, it is to begin with. But then I always hear other instruments, how they should sound. The closest I ever got to the sound I hear in my mind was on individual bands in the *Blonde on Blonde* album. It's that thin, that wild mercury sound. It's metallic and bright gold, with whatever that conjures up. That's my particular sound. I haven't been able to succeed in getting it all the time. Mostly, I've been driving at a combination of guitar, harmonica and organ, but now I find myself going into territory that has more percussion in it and [*pause*] rhythms of the soul.

PLAYBOY: Was that wild mercury sound in *I Want You*?

DYLAN: Yeah, it was in *I Want You*. It was in a lot of that stuff. It was in the album before that, too.

PLAYBOY: *Highway 61 Revisited*?

DYLAN: Yeah. Also in *Bringing It All Back Home*. That's the sound I've always heard. Later on, the songs got more defined, but it didn't necessarily bring more power to them. The sound was whatever happened to be available at the time. I have to get back to the sound, to the sound that will bring it all through me.

PLAYBOY: Can't you just reassemble the same musicians?

DYLAN: Not really. People change, you know, they scatter in all directions. People's lives get complicated. They tend to have more distractions, so they can't focus on that fine, singular purpose.

PLAYBOY: You're searching for people?

DYLAN: No, not searching, the people are there. But I just haven't paid as much attention to it as I should have. I haven't felt comfortable in a studio since I worked with Tom Wilson. The next move for me is to have a permanent band. You know, usually I just record whatever's available at the time. That's my thing, you know, and it's—it's legitimate. I mean, I do it because I have to do it that way. I don't want to *keep* doing it, because I would like to get my life more in order. But until now, my recording sessions have tended to be last-minute affairs. I don't really use all the technical studio stuff. My songs are done live in the studio; they always have been and they always will be done that way. That's why they're alive. No matter what else you say about them, they are alive. You know, what Paul Simon does or Rod Stewart does or Crosby, Stills and Nash do—a record is not that monumental for me to make. It's just a record of songs.

PLAYBOY: Getting back to your transition from folk to rock, the period when you came out with *Highway 61* must have been exciting.

DYLAN: Those *were* exciting times. We were doing it before anybody knew we would—or could. We didn't know what it was going to turn out to be. Nobody thought of it as folk-rock at the time. There were some people involved in it, like The Byrds, and I remember Sonny and Cher and the Turtles and the early Rascals. It began coming out on the radio. I mean, I had a couple of hits in a row. That was the most I ever had in a row—two. The top 10 was filled with that kind of sound—the Beatles, too—and it was exciting, those days were exciting. It was the sound of the streets. It still is. I symbolically hear that sound wherever I am.

PLAYBOY: You hear the sound of the street?

DYLAN: That ethereal twilight light, you know. It's the sound of the street with the sunrays, the sun shining down at a particular time, on a particular type of building. A particular type of people walking on a particular type of street. It's an outdoor sound that drifts even into open windows that you can hear. The sound of bells and distant railroad trains and arguments in apartments and the clinking of silverware and knives and forks and beating with leather straps. It's all—it's all there. Just lack of a jackhammer, you know.

PLAYBOY: You mean if a jackhammer were—

DYLAN: Yeah, no jackhammer sounds, no airplane sounds. All pretty natural sounds. It's water, you know, water trickling down a brook. It's light flowing through the—

PLAYBOY: Late-afternoon light?

DYLAN: No, usually it's the crack of dawn. Music filters out to me in the crack of dawn.

PLAYBOY: The "jingle jangle morning"?

DYLAN: Right.

PLAYBOY: After being up all night?

DYLAN: Sometimes. You get a little spacy when you've been up all night, so you don't really have the power to form it. But that's the sound I'm trying to get across. I'm not just up there re-creating old blues tunes or trying to invent some surrealistic rhapsody.

PLAYBOY: It's the sound that you want.

DYLAN: Yeah, it's the sound and the words. Words don't interfere with it. They—they—punctuate it. You know, they give it purpose. [*Pause*] And all the ideas for my songs, all the influences, all come out of that. All the influences, all the feelings, all the ideas come from that, I'm not doing it to see how good I can sound, or how perfect the melody can be, or how intricate the details can be woven or how perfectly written something can be. I don't care about those things.

PLAYBOY: The sound is that compelling to you?

DYLAN: Mmm-hnh.

PLAYBOY: When did you first hear it, or feel it?

DYLAN: I guess it started way back when I was growing up.

PLAYBOY: Not in New York?

DYLAN: Well, I took it to New York. I wasn't born in New York. I was given some direction there, but I took it, too. I don't think I could ever have done it in New York. I would have been too beaten down.

PLAYBOY: It was formed by the sounds back in the ore country of Minnesota?

DYLAN: Or the lack of sound. In the city, there is nowhere you can go where you don't hear sound. You are never alone. I don't think I could have done it there. Just the struggle of growing up would be immense and would really distort things if you wanted to be an artist. Well . . . maybe not. A lot of really creative people come out of New York. But I don't know anyone like myself. I meet a lot of people from New York that I get along with fine, and share the same ideas, but I got something different in my soul. Like a spirit. It's like being from the Smoky Mountains or the backwoods of Mississippi. It is going to make you a certain type of person if you stay 20 years in a place.

PLAYBOY: With your love of the country, what made you leave Woodstock in 1969 and go back to the Village?

DYLAN: It became stale and disillusioning. It got too crowded, with the wrong people throwing orders. And the old people were afraid to come out on the street. The rainbow faded.

PLAYBOY: But the Village, New York City, wasn't the answer, either.

DYLAN: The stimulation had vanished. Everybody was in a pretty down mood. It was over.

PLAYBOY: Do you think that old scene you've talked about might be creeping back into New York?

DYLAN: Well, I was there last summer. I didn't sense any of it. There are a lot of rock-and-roll clubs and jazz clubs and Puerto Rican poetry clubs, but as far as learning something new, learning to teach . . . New York is full of teachers, that is obvious, but it is pretty depressing now. To make it on the street, you just about have to beg.

PLAYBOY: So now you're in California. Is there any kind of scene that you can be part of?

DYLAN: I'm only working out here most, or all, of the time, so I don't know what this town is really like. I like San Francisco. I find it full of tragedy and comedy. But if I want to go to a city in this country, I will still go to New York. There are cities all over the world to go to. I don't know, maybe I am just an old dog, so maybe I feel like I've been around so long I am looking for something new to do and it ain't there. I was looking for some space to create what I want to do. I am only interested in that these days. I don't care so much about hanging out.

PLAYBOY: Do you feel older than when you sang, "I was so much older then. I'm younger than that now"?

DYLAN: No. I don't feel old. I don't feel old at all. But I feel like there are certain things that don't attract me anymore that I used to succumb to very easily.

PLAYBOY: Such as?

DYLAN: Just the everyday vices.

PLAYBOY: Do you think that you have managed to resist having to grow up or have you found a way of doing it that is different from conventional growing up?

DYLAN: I don't really think in terms of growing up or not growing up. I think in terms of being able to fulfill yourself. Don't forget, you see, I've been doing what I've been doing since I was very small, so I have never known anything else. I have never had to quit my job to do this. This is all that I have ever done in my life. So I don't think in terms of economics or status or what people think of me one way or the other.

PLAYBOY: Would you say you still have a rebellious, or punk, quality toward the rest of the world?

DYLAN: Punk quality?

PLAYBOY: Well, you're still wearing dark sunglasses right?

DYLAN: Yeah.

PLAYBOY: Is that so people won't see your eyes?

DYLAN: Actually, it's just habit-forming after a while. I still do wear dark sunglasses. There is no profound reason for it, I guess. Some kind of insecurity. I don't know. I like dark sunglasses. Have I had these on through every interview session?

PLAYBOY: Yes. We haven't seen your eyes yet.

DYLAN: Well, Monday for sure. [*The day that* Playboy *photos were to be taken for the opening page.*]

PLAYBOY: Aside from the dark glasses, is it something in the punk quality of Elvis or James Dean that makes you dress a certain way or act a certain way?

DYLAN: No. It's from the early 1960s. Elvis was there. He was there when there wasn't anybody there. He was Elvis and everybody knows about what Elvis did. He did it to me just like he did it to everybody else. Elvis was in that certain age group and I followed him right from "Blue Moon in Kentucky." And there were others; I admired Buddy Holly a lot. But Elvis was never really a punk. And neither was James Dean a punk.

PLAYBOY: What quality did Dean represent?

DYLAN: He let his heart do the talking. That was his one badge. He was effective for people of that age, but as you grow older, you have different experiences and you tend to identify with artists who had different meanings for you.

PLAYBOY: Let's talk some more about your influences. What musicians do you listen to today?

DYLAN: I still listen to the same old black-and-blue blues. Tommy McClennan, Lightnin' Hopkins, the Carter Family, the early Carlyles. I listen to Big Maceo, Robert Johnson. Once in a while, I listen to Woody Guthrie again. Among the more recent people, Fred McDowell, Gary Stewart. I like Memphis Minnie a whole lot. Blind Willie McTell. I like bluegrass music. I listen to foreign music, too. I like Middle Eastern music a whole lot.

PLAYBOY: Such as?

DYLAN: Om Kalthoum.

PLAYBOY: Who is that?

DYLAN: She was a great Egyptian singer. I first heard of her when I was in Jerusalem.

PLAYBOY: She was an Egyptian singer who was popular in Jerusalem?

DYLAN: I think she's popular all over the Middle East. In Israel, too. She does mostly love and prayer-type songs, with violin and drum accompaniment. Her father chanted those prayers and I guess she was so good when she tried singing behind his back that he allowed her to sing professionally, and she's dead now but not forgotten. She's great. She really is. Really great.

PLAYBOY: Any popular stuff?

DYLAN: Well. Nana Mouskouri.

PLAYBOY: How about the Beatles?

DYLAN: I've always liked the way George Harrison plays guitar—restrained and good. As for Lennon, well. I was encouraged by his book [*In his Own Write*]. Or the publishers were encouraged, because they asked me to write a book and that's how *Tarantula* came about. John has taken poetics pretty far in popular music. A lot of his work is overlooked, but if you examine it, you'll find key expressions that have never been said before to push across his point of view. Things that are symbolic of some inner reality and probably will never be said again.

PLAYBOY: Do you listen to your own stuff?

DYLAN: Not so much.

PLAYBOY: What about your literary influences? You've mentioned Kerouac and Ginsberg. Whom do you read now?

DYLAN: Rilke. Chekhov. Chekhov is my favorite writer. I like Henry Miller. I think he's the greatest American writer.

PLAYBOY: Did you meet Miller?

DYLAN: Yeah, I met him. Years ago. Played Ping-Pong with him.

PLAYBOY: Did you read *Catcher in the Rye* as a kid?

DYLAN: I must have, you know. Yeah, I think so.

PLAYBOY: Did you identify with Holden Caulfield?

DYLAN: Uh, what was his story?

PLAYBOY: He was a lonely kid in prep school who ran away and decided that everyone else was phony and that he was sensitive.

DYLAN: I *must* have identified with him.

PLAYBOY: We've been talking about the arts, and as we've been speaking, you've been in the midst of editing your first film, *Renaldo & Clara*. What do you feel you can do in films that you can't do in songs?

DYLAN: I can take songs up to a higher power. The movie to me is more a painting than music. It *is* a painting. It's a painting coming alive off a wall. That's why we're making it. Painters can contain their artistic turmoil: In another age, moviemakers would most likely be painters.

PLAYBOY: Although *Renaldo & Clara* is the first movie you've produced, directed and acted in, there was a documentary made in 1966 that marked your first appearance in a film—*Don't Look Back*. What did you think of it?

DYLAN: *Don't Look Back* was . . . somebody else's movie. It was a deal worked out with a film company, but I didn't really play any part in it. When I saw it in a moviehouse, I was shocked at what had been done. I didn't find out until later that the camera had been on me all the time. That movie was done by a man who took it all out of context. It was documented from his personal point of view. The movie was dishonest, it was a propaganda movie. I don't think it was accurate at all in terms of showing my formative years. It showed only one side. He made it seem like I wasn't doing anything but living in hotel rooms, playing the typewriter and holding press conferences for journalists. All that is true, you know. Throwing some bottles, there's something about it in the movie. Joan Baez is in it. But it's one-sided. Let's not lean on it too hard. It just wasn't representative of what was happening in the 1960s.

PLAYBOY: Don't you feel it captured the frenzy of your tour, even though it focused on you in terms of stardom?

DYLAN: I wasn't really a star in those days, any more than I'm a star these days. I was very obviously confused then as to what my purpose was. It was pretty early, you know. "The Times They Are A-Changin'" was on the English charts then, so it had to be pretty early.

PLAYBOY: And you didn't really know what you were doing then?

DYLAN: Well, look what I did after that. Look what I did after that. I didn't really start to develop until after that. I mean. I did, but I didn't. *Don't Look Back* was a little too premature. I should have been left alone at that stage.

PLAYBOY: You were involved in another movie around that period—1966—that was never released, called *Eat the Document*. How did that happen?

DYLAN: That started as a television special. I wasn't the maker of that film, either. I was the—I was the victim. They had already shot film, but at that time, of course, I did—I had a—if I hadn't gotten into that motorcycle accident, they would have broadcast it, and that would have been that. But I was sort of—I was taken out of it, you know, and—I think it was the fall of that year. I had a little more time to, you know, concentrate on what was happening to me and what had happened. Anyway, what had happened was that they had made another *Don't Look Back*, only this time it was for television. I had nothing better to do than to see the film. All of it, including unused footage. And it was obvious from looking at the film that it was garbage. It was miles and miles of garbage. That was my introduction to film. My film concept was all formed in those early days when I was looking at that footage.

PLAYBOY: From looking at those miles of garbage, you got your concept of film?

DYLAN: Yeah, it was mostly rejected footage, which I found beauty in. Which probably tells you more—that I see beauty where other people don't.

PLAYBOY: That reminds us of a poem you wrote for the jacket of an early Joan Baez album, in which you claimed that you always thought something had to be ugly before you found it beautiful. And at some point in the poem, you described listening to Joan sing and suddenly deciding that beauty didn't have to start out by being ugly.

DYLAN: I was very hung up on Joan at the time. [*Pause*] I think I was just trying to tell myself I wasn't hung up on her.

PLAYBOY: OK. Would you talk some more about the film concept you got from the rejected footage?

DYLAN: Well, up until that time, they had been concerned with the linear story line. It was on one plane and in one dimension only. And the more I looked at the film, the more I realized that you could get more onto film than just one train of thought. My mind works that way, anyway. We tend to work on different levels. So I was seeing a lot of those levels in the footage. But technically, I didn't know how to do what my mind was telling me could be done.

PLAYBOY: What did you feel could be done?

DYLAN: Well, well, now, film is a series of actions and reactions, you know. And it's trickery. You're playing with illusion. What seems to be a simple affair is actually quite contrived. And the stronger your point of view is, the stronger your film will be.

PLAYBOY: Would you elaborate?

DYLAN: You're trying to get a message through. So there are many ways to deliver that message. Let's say you have a message: "White is white." Bergman would say, "White is white" in the space of an hour—or what seems to be an hour. Buñuel might say, "White is black, and black is white, but white is really white." And it's all really the same message.

PLAYBOY: And how would Dylan say it?

DYLAN: Dylan would probably not even say it. [*Laughs*] He would—he'd assume you'd know that. [*Laughs*]

PLAYBOY: You wriggled out of that one.

DYLAN: I'd say people will always believe in something if they feel it to be true. Just knowing it's true is not enough. If you feel in your gut that it's true, well, then, you can be pretty much assured that it's true.

PLAYBOY: So that a film made by someone who feels in his guts that white is white will give the feeling to the audience that white is white without having to say it.

DYLAN: Yes. Exactly.

PLAYBOY: Let's talk about the message of *Renaldo & Clara*. It appears to us to be a personal yet fictional film in which you, Joan Baez and your former wife, Sara, play leading roles. You play Renaldo, Baez plays a "woman in white" and Sara plays Clara. There is also a character in the film called Bob Dylan played by someone else. It is composed of footage from your Rolling Thunder Revue tour and fictional scenes performed by all of you as actors. Would you tell us basically what the movie's about?

DYLAN: It's about the essence of man being alienated from himself and how, in order to free himself, to be reborn, he has to go outside himself. You can almost say that he dies in order to look at time and by strength of will can return to the same body.

PLAYBOY: He can return by strength of will to the same body . . . and to Clara?

DYLAN: Clara represents to Renaldo everything in the material world he's ever wanted. Renaldo's needs are few. He doesn't know it, though, at that particular time.

PLAYBOY: What are his needs?

DYLAN: A good guitar and a dark street.

PLAYBOY: The guitar because he loves music, but why the dark street?

DYLAN: Mostly because he needs to hide.

PLAYBOY: From whom?

DYLAN: From the demon within. [*Pause*] But what we all know is that you can't hide on a dark street from the demon within. And there's our movie.

PLAYBOY: Renaldo finds that out in the film?

DYLAN: He tries to escape from the demon within, but he discovers that the demon is, in fact, a mirrored reflection of Renaldo himself.

PLAYBOY: OK. Given the personalities involved, how do you define the relationship between you, your personal life, and the film?

DYLAN: No different from Hitchcock making a movie. I am the overseer.

PLAYBOY: Overseeing various versions of yourself?

DYLAN: Well, certain truths I know. Not necessarily myself but a certain accumulation of experience that has become real to me and a knowledge that I acquired on the road.

PLAYBOY: And what are those truths?

DYLAN: One is that if you try to be anyone but yourself, you will fail; if you are not true to your own heart, you will fail. Then again, there's no success like failure.

PLAYBOY: And failure's no success at all.

DYLAN: Oh, well, we're not looking to succeed. Just by our being and acting alive, we succeed. You fail only when you let death creep in and take over a part of your life that should be alive.

PLAYBOY: How does death creep in?

DYLAN: Death don't come knocking at the door. It's there in the morning when you wake up.

PLAYBOY: How is it there?

DYLAN: Did you ever clip your fingernails, cut your hair? Then you experience death.

PLAYBOY: Look, in the film, Joan Baez turns to you at one point and says. "You never give any straight answers." Do you?

DYLAN: She is confronting Renaldo.

PLAYBOY: Evasiveness isn't only in the mind: It can also come out in an interview.

DYLAN: There are no simple answers to these questions. . . .

PLAYBOY: Aren't you teasing the audience when you have scenes played by Baez and Sara, real people in your life, and then expect the viewers to set aside their preconceptions as to their relationship to you?

DYLAN: No, no. They shouldn't even think they know anyone in this film. It's all in the context of Renaldo and Clara and there's no reason to get hung up on who's who in the movie.

PLAYBOY: What about scenes such as the one in which Baez asks you, "What if we had gotten married back then?"

DYLAN: Seems pretty real, don't it?

PLAYBOY: Yes.

DYLAN: Seems pretty real. Just like in a Bergman movie, those things seem real. There's a lot of spontaneity that goes on. Usually, the people in his films know each other, so they can interrelate. There's life and breath in every frame because everyone knew each other.

PLAYBOY: All right, another question: In the movie, Ronnie Hawkins, a 300-pound Canadian rock singer, goes by the name of Bob Dylan. So is there a real Bob Dylan?

DYLAN: In the movie?

PLAYBOY: Yes.

DYLAN: In the movie, no. He doesn't even appear in the movie. His voice is there, his songs are used, but Bob's not in the movie. It would be silly. Did you ever see a Picasso painting with Picasso in the picture? You only see his work. Now, I'm not interested in putting a picture of myself on the screen, because that's not going to do anybody any good, including me.

PLAYBOY: Then why use the name Bob Dylan at all in the movie?

DYLAN: In order to legitimize this film. We confronted it head on: The persona of Bob Dylan is in the movie so we could get rid of it. There should no longer be any mystery as to who or what he is—he's there, speaking in all kinds of tongues, and there's even someone else claiming to be him, so he's covered.

This movie is obvious, you know. Nobody's hiding anything. It's all right there. The rabbits are falling out of the hat before the movie begins.

PLAYBOY: Do you really feel it's an accessible movie?

DYLAN: Oh, perfectly. Very open movie.

PLAYBOY: Even though Mr. Bob Dylan and Mrs. Bob Dylan are played by different people—

DYLAN: Oh, yeah.

PLAYBOY: And you don't know for sure which one *he* is?

DYLAN: Sure. We could make a movie and *you* could be Bob Dylan. It wouldn't matter.

PLAYBOY: But if there are two Bob Dylans in the film and Renaldo is always changing. . . .

DYLAN: Well, it could be worse. It could be three or four. Basically, it's a simple movie.

PLAYBOY: How did you decide to make it?

DYLAN: As I said. I had the idea for doing my own film back in '66. And I buried it until '76. My lawyer used to tell me there was a future in movies. So I said, "What kind of future?" He said, "Well, if you can come up with a script, an outline and get money from a big distributor." But I knew I couldn't work that way. I can't betray my vision on a little piece of paper in hopes of getting some money from somebody. In the final analysis, it turned out that I had to make the movie all by myself, with people who would work with me, who trusted me. I went on the road in '76 to make the money for this movie. My last two tours were to raise the money for it.

PLAYBOY: How much of your money are you risking?

DYLAN: I'd rather not say. It is quite a bit, but I didn't go into the bank. The budget was like $600,000, but it went over that.

PLAYBOY: Did you get pleasure out of the project?

DYLAN: I feel it's a story that means a great deal to me, and I got to do what I always wanted to do—make a movie. When something like that happens, it's like stopping time, and you can make people live into that moment. Not many things can do that in your daily life. You can be distracted by many things. But the main point is to make it meaningful to someone.

Take *Shane*, for example. That moved me. *On the Waterfront* moved me. So when I go to see a film, I expect to be moved. I don't want to go see a movie just to kill time, or to have it just show me something I'm not aware of. I want to be moved, because that's what art is supposed to do, according to all the great theologians. Art is supposed to take you out of your chair. It's supposed to move you from one space to another.

Renaldo & Clara is not meant to put a strain on you. It's a movie to be enjoyed as a movie. I know nothing about film, I'm not a filmmaker. On the other hand, I do consider myself a filmmaker because I made this film: So I don't know.... If it doesn't move you, then it's a grand, grand failure.

PLAYBOY: Is there any way of avoiding the fact that people *will* undoubtedly make the assumptions we've been discussing—that your own myths will subvert what you say is the purpose of the movie?

DYLAN: Don't forget—I'm not a myth to myself. Only to others. If others didn't create that myth of Bob Dylan, there would be no myth of Bob Dylan in the movie.

PLAYBOY: Would there even be a movie? Or the money to finance it?

DYLAN: I doubt it.

PLAYBOY: So aren't you caught in a bind?

DYLAN: You mean by talking out of both sides of my mouth?

PLAYBOY: Well, you've made a film that you'd like people to take on its own merits, with characters you'd like them to accept: yet the main reason people will see it is that they'll want to know about Bob Dylan and Joan Baez and Sara Dylan—

DYLAN: I would hope so, yeah.

PLAYBOY: How do you get around that?

DYLAN: What's there to get around?

PLAYBOY: Your stated purpose that people shouldn't take their preconceptions to the film.

DYLAN: Well, they shouldn't. No, I don't know how to get around that.

PLAYBOY: Could it be that the movie is really intended to take on the gossip about you head-on?

DYLAN: There's truth to that. It does take it on in the sense that gossip is information. Gossip is a weapon traveling through the air. It whispers.

But it does have a tremendous influence. It's one of the driving forces. How did we start talking about gossip?

PLAYBOY: Well—

DYLAN: OK, gossip. What we're doing now is gossiping.

PLAYBOY: In what sense?

DYLAN: We would have more in common if we went out fishing and said nothing. It would be a more valuable experience, anyway, than sitting around and talking about this movie, or life and death, or gossip, or anything we've been talking about. I personally believe that. That's why I don't sit around and talk too much.

PLAYBOY: All right, since there aren't any fishing rods around, let's continue gossiping for a while longer.

DYLAN: OK.

PLAYBOY: One last try: Is there anything to the interpretation that this movie was made in the spirit of "All right, if all you people out there want to talk about Dylan breaking up with his wife, about his having an affair with Joan Baez, I'll just put those people into my film and rub people's noses in the gossip, because only I know the truth"?

DYLAN: It's not entirely true, because that's not what the movie is about. I'm not sure how much of Bob Dylan and Joan Baez concern anybody. To me, it isn't important. It's old news to me, so I don't think it's of much interest to anybody. If it is, fine. But I don't think it's a relevant issue. The movie doesn't deal with anything current. This is two years ago. I'm smart enough to know I shouldn't deal with any current subject on an emotional level, because usually it won't last. You need experience to write, or to sing or to act. You don't just wake up and say you're going to do it. This movie is taking experience and turning it into something else. It's not a gossipy movie.

PLAYBOY: We began this discussion of your movie by comparing filmmakers to painters. Were you as interested in painting as in, say, rock music when you were growing up?

DYLAN: Yeah, I've always painted. I've always held on to that one way or another.

PLAYBOY: Do you feel you use colors in the same way you use notes or chords?

DYLAN: Oh, yeah. There's much information you could get on the meaning of colors. Every color has a certain mood and feeling. For instance, red is a very vital color. There're a lot of reds in this movie, a lot of blues. A lot of cobalt blue.

PLAYBOY: Why cobalt blue?

DYLAN: It's the color of dissension.

PLAYBOY: Did you study painting?

DYLAN: A lot of the ideas I have were influenced by an old man who had definite ideas on life and the universe and nature—all that matters.

PLAYBOY: Who was he?

DYLAN: Just an old man. His name wouldn't mean anything to you. He came to this country from Russia in the 1920s, started out as a boxer and ended up painting portraits of women.

PLAYBOY: You don't want to mention his name, just to give him a plug?

DYLAN: His first name was Norman. Every time I mention somebody's name, it's like they get a tremendous amount of distraction and irrelevancy in their lives. For instance, there's this lady in L.A. I respect a lot who reads palms. Her name's Tamara Rand. She's for real, she's not a gypsy fortuneteller. But she's accurate! She'll take a look at your hand and tell you things you feel but don't really understand about where you're heading, what the future looks like. She's a surprisingly hopeful person.

PLAYBOY: Are you sure you want to know if there's bad news in your future?

DYLAN: Well, sometimes when the world falls on your head, you know there are ways to get out, but you want to know which way. Usually, there's someone who can tell you how to crawl out, which way to take.

PLAYBOY: Getting back to colors and chords, are there particular musical keys that have personalities or moods the way colors do for you?

DYLAN: Yeah. B major and B-flat major.

PLAYBOY: How would you describe them?

DYLAN: [*Pause*] Each one is hard to define. Assume the characteristic that is true of both of them and you'll find you're not sure whether you're speaking to them or to their echo.

PLAYBOY: What does a major key generally conjure up for you?

DYLAN: I think any major key deals with romance.

PLAYBOY: And the minor keys?

DYLAN: The supernatural.

PLAYBOY: What about other specific keys?

DYLAN: I find G major to be the key of strength, but also the key of regret. E major is the key of confidence. A-flat major is the key of renunciation.

PLAYBOY: Since we're back on the subject of music, what new songs have you planned?

DYLAN: I have new songs now that are unlike anything I've ever written.

PLAYBOY: Really?

DYLAN: Yes.

PLAYBOY: What are they like?

DYLAN: Well, you'll see. I mean, unlike *anything* I've ever done. You couldn't even say that *Blood on the Tracks* or *Desire* have led up to this stuff. I mean, it's that far gone, it's that far out there. I'd rather not talk more about them until they're out.

PLAYBOY: When the character Bob Dylan in your movie speaks the words "Rock 'n' roll is the answer," what does he mean?

DYLAN: He's speaking of the sound and the rhythm. The drums and the rhythm are the answer. Get into the rhythm of it and you will lose yourself; you will forget about the brutality of it all. Then you will lose your identity. That's what he's saying.

PLAYBOY: Does that happen to you, to the real Bob Dylan?

DYLAN: Well, that's easy. When you're playing music and it's going well, you do lose your identity, you become totally subservient to the music you're doing in your very being.

PLAYBOY: Do you feel possessed?

DYLAN: It's dangerous, because its effect is that you believe that you can transcend and cope with anything. That it is the real life, that you've struck at the heart of life itself and you are on top of your dream. And there's no down. But later on, backstage, you have a different point of view.

PLAYBOY: When you're onstage, do you feel the illusion that death can't get you?

DYLAN: Death can't get you at all. Death's not here to get anybody. It's the appearance of the Devil, and the Devil is a coward, so knowledge will overcome that.

PLAYBOY: What do you mean?

DYLAN: The Devil is everything false, the Devil will go as deep as you let the Devil go. You can leave yourself open to that. If you understand what that whole scene is about, you can easily step aside. But if you want the confrontation to begin with, well, there's plenty of it. But then again, if you believe you have a purpose and a mission, and not much time to carry it out, you don't bother about those things.

PLAYBOY: Do you think you have a purpose and a mission?

DYLAN: Obviously.

PLAYBOY: What is it?

DYLAN: Henry Miller said it: The role of an artist is to inoculate the world with disillusionment.

PLAYBOY: To create rock music, you used to have to be against the system, a desperado. Is settling down an enemy of rock?

DYLAN: No. You can be a priest and be in rock 'n' roll. Being a rock-'n'-roll singer is no different from being a house painter. You climb up as high as you want to. You're asking me, is rock, is the lifestyle of rock-'n'-roll at odds with the lifestyle of society in general?

PLAYBOY: Yes. Do you need to be in some way outside society, or in some way an outlaw, some way a—

DYLAN: No. Rock 'n' roll forms its own society. It's a world of its own. The same way the sports world is.

PLAYBOY: But didn't you feel that it was valuable to bum around and all that sort of thing?

DYLAN: Yes. But not necessarily, because you can bum around and wind up being a lawyer, you know. There isn't anything definite. Or any blueprint to it.

PLAYBOY: So future rock stars could just as easily go to law school?

DYLAN: For some people, it might be fine. But, getting back to that again, you have to have belief. You must have a purpose. You must believe that you can disappear through walls. Without that belief, you're not going to become a very good rock singer, or pop singer, or folk-rock singer, or you're not going to become a very good lawyer. Or a doctor. You must know why you're doing what you're doing.

PLAYBOY: Why are *you* doing what you're doing?

DYLAN: [*Pause*] Because I don't know anything else to do. I'm good at it.

PLAYBOY: How would you describe "it"?

DYLAN: I'm an artist. I try to create art.

PLAYBOY: How do you feel about your songs when you perform them years later? Do you feel your art has endured?

DYLAN: How many singers feel the same way 10 years later that they felt when they wrote the song? Wait till it gets to be 20 years, you know? Now, there's a certain amount of act that you can put on, you know, you can get through on it, but there's got to be something to it that is real—not just for the moment. And a lot of my songs don't work. I wrote a lot of them just by gut—because my gut told me to write them—and they usually don't work so good as the years go on. A lot of them *do* work. With those, there's some truth about every one of them. And I don't think I'd be singing if I weren't writing, you know. I would have no reason or purpose to be out there singing. I mean, I don't consider myself . . . the life of the party. [*Laughs*]

PLAYBOY: You've given new life to some songs in recent performances, such as "I Pity the Poor Immigrant" in the Rolling Thunder tour.

DYLAN: Oh, yes. I've given new life to a lot of them. Because I believe in them, basically. You know, I believe in them. So I do give them new life. And that can always be done. I rewrote "Lay, Lady, Lay," too. No one ever mentioned that.

PLAYBOY: You changed it to a much raunchier, less pretty kind of song.

DYLAN: Exactly. A lot of words to that song have changed. I recorded it originally surrounded by a bunch of other songs on the *Nashville Skyline* album. That was the tone of the session. Once everything was set, that was the way it came out. And it was fine for that time, but I always had a feeling there was more to the song than that.

PLAYBOY: Is it true that "Lay, Lady, Lay" was originally commissioned for *Midnight Cowboy*?

DYLAN: That's right. They wound up using Freddy Neil's tune.

PLAYBOY: How did it feel doing "Blowin' in the Wind" after all those years during your last couple of tours?

DYLAN: I think I'll always be able to do that. There are certain songs that I will always be able to do. They will always have just as much meaning, if not more, as time goes on.

PLAYBOY: What about "Like a Rolling Stone"?

DYLAN: That was a great tune, yeah. It's the dynamics in the rhythm that make up "Like a Rolling Stone" and all of the lyrics. I tend to base all my songs on the old songs, like the old folk songs, the old blues tunes; they are always good. They always make sense.

PLAYBOY: Would you talk a little about how specific songs come to you?

DYLAN: They come to me when I am most isolated in space and time. I reject a lot of inspiring lines.

PLAYBOY: They're too good?

DYLAN: I reject a lot. I kind of know myself well enough to know that the line might be good and it is the first line that gives you inspiration and then it's just like riding a bull. That is the rest of it. Either you just stick with it or you don't. And if you believe that what you are doing is important, then you will stick with it no matter what.

PLAYBOY: There are lines that are like riding wild bulls?

DYLAN: There are lines like that. A lot of lines that would be better off just staying on a printed page and finishing up as poems. I forget a lot of the lines. During the day, a lot of lines will come to me that I will just say are pretty strange and I don't have anything better to do. I try not to pay too much attention to those wild, obscure lines.

PLAYBOY: You say you get a single line and then you ride it. Does the melody follow after you write out the whole song?

DYLAN: I usually know the melody before the song.

PLAYBOY: And it is there, waiting for that first line?

DYLAN: Yeah.

PLAYBOY: Do you hear it easily?

DYLAN: The melody? Sometimes, and sometimes I have to find it.

PLAYBOY: Do you work regularly? Do you get up every morning and practice?

DYLAN: A certain part of every day I have to play.

PLAYBOY: Has your playing become more complex?

DYLAN: No. Musically not. I can hear more and my melodies now are more rhythmic than they ever have been, but, really, I am still with those same three chords. But, I mean, I'm not Segovia or Montoya. I don't practice 12 hours a day.

PLAYBOY: Do you practice using your voice, too?

DYLAN: Usually, yeah, when I'm rehearsing, especially, or when I'm writing a song, I'll be singing it.

PLAYBOY: Someone said that when you gave up cigarettes, your voice changed. Now we see you're smoking again. Is your voice getting huskier again?

DYLAN: No, you know, you can do anything with your voice if you put your mind to it. I mean, you can become a ventriloquist or you can become an imitator of other people's voices. I'm usually just stuck with my own voice. I can do a few other people's voices.

PLAYBOY: Whose voices can you imitate?

DYLAN: Richard Widmark. Sydney Greenstreet. Peter Lorre. I like those voices. They really had distinctive voices in the early talkie films. Nowadays, you go to a movie and you can't tell one voice from the other. Jane Fonda sounds like Tatum O'Neal.

PLAYBOY: Has your attitude toward women changed much in your songs?

DYLAN: Yeah; in the early period, I was writing more about objection, obsession or rejection. Superimposing my own reality on that which seemed to have no reality of its own.

PLAYBOY: How did those opinions change?

DYLAN: From neglect.

PLAYBOY: From neglect?

DYLAN: As you grow, things don't reach you as much as when you're still forming opinions.

PLAYBOY: You mean you get hurt less easily?

DYLAN: You get hurt over other matters than when you were 17. The energy of hurt isn't enough to create art.

PLAYBOY: So if the women in your songs have become more real, if there are fewer goddesses—

DYLAN: The goddess isn't real. A pretty woman as a goddess is just up there on a pedestal. The flower is what we are really concerned about here. The opening and the closing, the growth, the bafflement. You don't lust after flowers.

PLAYBOY: Your regard for women, then, has changed?

DYLAN: People are people to me. I don't single out women as anything to get hung up about.

PLAYBOY: But in the past?

DYLAN: In the past, I was guilty of that shameless crime.

PLAYBOY: You're claiming to be completely rehabilitated?

DYLAN: In that area, I don't have any serious problems.

PLAYBOY: There's a line in your film in which someone says to Sara, "I need you because I need your magic to protect me."

DYLAN: Well, the real magic of women is that throughout the ages, they've had to do all the work and yet they can have a sense of humor.

PLAYBOY: That's throughout the ages. What about women now?

DYLAN: Well, here's the new woman, right? Nowadays, you have the concept of a new woman, but the new woman is nothing without a man.

PLAYBOY: What would the new woman say to that?

DYLAN: I don't know what the new woman would say. The new woman is the impulsive woman. . . .

PLAYBOY: There's another line in your movie about "the ultimate woman." What *is* the ultimate woman?

DYLAN: A woman without prejudice.

PLAYBOY: Are there many?

DYLAN: There are as many as you can see. As many as can touch you.

PLAYBOY: So you've run into a lot of ultimate women?

DYLAN: Me, personally? I don't run into that many people. I'm working most of the time. I really don't have time for all that kind of intrigue.

PLAYBOY: Camus said that chastity is an essential condition for creativity. Do you agree?

DYLAN: He was speaking there of the dis-involvement with pretense.

PLAYBOY: Wasn't he speaking of sexual chastity?

DYLAN: You mean he was saying you have to stay celibate to create?

PLAYBOY: That's one interpretation.

DYLAN: Well, he might have been onto something there. It could have worked for him.

PLAYBOY: When you think about rock and the rhythm of the heartbeat—is it tied into love in some way?

DYLAN: The heartbeat. Have you ever lain with somebody when your hearts were beating in the same rhythm? That's true love. A man and a woman who lie down with their hearts beating together are truly lucky. Then you've truly been in love, m' boy. Yeah, that's true love. You might see that person once a month, once a year, maybe once a lifetime, but you have the guarantee your lives are going to be in rhythm. That's all you need.

PLAYBOY: Considering that some of your recent songs have been about love and romance, what do you feel about the tendency some people used to have of dividing your work into periods? Did you ever feel it was fair to divide your work, for example, into a political period and a nonpolitical period?

DYLAN: Those people disregarded the ultimate fact that I am a songwriter. I can't help what other people do with my songs, what they make of them.

PLAYBOY: But you *were* more involved politically at one time. You were supposed to have written "Chimes of Freedom" in the backseat of a car while you were visiting some SNCC people in the South.

DYLAN: That is all we did in those days. Writing in the backseats of cars and writing songs on street corners or on porch swings. Seeking out the explosive areas of life.

PLAYBOY: One of which was politics?

DYLAN: Politics was always one because there were people who were trying to change things. They were involved in the political game because that is how they had to change things. But I have always considered politics just part of the illusion. I don't get involved much in politics. I don't know what the system runs on.

For instance, there are people who have definite ideas or who studied all the systems of government. A lot of those people with college-educational backgrounds tended to come in and use up everybody for whatever purposes they had in mind. And, of course, they used music, because music was accessible and we would have done that stuff and written those songs and sung them whether there was any politics or not. I never did renounce a role in politics, because I never played one in politics. It would be comical for me to think that I played a role. Gurdjieff thinks it's best to work out your mobility daily.

PLAYBOY: So you did have a lot of "on the road" experiences?

DYLAN: I still do.

PLAYBOY: Driving around?

DYLAN: I am interested in all aspects of life. Revelations and realizations. Lucid thought that can be translated into songs, analogies, new information. I am better at it now. Not really written yet anything to make me stop writing. Like, I haven't come to the place that Rimbaud came to when he decided to stop writing and run guns in Africa.

PLAYBOY: Jimmy Carter has said that listening to your songs, he learned to see in a new way the relationship between landlord and tenant, farmer and sharecropper and things like that. He also said that you were his friend. What do you think of all that?

DYLAN: I am his friend.

PLAYBOY: A personal friend?

DYLAN: I know him personally.

PLAYBOY: Do you like him?

DYLAN: Yeah, I think his heart's in the right place.

PLAYBOY: How would you describe that place?

DYLAN: The place of destiny. You know, I hope the magazine won't take all this stuff and edit—like, Carter's heart's in the right place of destiny, because it's going to really sound—

PLAYBOY: No, it would lose the sense of conversation. The magazine's pretty good about that.

DYLAN: Carter has his heart in the right place. He has a sense of who he is. That's what I felt, anyway, when I met him.

PLAYBOY: Have you met him many times?

DYLAN: Only once.

PLAYBOY: Stayed at his house?

DYLAN: No. But anybody who's a governor or a Senate leader or in a position of authority who finds time to invite a folk-rock singer and his band out to his place has got to have . . . a sense of humor . . . and a feeling of the pulse of the people. Why does he have to do it? Most people in those kinds of positions can't relate at all to people in the music field unless it's for some selfish purpose.

PLAYBOY: Did you talk about music or politics?

DYLAN: Music. Very little politics. The conversation was kept in pretty general areas.

PLAYBOY: Does he have any favorite Dylan songs?

DYLAN: I didn't ask him if he had any favorite Dylan songs. He didn't say that he did. I think he liked "Ballad of a Thin Man," really.

PLAYBOY: Did you think that Carter might have been using you by inviting you there?

DYLAN: No, I believe that he was a decent, untainted man and he just wanted to check me out. Actually, as presidents go, I liked Truman.

PLAYBOY: Why?

DYLAN: I just liked the way he acted and things he said and who he said them to. He had a common sense about him, which is rare for a president. Maybe in the old days it wasn't so rare, but nowadays it's rare. He had a common quality. You felt like you could talk to him.

PLAYBOY: You obviously feel you can talk to President Carter.

DYLAN: You *do* feel like you can talk to him, but the guy is so busy and overworked you feel more like, well, maybe you'd just leave him alone, you know. And he's dealing with such complicated matters and issues that people are a little divided and we weren't divided in Truman's time.

PLAYBOY: Is there anything you're angry about? Is there anything that would make you go up to Carter and say, "Look, you fucker, do *this!*"?

DYLAN: Right. [*Pause*] He's probably caught up in the system like everybody else.

PLAYBOY: Including you?

DYLAN: I'm a part of the system. I have to deal with the system. The minute you pay taxes, you're part of the system.

PLAYBOY: Are there any heroes or saints these days?

DYLAN: A saint is a person who gives of himself totally and freely, without strings. He is neither deaf nor blind. And yet he's both. He's the master of his own reality, the voice of simplicity. The trick is to stay away from mirror images. The only true mirrors are puddles of water.

PLAYBOY: How are mirrors different from puddles?

DYLAN: The image you see in a puddle of water is consumed by depth: An image you see when you look into a piece of glass has no depth or life-flutter movement. Of course, you might want to check your tie. And, of course, you might want to see if the makeup is on straight. That's all the way. Vanity sells a lot of things.

PLAYBOY: How so?

DYLAN: Well, products on the market. Everything from new tires to bars of soap. Need is—need is totally overlooked. Nobody seems to care about people's needs. They're all for one purpose. A shallow grave.

PLAYBOY: Do you want your grave unmarked?

DYLAN: Isn't that a line in my film?

PLAYBOY: Yes.

DYLAN: Well, there are many things they can do with your bones, you know. [*Pause*] They make neckpieces out of them, bury them. Burn them up.

PLAYBOY: What's your latest preference?

DYLAN: Ah—put them in a nutshell.

PLAYBOY: You were talking about vanity and real needs. What needs? What are we missing?

DYLAN: There isn't anything missing. There is just a lot of scarcity.

PLAYBOY: Scarcity of what?

DYLAN: Inspirational abundance.

PLAYBOY: So it's not an energy crisis but an imagination crisis?

DYLAN: I think it's a spiritual crisis.

PLAYBOY: How so?

DYLAN: Well, you know, people step on each other's feet too much. They get on each other's case. They rattle easily. But I don't particularly stress that. I'm not on a soapbox about it, you know. That is the way life is.

PLAYBOY: We asked about heroes and saints and began talking about saints. How about heroes?

DYLAN: A hero is anyone who walks to his own drummer.

PLAYBOY: Shouldn't people look to others to be heroes?

DYLAN: No: When people look to others for heroism, they're looking for heroism in an imaginary character.

PLAYBOY: Maybe that in part explains why many seized upon you as that imaginary character.

DYLAN: I'm not an imaginary character, though.

PLAYBOY: You must realize that people get into a whole thing about you.

DYLAN: I know they used to.

PLAYBOY: Don't you think they still do?

DYLAN: Well, I'm not aware of it anymore.

PLAYBOY: What about the 1974 tour? Or the Rolling Thunder tour of 1976?

DYLAN: Well, yeah, you know, when I play, people show up. I'm aware they haven't forgotten about me.

PLAYBOY: Still, people always think you have answers, don't they?

DYLAN: No, listen: If I wasn't Bob Dylan, I'd probably think that Bob Dylan has a lot of answers myself.

PLAYBOY: Would you be right?

DYLAN: I don't think so. Maybe he'd have a lot of answers for *him*, but for me? Maybe not. Maybe yes, maybe no. Bob Dylan isn't a cat, he doesn't have nine lives, so he can only do what he can do. You know: not break under the strain.

If you need someone who raises someone else to a level that is unrealistic, then it's that other person's problem. He is just confronting his superficial self somewhere down the line. They'll realize it, I'm sure.

PLAYBOY: But didn't you have to go through a period when people were claiming you had let them down?

DYLAN: Yeah, but I don't pay much attention to that. What can you say? Oh, I let you down, big deal, OK. That's all. Find somebody else. OK? That's all.

PLAYBOY: You talked about a spiritual crisis. Do you think Christ is an answer?

DYLAN: What is it that attracts people to Christ? The fact that it was such a tragedy, is what. Who does Christ become when he lives inside a certain person? Many people say that Christ lives inside them: Well, what does that mean? I've talked to many people whom Christ lives inside: I haven't met one who would want to trade places with Christ. Not one of his people put himself on the line when it came down to the final hour.

What would Christ be in this day and age if he came back? What would he be? What would he be to fulfill his function and purpose? He would have to be a leader, I suppose.

PLAYBOY: Did you grow up thinking about the fact that you were Jewish?

DYLAN: No, I didn't. I've never felt Jewish. I don't really consider myself Jewish or non-Jewish. I don't have much of a Jewish background. I'm not a patriot to any creed. I believe in all of them and none of them. A devout Christian or Moslem can be just as effective as a devout Jew.

PLAYBOY: You say you don't feel Jewish. But what about your sense of God?

DYLAN: I feel a heartfelt God. I don't particularly think that God wants me thinking about Him all the time. I think that would be a tremendous burden on Him, you know. He's got enough people asking Him for favors. He's got enough people asking Him to pull strings. I'll pull my own strings, you know.

I remember seeing a *Time* magazine on an airplane a few years back and it had a big cover headline, "Is God Dead?" I mean, that was—would you think that was a responsible thing to do? What does God think of that? I mean, if you were God, how would you like to see that written about yourself? You know, I think the country's gone downhill since that day.

PLAYBOY: Really?

DYLAN: Uh-huh.

PLAYBOY: Since that particular question was asked?

DYLAN: Yeah; I think at that point, some very irresponsible people got hold of too much power to put such an irrelevant thing like that on a magazine when they could be talking about real issues. Since that day, you've had to kind of make your own way.

PLAYBOY: How are we doing, making our own way?

DYLAN: The truth is that we're born and we die. We're concerned here in this life with the journey from point A to point Z, or from what we think is Point A to point Z. But it's pretty self-deluding if you think that's all there is.

PLAYBOY: What do you think is beyond Z?

DYLAN: You mean, what do I think is in the great unknown? [*Pause*] Sounds, echoes of laughter.

PLAYBOY: Do you feel there's some sense of karmic balance in the universe, that you suffer for acts of bad faith?

DYLAN: Of course. I think everybody knows that's true. After you've lived long enough, you realize that's the case. You can get away with anything for a while. But it's like Poe's "The Tell-Tale Heart" or Dostoyevsky's *Crime and Punishment*: Somewhere along the line, sooner or later, you're going to have to pay.

PLAYBOY: Do you feel you've paid for what you got away with earlier?

DYLAN: Right now, I'm about even.

PLAYBOY: Isn't that what you said after your motorcycle accident—"Something had to be evened up"?

DYLAN: Yes.

PLAYBOY: And you meant . . . ?

DYLAN: I meant my back wheel had to be aligned. [*Laughter*]

PLAYBOY: Let's take one last dip back into the material world. What about an artist's relationship to money?

DYLAN: The myth of the starving artist is a myth. The big bankers and prominent young ladies who buy art started it. They just want to keep the artist under their thumb. Who says an artist can't have any money?

Look at Picasso. The starving artist is usually starving for those around him to starve. You don't have to starve to be a good artist. You just have to have love, insight and a strong point of view. And you have to fight off depravity. Uncompromising, that's what makes a good artist. It doesn't matter if he has money or not. Look at Matisse: he was a banker. Anyway, there are other things that constitute wealth and poverty besides money.

PLAYBOY: What we were touching on was the subject of the expensive house you live in, for example.

DYLAN: What about it? Nothing earthshaking or final about where I live. There is no vision behind the house. It is just a bunch of trees and sheds.

PLAYBOY: We read in the papers about an enormous copper dome you had built.

DYLAN: I don't know what you read in the papers. It's just a place to live for now. The copper dome is just so I can recognize it when I come home.

PLAYBOY: OK, back to less worldly concerns. You don't believe in astrology, do you?

DYLAN: I don't think so.

PLAYBOY: You were quoted recently as having said something about having a Gemini nature.

DYLAN: Well, maybe there are certain characteristics of people who are born under certain signs. But I don't know, I'm not sure how relevant it is.

PLAYBOY: Could it be there's an undiscovered twin or a double to Bob Dylan?

DYLAN: Someplace on the planet, there's a double of me walking around. Could very possibly be.

PLAYBOY: Any messages for your double?

DYLAN: Love will conquer everything—I suppose.

January 1971

MAE WEST

A candid conversation with the indestructible queen of vamp and camp

Twenty-eight years ago, Mae West completed her 10th and then-final film—eight of them for Paramount Pictures, which she had saved from mendicancy during the Depression years, when she was the greatest phenomenon in show business, as Mae would be the first to tell you. Along with Garbo and Shirley Temple, she was the hottest box-office draw in the land and probably the best-known, most photographed person on earth. "I was better known than Einstein, Shaw or Picasso," she modestly admits. She was also the world's highest-paid and most quoted entertainer, historical monument and prepotent image of ribald sex—which she had shown the world was inherently hilarious.

Princeton scientists designed a magnet in the shape of her torso. The Department of the Interior tried to name twin lakes after her but was hooted down by the bluenoses. A twin-diesel engine was named for her on the Super Chief. Author Hugh Walpole applauded her mockery of "the fraying morals and manners of a dreary world." Critic George Jean Nathan called her "the Statue of Libido." The Dakota Indians made her a tribe member as Princess She-Who-Mountains-in-Front. Salvador Dali designed a sofa of red silk from an enlarged photograph of Mae's lips. And during World War II, R.A.F. fliers named an appropriately pneumatic life jacket after her, thus immortalizing Mae in *Webster's*.

By 1943, however, she had dimmed to a faint ember of the old flame—or so it seemed. Her final movie, *The Heat's On*, was a dreary failure; even Mae didn't like it, and Mae likes almost everything that features Mae. When critics wrote that "the heat is definitely off," she turned her impressive (40") bosom away from Hollywood and flounced back to the stage that had spawned her brazen swagger, adenoidal drawl and outrageous double-entendres.

Gamely and irrepressibly, she opened on Broadway in a lubricous mediocrity called *Catherine Was Great*, which she had written for herself years before. The critics lambasted the play; John Chapman wrote: "I'm afraid it's going to be a bust, which will give Miss West one more than she needs." But a new generation of audiences had come along since Mae's stage triumphs of the 1920s and they wanted to see her. They went in droves, less aroused, perhaps, than curious. "Like Chinatown and Grant's Tomb," wrote one critic, "Mae West should be seen at least once." And after each performance, she captivated them with a tart little curtain speech: "Catherine was a great empress. She also had 300 lovers. I did the best I could in a couple of hours"—she had successfully knocked off 14 suitors in a mere three acts.

It was art imitating life. In the course of her long, much-publicized and continuing love life, Mae had democratically—and inexhaustibly—befriended businessmen, lawyers, politicians, tenors, judges, Mexican wrestlers, French importers, Italian leading men and chorus boys. Mae was still going strong—on stage and off—at 56, when she resurrected *Diamond Lil* (first produced in 1928) as the starring vehicle for still another comeback. "After all," said Mae, "I'm her and she's me and we're each other. Lil and I, in my various characterizations, climbed the ladder of success, wrong by wrong." In London, she was feted by royalty ("Hell, I'm royalty, too") and eternalized in wax at Madame Tussaud's.

By the mid-1950s, however, Mae began to seem something of a wax figurine herself—to everyone but Mae. Looking around for new conquests, she surrounded herself with an entourage of loinclothed muscle men and for three years proceeded to break nightclub records all over the country. Asked if she realized how much she was doing to belittle the male, Mae seemed baffled for a second and then answered in her fashion: "It's my personality and it's *unique*. I'm the regal, dignified type. That's not a posture you learn in school, dear. It's the way you look at the world." From the day she first appeared on stage at an Elks Club show in her native Brooklyn at the age of seven and literally screamed for the spotlight, Mae had looked at the world as if it had been created just for her; and at 60, she saw no reason to change her mind.

There were a few TV appearances in the early 1960s—most notably, her show-stealing Oscar turn with Rock Hudson—several rock-'n'-roll albums, a couple of movie offers that she spurned because "they were wrong for my personality," a surprisingly circumspect autobiography (which now retails for $15.95 in arcane bookshops); but Mae's raffish hussy image gradually drifted into a kind of silly soft focus and nobody cared much anymore. Mae herself was too rich and too self-possessed to care, either, especially since muscular young men still came up to see her sometimes—and to sample her beldam favors in the boudoir.

Rumors of her professional demise, however, were still premature. Taste makers of the 1960s saw Mae as a delicious example of pop art and began to call her the queen of camp—an old word that found new meaning when the dead or superannuated darlings of the 1920s and 1930s became the property of pop posters and late-night television. Mae West film festivals swept the land. When *I'm No Angel* and *She Done Him Wrong* (the film version of *Lil*) were double-billed in Los Angeles, they outpulled all other pictures then in release from Universal, which now owns her old celluloid. And in two recent personal appearances—one at the Academy Award Theater in Hollywood, the other at USC's highly regarded cinema fraternity—Mae got tumultuous standing ovations.

Nowadays, the grandchildren of her first fans join her burgeoning international fan club, titter at her old flicks, write her gushy love letters, send her roses by the truckload, collect such Westiana as life-size cutouts—and even give her diamonds, Mae's longtime trademark. Whole football teams visit her home with a frequency that distresses their coaches. And Mae West jokes are in again (e.g., Mae on phone to Chinese laundry: "Where the hell is my laundry? Get it over here right away." Chinaman on arrival: "I come lickety-split, Miss West." Mae: "Never mind that. Just gimme the laundry.").

To cap it all, as everyone knows by now, Mae has returned to the screen in living offcolor—as a man-eating actors' agent in Gore Vidal's fetid garden of sexual reverses, *Myra Breckinridge*. Attending the Manhattan premiere, she was mobbed by 2000 unglued fans. At 78, she gets top billing and roughly $500,000, still thinks of herself as sex queen regnant ("Glamorwise, I'm the greatest thing since Valentino") and scorns the sharper curves of her co-star, Raquel Welch, to whom she refers simply as "the other woman."

Paradoxically—since she mostly burlesques sex rather than makes it desirable—Mae is real and Raquel is not, to many who know them both. "Mae is as strong as steel, loves sex, knows it's good and makes no bones about it," says *Myra* director Michael Sarne. "She is disciplined both physically and mentally. She does what's good for Mae. She always has, which is ultimately what every woman wants to do and few ever do. She is purely selfish and is perfectly honest about it. Raquel has the same selfish, ruthless drive as Mae, but she's not real at all. She's afraid of sex, but *she* is the myth. The legend, Mae West, is the real woman, the real sex symbol."

Today, most of Mae's time is taken up, as it always has been, with the care and feeding of Mae West. With a personal fortune estimated somewhere between $5 million and $15 million (mostly in real estate), she lives in a satiny cocoon with a fawning retinue that includes a maid, three secretaries, a Filipino butler-chauffeur whom she cast in *Myra* (along with several fans) and an ex-wrestler-bodyguard-companion with wall-to-wall shoulders. She assiduously avoids abrasive situations ("tears down the nerves") and still keeps her private life very private, but admits to being sexually active, rarely goes to parties or screenings, seldom reads anything but her fan mail, consults psychics before making important decisions, pampers herself interminably (everything from exercise to two colonics a day), scribbles dialogue on little note pads and appears to care little for the world outside her hermetically sealed pink shell.

Each of her three homes—a ranch in the San Fernando Valley, a 22-room beach house featuring murals of naked men with golden phalluses and disembodied testicles floating like pink clouds across blue Oriental skies, and the white-and-gold Louis XIV apartment she has had since she first went to Hollywood in 1932—is the very essence of Mae West: a cheerfully extravagant vulgarity. "God, do you know she keeps hand towels—*hand towels*—pinned to her white-satin couch?" a famous writer exclaimed recently.

It's true. Interviewer C. Robert Jennings sat on several of her couches during five conversations with Mae. When he arrived for his first visit, she made a grand sashaying entrance in a long, multicolored pastel hostess gown that effectively hid her high platform shoes (she's only 5'3"). "Oh, hello, dear," she said, blue eyes twinkling merrily. "How *are* ya? Siddown and take it easy. I do some of my best work on this couch." The only competition was Tom Jones on the hi-fi.

"Mae was a bundle of contradictions," reports Jennings, "at once illiterate and smart, demure and demonic, sweet old lady and shrewd little cookie cutter. But mostly she was warm, funny, gracious and surprisingly unsparing about herself. Once she got to know me, she didn't undulate with hand on hip; nor did she talk in epigrams and aphorisms. But she hasn't lost her randy sense of comedy—as I discovered when I asked my first question."

PLAYBOY: Since you clearly don't need the money, why did you choose to make a comeback in *Myra Breckinridge*, at the age of 77?
WEST: Seventy—*sex*, dear. But I could pass for 26. And it's not a comeback. I've never been away, never stopped. Since my last picture, I've broken in three plays, toured for years with my muscleman act, made four record albums, written my book, appeared several times on TV and finished screenplays from two of my plays, plus all my own dialogue for *Myra*. I felt it was somethin' my public would want me to do. I always like to give 'em what they want. And they were *demandin'* I come back. My fans are crazy to see me again. They're the young and they adore me. Mae West is a whole new thing to them, 'cause it's a whole new generation. I get 'em in their teens now. They even gimme diamonds. The public is so starved for me I took this part just to give 'em a break, ya know what I mean? I mean, it's not *my* movie, but they're referrin' to it in New York as "the Mae West movie." People are rushin' to see it because of *me*.
PLAYBOY: How do you feel about the criticism that's been leveled at *Myra*?
WEST: This is *controversy*! This is *marvelous*! This is *box* office! Thanks to what they're sayin', people are just runnin' to see the picture. All my biggest hits were controversial. As Hearst said in an editorial in the 1930s, "Isn't it time Congress *did* something about Mae West?" When Fox was protestin' the X ratin' for *Myra*, I said, "Are they crazy? I'd be *insulted* if a picture I was in didn't get a X ratin'." Don't forget, dear, I *invented* censorship.
PLAYBOY: How would you describe your role in the film?
WEST: Well, when they first mentioned the book, I thought they wanted me for the title role, 'cause I star in *everything*, ya know, so I told 'em,

"Never." It didn't grab me. I like my sexes stable. Myra can change her sex, but they're not gonna change *mine*. But then they said they wanted me to play Letitia Van Allen, who's sort of Agent S-E-X, not 007. I change my hat for every man and I change my men like I change my clothes. I run this agency for fun and I handle leadin' men *only*, and I end up ownin' everything, so I feel kinda at home in the part. It's not at all like the character in the book—I read parts of it; my fans would have a *fit* if it were. I know what my audience expects of me and I give 'em what they want.

In the book, Letitia meets a passionate young student who puts her in the hospital. In my version, I put *him* in the hospital. See what I mean? That's my personality. When I enter, there are 19 or 20 men waitin' outside my boudoir-office, all handsome and healthy; I picked most of 'em myself. "I'll be right with ya, boys," I say. "Get out your *résumés*." That was an innocent line when I thought of it, but when I said it, it broke everybody up. Like somebody says, "It warms the cockles of my heart," and I say, "Warms the *what*? Oh, yeah." Every time I say anything, there has to be a laugh. Why, I can't even say my prayers: "Now I lay me"—that's as far as I can get and they break up. But I never even meant "Come up and see me sometime" to be sexy.

PLAYBOY: Since so much of *Myra* was cut in editing, would you give us a random sampling of some of your other lines?

WEST: Yeah, sure. Once inside my office, I say to my male secretary, "You gotta mob here today and I'm a little tired. One of those guys'll have to go." Then a dumb stud comes in and says all he wants is my respect. I say, "Watch it, you're gonna kill the deal." Honey, I'm doin' and sayin' things that woulda given Adolph Zukor apoplexy when I was at Paramount. I got a lot of blame for bringin' on censorship in the 1930s, and I may just do it again this time around. If *Myra* doesn't stir 'em up, I don't know what will.

PLAYBOY: By today's standards, that dialogue sounds rather tame. Do you say anything that might be more censorable?

WEST: Sin *what*, dear?

PLAYBOY: What else do you say that's suggestive?

WEST: *Everything.* At one point, I say, "They're gonna give me an award," and Myra asks, "What, an Oscar?" And I say, "No, a golden phallus." Then I add, "Someday we'll have our own stable of studs—a boy bank where credit is always good. Sort of a lay-a-day plan." And Myra says, "God bless America." Everybody screamed on the set. In another scene,

I tell Myra, "The guy's a terrific bang. I wouldn't say he's exactly a sex maniac, but he'll do until one comes along." In the orgy scene, I come in on all these people doin' it, ya know, and I say, "Umm, guess this is what they mean by lettin' it all hang out." And in a hospital scene, one veteran from Vietnam complains that his arm screws off and another that his leg screws off and I say, "Well, come up and see me sometime and I'll show ya how to screw your *heads* off."

PLAYBOY: Did you know that many people have called *Myra* "the dirty *Cleopatra*"?

WEST: Oh, I'm never dirty, dear. I'm interestin' without bein' vulgar. I have—*taste*. I *kid* sex. I was born with sophistication and sex appeal, but I'm never vulgar. Maybe it's breedin'—I come from a good family, descended from Alfred the Great. In the script, I have a line, "I've got the judge by the . . . ," but I never say the word, just make the motions [*cupping her hand*]. I wouldn't use any four-letter words, dear. I don't like obscenity and I don't have to do it at any time. They thought I might be willing for *Myra*, because it's in vogue now, but I won't. I just—suggest.

PLAYBOY: Nudity's in vogue now, too. How do you feel about it?

WEST: Nudity should come under the headin' of art, not sex. But nowadays, they just throw in a naked body to help the plot, 'cause all the great plots have been done, and it's monotonous. I guess they think the younger generation wants to see somethin' different. Maybe they do, but not naked bodies, 'cause they've got all the sex they can handle—at least, so I'm told. Anybody can go to the beach, where they got people with real good bodies—but that don't make it, either. I saw *Hair*—and it went to sleep on me. My advice for those gals who think they have to take their clothes off to be a star is, baby, once you're boned, what's left to create the illusion? Let 'em *wonder*. I never believed in givin' 'em too much of me. I let the other woman in *Myra* do that.

PLAYBOY: There's been a lot of talk about how you and the other woman, as you call Raquel, clashed behind the scenes. What really happened?

WEST: I never gossip, dear. And I hate arguments. I don't like to down things. I like to think positive. I avoid anything that upsets me. That's my philosophy.

PLAYBOY: But you could hardly have avoided Miss Welch. Can't you tell us what happened, in your disagreement over costumes, for example?

WEST: Well, the director suggested I wear black and white throughout the picture. The other woman was gonna wear blues and reds. I only have two scenes with her. She thought I was gonna wear black velvet with white-mink trim, so she went out and got herself a black dress with a white collar. They told her not to wear it. She did anyway, but we fooled her, 'cause I came in with this *white* dress and *black* trim. Now she couldn't change to a white one. In the next scene [since cut], I was wearin' an all-white negligee with ostrich feathers and she got into a long, full red thing with a hood. Honest to Christ, she looked like Little Red Riding Hood. Reggie Allen, the set designer, is an old friend of mine and he filled the place with red so her dress didn't mean a thing. She couldn't stand it and she complained to her agent, who screamed to Dick Zanuck. I don't know why she was so vicious. She should be glad I'm in the picture; a lot more people will see her.

PLAYBOY: We understand there was a bit of friction concerning you and another star at the studio—Barbra Streisand. Why was that?

WEST: I never met her, dear. But when I came on the picture, they told me I had her dressin' room from *Hello, Dolly!* I said, don't tell *me* "somebody else's room." It's Mae West's room. I'm in a class by myself. I star in everything and I break records all over the world. My *ego's* breakin' records. If I can't break a record at whatever I do, it don't mean anything to me. So they redecorated the dressin' room just for me.

PLAYBOY: Many film critics compared Miss Streisand's characterization in *Dolly* to Mae West. One magazine even called it *The Mae West Story*. How do you feel about it?

WEST: Streisand has the unmitigated *gall* to imitate me. It'll hurt my *Diamond Lil*, which I'm bringin' to the screen again, in color and with new music. Streisand conflicts with her. If it wasn't for *Dolly* bein' at Fox, too, I think I'd have gone in there and had 'em take some of it out. She needs a little sex quality in there and she knows imitatin' me is the best way she can get it. But she'd better forget it.

PLAYBOY: Barbra said in an interview that she'd love to meet you but she didn't want to bother you.

WEST: She didn't wanna bother to ask if she could *imitate* me—take it and ask after. Well, it might interest her to know that David Merrick wanted *me* to do *Dolly*. But I didn't wanna be a Dolly. I'm me. I'm unique. But even Edie Adams on those cigar commercials is sayin', "Pick one up and smoke it sometime." I gotta *watch* these things?

PLAYBOY: But people have imitated you all your life.

WEST: The gay boys, sure. I *like* some of the gay boys doin' imitations of me. At a drag ball here recently, there were 16 Mae Wests and not one of that other woman. I always win the prizes, too.

PLAYBOY: How do you account for your homophile following?

WEST: Homo what, dear?

PLAYBOY: Homosexual.

WEST: I've always had it, dear. They're crazy about me 'cause I give 'em a chance to play. My characterization is sexy and with humor and they like to imitate me, the things I say, the way I say 'em, the way I move. It's easy for 'em to imitate me, 'cause the gestures are exaggerated, flamboyant, *sexy*, and that's what they wanna look like, be like, feel like. And I've stood up for 'em. They're good kids. I don't like the police abusin' 'em, and in New York I told 'em, "When you're hittin' one of those guys, you're hittin' a woman," 'cause a *born* homosexual is a female in a male body. There's another kind of homosexual—it depends on his environment and opportunities—but that's just another form of masturbation. I saw *The Sergeant* and felt awful depressed; it wouldn't have hurt that kid to give in a little to Rod Steiger. I've liked 'em ever since vaudeville, when I used to take some of the chorus boys home. My mother, whom I was crazy about, loved 'em 'cause they'd fix her hair and her hats. They were all humorous, sweet, talented and, some, geniuses.

PLAYBOY: Have you ever had a homosexual problem yourself?

WEST: I hope not. I said in my book I never had any interest in a woman as a love object. I've liked the boys for as long as I can remember. When I was 12, I'd have about six of 'em around me and we'd sing and talk and hug and kiss and I'd play with their—umm, *you* know [*makes groping motions with both hands*]. They called me Peaches. But I didn't know then I had this *sex* personality.

PLAYBOY: You've just completed a screenplay based on your homosexual play, *The Drag*, which you wrote in the 1920s but never took to Broadway. Why are you reviving it?

WEST: Censorship has changed, dear. Back in the 1920s, the city fathers asked us to keep it out of New York—and I had already served time in jail for corruptin' the morals of youth with my first play, *Sex*. So we opened in Paterson, New Jersey, and we were gettin' up to $50 a seat: They came from all over the country to see it. Caused a scandal. I was always ahead of my time, dear. It had a cast of 60 and it *glorified* homosexuals. The big scene is a dance, with about 40 of 'em in drag—I even had taxicab and truck-driver types in drag. I directed it but didn't appear in it. They never used the word sex, but I had screamin' gay great-lookin' guys flauntin' it out all over the place. There were at least a dozen curtain calls after each of the three acts and it took an hour to empty the theater—everyone wanted to visit the actors, even though a great percentage of the audiences were women. The time's right to do it on the screen, but *The Boys in the Band* is doin' the same thing I did and I hear *A Patriot for Me* copied my drag ball scene from *Sex*—the oddest party ever produced for the stage. I'm waitin' for the right producer to put the movie together. I've got a part in it that would make a *star* out of Rex Reed.

PLAYBOY: Was *The Drag* the first homosexual play in America?

WEST: The first realistic one about men, I think. I used comedy to make mine interestin', but I wanted to show the tragic *waste* that was spreadin' into our society when people were shocked by it in any form but didn't do anything about it. It starts seriously in a doctor's office and this doctor says 5 million—now about 20 million, I'm told—people in this country alone are gay and civilization has done nothin' to cure them.

PLAYBOY: In a recent Mae West film festival in Los Angeles, you were billed as the queen of camp. What does the word camp mean to you?

WEST: Camp is the kinda comedy where they imitate me. In the 1920s and 1930s, the gay crowd was usin' it. It's finally gotten out to the public. In *The Drag*, I used phrases like, "Oh, let your hair down, Mary" and "drag queen" and "She dished and dished and dished" and "All night she camped all over the place." Camp is bein' funny and dishy and outrageous and sayin' clever things. I'm always sayin' somethin' sexy and campy and they like to sound that way, too. That's one way they feel they *can*, since they feel they're not, you know, naturally sexy.

PLAYBOY: Do you feel *you're* naturally sexy, or are you just a parody of sex?

WEST: Even at the beginnin', it was natural with me. I feel sexy all the time. I can't remember not feelin' sexy. And I didn't parody sex consciously. 'Cause at first, I played more straight dramatic parts, though they wouldn't let me even murder a woman, except in self-defense, like in *Lil*. So I began to pad it up with funny lines, exaggerate my delivery and body movements more and more. Especially in movies, when I had school kids in the audience, so I put in that element to *please* 'em. But the censors wouldn't even let me sit on a guy's lap, and I'd been on more laps than a napkin. They called it suggestive, not sexy, in those days. Vampy parts I did most. I was good at makin' humorous remarks—five or six right after another—but it was always on the sex angle that the comedy came through. I'd even write decoy lines for the censors to cut so I could keep the rest, like, "Is that a gun in your pocket or are you just glad to see me?"

PLAYBOY: What about funny but sexless lines like "Beulah, peel me a grape"?

WEST: That came from Boogie, my monkey. You know I keep monkeys. They're my babies. Boogie loved grapes and he never ate one before peelin' it. Very fastidious. Anyway, after that picture [*I'm No Angel*], I was the most famous and popular motion-picture star in the world.

PLAYBOY: Garbo was popular then, too—did you know her?

WEST: No, not then, 'cause Hollywood people never met, they never mixed here, unless they were on the same picture or at the same studio. They had their own parties and I didn't go to parties. I kept Hollywood at a distance. But not long ago, my dear friend George Cukor called and said Garbo was in town and wanted to meet me. She loved my pictures and I liked hers and she always conducted herself right. I didn't know what I'd talk about, so I decided to talk about myself. When she came in, I said, "Hello, dear," and I kissed her on the cheek. She seemed startled at first, but I just wanted her to feel at ease. She's still a very beautiful woman, but she didn't say much. Certain people you don't have to talk much with, though; you say a few words and they understand. Garbo does more thinkin' than talkin'. I don't do much talkin', either, unless I'm asked.

PLAYBOY: You said you didn't go to parties in the old days. Why not?

WEST: Between pictures, I was too busy writin' to mingle in the old days. I was always scribblin', anywhere—in cars, in bed, on anything, scraps, paper bags. Also, I never drank, and you don't enjoy a party very much out here if you don't drink. I may have tasted crème de menthe or sweet wine a few times, but I realized quite a long time ago it wasn't good for ya; it kills the vitamins in your food. So I steered away from parties, especially the wild ones.

PLAYBOY: In addition to Garbo, were there any of the other old stars you admired?

WEST: Well, I always said Chaplin was the only other person who could write his own pictures and star in 'em, too. Theda Bara had a nice mean quality and Clara Bow had cute sex. But mine was more sultry and sophisticated and really did the job. It was *how* I said my lines and what I *did* when I said 'em. L.B. Mayer tried to get me to write stories for the blonde one [Harlow]. "Give her a sophisticated story," he says. And I says, "If I got good ideas, L.B., I gotta keep 'em for myself." Lana did very well, too, but there's nobody like me. Nobody in my class.

PLAYBOY: We read somewhere that you OK'd Marilyn Monroe to play your life story.

WEST: Never. She didn't have the *speakin'* voice to play me, though she was nearest in looks to myself. I found Marilyn very attractive and the type the masses like; they thought they had another Mae West with her. But she couldn't talk. And she had to be surrounded by two or three names, 'cause she couldn't build a story for herself like I could.

PLAYBOY: You sort of made yourself the leading man, so to speak, didn't you?

WEST: Well, I do dominate my pictures. Everything is written around me, and that includes men. A forceful, dominatin' sex personality that requires multiple men, like I always had in real life. If they build the man up equally, it's no good for me. I carry the sex interest, the love interest, the drama and the humor—and sometimes the tragedy. I'm also the heavy. There are very few personalities in history that could do that, if any. I'm my own original creation.

PLAYBOY: Yet W.C. Fields held his own in My *Little Chickadee* and shared screenwriting credit with you, too, didn't he?

WEST: For your information, dear, I wrote *all* of My *Little Chickadee* and Bill asked me if he could put in a few lines and then he wrote about three minutes for himself—where he talks to a fly on the bar. He finally got his name up there, 'cause he gave 'em a lot of trouble about it. He was just tryin' to get back at me, 'cause I had him thrown off the set.

PLAYBOY: Why?

WEST: I had a clause in my contract that if he drank, he'd have to leave the set. "Not even a small beer?" he pleaded. "No," I says. "And those cigars are more than I can take." Three weeks later, he comes on the set tight and says, "Who stole the cork outa my lunch?" And I says, "Pour him outa here."

PLAYBOY: You mentioned multiple men in your life. Who were some of them?

WEST: I'm not a kiss-and-tell. I never flaunted my affairs in public, never talked about my men by name, except for Joe Schenck of the vaudeville team, but that wasn't a *sex* love affair; and my husband, Frank Wallace, who I married secretly when I was 17. It was a mistake—he was a problem and I sent him off on a solo tour. But I had warned him I didn't love him. I told him, "There's just this physical thing between us. You don't appeal to my finer instincts." But I never was the cottage-apron type. For years, my manager was wild about me and he was very possessive and jealous of my other romances. He taught me that you've gotta conserve your sex energy in order to *do* things. This is the way you store up power for your creative work, he says. I didn't know that. I thought you just *do* it. Sex. It was through this knowledge that I started to really write, and when I started a picture, I'd stop all my sex activities and put that energy into my work. I'd get absorbed in the play and the sexiness of *that*. It was a goal. Up until then, I just *did* it all the time. But it was too much, 'cause my mind was divided.

PLAYBOY: How many lovers have you had?

WEST: Oh, God, I don't remember, there were so many. I was never interested in the score, though—only the game. Like my famous line, "It's not the men in my life that counts but the life in my men."

PLAYBOY: What kind of man makes the worst lover?

WEST: Men that drink. I've never had a drunken sweetheart. But there's potential in most all of 'em. You just have to know how to bring it out. One of my first affairs was with a virgin, though he was well into his 20s. Very shy. I initiated him and found it fascinatin', teachin' him things, but I understand he's lived a life of celibacy ever since.

PLAYBOY: What type makes the best lover?

WEST: Male. When people ask me what kind of man I prefer, I always say I like two types: foreign and domestic. Find a man of 40—when he's ripened. I look for personality, not handsomeness. And like the line in a song of mine, I prefer "a guy that takes his time."

PLAYBOY: What was your most memorable affair?

WEST: Two I remember best. One was this charmin' Frenchman who would pick me up in his car after *Diamond Lil* and take me over to this other theater where I was rehearsin' *Pleasure Man*. It was love on the run, 'cause I was havin' an affair with him and my manager at the same time, see. I liked to muss the Frenchman's wavy black hair. We met anyplace we could—dressin' rooms, elevators, the back seat of his car or my limousine. A kind of hit-and-run affair, you might say—until his wife showed up. I didn't know he was married. I've never knowingly had an affair with a married man. Anyway, I saw a guy in the show I liked, but I was afraid to start a *third* affair, so I says, I'll have *him* when I get to Chicago. He was a 26-year-old boxer. My manager fired him from the show, but out on the road, he met me at my hotel.

PLAYBOY: And?

WEST: It was somethin'. We were at it from Saturday night till four the next afternoon. I had a dozen of those rubber things, ya know, and he went through 'em and did it 10 *more* times by mornin'. That's 22 times from 11 to seven. I said, "I'm kinda tired and I think we ought to get some sleep." Three or four hours later, he went another four times and then had lunch. Oysters, if I remember correctly. He'd been married and divorced and said he'd only done it one or two times a night until then. Three at the most. But he'd had his eye on me and it'd been buildin' up in him for a long time. You see, men don't know their own *capacity*. You can never tell about the capacity of a person.

PLAYBOY: Considering the fact that you were born in the Victorian age, how did you manage to escape the puritan sense of sin and guilt that afflicted most of your contemporaries and even later generations?

WEST: My mother thought I was the greatest thing on earth and she liked me to play with the boys. Then there was the thing I put in my book: that if Kinsey is right, I only did what comes naturally, what the average person does secretly, drenchin' himself in guilts and phobias 'cause of his sense of sinnin'. I never felt myself a sinner. I've always believed in sex. Sex is natural and what's natural isn't nasty.

PLAYBOY: You seem partial to boxers and muscle men, but there's a theory that bodybuilders tend to pass up sex in their preoccupation with physical fitness.

WEST: Just because they build up their bodies doesn't mean they don't have the *capacity*. The point is, they're all good healthy specimens—don't drink or smoke—and that's what I like. It's true that muscle men use up their energy and strength buildin' their bodies up and some of 'em are like one a night, some like a couple times a night. Fighters have to watch themselves. Wrestlers are sexier, 'cause they don't have to train a lot, so they have sex on their minds more and it's in the mind that it starts. I like 'em all, but there's a few I like a little *more*.

PLAYBOY: Did you know that at a USC banquet a year ago, one of the football coaches said, "We'll have a pretty good year if we can find a way to keep the boys away from Mae West's apartment"?

WEST: Sure, they come up and see me. They're great-lookin' boys. I like 'em 'cause they take care of their bodies. I always said I adore football players; their passes are so forward.

PLAYBOY: Have you ever been in love with any of your conquests?

WEST: Some of my affairs reached great heights. They were very deep, hittin' on all the emotions. You can't get too hot over anybody unless there's somethin' that goes along with the sex act, can you? But I concentrate on myself most of the time; that's the only way a person can become a star in the true sense. I never wanted a love that meant the surrender of my self-possession. I saw what it did to other people when they loved another person the way I loved myself, and I didn't want that problem. I had to stay in command of my career.

PLAYBOY: Then your career was everything?

WEST: It was first and it still is. I do nothin' but look after myself and my work. Good reviews is my favorite reading matter.

PLAYBOY: Do you miss never having had children?

WEST: I never wanted children. I was afraid it might change me mentally, physically and psychologically. Motherhood's a career in itself. I like other people's children, but I wouldn't want any of my own. You see, dear, a woman who's married and has children can't be a sex symbol. Men feel you belong to someone else. You're the sex symbol to your husband only and you *should* be, especially if you have children. You may be attractive, but you can't be a sex symbol for the masses, for the industry, for the world. Like myself. Years ago, a star wouldn't even tell if she was married. If she had children, she had to hide 'em. Even the enthusiasm for Elvis isn't there since he married—but that's human nature. When you're single, everybody feels you're *theirs*. This helped the Mae West character, but it also got me in a lotta trouble.

PLAYBOY: How?

WEST: Even back in vaudeville, my manager would come and say, "Mae, you'll have the church after us sure," and I'd have to take out a song or change it. My first play, *Sex*, started an epidemic of sex plays; and this was at a time when the *word* had never even been mentioned before, except clinically. But most of these plays closed down 'cause they didn't have a good story—or Mae West. So I came into pictures and I brought my own audience. The theaters were empty. Paramount was losin' 1700 theaters and havin' 'em turned into office buildin's. My first picture, *Night After Night*, wasn't really a Mae West movie, but I wrote my own dialogue and George Raft said I stole everything but the cameras. I came in next with *She Done Him Wrong* and broke all records and saved the studio and the theaters. *I'm No Angel* did the same thing, attracted so much attention that all the other studios tried to get their own Mae West. I wrote *I'm No Angel*, too—it's all about this girl who lost her reputation but never missed it. Then the church got after me. A couple of priests came to see me and one of 'em, a handsome guy, said, "A woman told me in the confessional, 'Father, I have sinned. I've committed adultery. It was that Mae West movie that drove me to it.'"

PLAYBOY: You had some trouble with the networks, too. Didn't NBC ban you for a dozen years or so?

WEST: Yeah, but you know, it's hard to be funny when you have to be clean. It happened 'cause of somethin' I said on the Charlie McCarthy show. All I did was ask Don Ameche, who was playin' Adam to my Eve, "Would you like to try this apple sometime, honey?" Then I invited Charlie to come up and play in my woodpile sometime.

PLAYBOY: There was also a *Person to Person* interview with you that was never aired. Why?

WEST: Oh, that was when I took Charles Collingwood back to my famous bedroom and he asked me why I had so many mirrors on the ceilin' and everywhere. I said, "They're for personal observation. I always like to know how I'm doin'." He had to change the subject fast, ya know, so he asked me about current events and I says: "I've always had a weakness for foreign affairs." That was about all. Oh, yeah, they asked me if I had any advice for the young and I said, "Sure. Grow up." So they refused to put the show on. But I believe in censorship. After all, I made a fortune out of it.

PLAYBOY: Haven't you ever gotten tired of being Mae West—sustaining that larger-than-life erotic image?

WEST: You can't get enough of a good thing, in my opinion. My career is built on doin' things the right way, *my* way—and my way is the easy way.

PLAYBOY: Haven't you ever felt the need for something beyond self-gratification?

WEST: In November 1941, I had an experience that changed my life. I was at the peak of my career. I was rich, successful and bored stiff. I was tired of workin'. I had everythin' and nothin'. I decided to devote six months to explorin' the unknown, religion and how the soul works. I was always interested, but I could never find the real thing. Then I met this spiritualist, Reverend Kelly, and he was really great. Anything metaphysical was called spiritualism then, and I was one of the original people that got 'em off that. I had gone through Tarot cards, fortune-tellin', the whole bit—but I wanted *proof*. I used to go to Sunday school and get headaches. It was always hard for me to believe anything, 'cause nothin' could be *proven*.

Then I met a woman who taught me to meditate, to go "into the silence." You've gotta leave your conscious mind a blank and do it in the dark, 'cause if you see things, your mind is workin'. It took me over a week to do it for two minutes. 'Cause the forces come in and work on the part of the mind that we dream with—that's the psychic eye, ya know what I mean? Within two and a half weeks, I was able to do it for 25 minutes, leave the mind a blank—but nothin' came in. Then one morning, this angelic voice said, "Good mornin', dear." Sounded like a child's voice; it was like inside my ear. I found out that it's a little spirit called Juliet who generally comes to beginners through the inner ear. Later, a man's voice came from my solar plexus. "Am I imaginin' things?" I asked Reverend Kelly. He said the mind—the intelligence that lives within our bodies—is so powerful that it can survive death and come through walls or anyplace, like electricity. One time, Reverend Kelly brought Mario Lanza back. But I had to quit foolin' around with the forces myself.

PLAYBOY: Why?

WEST: They started to bother me so much I couldn't sleep. I saw one face after another, mostly men, dressed in period clothes with monocles, like from another century, sayin' "thee" and "thou." Finally, I had to tell 'em to leave. They formed a whole circle of heads over my bed, just under the ceilin'. I said, "I gotta get up and go to work. I believe, I believe. Please go away." And they did.

PLAYBOY: Have they made any surprise visits since then?

WEST: No, but if I wanted 'em now, they'd come. I know how to go into the unknown. I see Dr. Ireland from time to time; Reverend Kelly introduced me to him before he passed on. He's got great psychic powers. I wasn't sure about doin' *Myra*, didn't know the director, until Dr. Ireland told me I should go ahead, that the director's got determination and is a wonderful person. If Ireland likes him, he must be all right. But he told me to beware of a certain man in the movie; I asked Sarne if it was him, but it turned out to be Rex Reed. I hear he's been talkin' about me on TV. Well, if he has, it's *jealousy*.

PLAYBOY: Has your interest in the occult affected your thoughts on death?

WEST: I never think of death, dear.

PLAYBOY: Not even when friends and colleagues die?

WEST: Nobody I ever knew outside of my mother's and father's death affected me. I nearly went out of my mind when my mother died, but there's a lot of things I hadn't learned then. I didn't believe in the hereafter then. If I had the same understandin' I have now—that her soul's still around—it wouldn't have affected me that way.

PLAYBOY: We have a hunch you'll live to be 150. How do you keep in such good shape?

WEST: My mother was a health nut and my father was an athlete. Like I said, I don't drink and I don't smoke, and it's still in my contract that I don't have any smokin' around the set when I'm workin', 'cause I can't take it. Even in a restaurant, it spoils your whole dinner, especially cigars, and when I go to my favorite restaurant, Perino's, they don't let 'em smoke around me. I missed all the childhood sicknesses, too. I get a cold about every 10 years. In 1959, I had my chest X-rayed and they told me I have double thyroid glands, which gives you extra sex energy; that's a lotta thyroid, dear. So that's in my favor, too. Also, if you have proper food and keep your insides clean, you'll live a long life; I smell just as sweet at either end. The body renews itself all the time. With proper food and proper cleanin' of the system, age won't set in. People age from *within*, but it shows from without. The doctors told me, "Your lungs are as clear as a bell"—even with the smog. I only breathe in clean air from the air conditioners in all my houses and my car, and I drink nothin' but bottled spring water. I even bathe in it.

Also, I don't take pills, I never had a face-lift and I don't even take vitamins. My skin was always very good—here, feel it; it's the skin of a little girl. [*It is.*] I massage it with cocoa butter and lanolin, heated and mixed. I still have all my own teeth; my mother wouldn't permit me to eat candy as a child. And I'm solid, strong [*flexes muscles*]. I'm always exercisin'—stretchin' exercises—and I use dumbbells. I walk on the beach and my ranch. I have a walkin' machine here. I also massage my breasts; you should do it yourself, 'cause the muscle under the arm doin' the massagin' holds the bust up and keeps the breasts firm. [*She demonstrates.*] Breast exercises stimulate the whole body an' glands an' everything, ya know?

PLAYBOY: Looking back on a long and full life, how do you see yourself and what do you think of what you see?

WEST: I see myself as a classic. I never loved another person the way I loved myself. I've had an easy life and no guilts about it. I'm in a class by myself. I have no regrets. Who else can do what I'm doin' now and look the way I look? That's why I never wanted to be anybody else. Look at Betsy Ross—all she ever made was a flag. If I wanted to be somebody in history—Florence Nightingale or Madame de Pompadour or Catherine the Great, who was a preincarnation of myself—I'd just write a play for myself about 'em. The only other thing I ever wanted to be was a lion tamer. Lions are the most beautiful of all the animals, so *massive*; I just wanted to hug 'em when my father took me to the zoo. But I became a *man* tamer instead. A reporter asked me recently what I wanted to be remembered for and I told him, "*Everything.*" That about sums it up.

PLAYBOY: Thank you very much, Miss West. You've been most generous with your time.

WEST: It was *fun* for me, dear. I always enjoy talkin' about myself. Goodnight, love. And come up any time.

June 1973

WALTER CRONKITE

A candid conversation with America's most trusted television newsman

In commenting on the demise of *Life* magazine last autumn, former chief editorial writer John K. Jessup remarked, "Except maybe for Walter Cronkite, there is no more focal point of national information cutting across these special interests, no cracker barrel, no forum, no well." Certainly, if God had set out to create a prototypical middle American, He could have done little better than limn the image of the sad-eyed 56-year-old man—at his CBS anchor desk in New York—whose military-drum-roll voice, sending modulator needles flickering toward the bass registers, has become part of our collective consciousness. *Time* magazine has described Cronkite as "the single most convincing and authoritative figure in television news," and a survey conducted by Oliver Quayle and Company to measure trust in prominent figures showed Cronkite leading everyone—including presidential candidates Richard Nixon, Edmund Muskie, Hubert Humphrey and George McGovern.

But while Cronkite is regarded by the public as a fatherly, sympathetic figure, he has a rather more volatile reputation among his colleagues in the broadcast industry, where he's known as a tough, jealous and outspoken guardian of newsmen's rights. When Vice President Agnew made his now-famous speech in Des Moines in 1969, sneering at TV news commentators as "a tiny, enclosed fraternity of privileged men elected by no one and enjoying a monopoly sanctioned and licensed by government," Cronkite was among the first broadcasters to join the battle. Agnew's speech, he charged, was "a clear effort at intimidation." In May 1971, while most network news executives were taking refuge in corporate anonymity, Cronkite lashed out at the Nixon administration for committing "a crime against the people" by trying to prevent TV from doing its job as the people's observer of the performance of their elected representatives.

This position at the barricades is, in fact, a highly distasteful one for the Missouri-born, Texas-educated dentist's son, who has avowed no greater desire in his 22 years at CBS than to be where the news is. "Punditry doesn't really appeal to me," he once told TV critics in New York. Cronkite joined United Press after his college days at the University of Texas and, when World War II broke out, he became a top U.P. correspondent—filing eyewitness dispatches from the Battle of the North Atlantic in 1942, landing with the invading Allied troops in North Africa in November of that year, taking part in the Normandy beachhead assaults in 1944, dropping into Holland with the 101st Airborne Division and riding with General Patton's Third Army to the rescue of encircled American troops at the Battle of the Bulge in December 1944. After the war, Cronkite re-established U.P. bureaus in Belgium, Holland and Luxembourg, and he was chief U.P. correspondent at the Nuremberg trials of Göring, Hess and other Nazis before becoming U.P.'s chief correspondent in Moscow. Returning home in 1948, he broadcast events in Washington for a group of Midwestern radio stations before joining CBS News, where he became managing editor in 1963.

Before and since going to CBS, he has been present at most of the major news events of his time; perhaps his strongest identification in recent years has been with coverage of the United States space program, for which he has received two Emmy awards. He has also been a fixture of CBS's political-convention coverage from its infancy in 1952 through the 1972 campaign—with one important, and humiliating exception. In 1964, CBS pulled Cronkite out of his anchorman's post for the Democratic Convention, substituting Roger Mudd and Robert Trout in an attempt to counter the rating success of NBC's Chet Huntley and David Brinkley. Cronkite's professional pride was deeply hurt, but he accepted the decision without public or private comment—and was back in the driver's seat after TV critics and the public voiced loud displeasure. Never again has he been so cavalierly treated by his network.

Though he has always cherished his old wire-service-bred belief in objectivity, Cronkite has occasionally departed from his impersonal role. Sometimes the departures were unintentional—as when his voice broke with emotion in November 1963 as he announced President Kennedy's assassination, and when he gleefully chortled "Oh, boy!" on witnessing the blast-off of *Apollo 11* for the moon in July 1969. Sometimes they were deliberate: In March 1968, after a two-week visit to Vietnam, he concluded several newscasts with ringing statements of his view that the administration was wrong in its policies there. And on at least one on-the-air occasion, Cronkite got just plain mad. During the 1968 Democratic National Convention in Chicago after seeing a CBS correspondent punched on the convention floor by security officers, he fumed: "If this sort of thing continues, it makes us, in our anger, want to just turn off our cameras and pack up our microphones and our typewriters and get the devil out of this town and leave the Democrats to their agony."

He didn't pack up, of course. He hung in there and saw the story through, as he has ever since his first days as a wire-service reporter. Thoroughness is a Cronkite hallmark—as evidenced in two of last year's most incisive news specials: a three-part series on the controversial U.S. Soviet wheat deal and an in-depth report on the Watergate scandal, both of which he put together after returning from trips with President Nixon's entourage to China and the Soviet Union.

It's likely that Walter Cronkite has talked, on-mike, with more of the world's headline makers than has any other living American—with the possible exception of Henry Kissinger—and many of his interviews have been considered landmarks of broadcast journalism. In September 1963, he inaugurated *The CBS Evening News with Walter Cronkite*, network TV's first half-hour, five-day-a-week news broadcast, with an exclusive conversation with President Kennedy. Among his other subjects: Egypt's President Anwar El-Sadat, Israel's Premier Golda Meir, Yugoslavia's President Tito, West Germany's Chancellor Willy Brandt, Britain's Prince Philip, and Daniel Ellsberg, the man who released the Pentagon papers. Most recently, Cronkite conducted a series of four interviews with former President Lyndon Johnson, the last taking place just 10 days before Johnson's death in January.

To get a summing up of Cronkite's own feelings about his 40 years in journalism and about the current contretemps between the government and the press, *Playboy* assigned *Chicago Sun-Times* TV critic Ron Powers to interview Cronkite in New York. His report:

"Walter Cronkite is a Walter Mitty in reverse: He is a famous man who has fantasies of being ordinary. His office—a pristine cubbyhole just off the *Evening News* set at CBS's big broadcast barn on West 57th Street in New York—proves it. There are the obligatory 'serious books' about presidents and nations, the plastic-lined wastebasket, the three TV sets and the 'Facts on File.' But there is also a large, sentimental oil painting of a sailing boat (boating is Cronkite's favorite recreation), a box of chocolates and a cardboard-cutout statue of *Apollo* spacemen, a grade-schooler's gift that Cronkite keeps as a souvenir.

"He never loosened his necktie as we talked, but he propped his feet up on his desk and alternately clasped his hands behind his head and fiddled with his stretch socks. At one point he interrupted the interview to take a phone call from some dignitary; the one snatch of conversation I heard was, 'This is between you and me and the fence post. . . .' He coughed frequently—blaming it on a cold—and his voice in conversation was surprisingly low, as though he were trying to protect the throat that had recently undergone surgery for removal of a benign tumor. (He insisted he was fine now.) His eyes, so penetrating on the screen, seem pale and sensitive in person. He has the old-time journalist's knack of forming his thoughts into cogent, parsable sentences as he speaks, and he displayed a gift for the lyric phrase when talking of his reveries at the helm of his boat or of memories of childhood days in Texas.

"I frequently sensed a mild, resigned puzzlement that the life of a superstar had come to him. He was unfailingly courteous with me, but on the topic that was obviously foremost in his mind—current government ploys to muffle newsmen in the pursuit of their work—he was neither mild nor resigned. He was visibly steamed, in fact, when we discussed the subject, which I broached in my first question."

PLAYBOY: You are perhaps the most outspoken of all newsmen in defending broadcasters' rights against government intimidation. In fact, you have used the word conspiracy in describing the Nixon administration's efforts to discredit the press. How would you characterize this conspiracy?

CRONKITE: Let me say, first of all, that after I used the word conspiracy the first and only time, in a speech to the International Radio and Television Society in New York a couple of years ago, I began to regret the use of the word—only because I found that there were still people who equated conspiracy with some of the witch-hunts of the past. The word has nearly lost its true meaning. Having said that, I still feel that this is basically what has taken place: a well-directed campaign against the press, agreed upon in secret by members of the administration. I can't see how it's possible to have such an orchestrated, coordinated campaign without some prior plan and agreement—which really comes out to be a conspiracy.

PLAYBOY: Can you trace it to one person in the administration?

CRONKITE: I certainly think that the president has to be held accountable, since he's the boss.

PLAYBOY: Do you attribute Nixon's hostility toward the press to his personal bitterness about the way the press has treated him?

CRONKITE: I think that may be true, although it's very hard to ascribe motivation to anybody. Circumstantially, the evidence would point to that. Certainly, he's had his bouts with the press before; his disappointments have been shown in public. There is the case of the 1962 gubernatorial concession statement in California. There is his failure just in recent months, at a very critical time in history, to appear more frequently before the press and the public to explain the workings of the administration. I think all these things point to that general attitude toward the press.

I don't know what happened inside the administration. I don't know at what point its members decided that it would be wise to attempt to bring down the press's credibility in an attempt to raise their own. But I think that's what has happened. It's sort of like that U tube we used to see in physics class that shows the countereffects of pressure: When you put pressure on one side and the level goes down, the level of the water on the other side has to rise. Extending that theory, if you could lower the credibility of the press, you could raise the credibility of the politicians. That must be the underlying theory in their attack.

PLAYBOY: Who, besides the president, are the men involved in this attack?

CRONKITE: I'd include almost everybody on the White House staff. You've got Herb Klein and Ron Ziegler to be considered in there. You've also got the advisors, Bob Haldeman and John Ehrlichman, and the speechwriter, Pat Buchanan. Of course, it's unfair in a way to lump them all together, because I don't know who in that group might be raising a dissenting voice and suggesting that this is *not* the way to go about handling the press relations of this administration.

PLAYBOY: Nearly all politicians have felt the need to control the press to some degree. Is this administration simply more sophisticated than its predecessors in the techniques of applying pressure effectively?

CRONKITE: I don't know that they're any more sophisticated, but they're the first ones who have deliberately set out to *use* those techniques.

PLAYBOY: What has been the chronology of this attack? Was Vice President Agnew's 1969 Des Moines speech—in which he attacked the "tiny, enclosed fraternity of privileged men"—the start of it all?

CRONKITE: I think that was the open declaration in the battle. Before that, it was simply felt that this administration's antagonism had been about like the antagonism shown by previous administrations, Democratic as well as Republican—particularly Democratic—toward the press. An adversary relationship, we all agree, is a good thing. But the Agnew attack suddenly became a matter of administration policy and, more than that, a threat to use governmental weapons against the press. Then following Agnew's speech, there was a tightening in attitudes on the part of press-relations people in the government. It was a subtle thing.

PLAYBOY: Not being cooperative with reporters?

CRONKITE: Yes. And clearly displaying a feeling that they felt they were under pressure from the press but that they were going to be protected higher up. They took the hard line.

PLAYBOY: There have been private complaints by news executives of other networks about rather direct applications of this hard line. They say that staff aides of the FCC, and sometimes administration staff people, upon hearing that a controversial documentary is in the works, will telephone the station managers of affiliate stations and remind them that their license is coming due for renewal in a few months. They raise that reminder in connection with whether the station manager is going to clear the documentary for broadcast or not. Has that happened at CBS?

CRONKITE: I haven't heard anything like that here at CBS, but that doesn't mean it doesn't happen.

PLAYBOY: In December of last year, Clay T. Whitehead, who is President Nixon's communications advisor, announced to a journalism fraternity in Indianapolis that a bill was in the works that would place a local station's license in jeopardy if the station couldn't "demonstrate meaningful service to the community." Whitehead said "the community-accountability standard will have special meaning for all network affiliates. They should be held accountable to their local audiences for the 61 percent of their schedules that are network programs." Whitehead used the words bias and balance in defining this accountability. What do you think is behind such a requirement?

CRONKITE: I think the administration would like to deflate, if possible, the power of the network news programs. But I don't know how in the world local station owners could do that. I think it's impossible. On the basis of what knowledge are they going to edit locally what we broadcast nationally? They don't have the sources of information available at their fingertips, as we do. Are they going to challenge a statement made by a network news correspondent in Saigon? How are they going to do that? Are they simply going to decide it doesn't sound right to them? Or it doesn't sound fair to them? I think this is what Mr. Whitehead would like to impose.

PLAYBOY: Why?

CRONKITE: This administration clearly feels that its strength is out in the country, in the smaller communities, the land of the great silent American, as they would have it. The networks, this thinking goes, are more "liberal" in their outlook than the individual stations. I think they might be fooled in that assumption if they began to tamper with the flow of news. But the other part of Whitehead's proposition was the carrot dangling at the end of the stick: an increase in the license term to five years, instead of the present three. This would mean vast savings in legal fees for the station owner. The bill would also assure the owner that if anyone challenged his license, it would be up to the challenger to present proof that the station hadn't performed its function, rather than the station owner's responsibility, as now defined by law, to prove he'd done a good job. And that, obviously, is very appealing—and rather insidious as a temptation to "cooperate" with the government. But I think most station owners know there's no practical way they can exercise any real judgment over network programming, either entertainment or news.

PLAYBOY: They could decide to cancel the network feed.

CRONKITE: Yes, they certainly could. I would assume that that's the intent of the Whitehead proposal, in its ultimate: If the networks don't shape up by reflecting community attitudes, then the only recourse of the local station is to cancel them. Which means that you would be frozen in the establishment attitude of each individual community. If network news didn't coincide precisely with the view at the local level, off the air we'd go. If enough local stations did that, you wouldn't have network news any longer. But I don't think that's likely to happen.

PLAYBOY: Wouldn't it be possible for local-station anchormen to use the same sources of information that you have at the network level and to give their own national newscasts?

CRONKITE: Certainly. They can use the AP and the UPI, just as we do. But the great bulk of our reporting is with our own network correspondents, our own film crews around the world. I don't know who would supply the local stations with film. There have been attempts at syndicated news-film services that haven't been successful. I think it would be fine to have a television news association similar to the AP or the UPI, an association in which you would have a staff of foreign correspondents and foreign film crews. But it's a very expensive proposition, and it would cost the local stations a great deal more than the present system of taking network news, which is subsidized by the network.

PLAYBOY: You had lunch with Mr. Whitehead recently. Did you raise these arguments with him?

CRONKITE: Yes, it was a diplomats' day; we had a "frank and open discussion." And, as the diplomats say privately, it didn't come to anything. We had, I must say, a quite pleasant lunch, but we have a fundamental disagreement on these matters.

PLAYBOY: What's the nature of your disagreement?

CRONKITE: Well, it gets down to a couple of things. First, Mr. Whitehead suggests that he's not really trying to get at network news; that's not the purpose of the license-renewal bill. If that wasn't the intent, I asked him, why did he make that speech to a journalism fraternity? And he said. "Well, it just seemed like a good forum at the time." I found that a little disingenuous. Then, secondly, he maintains that the administration feels network news must exercise a greater degree of "professional responsibility." I really couldn't get a definition from him of just what that "professional responsibility" is. I'd have a hard time defining professional responsibility myself. But my hackles rise when I hear it suggested that we're *not* responsible. We in broadcast news have ethics we defend and maintain as strongly as a doctor or a lawyer does; in fact, a lot *more* strongly than some doctors and lawyers I know.

PLAYBOY: Doctors and lawyers have rather well-defined codes of professional standards, but journalists don't. Do you think they should?

CRONKITE: I don't really see that they need to be imposed, and I see some dangers in it. Freedom of press and speech seems to imply that anybody can write or speak out, whether he's literate or not. Erecting standards would also suggest that you're going to legislate against the underground press, and I think that would be a mistake. If you're going to accept journalists only if they conform to some establishment norm, you won't have the new blood and free flow of new ideas that are absolutely essential to a vital press. I don't know that Tom Paine could have passed a journalism-review test.

PLAYBOY: One standard that government already confers on broadcasters is the so-called fairness doctrine, which requires that both sides of controversial issues be presented. You have said you favor its elimination because it imposes artificial and arbitrary standards of balance and objectivity.

CRONKITE: Yes. I think the only way to free radio and television news broadcasting from the constant danger of government censorship is to free it from any form of government control. The only way to do that is to limit the licensing practice to a technical matter of assignment of channels.

PLAYBOY: Whitehead agrees with you on this. But he cites three "harsh realities" that he says make it impossible to eliminate the fairness doctrine at this time. The first is "a scarcity of broadcasting outlets," which he feels limits the range of viewpoints expressed on the air.

CRONKITE: I think that's false. There are certainly a limited number of bands on the open-broadcast spectrum, but we've got cable TV, which provides a multitude of outlets, coming along now. And even over the airwaves, how many outlets do you need to have enough? In almost every community today, the number of television stations is limited solely by economic viability. So where is this monopoly they keep talking about? It doesn't exist. You've got more television networks serving out news than you've got wire services.

PLAYBOY: Whitehead's second argument is that a great deal of economic and social power is concentrated in the networks. CBS, for example, does research and development in military and space technology, owns two publishing houses and has phonograph-record, record-club and film-communications divisions.

CRONKITE: That's right. We're big. And we're powerful enough to thumb our nose at threats and intimidation from government. I hope it stays that way.

PLAYBOY: But are you powerful enough to broadcast in your own interest, as opposed to the public interest?

CRONKITE: That danger probably exists. I couldn't deny it. But there are an awful lot of journalists who wouldn't work for networks if they did that. That's the first line of defense. The second line of defense, which I admit is a matter of trust, is that none of the network managements is as venal as that. At least they haven't shown that side to me. I've been here for 22 years and I just don't think that's likely.

PLAYBOY: Whitehead again: "There is a tendency for broadcasters and the networks to be self-indulgent and myopic in viewing the First Amendment as protecting only their rights as speakers. They forget that its primary purpose is to assure a free flow and wide range of information to the public." Comment?

CRONKITE: That's absolutely what we ought to be doing. But that's not just what we're supposed to be doing; that's what we *are* doing.

PLAYBOY: Do you think the local-station license-renewal bill will succeed?

CRONKITE: I have a feeling that it won't simply because I believe that there are enough congressmen today who are alert to the dangers to our free speech and free press that they would go very slow on anything of this kind. I think that this awareness is increasing in the country. Now, I'm afraid that we in the news media aren't popular with politicians, with any political party or any political creed. I mean, all we have to do is go back four years to remember the furor that was raised in Congress after the Democratic Convention of 1968 by Democrats who were shocked at the coverage that we dared give their clambake in Chicago. Now it's the Republicans in power.

PLAYBOY: You say you believe that Congress will be alert to the dangers posed to free speech, yet you say the news media aren't popular with politicians. If that's true, wouldn't Congress be likely to vote in favor of restrictive legislation?

CRONKITE: No. I don't think so. I don't think you have to equate popularity or unpopularity with rational consideration of a given issue. I think a lot of congressmen will vote to support an institution they have disagreements with if the issues involved are important enough to transcend their own personal bias, as I think the issues in this bill clearly are. Those in command are never going to appreciate the press. It's fundamental that they shouldn't. When they do, we'd better look to our profession to find out what's wrong.

PLAYBOY: Do you think what some editorial writers have called the "chilling effect" of the Whitehead bill may have been achieved simply by its being brandished as a potential weapon?

CRONKITE: There is a chill right now on newspapers, and on broadcast news in particular. We feel it to a certain extent here at the network level, where we have the greatest strength. That's why they're after us first.

PLAYBOY: What form does this pressure take?

CRONKITE: We feel it on us with each item we report: that it's going to be questioned by the administration, and in the higher echelons of the network, and among our affiliates. We may be called upon to explain an item, why we used it, why we chose that particular wording. This is a shadow and a threat that constantly hangs over us.

PLAYBOY: Does that threat influence the content of the news?

CRONKITE: I don't think so. It's like a cold draft coming through the door, but I think we're kind of bundling up and putting on our mittens and continuing to do our job. I don't know of any story that hasn't been carried on the CBS Evening News because of a chilling effect, but I don't know that that can go on forever.

PLAYBOY: Besides the Whitehead bill, there have been other recent assaults on the press. Four reporters have been sent to jail for refusing to hand over confidential information to the courts; a fifth—Jack Anderson's legman Les Whitten—was handcuffed and his notes were impounded. And a Nixon-appointed Corporation for Public Broadcasting has removed virtually all news and public-affairs programming from public TV's 1973 schedule. Do you believe these incidents are all part of an orchestrated attack on freedom of the press?

CRONKITE: Yes, I do. I have no doubt at all that they amount to a very serious assault. This administration has tried to bring, and may have succeeded in bringing, the press to heel. It has tried to suggest in every possible way that the press has no privileges in this society, that, indeed, if anything, the press should be put under much closer scrutiny by society as a whole. And this, I think, is a dangerous philosophy. This campaign against press credibility, to divide the nation from the press, is continuing—and is being stepped up, as a matter of fact. I'm thinking of Agriculture Secretary Earl Butz's remark in late February, when he announced that the cost-of-food index had risen in January by the greatest percentage in 20 or 25 years—and then said. "Of course, the press is going to misinterpret this." That was quite a prejudgment, it seems to me. How do you misinterpret the fact that food prices have gone up by the greatest percentage in 20 or 25 years? Butz figures that food prices are going to be nasty and difficult for the administration to deal with, so let's put the blame somewhere else again.

PLAYBOY: Insofar as television is bearing the brunt of this attack, do you feel that CBS is the primary target—that the administration is still vindictive about *The Selling of the Pentagon* and your own news reports last summer on the Watergate affair and the Soviet wheat deal?

CRONKITE: I like to think that we've been in the forefront of the reporting and therefore in the forefront when the flak starts to fly. That doesn't alarm me. I'm not alarmed for CBS. I'm alarmed for the entire country.

PLAYBOY: News analysis on all the networks has dropped off since the administration's attacks began. There are fewer "instant analyses" of presidential addresses, for example.

CRONKITE: I'm not sure I agree with you. I think that we at CBS bend over backward to be sure that we get an analysis on after every major address. Even when commercial considerations might have dictated going immediately from the address to the next program, we've cut into the top of that program in order to get a few licks in.

PLAYBOY: But are these licks as tough as they used to be?

CRONKITE: I don't know. I guess I have to be candid and say that it seems to me that on occasion our guys have pulled their punches. But I've talked with them about it—not officially, because that's not part of my function—and I get the impression that they don't feel they have. But they do feel threatened. This question of "instant analysis," though, is one of the major phonies of the whole anti-network, anti-press campaign. As any newspaperman knows, it's rare that the press doesn't have a major presidential speech several hours in advance. The newspapers must get it set in type, the editorial writers must have a shot at it for the next day's paper. So there's nothing instant about analysis. The network analysts have longer than the print press to study a speech, in fact, because they don't deliver their analysis until after it's given.

PLAYBOY: What about the "instant analysis" that government spokesmen gave to *The Selling of the Pentagon?* Do you feel some of that criticism—for editorial bias and unfair editing—was justified?

CRONKITE: I think some of it *was* justified. I'm not a great defender of some of the editorial techniques used in *The Selling of the Pentagon*. I'm talking partly of rearranging the sequence of a military officer's conversation so that his remarks were taken out of context. I also think there was some emphasis on some aspects of Pentagon public relations that was kind of a bum rap. I think the firepower display and the touring exhibits are perfectly acceptable as Pentagon PR. I think the Pentagon *ought* to be showing the public what it's got and what we're buying for our money. How else is the public going to know? But the government was nitpicking in an effort to destroy the general theme and the impression given by *The Selling of the Pentagon*, which was fully justified.

PLAYBOY: What was that general theme?

CRONKITE: The exposing of a great propaganda organization that has been developed not primarily to inform the public but to keep it sold on a big military establishment.

PLAYBOY: Can you think of subsequent documentaries that have been as tough and crusading as that one? Many feel it was the last of its kind. And it was broadcast back in 1971.

CRONKITE: I don't think the documentaries are less tough. We just don't have as many of them on as we used to, on any of the networks. I think this is a function partly of having kind of worn out the market for them, temporarily. What we have instead now is the *60 Minutes* format, the Sunday-magazine format. And I don't believe that anybody can say that that is soft. It's damn tough stuff.

PLAYBOY: Do you think that the public's apparent declining interest in documentaries has anything to do with the administration's success in discrediting the press? Were you surprised, for example, at the low level of outrage following the Watergate exposé?

CRONKITE: I certainly was, very much so. I tie it to the fact that the people say, well, it's just another campaign-year press attack against Nixon.

PLAYBOY: Do you think the public really cares about freedom of the press any more? Or even about its own freedom of speech or assembly?

CRONKITE: I think people care in the abstract. But they don't understand the specifics. We did a poll on the Bill of Rights at CBS a couple of years ago. We asked people such specific questions as, "As long as there appears to be no danger of violence, do you think any group, no matter how extreme, should be allowed to organize protests against the government?" Something like 76 percent of the people said no, they don't have that right. But the same people *support* the constitutional guarantee of freedom of assembly. So they believe in the abstract but not in the specific. And this is our problem.

PLAYBOY: Implicit in the administration's attempts to force the networks to "balance" the news is a conviction that most newscasters are biased against conservatism. Is there some truth in the view that television newsmen tend to be left of center?

CRONKITE: Well, certainly liberal, and possibly left of center as well. I would have to accept that.

PLAYBOY: What's the distinction between those two terms?

CRONKITE: I think the distinction is both clear and important. I think that being a liberal, in the true sense, is being nondoctrinaire, nondogmatic, noncommitted to a cause—but examining each case on its merits. Being left of center is another thing; it's a political position. I think most newspapermen by definition have to be liberal; if they're not liberal, by my definition of it, then they can hardly be good newspapermen. If they're preordained dogmatists for a cause, then they can't be very good journalists; that is, if they carry it into their journalism.

As far as the leftist thing is concerned, that I think is something that comes from the nature of a journalist's work. Most newsmen have spent some time covering the seamier side of human endeavor; they cover police stations and courts and the infighting in politics. And I think they come to feel very little allegiance to the established order. I think they're inclined to side with humanity rather than with authority and institutions. And this sort of pushes them to the left. But I don't think there are many who are *far* left. I think a little left of center probably is correct.

PLAYBOY: Some critics believe that this left-of-center tendency produces a kind of conventional wisdom for liberals—a point of view that's common to most newsmen. During last summer's convention coverage, for example, George McGovern was repeatedly characterized as a likable but conniving bumbler and President Nixon as an unlovable but efficient manager running a closed shop. According to Richard Dougherty, senator McGovern's press secretary during the 1972 campaign, the press never rests until it has found a convenient tag. Then, unconsciously, it edits its coverage to fit this preconception. Is this a legitimate charge?

CRONKITE: God, it worries me more than almost any other single factor. It's a habit that I justify to myself because of the time element. You quickly label a man as a leftist or a conservative or something, because every time you mention him, it's almost impossible to explain precisely where he stands on various issues. But labeling disturbs me at every level of our society. We all have a tendency to do it.

PLAYBOY: Doesn't the fact that the same labels tend to be applied to the same people by all the networks—as well as by the print media—imply that there's a bit too much editorial camp-following in the news business?

CRONKITE: Don't forget that in political campaigns those who cover a candidate are all living and working together in the greatest intimacy. I mean, there's a lot of cross-fertilization, and these reporters become kind of a touchstone for the rest of the press. That's inevitable, I suppose. But the idea that there's some elitist liberal Eastern establishment policy line is absolutely mad.

PLAYBOY: To the extent that there is at least a tendency to group-think, what do you think the effect of it is?

CRONKITE: To the extent that there *is* an effect, I think it's to be deplored. But I don't know that there's anything you can do about it. We're perhaps all conditioned by similar backgrounds, similar experiences. And you'll find, I think, that if we do, indeed, react in a knee-jerk fashion to news stimuli, so do people in every other business.

PLAYBOY: Isn't that the essence of Vice President Agnew's charge—that newsmen are conditioned by similar backgrounds and experiences?

CRONKITE: Again, he's thinking of the elitist Eastern establishment as our common background and experience. I'm thinking about covering the police station in Louisiana in Howard K. Smith's case or North Carolina in David Brinkley's case. That's the kind of experience I'm talking about—experience of America, experience with the people, experience with the burgeoning and overburdening bureaucracy, experience with those who have a tough shake in life. That's the experience I'm talking about.

PLAYBOY: How do you feel about advocacy journalism—the kind of reporting that puts the sort of experience you mention in the service of a newsman's own personal convictions? Is it possible that there isn't enough of this—rather than too much, as Agnew claims—in the media?

CRONKITE: I think that in seeking truth you have to get both sides of a story. In fact, I don't merely think, I *insist* that we present both sides of a story. It's perfectly all right to have first-person journalism; I'm all for muckraking journalism; I'm all for the sidebar, the eyewitness story, the impression piece. But the basic function of the press has to be the presentation of all the facts on which the story is based. There are no pros and cons as far as the press is concerned. There shouldn't be. There are only the facts. Advocacy is all right in special columns. But how the hell are you going to give people the basis on which to advocate something if you don't present the facts to them? If you go only for advocacy journalism, you're really assuming unto yourself a privilege that was never intended anywhere in the definition of a free press.

PLAYBOY: In reporting an official statement that a newsman knows to be patently untrue, do you think that in the interest of presenting both sides of a story, he should feel an obligation to report also that it's a lie?

CRONKITE: I think you're probably obligated to report it—but you're also obligated to check the records first.

PLAYBOY: Can you think of a story in which a man who's been quoted has been shown by independent checking to be untruthful?

CRONKITE: Yes, that happens quite frequently. For example, there's a Pentagon announcement about the purchase of a new weapons system that's going to cost so much, and we point out that development costs have already run a lot more than that. This is a routine part of reporting.

PLAYBOY: The job of corroborating the facts in a story can be complicated by a newsman's closeness with his source. Jack Anderson and others say that most newsmen in Washington are so dependent on high-level sources, so impressed with being able to associate with the mighty, that they become their unwitting allies. Is this a fair appraisal of the Washington press corps?

CRONKITE: I think it's a serious problem, and not just for the Washington press corps. It's a serious problem for the county-court reporter, the police reporter in Sioux City or anywhere else. How close do you get to your sources? It's a hard decision. In order to protect your objectivity, you can turn your back on them socially; but by so doing, you can also cut yourself off from inside information.

PLAYBOY: Anderson insists that sources tell him things because they're afraid not to.

CRONKITE: Well, I think that's right. But I don't approve of everything Anderson does and everything he prints. He often has inadequate evidence. I think he takes the minor episodes and blows them into what appear to be major scandals. On the other hand, he's the one guy who's doing a consistent job of investigative journalism, at least on a daily basis in Washington. And I do agree with him that there are many reporters in Washington who deliberately seek social favors, to the considerable detriment of their reporting. But there are also a lot of lazy reporters who aren't high enough on the social scale, the impact scale, to get the big invitations. They simply find it's a lot easier to take the handouts and rewrite them than it is to do a day's work.

PLAYBOY: Another problem in Washington news coverage seems to handicap broadcast reporters more than the print press. The networks don't seem willing to spend the money for specialist reporters, and their general newsmen are shunted from story to story, never staying on one for a long time. Doesn't that handicap you?

CRONKITE: Yes, there's no question about it. It's part of our basic problem in network news, something the public should be aware of. The problem is lack of personnel. The reporters we have in the field are the best in the business, I think; most of them are graduates of newspapers and news services, and they are superb. But we don't have enough of them, and we're never going to—simply because we don't have the outlet for them. I mean, we may have room on the *Evening News* for maybe three or four reports on camera and a total of 10, 12 or 15 other items that are going to run 15 to 20 seconds each. It's pretty hard in those circumstances to economically justify maintaining a staff equivalent to that of the AP or UPI.

In television, we can introduce the public to the people who make the news. We can introduce them to the places where the news is made. And we can give them a bulletin service. In those three particulars, we can beat any other news medium. But for the in-depth reporting that's required for an individual to have a reasonably complete knowledge of his world on any given day—of the city and county and state—we can't touch it.

PLAYBOY: There is a famous story that the CBS news director once pasted up your transcript of the *Evening News* onto a dummy of *The New York Times*, and it covered less than the eight columns of the front page.

CRONKITE: Yes. The number of words spoken in a half-hour evening-news broadcast—words spoken by interviewees, interviewers, me, everybody—came out to be the same number of words as occupy two thirds of the front page of the standard newspaper. We are a front-page service. We don't have time to deal with the back pages at all.

PLAYBOY: In recent years, the television press has been criticized not merely for the superficiality with which it reports the news but for actually creating or transforming news events—riots, for example. Do you think that's a valid criticism?

CRONKITE: There's a very serious problem with that. Demonstrations have always been staged for the purpose of attracting attention. There's no purpose for a demonstration except to get public attention and—it's hoped—sympathy. Certainly, the demonstrators are going to be where the cameras are. Certainly, they're going to let us know in advance that the demonstration will take place. Certainly, they're hoping for live coverage. Certainly, if you have live coverage, it's going to be a more lively demonstration than if you don't have live coverage. But I don't think that we're responsible for the events. We unquestionably have an influence on them; but so does a newspaper reporter's or a still photographer's presence.

PLAYBOY: But TV camera crews are very conspicuous, whereas a newspaperman can be lost in the crowd.

CRONKITE: Lights are the biggest problem. And I guess for that reason the Chicago convention may have been the end of lighted demonstration coverage, because lights attract demonstrators like moths to a flame.

PLAYBOY: Television has been assailed at least as much for its coverage of the Vietnam War as for that of demonstrations against it here at home. Do you think we found out from television—soon enough, at least—what was really going on in Vietnam? In the early war years, network news executives seemed to subscribe to the conventional assumption that American generals and politicians were simply doing what had to be done to preserve freedom, and the war was covered accordingly. It wasn't until long afterward—1968 and later—that TV newsmen such as yourself began to express doubts about the justness of America's involvement in Indochina. Wasn't this lag in critical reporting one of broadcast news' great failures?

CRONKITE: I'm not sure I can give an entirely satisfactory answer. The coverage changed. Yes. It changed. It went through several periods. Let's go back to when American troops were first committed over there in sizable, easily identified units, as opposed to two or three American advisors working with the Vietnamese troops. Up to 1965, as our involvement deepened, we were increasing our coverage. We were doing stories on advisors out in the field, and the dangers to them, and the occasional death. But it wasn't a daily flow of combat film. For one thing, we weren't interested in endangering our correspondents to do that kind of thing. But in 1965, when we began committing total U.S. units, it was another story. Here were American boys fighting in a war. The news story became these boys at war. If you're going to do that honestly, you're going to have to go up where the blood is flowing. That's where the story is; the story's not back in the base camp. We were taking the war into the homes of America—and that's where it belonged. In a war situation, every American ought to suffer as much as the guy on the front lines. We ought to see this. We ought to be *forced* to see it.

PLAYBOY: But Vietnam wasn't just a visual story. It was a complex story of ideas, of political assumptions, of men's attitudes. To convey an understanding of the war on this level necessitated sophisticated reporting. How high was the journalistic quality of the TV newsmen who went over there in the early years? How about those guys who hung around the press headquarters in Saigon for the so-called "five o'clock follies"—those no-comment news conferences? How long did it take them to realize they had to stop taking handouts and find out what was really going on?

CRONKITE: I don't think there was any lag at all. As a matter of fact, I was surprised—and a little annoyed—at reporters during my 1965 visit over there. I had gone over believing in what we were doing; I came back concerned because I saw a buildup of forces far greater than our leaders ever told us we were likely to commit. That's when my disillusion began. But at first, when I arrived, as I say, I was annoyed at the skepticism of the reporters at the press conferences in Saigon. They were accepting nothing at the five o'clock follies. More than seeking information, they were indulging in what I considered self-centered bearbaiting, pleasing their own egos, showing how much they knew. And I was a little offended. I thought they shouldn't betray their extreme youthfulness. Maybe, I thought, they were a little wet behind the ears. I wondered why they didn't just do their jobs, ask the questions and then go on and get the story.

PLAYBOY: Didn't the military have a strong hand over there in directing the flow of news, deciding where a man could go with his camera?

CRONKITE: Yes, they did, but they always do in a war situation. And I think that the press ended up getting the truth anyway—and telling it.

PLAYBOY: Well, it wasn't a reporter who uncovered My Lai but a disgruntled soldier, Ronald Ridenhour, who tried for months to peddle his story to the press before *The New York Times* accepted it. There was great resistance on the part of the press to accept his version.

CRONKITE: That could very well be, because this sort of story comes to us quite frequently. There are a lot of things that, if we had the manpower and the time and so forth, we could investigate: the letters that come to us about conditions at mental institutions, or in prisons, or the welfare situation, that undoubtedly are true. But as for My Lai, had it come to us first, I don't know precisely how we would have handled it, but I can see where we would have had considerable difficulty in handling it. Here was one soldier's charge; we couldn't have just gone on the air with it. We would have had to go out and spend a tremendous amount of effort to check the thing out. A really overwhelming amount of effort. And we just haven't got the resources to do it.

I think that the attitude of a managing editor, faced with that tip, might very well have been, "God, that sort of thing goes on in all wars. It's probably not as bad as this soldier says it was. It's probably somewhere between that and not having happened at all. As a matter of fact, we've already reported several like that—obviously not as bad as that, but charges that civilians had been shot, and so forth." And just dismissed this story for that reason. My Lai, fortunately, *was* finally uncovered, to the very great credit of Seymour Hersh.

PLAYBOY: You were quoted as saying that if Daniel Ellsberg had brought the Pentagon papers to CBS, you wouldn't have run that story either.

CRONKITE: I didn't say that. Somebody else said it, I think. But I'm not sure that it's quite true. I think if he had brought them here, we would have gone to a newspaper and said, "Let's work together on this. Let us summarize them and you present the full text." But the Pentagon papers are a tough one. I don't know that if I were the editor of a newspaper, I would assign a reporter to try to get hold of the secret reports of the Pentagon. In fact, I'm pretty confident I wouldn't.

PLAYBOY: Why not?

CRONKITE: Because I think that going in from the outside to get hold of secret papers is legally indefensible. I don't think the press has a right to steal papers.

PLAYBOY: Isn't it just as legally indefensible to print papers stolen by someone else?

CRONKITE: No. Once they've come out of the secret files and are in circulation in any way whatsoever, I'd say then that the public is entitled to know whatever anybody else knows. But I don't think an individual is entitled to know what is inside secret files while they're still secret. Please understand, however, that I'm for complete declassification of secret papers. Overclassification is one of the areas in which the federal government is terribly culpable. But I think we have to get at it through legal means.

I don't believe we have any right to violate the law. I'm a real old-fashioned guy in that sense: I believe in law and order. I don't like the fact that the phrase has become a code word for bigotry and suppression of civil rights and a lot of other things. I don't believe in that for one damned ever-loving minute. But if you take the words for what they really mean, I think law and order are the foundation of our society. And I just don't believe that anybody should take it unto himself to violate the law, no matter what good he thinks can be achieved, because you can extend that right up to lynching. Now, what Ellsberg did is for his conscience to work on. I admire tremendously his courage and bravery and his fortitude in doing what he did. But I would never assign a man to do that for CBS.

PLAYBOY: So a public good came from something you oppose in principle.
CRONKITE: It's not clear yet that Ellsberg violated the law. The trial is still on as we talk today. Ellsberg, after all, was the *author* of much of this material. He was a participant in it, you know.
PLAYBOY: Whether or not Ellsberg is guilty of a crime, is there never an instance, in your opinion, in which breaking the law could be justifiable? What about civil disobedience as practiced by Martin Luther King?
CRONKITE: Clearly, there may come a time when civil disobedience and protest against what is considered an unjust law might be considered proper. I'm inclined to believe, though, that if I had to stand on absolutes, I'd prefer to stand on the absolute of law and order, even in such a case as that. I think there are means in our society to correct injustice, and I don't think that civil disobedience or sticks and stones provide the way to do it.

I'm glad that things have worked out to speed integration in this country; certainly, for 100 years we damn well did far too little—didn't do anything, in fact. I'm glad we've finally gotten off our behinds and gotten going here in the last couple of decades. We have probably been spurred to some degree by the demonstrations that the great Martin Luther King directed. So you've got to say, well, it works on occasion. But I still think the better way would be to do it within the law.
PLAYBOY: The opinions you've just expressed are stronger than any you've ever delivered on the air about this issue—which seems to reflect your views about the importance of remaining an objective reporter. Yet you departed from that policy when you returned from a visit to Vietnam in 1968 and advocated an early negotiated peace in a series of editorials at the end of your nightly newscast. Are you glad you did it?
CRONKITE: Glad? I'm not sure. In a lot of people's minds, it put me on a side, categorized me in part of the political spectrum. And I think that's unfortunate. It's a question in my mind now, looking back, weighing the long-term disadvantages with the short-term benefits. When I went over there, I didn't know what I was going to report back, actually. I didn't go over to do a hatchet job. I didn't go over to be anti-Vietnam, to be against American policy. I was leaning that way; I had been very disturbed ever since the 1965 buildup. I was particularly disturbed over the lack of candor of the administration with the American public, about the constant misleading statements as to the prospect of victory—the light-at-the-end-of-the-tunnel stuff. I thought—and I still think—that was the most heinous part of the whole Vietnam adventure. I had also

been disturbed about the vast overkill, about what we were doing to the people of Vietnam.

But even then, I was still living with my old feeling of sympathy for the original commitment, in line with Kennedy's promise that "we shall support any friend to assure the success of liberty." Nobody was kidding himself about the nature of the South Vietnamese regime, but we thought we were trying to create conditions that would promote the growth of democracy, give them a right to self-determination. So I went out in 1968 still basically believing in our policy but increasingly disenchanted with what we had actually been doing over there ever since 1965. Then, after the Tet offensive, Johnson and Westmoreland and McNamara were saying we had won a great victory—you know, "Now we've got them; this was their last great effort." And it was clearly untrue. That was what broke my back. That's why I felt I finally had to speak out and advocate a negotiated peace.

PLAYBOY: What do you think was the effect of your editorials?

CRONKITE: I think the effect was finally to solidify doubts in a lot of people's minds—to swing some people over to the side of opposition to our continued policy in Vietnam. I must be careful not to be immodest here, but I happen to think it may have had an effect on the administration itself.

PLAYBOY: On President Johnson?

CRONKITE: Yes, although he denied that to me personally. Not just about my reporting but about everybody else's. In fact, in our last conversation, 10 days before his death, he went over that ground again, as he did in almost every conversation. It weighed on him very much, apparently. He talked about the Tet offensive and he said a lot of people were sure it was Tet that really turned him off, and he said it wasn't so and that it wasn't my reports that did it, either.

PLAYBOY: Did Johnson ever confide in you about his feelings on the war? In the course of those last interviews you had with him, did he say anything that contradicted his public statements in office?

CRONKITE: No, never. It was one of the disappointments of the interviews we did. I thought, when he was out of office, that he would let his hair down and say, "Well, there were some points where I think we went wrong; there were some things I did that I wish, looking back on it, I hadn't done." But that never happened, either in personal conversation or in the interviews. And I think that's because he didn't entertain any such thoughts. Our private talks were reasonably personal. I'm sure he thought that they were confidential, and therefore there would have been no reason not to say it if he felt it. He was a loquacious man in person, and I believe these feelings would have flowed if he had felt them.

PLAYBOY: Another about-face for you in 1968 occurred at the Democratic Convention in Chicago. It seemed almost a coming-out for you in a lot of human ways. It was as though you had gotten fed up with being above the battle. You saw Dan Rather get punched out on the convention floor and you made a reference to thugs. And then you said you felt bad about having said that.

CRONKITE: Yes, I did.

PLAYBOY: Do you still?

CRONKITE: Yes. I know that outburst kind of makes me more human in the eyes of the public and therefore, perhaps, improves the impression that people may have of me—that I'm not just an automaton sitting there gushing the news each night. But I think that each network ought to have someone who really *is* above the battle. CBS has 24 minutes of news time every evening. I know I could do 22 minutes of news just as objectively as I'm trying to do it now, and then I could put on another hat and for two minutes I could give a scathing editorial opinion, analysis, commentary, whatever you want to call it. It would be right out of the guts and depths of my soul each day, and it probably would be a pretty good piece. I'd like to think, what was revealed about me in those two minutes wouldn't affect the objectivity with which I conducted myself for the 22 other minutes of that program. But I can't for one minute expect anybody else—except, perhaps, another journalist—to believe that.

PLAYBOY: Some critics have discerned traces of editorializing in other facets of your coverage. During the space flights, for example, you were affectionately referred to as "the other astronaut," and your enthusiasm was obvious.

CRONKITE: Well, I can see why they would come to that conclusion. I don't fault them for coming to it. I was a space booster; I believed in that program. But I don't think that affected my criticizing the program, which I did on many occasions. I thought they should have gone with an extra *Mercury* flight, for instance. There were a lot of things in *Mercury* and *Gemini* and *Apollo*—in the matter of equipment and delays and some of the usual hardware problems—that I didn't think were handled right. And I talked about that during the space shots. I didn't ever pull those punches. But that in no way dimmed my excitement over man in space. I think it was the most exciting adventure of our time and probably of centuries; probably since the original explorations of the New World. I have no apologies to make for that.

Now, of course, it's fashionable to criticize all the money that was spent—"We should have used it here on Earth" and all that sort of thing—but I still don't think that's right. If you could guarantee that the $24 billion would have been spent on our cities instead of on space, then I would be inclined to agree that the money was perhaps not apportioned in the right fashion. But you know it *wouldn't* have gone to the cities. I think history is finally going to have to make some decisions on this matter. I think that those who are being critical are going to have to eat some words before the whole thing is over, because I think we're going to find that space is terribly valuable to us.

PLAYBOY: In your coverage of President Nixon's trips to China and Russia, did you feel you even had a chance to be objective, or did you feel that you were merely part of an entourage?

CRONKITE: Well, you can't help but feel you're part of an entourage when you're transported, fed, babied by management. But I didn't feel I was part of an ideological entourage. They had my body and I hoped they would deliver it back to the United States intact at the end of the trips; but they didn't buy my brain and soul. The problem in China was that, for one thing, there wasn't a hell of a lot of substance to the trip. The great story in China was clearly the Marco Polo aspect of going in and seeing this country for the first time, with live cameras in the streets of Peking and Shanghai, and that sort of thing. There wasn't any substance we could get hold of; we didn't know what Nixon and Chou En-lai were talking about; we weren't told. So the story was, to me, the president of the United States being there and the pictures of the place. That's what we covered. Yet people said back here we should have had more substance. So then we go to Russia, where the story is *all* substance. I mean, there was one agreement after another—in a country we had seen a hundred times on television. And people said, "Why didn't we get to see more of the Soviet Union?"

PLAYBOY: On news events such as these, you're not only a correspondent but part of management as well. In fact, your title is managing editor of CBS News. How much editorial responsibility do you have?

CRONKITE: It's about like being managing editor of a newspaper. When I assumed that title, some of my friends in the press were critical—not in their columns but they suggested it was some kind of show-business gimmick, a title that had been lifted from the ancient and honorable print media. But when I pointed out what I did, I think I pretty well convinced them it was a sensible title. I participate in making assignments, in the decisions about what will be covered, future programming plans—what we're going to go after and, ultimately, what goes into the program. And I edit the copy. Every word that's said goes through my hands and is usually touched by my hands in some way. I edit almost every piece, rewrite many of them and originally write some of them.

PLAYBOY: If you were to quit tomorrow—

CRONKITE: There's a great idea.

PLAYBOY: Would the public get a substantially different picture of the news from CBS?

CRONKITE: Not really. I'm not sure, though, that some of the things I eventually hope to accomplish around here would be quite as easily and quickly done by somebody else, because I think I've established a certain degree of credibility with the public and with my employers as to my honesty and integrity. There's a mutual trust there. On that particular score, I may have a value beyond that of the daily broadcaster.

PLAYBOY: Actually, you're not only a network newsman but a TV star. Does that status affect the way you're able to cover a story?

CRONKITE: It's a major handicap. There's an advantage to it, quite obviously, in that I can reach people more easily than a less-well-known newsman could. This works around the world, I find. I get in to see heads of state, usually through their American representatives, ambassadors or whatnot, just because they've seen television coverage. But, on the other hand, just like the camera that appears at the scene of a riot, when I appear I change the nature of the situation. I can't go to a bar and take in an average conversation, because it changes when I'm there: They're talking to the press.

And the same thing is true even when I meet important people. Yesterday a journalist who was doing an interview with a very important person in Washington told me he thought that his interview subject was arrogant and domineering. Well, I haven't seen either of these characteristics in this man, and I said so. My friend said, "Well, he probably *isn't* that way with you. With you, he probably feels he's dealing with an equal, or has some fear of your power, and therefore is much more courteous, much more willing to exchange ideas." And I suppose that's true. But I think if I have enough time, I can break down most barriers. I think if I went back to that hypothetical bar for two or three days in a row, I'd find that I was accepted as a fairly regular fellow and the facade would wither away.

PLAYBOY: How do you feel about the personal side of being a television star? Do you like to be recognized, sign autographs and all that?

CRONKITE: Well, the autograph thing is flattering; that's exactly the word for it. But it's exceedingly tiring. It'd be nicer if you could turn it on once every few months, as sort of an ego builder, and then turn it off again. It's not fun to be the center of attention all the time. You know that people's eyes are on you. My wife and I like to dance, and we don't do it very often, but just the other night we were at a big occasion, an opening in New York, and we were Joel Grey's guests. In the early stage of the evening, at the Waldorf, we were dancing; but we suddenly realized, heck, everybody's kind of watching us dance. And that's not fun. I'm not an exhibitionist—at least not quite in that sense. I'd like to be a song-and-dance man; that's my secret ambition, but—

PLAYBOY: Wait a minute. You've always wanted to be a song-and-dance man?

CRONKITE: I've always thought one of the great things in life would be to entertain people with songs and dances and funny sayings. But it's just a fantasy. Another Walter Mitty dream.

PLAYBOY: Has your wife enjoyed the celebrity life?

CRONKITE: I think so, to about the same extent I have. That is, I can't deny it's nice getting a good table in a crowded restaurant without a reservation—a few emoluments of that kind. But I think both of us would have liked a more quiet life.

PLAYBOY: How do you escape? What do you do for privacy and enjoyment?

CRONKITE: Well, I enjoy totally escapist reading: I duck into historical sea stories. I enjoy the C. S. Forester kind of stuff—and there are 10,000 imitators of Horatio Hornblower who kind of keep me going. It's about a simpler period, a romantic period—strong men doing daring deeds, and a rather simplified moral code—and that makes it rather easy to take. I really enjoy solitude and introspection. That's why I like sailing. I like sitting in the cockpit of my boat at dusk and on into the night, gazing at the stars, thinking of the enormity, the universality of it all. I can get lost in reveries in that regard, both in looking forward to a dreamworld and in looking back to the pleasant times of my own life.

PLAYBOY: Tell us about that dreamworld.

CRONKITE: Oh, my dreamworld personally is to just take off on that boat of mine and not have to worry anymore about the affairs of mankind, and about reporting them, and taking the slings and arrows from all sides as we do today, since we can't seem to satisfy anybody. After 10 years of it here in this particular spot, it gets tiresome. I'd like to be loved, like everybody else.

PLAYBOY: Do you feel the slings and arrows personally?

CRONKITE: Yes, I do. Most of them aren't directed at me personally, but they disturb me deeply anyway. And the criticism comes from both sides. The conservative press picks up the administration line and hammers that back at us; and the liberal press snaps at us all the time about the things you've been bringing up, quite justifiably: about space, about civil rights, about our coverage of the war. So my dreams are to not have to fight the battles anymore.

My dreams for the world are the same. I get fearful about what the world is coming to. You know, most people are good; there aren't very many really evil people. But there are an awful lot of selfish ones. And this selfishness permeates society. It keeps us from the beauty of where we could go, the road we could travel. Instead of being always on these detours and bumbling along side roads that take us nowhere, we could be on a smooth highway to such a great world if we could just put these self-interests aside for the greatest good of the greatest number. It applies to the industrialist who puts out a product into which he builds obsolescence, and to the guy up in Harlem who throws his garbage out the third-floor window. It's everybody's fault. I just find it hard to understand how man could come so far, how he can be so damn smart and at the same time be so damn stupid.

PLAYBOY: You're not alone in being discouraged with contemporary society; some writers are beginning to call the age we live in "postconstitutional America." They view with particular alarm such trends as the tendency toward unregulated, unlimited surveillance. What's your opinion?

CRONKITE: I can't decry it enough. I just don't see how we can live that way. It's not America, and it's not what we believe this country stands for. It's so terrible that I'm convinced there's going to be a great revulsion to it. I think we've come as close as we can to living in a kind of chaotic police state—and I say chaotic because it doesn't have any central headquarters; everybody's doing it. We're living in a state where no one can trust his telephone conversations, nor even his personal conversations in a room, in a bar or anywhere else.

PLAYBOY: Have you ever suspected that your phone was tapped?

CRONKITE: Oh, yes. My home phone and the one here at my office. I think anybody in the public eye—even in private business—who believes that his conversations are sacred today is living in a fool's paradise.

PLAYBOY: The Justice Department, in utilizing such tactics as bugging, stop-and-frisk searches, no-knock raids and preventive detention, has claimed these steps are necessary to control crime. Do you agree?

CRONKITE: I think this erosion of due process is reprehensible. Of course, we do have a serious crime problem in this country, there's no doubt about that. We've got to take off our gloves and somehow or other wade into this problem of crime and face quite openly its relationship to the slum living conditions of a large part of our population, and the resultant welfare circumstances in which they live, the resultant slippage in moral standards—that is, honesty, integrity, hard work and all those old fundamentals.

PLAYBOY: The increase of street crime has been blamed by some on Supreme Court decisions that conservatives feel protected the rights of criminals at the expense of their victims. More recently, it's been the liberals who have attacked the Court, particularly since its decisions have begun to be redirected by its Nixon appointees. Where do you think the Supreme Court is headed?

CRONKITE: Reading the past and looking at this Court now, in view of the most recent major decision, the abortion decision, I think it's impossible to predict the course of the Supreme Court. And I think one makes a mistake to do so. I think in our history we've been very lucky in our Supreme Court Justices, even as we have with our presidents. For different reasons, perhaps, but the system seems to work pretty well. I've been appalled by a couple of recent Supreme Court decisions, but I was appalled by a couple of Warren Court decisions, too.

PLAYBOY: What decisions of the Burger Court have you found appalling?

CRONKITE: Well, primarily the matter of subpoena of newspapermen and their responsibility to reveal sources. I think that was disastrous, absolutely disastrous. But where the Court is going, where it's going to end is anybody's guess. It's a more conservative Court, to judge by its performance so far; but look at some of the people who, after coming on the Court, have taken positions that seemed absolutely antithetical to their past records. Justice Hugo Black was one of the most controversial men to go on the Supreme Court, I suppose. And he turned out to be one of the greats.

PLAYBOY: Isn't the current Court among the most political in American history?

CRONKITE: Well, I suppose that people of liberal persuasion would be inclined to think that, even as people of a conservative persuasion were inclined to think that the Warren Court was a terribly political Court. I'm very hesitant about criticizing the Supreme Court at this point. I think it has every promise of being a fair Court, if it goes down the line. I'd hate to prejudge it at this stage.

PLAYBOY: Are you concerned about backsliding in the enforcement of earlier Court decisions in the area of civil rights?

CRONKITE: Well, yes, though I don't know that it's any more than a swing of the pendulum. But it's to be regretted, because I believe we were making progress. As for busing, though, I've got to be honest about it: That never seemed to me to be the right solution. I think breaking down housing patterns—mixing up the neighborhoods, to use the phrase of some people—is the answer, rather than putting kids in buses for three, four and five hours a day. I don't care whether you're black or white, the neighborhood school is a fundamental concept. Admittedly, I've always believed that you must break down the patterns of segregation and prejudice through schooling; you've got to start with the child. But I think that busing, as hard as it's been to sell to people, is too easy a solution. I think that other solutions—like housing integration and equal employment opportunity—may be tougher, may take longer, may be more expensive, but I think they've got to be better.

PLAYBOY: Would it be fair to describe your position on race relations—and most other issues—as middle of the road?

CRONKITE: I think it probably would. I just don't understand hard-shell, doctrinaire, knee-jerk positions. I don't understand people not seeing both sides, not seeing the justice of other people's causes. I have a very difficult time penetrating what motivates such people. I'm speaking now of the particularly militant left as well as the particularly militant right. But I'm also speaking of people in that great center, whom I sometimes despair of when they accept so glibly the condemnation of other factions within our society—whether it's welfare people or the rich.

There are many people in this silent America who are bitter against the rich. We forget that. You know, from my Midwestern background, I know the Archie Bunkers of Kansas City; they're really basically my own family. I know exactly how they felt about all other walks of society, the lower classes as well as the upper. Unless you were a 32nd-degree Mason living on Benton Boulevard in Kansas City, Missouri, and a white Protestant, there was something a little wrong with you.

PLAYBOY: With that kind of background, where did you get your sense of fairness?

CRONKITE: From my parents. My father was a liberal when he was a young man. Though he's basically kind of set in his ways, as older people are inclined to be, he was terribly upset over the treatment of blacks when we moved to Texas. He went down to teach at the University of Texas Dental School in Houston, and also to practice. And the very first crack out of the box, the first social occasion we went to, we were sitting on the porch of the rich sponsor down there, in a fancy section of town—such a fancy section it didn't have alleys—and we ordered ice cream. In those days, nobody had a freezer, so you ordered it from the drugstore. A young black delivery boy brought it over.

There wasn't any alley, as I say, and he parked his motorcycle out in front of the place and walked up the front walk, across the lawn. And this fellow sat, with rage obviously building in him, and watched him come up the walk. When this young man set his foot on the first step of the porch, this fellow leaped out of his chair and dashed across the porch and smacked him right in the middle of the face. He said, "That'll teach you niggers to walk up to a white man's front door." And my father got up and said, "We're leaving." We almost went back to Kansas City. Growing up in the South, one's attitudes are affected quite seriously by such early experiences.

PLAYBOY: Do any other such experiences come to mind?

CRONKITE: Well, there was another one that also involved ice cream. This time *I* was the drugstore delivery boy; I did bicycle deliveries and we had a couple of blacks who used motorcycles for more distant orders. They were both great guys. One of them was a particularly close friend of mine—as close as you could be in the environment of Houston at that time. We weren't about to go out together anywhere, but we were good friends at the drugstore and sat out back and pitched pennies and shot crap and a few things like that.

As I say, he was a very nice guy, came from a nice family. His mother was a washerwoman, his father was a yardman, but they had great dignity. He had three or four brothers and sisters. Anyway, one night, as he parked his motorcycle and was walking between two houses to deliver some ice cream to the back door, he was *shot* by one of the occupants—the one who hadn't ordered the ice cream. He was listed as a peeping Tom and the murder was considered justified. Incredible. I mean, this guy was no more a peeping Tom than I was—maybe less so. Of course, if he'd gone to the front of the house, the guy who ordered the ice cream might have shot him. I almost never got over that case.

PLAYBOY: When did you decide to become a journalist?

CRONKITE: About the time I started junior high school. I became the happy victim of childhood Walter Mittyism, and it's never really gone away. *The American Boy* magazine ran a series of short stories on careers. They were fictionalized versions of what people did in life. And there were only two that really fascinated me at that point. One was mining engineering and the other was journalism. Anyway, I started working on the high school paper in Houston and I found that was what I wanted to do. In fact, that's really *all* I wanted to do. I didn't want to go to school anymore. But I did. I worked my way through the University of Texas in Austin as a newspaper reporter and did a little radio. Did a lot of other things, too, such as working in a bookie joint for a while.

PLAYBOY: What was your job there?

CRONKITE: Announcer.

PLAYBOY: In a bookie joint?

CRONKITE: On the public-address system. When they hired me, they said, "You sit back here in this room, and as the stuff comes over, you read it out over the P.A. system." Well, I'd never been in a bookie joint before, so I gave them the real Graham MacNamee approach on this, describing the running of the race. A mean character ran the place, a guy named Fox, and he looked like one. He came dashing into the room and said, "What the hell do you think you're doing? We don't want entertainment, we just want the facts!"

PLAYBOY: Your first critic.

CRONKITE: Yeah!

PLAYBOY: When you got out of school, according to your bio, you joined United Press and later covered World War II for them, and among the dispatches you filed was one from the belly of a Flying Fortress during a bombing raid over northern Germany. Under those circumstances, was it good copy?

CRONKITE: Well, it had a dramatic lead. Homer Bigart, who was then a correspondent for the *New York Herald Tribune*, and I were at the same base. We were heading for the bomber command headquarters, outside London, to be debriefed after a long day's raid over Germany. We were both tired and I said, "Homer, I think I've got my lead: 'I've just returned from an assignment to hell. A hell at 17,000 feet, a hell of bursting flak and screaming fighter planes.'" I just recited it. I don't know if you knew Homer Bigart, but he stuttered very badly in those days—and he turned to me and put his hand on my arm and said, "Y-y-y-y-y-you wouldn't."

PLAYBOY: Did the experience teach you anything about war?

CRONKITE: I didn't need to be taught anything about war. I had already learned about it. But I still didn't understand—and don't understand today—how men can go to war. It's irrational, it's unbelievable. How can people who call themselves civilized ever take up arms against each other? I don't even understand how civilized people can carry guns.

PLAYBOY: Were you under fire as a correspondent?

CRONKITE: Lots. People take a look at my record, you know, and it sounds great. I'm embarrassed when I'm introduced for speeches and somebody takes a CBS handout and reads that part of it, because it makes me sound like some sort of hero: the battle of the North Atlantic, the landing in Africa, the beachhead on D-day, dropping with the 101st Airborne, the Battle of the Bulge. Personally, I feel I was an overweening coward in the war. Gee, I was scared to death all the time. I did everything possible to avoid getting into combat. Except the ultimate thing of not doing it. I did it. But the truth is that I did everything only once. It didn't take any great courage to do it once. If you go back and do it a second time—knowing how bad it is—that's courage.

PLAYBOY: After the war, you stayed on in Europe with United Press, finally returning to this country in 1948. Two years later, you joined CBS News in Washington, as a correspondent. Since CBS is a large, competitive organization, how did you manage to rise to your present position there?

CRONKITE: I was just plain old lucky to be in the right place at the right time. But I think that to take advantage of luck, you've got to have some ability to do the job. As far as the ability to work on camera is concerned, that part of it was an absolute accident. I never trained for it; I'm just lucky to have it. Whatever it is, it seems to work. I was also ambitious as a young man and pushed myself along, not to become president of United Press but because I wanted to be where the story was. So I pushed to get where I could go. And I guess the whole thing just built up into a store of experience, and with experience came a certain amount of knowledge.

PLAYBOY: In the years since you've been reporting the news at CBS, we've seen America's belief in its own rightness and invincibility crumble, its moral sense lost, or at least mislaid. Has it been shattering to you—as a man who believes in the system—to see all this happen?

CRONKITE: No, not shattering. I'm still sitting here and doing my work; I'm not in a mental institution—although maybe some think I should be. But it *has* eaten at me. Sometimes I think about early retirement, simply to get out of the daily flow of this miserable world we seem to live in. But shattering? I have to say no. I think at times, though, that maybe I'm not as sensitive as I ought to be, that I ought to have gone nuts by now, covering all of this and seeing it firsthand. I sometimes wonder if maybe I'm not really a very deep thinker or a deeply emotional individual.

PLAYBOY: Are you serious about early retirement?

CRONKITE: Oh, I don't suppose it'll happen, at least not in the foreseeable future. I've just negotiated a rather lengthy extension of my contract.

PLAYBOY: So you wouldn't have accepted that Democratic Vice-Presidential offer we heard about, had it been made by George McGovern.

CRONKITE: No, I don't think so. Well, I don't know. I don't know what I would do with a political opportunity if it actually came down the pike.

PLAYBOY: Would you really have considered it?

CRONKITE: Well, if it were seriously tendered—and this is all so hypothetical, because it never was, you know, let's be perfectly honest about it. As I reconstructed it, the McGovern people were sitting around in a meeting and somebody simply said, "Look, I just saw a poll that said Walter Cronkite was the most trusted man in America, what about him?" And I think that's just about as far as it went. Nobody said that there were loud guffaws, but it would have gotten back to me directly if they had gotten any more serious than that. If they *had* gone any further with it, though, they would have uncovered the fact that I'm not a registered Democrat. I'm not a registered anything. I'm a total independent.

PLAYBOY: Do you have any other skeletons in your closet?

CRONKITE: Well, I'm just not going to talk about them!

PLAYBOY: Have you ever seen yourself as a statesman?

CRONKITE: Well, I must admit I've seen myself as a senator. I see it in a very romantic way, jousting for justice and that sort of thing, on the floor of the Senate. But I don't know how effective I'd be in the political infighting. And I think we forget how hard public servants work. When you see them in action in Washington, you appreciate that they work awfully hard, long and tough hours. It must also be the most frustrating job in the world, spinning wheels as they do so much of the time. I really wouldn't want to undertake all of that. Far less would I ever want to be president. Even if I were temperamentally suited for the job, which I'm not, I wouldn't regard myself as qualified—except perhaps by good intentions.

PLAYBOY: Do you think Nixon is qualified for the job—temperamentally or professionally?

CRONKITE: Well, whether or not I agree with some of the things he's done as president, there's no question that he's had plenty of experience to qualify him for the job. As for his temperament, I think it's regrettable, particularly for a man in his position. I guess I just don't understand a man like Nixon—the completely private man. To stand off and almost hold your hands up and say, "Don't come any closer"—that bothers me in anybody, whether it's President Nixon or my next-door neighbor. It must be terribly sad and lonely to be so aloof, to be unable to throw one's arms around one's fellow man and hug him to you. I think President Nixon would like not to be that way; I think he'd like to be an outgoing lovable man. But he knows he's not; it's not in his makeup. Somewhere in his genes, he just didn't come out that way. I think it bothers him, and I think it may affect a lot of his thinking.

You understand that I'm doing this analysis from about as remote a position as one can have. As you well know, I'm not exactly one of the inner circle. As a matter of fact, I'm cut off from the White House today, presumably because of my outspokenness about the war and about administration attacks on freedom of the press. I regret this very much. I'm very sad, at this stage in my professional life—where, rightfully or wrongly, I have acquired a large audience and some prestige—that people in high places aren't inclined to invite me into their groups.

On occasions when I've been with President Nixon—and they've been fairly rare, countable on the fingers of one hand—I've had a tremendous feeling of wanting to reach out to him. I wanted to kind of help him. I wanted to say, "Look, let's let our hair down and talk about these problems." I have no doubt that this man wants to do what's right. But, as I said, I think what he's trying to do in several cases is absolutely dead wrong. I think that the attack on the press is so antithetical to everything that this country stands for that I just can't understand it.

I would love to be able to shut up about all of this. I don't want to stand out here as a spokesman for the free press against the president of the United States and against his administration. That's not a comfortable thing to have to do. The attacks haven't come from our side, though. We're like the troops in the trench during a cease-fire that's being violated by the other side. You know, if we could just lay down our arms and say, "Come on, the Constitution says we have free speech and a free press, and broadcasting ought to be a part of it; now let's just admit that and acknowledge that this is the way this country has always run, and let's run it that way." Gosh, that would be great.

I just don't understand why the administration took this position in the first place. The press wasn't that anti-Nixon in 1968 or 1969. I think most of the liberals in this country would say the press was cozying up to him, if anything. And yet, whammo, this whole explosive attack on the press. It all gets back a little bit, I think, to the president's personality, to his remoteness. He has never been able to sit down with newsmen, put his feet up, get out the bourbon bottle and say, "Come on, gang, let's have a drink; you guys sure laid it into me today." That's the sort of thing that goes on all over Capitol Hill every afternoon. And I think that because President Nixon can't do that, his aloofness grew into coolness, into misunderstanding of the press, and then into antagonism toward the press and eventually into a campaign against it.

PLAYBOY: Why does so much of the public seem to acquiesce in this campaign? Is it something about the times we live in?

CRONKITE: I think you put your finger on it right there. It's a revolutionary time and people are never comfortable in a period of revolution. I think they try to regain some sense of security through the use or threat of force. But force isn't the mainstay of our democratic system. Dialogue—debate is, and that's regarded with suspicion and indifference by most people at this particular moment in history. I suppose it's only human, when you're backed into a corner in debate, to get mad, to lash out with your fist or to leave the room as a last resort. I think that's what's happening today. Demands for law and order are translated into suppression. As I said before, I believe in law and order, not as a code word but as a keystone—along with freedom and justice—of the democratic process. We've got to stand for law and order. But when the effect of maintaining order is to chip away at the Bill of Rights, to suppress dissent and debate, then I think we're in very serious trouble.

I think these charges by the administration fall on receptive ears in much of our country, among so many classes of people, because they feel so afraid, so unable to understand, let alone cope with, the tumultuous times we live in, so helpless to hang onto the values they were taught to believe in, so threatened by the revolutionary changes they see going on around them, that they're looking for scapegoats—and the press is a handy one. It's tragic that they can't see the press as the bulwark of their own freedom. I suppose the only reason I keep going, the only reason I haven't been shattered by all this, as I said earlier, is that basically I have hope that it's all going to turn around. In time, I think there'll be a new tolerance, and with it will come a strong resistance to all of these pressures against our liberty.

PLAYBOY: Where will this resistance come from?

CRONKITE: I think it'll come from the people. You know, we've shown amazing resilience all these years of the American experience. We go through these dark periods, but eventually we come back into the shining light of day. And I think we'll come back again.

May 1972

HOWARD COSELL

A candid conversation with the fustian oracle of sport

Over the past 16 years, Howard Cosell has earned an enviable reputation for "bringing to the light of public scrutiny," as he might put it, sports' most controversial dealings and misleadings. He has also earned an unenviable reputation as an opinionated son of a bitch. As a result of both, Cosell has become the best-known and most-listened-to sports commentator in the business. Cosell's pontificating commentaries and melodramatic inquisitions—his trademarks—have made him a topic of hot debate among athletes as well, whose opinions of his worth run the gamut from Joe Namath's glowing appraisal, "He's the best there is," to Dick Butkus's succinct estimate, "Horseshit!"

Submitting to an interview with Cosell has been likened to opting for brain surgery without anesthesia, yet even his detractors are forced to admit that he has been the one sportscaster able to gain the confidence of sports' most iconoclastic performers. In fact, a good deal of Cosell's notoriety stems from his support for such maverick athletes as Namath, former Cleveland footballer Jim Brown, Muhammad Ali, Tommie Smith and John Carlos—both of whom raised their fists in black-power salutes when presented with medals at the 1968 Olympics—and, most recently, Duane Thomas of the Dallas Cowboys. Says Cosell, in his distinctively lilting Brooklynese, "Coach Tom Landry said he thinks the Cowboys could win another Super Bowl without Thomas, who, in my opinion, just happens to be the best running back in pro football. I'd like to see Landry try it." The observation was typical of Cosell's penchant for direct confrontation with the sports establishment, and whether he's regarded as an irritant or an inspiration, such remarks have caused much of the American public to regard him as the last polysyllabic word on athletic endeavor. For a man who had never confronted a microphone professionally before the age of 36, Cosell has clearly come a long way.

The son of a credit clothier, he was born in Winston-Salem, North Carolina on March 25, 1920. The family moved north a few years later and Cosell grew up in Brooklyn, where life was not without its difficulties. "I remember having to climb a back fence and run because the kids from Saint Theresa's parish were after me. My drive, in a sense, relates to being Jewish and living in an age of Hitler," he recently told a writer. Cosell was a student at New York University, attended NYU Law School and was admitted to the bar at 21. "I'd never really wanted to become a lawyer," he has said. "I guess the only reason I went through with it was because my father worked so hard to have a son who'd be a professional. I remember him going to the bank every three months to renew a loan that allowed me to stay in school." Before Cosell was fully decided on a career, however, America had entered World War II and in February 1942, he enlisted as a private in the army Transportation Corps.

After four and a half years, Cosell left the Service—as a major—and in 1946 set up legal offices on Broad Street in Manhattan, where he became friendly with another new tenant and fledgling barrister, labor negotiator Theodore Kheel. For the next 10 years, Cosell steadily built up his practice, and his clients came to include people in theater, radio, television and sports (he served as Willie Mays's counsel). Through a series of acquaintances, he was asked to incorporate little-league baseball in New York—which he did—and soon afterward, he was contacted by ABC Radio, which wanted to use the name Little League in connection with a Saturday morning public-service program it was planning. Cosell agreed on the condition that the show be noncommercial. Asked to host the show without pay, Cosell said yes. The format of the program called for the Little Leaguers to ask questions of the pros. Cosell wound up writing the questions, if one can imagine eight-year-olds mouthing supercilious Cosellisms. The 15-minute program, projected for a six-week summer run, was eventually expanded to a half hour and lasted five and a half years.

By 1956, the series' popularity led ABC to offer Cosell a professional broadcasting job. His six-week contract called for 10 five-minute weekend shows, for which he was paid a below-scale $25 each. The following year, his *Sports Focus* became a summer replacement for *Kukla, Fran & Ollie*; it lasted 18 months and remains the only nighttime sports-commentary show ever attempted on TV. Cosell's radio audience, meanwhile, continued to grow, and in 1961 he went on the nightly ABC-TV New York news, where he remained until June of last year, when he asked to leave and was replaced by former baseball player Jim Bouton.

During those years, Cosell formed his own production company and produced such sports specials as *Run to Daylight*, a study of the Green Bay Packers under Vince Lombardi, which is still the most highly acclaimed TV sports documentary ever made. While he was thus occupied, Cosell also began appearing regularly on *Wide World of Sports*, where his haughtily contentious analyses of heavyweight boxing caused both the TV ratings and his audience's blood pressure to rise. When ABC decided in 1970 to gamble on televising pro football on Monday nights, the natural choice was Cosell as half of a very colorful team of "color" commentators; the other half was former Dallas Cowboy quarterback Don Meredith. Although a well-known commodity then, Cosell has since become a household name and now not just New Yorkers but fans all over America have a chance to jeer at him regularly.

In an effort to find out whether he's really as mean—or as knowledgeable—as he likes people to think, *Playboy* sent former Associate Editor Lawrence Linderman to interview Cosell. Reports Linderman, "The first thing that struck me was his appearance. No one else could possibly resemble Howard Cosell. A shade over six feet tall, he's all angles and slouch; depending on which way he decides to aim his torso, his legs seem to be either two feet in front or in back of the rest of him. His features, highlighted by a long arrow-shaped nose, are also sloping and angular and he is blessed with a face that only his loving wife and two children could find appealing.

"Though he likes to give the impression of being the original tough-minded hard-ass, Cosell is an emotional soft touch for any underdog. To a very real extent, he feels he is a champion of the downtrodden, and to a very real extent, he is. Socially, however, he is something else again. When he enters a room, Cosell—an outrageous showoff—makes his presence felt immediately, usually through put-ons that can unintentionally insult people who don't know him. Introduced to an attractive woman with her husband in tow, he once said, 'You're a girl of rare and great beauty, my dear; it must thoroughly break your heart to know that you've so obviously married beneath yourself.' But he can also encounter an old friend like Muhammad Ali and convulse him for 10 minutes with a lecture on how he would still be an unknown if not for the TV buildup given him by the master. He's been known to conclude this straight-faced peroration by craning his neck upward at Ali and adding, 'I made you, Muhammad, and I can break you.'

"When he's not clowning, Cosell spends a good deal of his time making and keeping himself an authentic expert on sports, especially football. The night Fran Tarkenton was traded to Minnesota by the Giants, Cosell immediately began calling various players and football insiders to get their opinions of the trade. Then he cabbed down to Duncan's, an East Side pub owned by Duncan MacCalman, the Giants' Tucker Frederickson and former New York Jet Bill Mathis, to discuss the trade with all the players gathered there that night.

"Cosell probably works far too hard. The hectic schedule he maintains catches up with him by early evening. Whenever I stretched our taping sessions beyond an hour's length, his voice would begin to crack and there was no mistaking how tired the man was—to the point where his hands started to shake. What makes Howard run? 'I earn a lot of money speaking at dinners,' he says, 'but I really could make twice as much as I do and I'd still have to turn down most of the invitations. I guess the real reason I go out to meet the public is to try to offset the image I have of being such a bastard.' Cosell's remark provided a logical opening for our interview, which I decided to begin as he might one of his own."

PLAYBOY: We're talking to Howard Cosell, beloved albeit beleaguered dean of television sportscasters. Tell us, Howard, is the acerbic and abrasive manner in which you conduct yourself on the air a professional personality—or do you seriously expect the American people to believe that you're that way all the time?
COSELL: That's not a professional manner, that's me. But *I* don't think I'm intentionally acerbic or abrasive. I haven't recently heard anyone call Mike Wallace acerbic and abrasive, nor Harry Reasoner, nor Dan

Rather, nor Walter Cronkite. Why not? We all know why not: As newsmen, they're *expected* to ask critical questions relating to issues and figures the public has a reasonable right to know about. Well, I'm doing the same thing in sports, but it's a field in which straight, honest reporting has never really been attempted. Instead, people in this country have grown up with the carefully propagated notion that sport is somehow different, that it's a privileged sanctuary from real life, a looking-glass world unto itself.

Through the years, the legend that owners have fostered, that the various sports commissioners have endorsed and that even my own industry has seen fit to perpetuate is a fairy tale in three parts: first, that every athlete is a shining example of noble young manhood; second, that every athletic competition is inherently pure; and, third, that every owner is a selfless, dedicated public servant concerned only with the public entertainment and utterly unconcerned with profit. That's been the myth of American sport and a lot of people have been indoctrinated by it, particularly those over 40 years of age.

So I'm a shock treatment to them, because I won't let them live with the legend. Young people, however, don't buy the fairy tale of sport, nor should they be expected to. Young people know that some athletes drink, some are on drugs, some are racists, and that they can go to any street in any town or city in America and find it there. In other words, they know that sport is just part of the fabric of real life, that it's human life in microcosm, and that the very maladies and virtues that exist in society must exist in sport. It's as simple as that.

PLAYBOY: You say that sport is life in microcosm, but you've also said that it's "the toy department of life." Which do you believe?

COSELL: I suggest that they aren't in conflict. Sport is the toy department of human life in this sense: It doesn't really matter who wins or loses a game. The contest in the arena fulfills the primary function of sport, which is escape. In the face of the stress and complexities of daily existence, people *have* to have escape.

PLAYBOY: Could it be that by introducing into sport the kinds of worries and concerns that plague so many areas of modern life, you make it less than a total escape—and therefore partially defeat what you feel is its primary function?

COSELL: That's entirely possible, I suppose, but that doesn't mean I'm wrong to do it. I feel that my job as a journalist is to be constantly concerned with the vital issues in sport. One vivid example would be the three and a half years of idleness that were forced upon Muhammad Ali. As a lawyer who practiced

for 10 years, I knew that, constitutionally, Ali had to win. I honestly believe that much of the antagonism toward me relates back to the Ali case.
PLAYBOY: Why?
COSELL: Because I took an unpopular stand. Many people were offended by the idea that a boxing champion would declare himself to be a conscientious objector. But that was a matter for the courts to decide. My support of Ali had to do only with the fact that his championship and his right to earn a living had been unfairly taken from him. On April 28, 1967 at 701 San Jacinto Street in Houston, Texas, Muhammad Ali arrived in answer to a call for military induction and he refused to take the one step forward that would have made him a member of the United States army. As a citizen he had a right to do that, and as a citizen he knew he would have to face the consequences. Under the law, if he were deemed a valid conscientious objector, he'd be excused from military service. If not, he could be sent to jail. Within a matter of minutes after Ali chose not to step forward, Edwin Dooley, a politically appointed boxing commissioner of New York State, stripped him of his championship and of his license to fight—in other words, of his right to earn a living.

Mr. Dooley, a former congressman, was doing the popular thing. But there had been no arraignment, there had been no grand-jury hearing, no indictment, no trial, no conviction, no appeal to a higher court, and in a matter such as this, with the Supreme Court likely to hear such a case, there had been no appeal to the Court of last resort. In other words, due process of law had not even been initiated, let alone exhausted—and under the Fifth Amendment of the Constitution of the United States, the fundamental law of this land, no person may be deprived of life, liberty or property without due process of law. Secondly, in all the years of Muhammad Ali's enforced idleness, the New York State Boxing Commission's action was adopted by every state in the country. Ali couldn't fight anywhere in America and, since he was stripped of his right to leave the country, he couldn't fight overseas, either.

But during these years, New York and other states were licensing men to box who had been deserters from the army. So when the Ali case came before the Southern District New York Federal Court, Judge Walter Mansfield determined that Ali had been denied his rights under the 14th Amendment of the Constitution, which provides equal protection under the law. Thus, Ali got back the right to earn his livelihood. The whole story was an ugly chapter in American history and it points up a lesson we learned a couple of centuries ago but which America has to keep learning: that what is popular is not always right and what is right is not always popular. I was right to back Muhammad, but it cost me.

PLAYBOY: Did you suffer financially because of it?

COSELL: Not at all, but it caused me major enmity in many areas of this nation. During that period, thousands upon thousands of letters were written to my company, and when I began the Monday-night football telecasts in 1970, the overwhelming majority of mail typically asked the American Broadcasting Company to "get that nigger-loving Jew bastard off the air." The Ali episode also triggered threats on my life. I'm not trying to be dramatic, but the fact remains that I received a number of phone calls warning me that I was about to be killed. Occasionally, the notion of a sports announcer stirring up people to such a degree strikes me as ludicrous, but when I reconsider the Ali case, it's clear that the issue involved was hardly frivolous and does indeed account for the hostility many misguided people have for me.

PLAYBOY: Why are you even more unpopular with sportswriters than with the public?

COSELL: There are very definite reasons that motivate members of what I call the old-world sporting press to attack me. Most of them are not men of education, and it hasn't been an easy thing for these people to see life pass them by in philosophical terms they don't even understand. The old-world press relates to an era that's past. Most of these men began as—and still are—baseball writers, and they can't abide the diminution in importance of their beloved sport. Baseball simply doesn't hold the place it once did within the spectrum of sport, and whereas the baseball writer's beat was once the most prestigious job in a sports department, it has now shifted to the men covering football.

Further, the old-world sportswriters don't understand many of the contemporary figures in sport today. Dick Young of the New York *Daily News*, a man who has devoted the past three years of his life to downing me almost daily, has feelings about Ali that are entirely antithetical to my own, nor have he and other members of the old-world press ever taken kindly to Joe Namath, another controversial figure I've been known to support. So there is a coterie of newspaper sportswriters who don't care for me and my work. But as Harry Truman once said, "If you can't stand the heat, get out of the kitchen." I'm not about to get out of the kitchen, especially when I consider the sources of the heat; the background, education and perception of my more rabid critics just don't stand up to my own. If that makes me egotistical, I'll accept the tag.

PLAYBOY: You seem to have earned a good deal of enmity among TV sports announcers as well as among sportwriters. Were you surprised when Ray Scott of CBS attacked you, in *The Detroit Free Press*, for bringing to football "an air of false controversy"?

COSELL: One virtue of this interview may be that after reading it, people will think twice before calling *me* relentless. I've known Ray Scott for many years. He's a decent man and a competent sports announcer for CBS. Scott is not malicious and he's achieved a place in the world of sports announcing, but I don't agree with a single thing he said in that article and I don't think even *he* does. But I can understand his saying what he said, for TV sports announcing is a highly competitive, cutthroat business with very few jobs, many of which are attained through opportunism, luck, circumstance and only occasionally through what I like to think of as being some dedication, perseverance, brains and talent. That's why I've gotten to the top in my industry. One of the many clichés that Alvin Pete Rozelle has uttered turns out to be true: If you're successful, expect to be attacked.

PLAYBOY: How much of the success of ABC's *Monday Night Football* do you think is attributable to you, Don Meredith and Frank Gifford rather than to the sport itself?

COSELL: One could probably debate that subject forever. The best test, according to Roone Arledge, president of ABC Sports, is how we do when we broadcast lackluster games. Which brings up another avenue of attack we were subject to—the idea that we had an irresistible lineup of great games. Were the Jets and the St. Louis Cardinals a great matchup? In that second game of the year, we had two teams that had lost their openers, the Jets without Namath and the Cardinals obviously with very little going for them with or without their quarterback. Pittsburgh vs. Kansas City: The Chiefs scored 28 points in the second quarter to end a game that was a mismatch to begin with. St. Louis at San Diego: Each team went into the game at three up and five down. *That's* a lively prospect? When Miami beat the Chicago Bears 34 to 3, the game was over in the first quarter. But our ratings held up for all of those games, so maybe there *is* a chemistry that's right for the country in Dandy Don Meredith, Humble Howard Cosell and Faultless Frank Gifford. And if there is, we're not going to apologize for it.

PLAYBOY: There's no reason you should, yet you've often inveighed against the instant transformation of jocks into television sports announcers. Gifford has had the benefit of years of experience, but doesn't Meredith qualify as a classic case of jock turned broadcaster?

COSELL: Meredith's greatest value hasn't really been in terms of knowledgeability because he happened to play the game. The mere fact that a man has played football, basketball or baseball has nothing to do with the requirements of such a job. Don's value as a sports commentator lies in his ability to say things like, "Well, Roger Staubach is now four for four in the passing department. He's completed two to his team and two to the other." That comes over as such a *shock* compared with usual jock commentary that people eat it up. Don can get away with it because he's country, corn-pone, middle America. Of course, if Howard Cosell said the same thing, the reaction would be, "Who does that vicious son of a bitch think he is? Why, he's never even *played* the game!"

PLAYBOY: What was your reaction when you found out you were going to be teamed with Meredith?

COSELL: When Roone Arledge asked me about working with Dandy, I told him I'd be delighted to. I'd known Meredith when he played for the Cowboys—not intimately, but I'd responded to him personally. He's a delightful guy and I thought we could work well together, but I never dreamed it would work out as well as it has. Keith Jackson was the third man in the booth our first year and he's one of the finest announcers in the country, certainly close to being as good as Curt Gowdy of NBC, whom I consider the best play-by-play announcer in the business. Don't ask me who I think is the best color man in the business.

PLAYBOY: Howard, who do you think is the best color man in the business?

COSELL: Thank you for not asking me. I really believe *I'm* the best, for I have sought to bring to the American people a sense of the athlete as a human being and not as a piece of cereal-box mythology. My relationship with the men who play the game—*all* games—is probably unparalleled in this country, and I bring information about them to the public. But at the same time, because of my relationships not just with the athletes but also with the coaches and general managers, I have an overall view of sport as a further frame of reference. And you can add to these the irreverence with which I generally approach sport. Irreverence is probably the trademark of our Monday-night telecasts—and the reason why Dandy Don Meredith is worth his weight in gold.

PLAYBOY: Was Meredith confident that he could make the switch from quarterbacking to announcing?

COSELL: No. In fact, he almost quit before the broadcasts got started. We did a dry run of the first pre-season game of 1970, Kansas City at Detroit, with Keith Jackson, Dandy and me taping as if we were on the air. The three of us then viewed the tape in New York along with Roone Arledge and Chet Forte, our producer-director, both of whom were sharply critical of Meredith. Dandy, who'd had no broadcasting experience at all, was very upset at the session, but for other reasons. He is a terribly sensitive man, surprisingly creative and intelligent, who's been beset by a tremendous number of personal problems, including a couple of marriages that didn't work out. Don is also the father of a beautiful little girl named Heather, who was born blind and retarded. Dandy had to fly back to Dallas the night we were reviewing that tape, because the very next day he was institutionalizing the child; so he was uptight anyway, and here he was being strongly criticized.

He fully realized he wasn't a professional announcer by a long shot, and finally he said, "Look, fellas, this isn't really my bag, and I don't even know that much about football. I only know the Xs and Os Mr. Landry taught me at Dallas. So I'll just leave." I quickly took Roone and Chet aside and said, "Listen, Meredith can work out. Leave him to me." I then invited Dandy to have a drink with me at the Warwick Hotel across the street. When we were seated, I said, "Don, I know you're feeling down, but I think you'd be crazy to leave. You've got a style that's natural, you've got your own kind of flair and you're a personality. People are going to love you. And you've got something else: *me*. I'll lead you every step of the way. I can name 60 old-world sportswriters just waiting to put me down. I'll get all the heat, you'll get all the light and in the long run we're both gonna win." And Dandy looked at me and said with his usual eloquence, "Gol dang it, How, I'm with ya!"

PLAYBOY: You make a lot of jokes on the air about Meredith's career with the Dallas Cowboys. What did you really think of his abilities?

COSELL: Meredith was a good quarterback. One of the better quarterbacks—but not one of the great ones.

PLAYBOY: Do you think he was wise to retire when he did?

COSELL: Yes. I think Dandy had the capacity to be a great quarterback, but because of a poor personal relationship with his coach, Tom Landry, it was impossible. His retirement turned out to be lucky for ABC, because he's probably the most irreplaceable member of our broadcast team.

PLAYBOY: Since you brought up the subject of replacement, would you tell us why Keith Jackson was dropped from the telecasts last year in favor of Frank Gifford?

COSELL: That was Roone Arledge's decision. Roone has great belief in Frank Gifford and feels he is a very valuable man to have in a company lineup of announcers. He was concerned, of course, about the morality of replacing Keith, who had done a fine job, and who'd done it just the way he was asked to. Arledge told me, "That's my problem and I'll make it up to him. He'll be paid more, he'll do more NBA basketball and he'll go back to college football. There's no way I want to lose this guy." But Roone felt we needed Gifford on Monday nights.

PLAYBOY: Are the three of you as friendly as you seem to be on TV?

COSELL: I think so in every respect. Dandy and Frank are best friends, and Frank actually got Meredith his job. We'd wanted Gifford on the show the first year and Frank wanted to be with us but couldn't because of his contract, so he recommended Dandy instead. Meredith and I became very close very quickly. When Gifford joined us last year, there was nothing less than amiable between Frank and me but, to be perfectly honest, certain tensions were there. Frank was feeling his way along; he didn't want to appear insecure and I didn't want to appear overriding. But by the fourth or fifth week, all of that had disappeared. Frank kept getting looser and looser, until he was as ready to laugh as Dandy and I were.

PLAYBOY: Is the comedy on the telecasts rehearsed?

COSELL: No, nothing is. I don't see Don and Frank until about noon of every Monday game, when we have a meeting with the producer-director. Occasionally, though, things happen just before a game that really get us in a great state of mind for the show. Our eighth telecast of the year, for example, took place in Baltimore, and it was a crucial game for both the Colts and the Los Angeles Rams. An hour before game time, I elected to go into the Colts' dressing room, which I'm really not supposed to do, but I'm very friendly with Carroll Rosenbloom, the team's owner, and Don Klosterman, the Colts' general manager. As I walked in, I stumbled over Tom Matte's foot, so I immediately broke the silence in the dressing room by announcing in my most blustery way, "There he is, Tom Matte, number 41. Does nothing well, but somehow everything well enough to win. And thus typifies this curiously unspectacular but nonetheless championship Colt team." All the players begin laughing and even John Unitas, who's sitting next to me, is smiling, and then cracks himself up further by saying wittily, "You're talking through your asshole, Howard." Anyway, in a corner of the dressing room, I see Rosenbloom chatting with Vice president Agnew, who's a rabid Colts rooter. Rosenbloom sees me and, with an obvious measure of resignation, says, "Mr. Vice president, do you know this man?" The Vice president says, "Why, yes, Carroll, Howard and I have worked the banquet circuit together." I reply, "Absolutely true, Mr. Vice president, but presently irrelevant. Tell me, sir, what is your position on Jewish ownership?" I said it loud enough for all the players to hear and I thought Klosterman was going to hide in the shower. Rosenbloom shakes his head and begins muttering, "I might have known what to expect from Cosell."

I then suggest to Agnew that it would be a nice gesture to go from cubicle to cubicle and wish the players luck. So we go around the locker room together and I see us approaching four black players—John Mackey, an old friend of mine, Willie Richardson, Ray May and Roy Hilton. Just as we get within earshot, I say, "Then your conclusion, Mr. Vice president, is that this team is saddled with too many blacks?" The black players know me, of course, and start giggling, and Agnew recovers instantly. "I didn't put it *that* way, Howard," he answers almost peevishly. "What I said was that an intelligent re-examination of the quota is in order." He really has a hell of a sense of humor and is a good sport. Agnew agreed to do an interview with me to open the telecast, and after it was concluded, I turned the mike over to Dandy, who said, "I hope you all noticed that the Vice president is wearing a Howard Cosell wrist watch." Believe me, we were *very* loose for that game.

PLAYBOY: Aside from being irreverent, do you feel that your Monday-night football telecasts have made any contribution to televised sports?

COSELL: Well, we've tried to eliminate the immense amount of jargon used by sportscasters to convince the public that football is a hopelessly complex game. After all, how many times can people hear that one team is "isolating a setback on a linebacker"? That theme has become the most redundant of all refrains, because it's the most obvious way to combat a zone defense, which, in turn, is presented to us as if it were a work of Aristotelian logic. We try to talk about football in plain English and treat it as no more than what it is: a game.

Monday Night Football has made one other major contribution to sports, I think. I would say that Dandy Don Meredith's erratic march to the Emmy, the most treasured of all broadcast awards, has to be regarded as one of the great feats of modern times. He did it in his very first year of TV work, and that season will always be filled with priceless memories for me. The first step in Don's countdown to Emmy came on the very first Monday-night telecast: Cleveland 31, Jets 21, Cleveland gaining about 180 yards, the Jets gaining over 500 yards, people in New York complaining that I hate Namath and people in Cleveland complaining that I hate the Browns. In that game, Dandy Don gave unmistakable evidence he was on his way by establishing his profound understanding of pass interference. He made that very clear by saying, "I don't know what it is, but it's a no-no."

By our fifth game, however, he really showed just what a classy announcer he had become. The Washington Redskins were meeting the Oakland Raiders and during our Monday meeting, Roone Arledge said, "We've got a fantastic game tonight, fellas: the two great quarterbacks, Sonny Jurgensen versus Daryle Lamonica. Howie, it's a terrific opportunity for you to lead Dandy into anecdotes about the quarterbacks." And I said, "Roone, we've got an instant disaster on our hands. Washington doesn't belong on the same field with Oakland." Arledge answered, "Listen, any time Oakland scores, Washington can come right back with Jurgensen's passes." OK, I would lead Meredith into stories about the quarterbacks.

So the game begins with Washington kicking off and Oakland returning the ball 52 yards upfield. On the first play from scrimmage, Lamonica hands off to number 35, Hewritt Dixon, and up the middle he goes for 48 yards and a touchdown. Oakland 7, Washington 0. After Oakland kicks off, Washington goes nowhere in three downs, and they're on their own eight in a punting situation. A bad snap and Oakland gets the ball deep in Redskin territory. First play, Lamonica to Warren Wells for a touchdown. Oakland 14, Washington 0, and we're not two minutes into the game. Arledge buzzes me from the booth: "Well, Lamonica threw a TD pass, so lead Dandy into an anecdote about Daryle." Right. "Dandy," I say over the air, "Daryle really knows how to capitalize on a break, doesn't he?" Meredith gets right with it. "He sure does, Howard. That reminds me, Daryle and I were on ABC's *The American Sportsman*"—and Meredith proceeds to tell America how he caught a really bad case of amoebic dysentery while hunting in Africa for the network's show. Keith Jackson has his head in his hands, I'm roaring and Dandy's the only guy in the booth able to talk. Arledge buzzes me again: "You hear what I heard? What do we do?" I say, "We wait to hear from the FCC." Says Arledge, "Fuck the anecdotes."

After that, Arledge runs away to Europe and we are now in Three Rivers Stadium in Pittsburgh, with the Steelers playing the Cincinnati Bengals in a driving rain. The game is an absolute fiasco, we are wet and cold and all of us are bored to tears at the start of the second quarter. Then a retread middle linebacker for the Steelers, number 58, Chuck Allen, makes a tackle after moving a half foot to his right. Chet Forte buzzes me from the booth and asks, "Should we replay that?" I say, "Why not? We have nothing better to do. And in the jargon of the ex-athlete, we will call it a demonstration of lateral pursuit." Forte tells me to lead Dandy into an anecdote about Allen. Fine. "Dandy," I say, "our old friend number 58 made that play, a real beauty. Take over." Dandy wakes up and instantly is in command. "Yeah, How, that's our old buddy number 58," he says, checking the Cincinnati chart, "Al Beauchamp, and look at that lateral pursuit." I break up and Forte buzzes me. "Howard," he says, "the fucker had the wrong player on the wrong team. What do we do?" I suggest we let 10 minutes go by and then I'll allude to it with a jocular throwaway. That's not good enough for Chet, who buzzes Dandy. "Listen, you stupid son of a bitch," he tells Meredith, "you had the wrong player on the wrong team. Not another word unless Howard asks you a direct question." Dandy takes his earphones off, turns to me and asks, "What's bugging *him*?" And I say, "Dandy, forget it. You *know* the guy chokes up when Arledge isn't around." I knew then that Meredith had an Emmy locked up. I wish all aspects of football could be as much fun for me as covering the games. If football weren't becoming so institutionalized an American rite, I'd enjoy it much, much more.

PLAYBOY: In terms of football as a national rite, how do you feel about the patriotic displays that now precede games—the playing of the national anthem, the jet-aircraft flyovers and similar demonstrations?

COSELL: I think that every time they run up the flag and fly the airplanes and everything else, they should also hold an antiwar demonstration on the field. I don't buy any of it. I don't equate professional football, major-league baseball or any other sport in this country with motherhood, apple pie and patriotism. That's part of the old-world motif that's gone forever, and young people don't buy it, either. Furthermore, I don't think the playing of our national anthem is a fitting beginning for a football game or basketball game or boxing match or *any* athletic contest; that opinion will probably result in 50,000 more hate letters directed my way. But how is it an evidence of patriotism to sing or hear the national anthem played before a game? That's a cheap and easy thing, and 200 million Benedict Arnolds could subscribe to it and it still wouldn't make them patriots. Some of the military pageantry before games is just as embarrassing. Before last year's Super Bowl, we had the North against the South in a replay of the Civil War, and the Sugar Bowl was filled with the sounds of gunfire as a mock battle was conducted. It was disgraceful.

Likewise, I feel that playing the anthem before a game debases it and cheapens the real meaning of patriotism. The importance that our society attaches to sport is incredible. After all, is football a game or a religion? Do they play it in Westminster Abbey? The people of this country have allowed sports to get completely out of hand. Can you imagine that colleges actually were once places of education and not communities whose fondest wish is to produce undefeated football and basketball teams?

PLAYBOY: ABC, which televises major college football, will undoubtedly be pleased to learn your opinion of big-time college sport. Do you have a quarrel with it?

COSELL: Purely and simply, I'm against big-time college sport, at least the way it's conducted in this country. I think big-time college sport is corruptive and hypocritical. When a great university spends a good deal of its time and money—which they almost all do—on the importation of a 6'11½" young man because he can drop a ball through a hoop, it's a distortion of emphasis and values that redounds to a school's discredit. Young people are corrupted at the very beginning by college recruiters who descend upon them offering blandishments—many of them illegal under NCAA rules. So why should the country be surprised when athletes thus corrupted take the next highest bid and engineer basketball scandals? Why is it that every 10 years in recent decades we've had a basketball scandal? Who knows, maybe we're ready for another one. Basketball is the slot-machine game of sports, the easiest one to dump. There are guys who've perfected the great dump shots—back rim–front rim–back rim—and out, and you can't tell a damn thing. But it's happened. I'm not going to name names, because I'd be subject to legal responsibility. And how can you really blame the young men involved, many of whom are from the ghetto, who are in some cases black, in other cases white, but all of whom are corrupted by the great institutions that entreat them to attend without regard to their pursuit of education or anything else? In the face of the kind of shameful recruiting that goes on, nobody should be surprised if and when the next dumping scandal occurs, because the colleges have been asking for it.

PLAYBOY: Would you give us some examples of what you define as corruptive athletic recruiting?

COSELL: Certainly. I think it's a dreadful thing for a university president to allow a coach to advertise in *The Washington Post* for basketball players to come to his institution, which was done by Charles ("Lefty") Driesell of the

University of Maryland, brought in from Davidson to make Maryland a national basketball power. A much stronger and more absurd example concerned Steve Worster, who eventually starred for the University of Texas football team. When he was a senior at Bridge City High School, Steve was the most famous high school player in America. I asked his parents if we could go into their home and film Steve and his folks in conversation with scouts there to recruit him for their colleges. I couldn't believe what I saw. I couldn't believe that the scouts would allow us to record what they had to say. In came this guy from the University of Houston. "Steve," the scout said, "I want your parents to hear this. Leave aside the car and a good part-time job and everything else you can expect. Steve, how do you like it when you play? You like it a little bit cold, 54 degrees? You got it. Or maybe you like it warm, 74 degrees? You got it. Somewhere in between, say 64 degrees? You got that, too. Steve, we play in the Astrodome. Not only can you call the game for us, Steve—we'll let you call the *temperature!*" Can you believe this? This is what a college is for? See it in practice and you get sick to your stomach.

PLAYBOY: We're not trying to put words in your mouth, Howard, but you seem to be charging that the NCAA is inept at its job.

COSELL: I suppose if one accepts the fact that there has to be big-time college sports, the NCAA can be presumed to be doing a good job administratively, in the sense that it oversees scheduling and gives orderliness to the whole conduct of intercollegiate sports. But in the sense of adhering to the true purposes and doctrines of a college, in the sense of building the integrity and moral fiber of young people who happen to have a bent for athletics, I think it's doing a very *bad* job.

PLAYBOY: Perhaps the disillusioning college experience helps explain the cynicism with which many young players view a professional sports career—that is, if you believe veterans such as Mike Ditka of the Dallas Cowboys. He recently stated that today's athletes coming out of college are a new breed who regard their pro careers as a meal ticket and nothing more. Do you think the young pros of today differ greatly from their predecessors of a decade ago?

COSELL: Sure, there's a new breed of athlete, and although I didn't read the Ditka quote you just mentioned, I remember Mike very well and *his* concern for a meal ticket. During the pro-football war for talent, one of the men acquired by the Houston Oilers of the American Football League was Mike Ditka, then with the Chicago Bears, who received a reported $50,000 for signing. So I don't think he's immune to the notion of a meal ticket. But the athletes of today are indeed different from those who were active when I came into the business. They are men much more aware of the society of which they are a part. They want a voice in their future, and many of them don't want to give up the whole of life just to play football. Men like Dave Meggyesy, who quit the St. Louis Cardinals, George Sauer Jr., formerly of the New York Jets, and Chip Oliver, an erstwhile Oakland Raider, are no longer exceptions.

PLAYBOY: What about men who feel that football isn't their entire life but want to continue playing; will they necessarily come into conflict with their coaches, many of whom believe a pro's total existence must revolve around his sport?

COSELL: They'd have trouble with most of the current pro coaches, but not all of them.

PLAYBOY: Which coaches are considered the most doctrinaire?

COSELL: Don Shula is hard line. Hank Stram is surprisingly hard line. Dick Nolan is hard line. Tommy Prothro is not. Weeb Ewbank is not. Instead of giving you a rundown on every remaining pro coach, let me just say that most of the alleged new breed of athletes will come afoul of their coaches, but if the players are good enough, some of the toughest coaches will let things ride. This was true even of Vince Lombardi, probably the most disciplinary of coaches. The year Vince took over the Washington Redskins, he was watching the players report to training camp at Dickinson College in Carlisle, Pennsylvania. Sonny Jurgensen came in, Charley Taylor arrived, and then up comes this car and a mod kid jumps out with hair down to his shoulders and he's carrying a guitar. Lombardi looks at him with suspicion and spits out to his assistant, "Who the hell is *that*?" And the guy says, "That's Jerry Smith, the tight end." Lombardi, who'd been studying Redskins game films all winter and spring, says, "He can play. Let him keep the hair and guitar."

PLAYBOY: Do you think that Lombardi, who set the style for coaching authoritarianism, would be able to inspire today's young players to the excellence he achieved at Green Bay?

COSELL: Absolutely. Some men are exceptional, and Lombardi was an exceptional man. He would have been exceptional in *any* walk of life—in industry, government or education. The man was a classics scholar, you know, and he was very much misrepresented by a certain segment of the sporting press. Nobody has ever really written about the reason Vince quit coaching the Packers when he did. It related to a very hostile piece about him in *Esquire* magazine by Leonard Schecter and a call Lombardi got from his mother, who was in tears, and who told him, "This is not my son. How could they write this about you?"

PLAYBOY: Schecter portrayed Lombardi as a man so single-mindedly committed to victory that he drove his players as ruthlessly as any general would in a battle. Was that an inaccurate portrait?

COSELL: It very definitely was. Lombardi was fanatical *only* when drilling his team on the football field. And when Schecter's *Esquire* article came out, Vince felt it was a thoroughly scurrilous piece, utterly unfair, and it upset him terribly. When his mother called him about it, he really became distraught, because Vince was an Old World Italian, a very devoted family man. And he decided, hell, he'd lived a clean and decent life and had done his damnedest in his profession. He was well fixed for life and he just didn't want to take that kind of criticism anymore; he felt that if he became only a general manager and stepped out of coaching, the sportswriters would ease up on him. Vince was deeply affected by and sensitive to adverse press, and he never got over it.

PLAYBOY: Were you surprised when he later came out of retirement to coach the Redskins?

COSELL: No, not at all. I knew he was going to do it. In fact, he discussed it with me several times during his retirement period. Vince couldn't sit on the sidelines, he just couldn't. He loved that goddamn game; it was his whole life.

PLAYBOY: Lombardi set a standard of coaching excellence; are there currently any NFL coaches as good as he was?

COSELL: I think not. In my opinion, the three best coaches in professional football today are George Allen, Don Shula and Hank Stram, but they still cannot yet be compared to Lombardi—which is by way of illustrating how great Lombardi was, for Allen, Shula and Stram are really, fine, fine coaches.

PLAYBOY: Given the same personnel, what can these three do that other coaches can't?

COSELL: React, adjust, communicate—and win. There's no question that Don Shula and George Allen can do great things with a football team; their records prove it. Hank Stram gets a lot of criticism from the fans in Kansas City, who feel he's got the personnel to win every year. But that's illusory, because Hank hasn't had great running backs, and only one, Ed Podolak, has developed.

Of course, there are other excellent coaches in the NFL. Weeb Ewbank may be smaller than anybody else when it comes to evaluating players and their various talents. And because he had a unique appreciation for a very young Jets team, he was able to guide them to a Super Bowl championship. Weeb's weaknesses are different. He's also general manager and for him that's a bad situation; when you let him negotiate contracts with players, he can hurt the team badly. He'll save the team $2000 and cost it a quarter of a million. Verlon Biggs, the Jets' great defensive end, was traded to Washington over a meager salary difference of $1500—and he's the kind of player upon whom Super Bowl championships are built. I'm not singling out Ewbank for criticism; I criticized him for three years and I was wrong. I thought his ideas were obsolete; I thought he didn't discipline the team enough and I was wrong. I always wonder, though, about Namath under Lombardi, for Lombardi dreamed about coaching him. I think Namath could have been much greater than he has been.

PLAYBOY: How great is that?

COSELL: In terms of ability, no man has yet played the quarterback position who could really equal Joe Namath. His talent is unbelievable. John Unitas will tell you this, but John will also say, "Look at what he does with it." Joe is a young man who needs the discipline he would have gotten from Lombardi—not in his private life but in his thinking on the field. With all of his talents, he continues almost obsessively to make critical mistakes, such as challenging zone defenses when he shouldn't and thus giving up key interceptions. Namath does that constantly, so I don't think he's yet played as brilliantly as he can. The one time Namath did was in the Super Bowl, when he adhered religiously to the game plan, was totally disciplined, and then you saw the absolutely impeccable quarterback.

PLAYBOY: Is your high regard for Namath's abilities shared by many in the sports world?

COSELL: It is by people who work in professional football. There are at least five common yardsticks for the evaluation of a quarterback: reaction to pressure, quickness in setting up, quickness in delivery, leadership qualities and recognition of defenses. On a total rating of these five values, at five points apiece, Namath scores a 23 or 24, and the closest others rate is 18 or so: Len Dawson, John Brodie and Johnny Hadl, the exceptional and very underpublicized quarterback of the San Diego Chargers. Incidentally, if Unitas and Bart Starr weren't over the hill, they, too, would be up there. Then come the two young ones, Roger Staubach and Bob Griese, at the same level with Fran Tarkenton, who's a very fine quarterback and who may well take Minnesota to next year's Super Bowl. A more publicized quarterback like Roman Gabriel is well down on the list, but not nearly so far down as people like Bob Berry of the Atlanta Falcons and Jack Concannon of the Chicago Bears. Namath has all these players beat by a wide margin. His abilities are so vast that they are often his undoing.

PLAYBOY: In what way?

COSELL: His confidence in himself is awesome—as is his stubbornness. He thinks he can throw a pass anywhere, any time, regardless of defense, but he's human—and he can't. That's about the only thing Namath has to be disciplined into learning. Joe is an exceptional play caller and nobody, absolutely nobody, reads defenses better than he does; Namath is a terribly bright guy. I think Don Shula or George Allen could make him into the best quarterback ever to step on a football field. The only reason I don't mention Stram is that Namath wouldn't be good for Hank's offense; Joe can't run and Stram wants movement in a quarterback because of the Chiefs' offensive variations.

PLAYBOY: Is the quarterback the most important man on a team?

COSELL: In theory, yes, yet it has been documentarily established in recent years that you can win a title without a great quarterback. The Vikings went to a Super Bowl with Joe Kapp and last year the Cowboys got there with Craig Morton—where they were beaten by the Colts with Earl Morrall. What are these—great quarterbacks? Now you see teams winning games in the NFL with the likes of Bobby Douglass and Virgil Carter.

PLAYBOY: You pronounce these names as if each were a communicable disease. Are they really that bad?

COSELL: I don't think they're that bad, but the sense in which I relate to them is this: Throughout all its years, the NFL has carefully and effectively propagated the myth of its own invincibility. Presumably, every player was a superstar—and to be a quarterback in the NFL you had to be perfect, or so claimed the NFL. If it was true then, which it wasn't, it certainly isn't true now. The Bears won the title in 1963 with Billy Wade and the Browns won it in 1964 with Frank Ryan, hardly great quarterbacks by any stretch of the imagination. I think the NFL's finest achievement has been the masterful job of propaganda it's done about itself.

That's the real greatness of Joe Willie Namath: In a single afternoon, he punctured the entire myth of NFL superiority. And then, the next year, along came Kansas City to stick it to the Vikings in the Super Bowl. Conversely, that's the sad thing about Miami's loss to Dallas this year; now old-line NFL sportswriters and fans are chuckling as if they were club owners, such is their allegiance to the NFL. They're saying things like, "We still got the *real* teams—see what the Cowboys did to the Dolphins?" As if the Jets and Namath and the Chiefs and Stram never existed.

PLAYBOY: What are you predicting for next season?

COSELL: That we're going to witness the continued growth of the traditional NFL have-nots; the Eagles, the Bills, the Houston Oilers, the New Orleans Saints, the Atlanta Falcons, the New England Patriots and the Cincinnati Bengals are all on their way to becoming formidable teams. Miami, a have-not just a couple of years ago, has already moved up. Whereas the Bears, like the Giants, another traditional old-world power, are a declining team. The Green Bay Packers have declined, but I suspect they're going to improve dramatically quite soon. I think the Kansas City Chiefs will stay up there, especially if Len Dawson doesn't retire. The San Francisco 49ers have good personnel and will be contenders, and Dallas, of course, may well reappear in the Super Bowl. Minnesota, having acquired Tarkenton, will finally have an offense to go with its murderous defense, and Baltimore has excellent personnel everywhere but at quarterback, which may be a prepossessing problem. The New York Jets have a chance to be strong for many years if Namath can merely stand up; he's a *very* great player.

PLAYBOY: You're as generous with compliments as you are with criticism, but the criticism seems to be what you're known for.

COSELL: That's precisely the kind of reaction I've always encountered when dealing seriously with sport, and that really started with a show I did early in my career. When the New York Mets came into existence, ABC Radio broadcast their games and I was assigned to do a post-game show. Casey Stengel had been hired as the Mets' manager and, of course, he'd been at the helm of the New York Yankees during their string of pennant and World Series victories. Stengel was a welcome figure to have on the scene, but I knew that most of the Yankees who had played under him disliked the man, and soon after he took over the Mets, I saw why. In my opinion—and I said so on the air—Stengel was bad for young people. He didn't like them and he treated them badly. But he was revered by the fans and when I criticized him, I was immediately accused of doing it "to develop a name." What a ridiculous thing to think. I was taking my professional life in my hands by doing it. I wasn't then what I am now, and I was doing it because I'd seen exactly how Stengel treated his men. Like many an ex-Yankee, most Mets players didn't like him; they thought he was cruel and a big bag of wind.

PLAYBOY: Would you care to be more specific?

COSELL: I don't mind at all. There are 25 men on a baseball team and Stengel was the only manager I'd ever heard of who didn't know the names of many of his players, such was his abiding interest in them. I think what finally bothered me most about Stengel was the manner in which he would talk to the press about his players and their failings; he would really ridicule them. Now, they may have been lousy players—and, let's face it, the early Mets *were* lousy players—and it's perfectly all right for a manager to chew out his players in the dressing room. But there was hardly a need to strip young men of all their pride and self-respect in public. Stengel did that. Repeatedly.

PLAYBOY: Didn't any other members of the New York press point out these things?

COSELL: Never. The sportswriters loved Stengel because he gave them copy every day. And what we soon had in New York was a press that celebrated futility. That's all Stengel was there for, to promote public relations, and the team's ineptitude became a gay thing. Well, I thought it was a pathetic thing. There I was, living in an age where, in football, Vince Lombardi was pursuing a quest for excellence while, in baseball, Casey Stengel was creating a legend out of almost purposeful futility. Between the two, I'll go with Lombardi.

PLAYBOY: Did you disapprove of the way Stengel managed his team as well as the way he handled his players?

COSELL: I don't mind telling you I thought Stengel was a good manager. I'm tempted to add, "He knew the game," but how difficult is it to know the game of baseball? Little leaguers could manage a team successfully and the game is so simple that eight-year-olds can play it and understand it and sit in a grandstand and second-guess as well as any fan who's followed a team for 20 years. Since baseball broadcasters are usually hired by the team and therefore must act as shills, it created a stir when I did *my* post-game show. I then learned—by reading the newspapers—that I was being controversial to advance my career. But I've learned to live with even the most mindless criticism, which began to come my way when I first started to cover boxing.

PLAYBOY: Has prizefighting always been one of your favorite spectator sports?

COSELL: At that time, no. I was drawn to boxing initially because of my interest in Floyd Patterson. I was young in the business then and I learned, after doing a few interviews with Floyd, that a number of sportswriters didn't like me because I was producing exclusive material with him. I got caught up in the man's background. Floyd had attended the Wiltwyck School and, later on, one of the "600" public schools, both of which offered special training for the disturbed child—which Floyd was. As a little black kid growing up in the Bedford-Stuyvesant section of Brooklyn, Patterson used to hide in a hole in the subway and he'd sit there for hours until it was time to go home. He was a very undecipherable young man and in a real way, he fascinated me. Since I'd never really been a devotee of boxing, I suppose it would be accurate to think that Floyd was the catalyst for my interest in the sport.

PLAYBOY: Did you think he was a great fighter?

COSELL: If Patterson had been just a bit smaller, he probably would have been the greatest light-heavyweight champion in history. Floyd fought as a heavyweight at weights varying anywhere from the 180s up into the low 190s. Patterson's punching ability was little short of amazing for his size, and I mean to tell you he was as hard a puncher as I've seen. In fact, the strongest single punch I've ever seen in my life was the left hook with which Floyd knocked out Ingemar Johannson on June 20, 1960 in the fifth round of their title fight at the old Polo Grounds. I'll never forget the scene; blood was coming out of Johannson's mouth, his right leg was twitching and he was still out cold when I climbed into the ring. Whitey Bimstein, the trainer, was leaning over him and a chill went through me when I saw Johannson lying there like that. "My God, Whitey, is he dead?" I asked. And Bimstein, barely looking up at me, said, "The son of a bitch should be—I *told* him to watch out for the left hook."

PLAYBOY: Patterson, now 37, is well past his prime as a fighter, and supposedly is financially secure. Do you have any idea why he's still active in the ring?

COSELL: Yes, I know why he fights. Boxing gave Floyd a place in society that he never dreamed he could possibly have. And he has a tremendous gratitude to the sport for that. He put it to me in quite a moving way: "It's like being in love with a woman. She can be unfaithful, she can be mean, she can be cruel, but it doesn't matter. If you love her, you want her, even though she can do you all kinds of harm. It's the same with me and boxing. It can do me all kinds of harm, but I love it." Certainly, as a fighter, Floyd is little more than a shadow of what he was. I think his abilities had diminished sharply as far back as the first Liston fight, when he lost his championship to a man whose character seems to have improved in death as it never could have while he was alive.

PLAYBOY: What do you mean by that?

COSELL: I recently read that as a product of society and what it had made him, Charles ("Sonny") Liston was more honest in his own way than many a do-gooder—such as myself—who had verbally assaulted him while he was alive. What can I tell you? I despised Sonny Liston.

PLAYBOY: Why?

COSELL: He was a congenital thug with a record of more than 20 arrests and a number of felonies—really serious crimes—to his credit, or rather discredit. He was a cheap and ugly bully without morality and I had no use for him. It's just too easy a cop-out to say that Liston was a product of a society in which the black is a second-class citizen and all the rest of that line of reasoning. Sonny was a bad apple.

PLAYBOY: What were your dealings with him like?

COSELL: Unlike my dealings with any other man I've ever encountered in sport. The first time I met Sonny, I mean *really* met Sonny, was in September of 1962. He was getting ready for his first title fight with Patterson and he was training at Aurora Downs, a broken-down old race track about 30 miles outside Chicago. I was doing a radio broadcast of that fight with Rocky Marciano, who'd never met Liston either. We drove out to tape Liston for our prefight show, accompanied by Oscar Fraley, a good friend of mine who'd co-authored *The Untouchables* and who was the feature sportswriter for United Press. When we got to this seedy old place, we had to wait quite a while before an armed guard—patrolling behind a barbed-wire fence—got permission for us to enter. The ring had been set up in the middle of what had been the clubhouse, and the floor was littered with losing horse-race tickets, and all the betting windows were smashed in. The place was so ramshackle as to be almost beyond belief.

The whole thing was eerie. When we entered, Liston was in the ring, shadowboxing to a recording of *Night Train*. There were about five other people there, but no one would make a sound. Suddenly, from an upper level, Liston's wife comes down the stairs, says not a word to anyone but walks straight toward the ring and climbs in. And then she and Sonny start to do the twist to *Night Train*. And all this time, no one has said a word. I'm telling you, the scene was *weird*. I pulled Marciano aside and said, "Look, as soon as the Listons finish dancing, the smart thing for us to do, champ, since you were the greatest, is for *you* to do the interview." Rock looks at me and says, "I want no part of it. You think I'm nuts?" So I turn to Fraley and before I can say anything, he says, "I wanna go home."

PLAYBOY: Did you?

COSELL: Not yet. A few minutes later, his manager talks to Sonny about us and from the ring Liston looks over balefully, gives us a sinister stare and then shouts, "Goddamn it, I ain't talking to no one! No one, you understand?" We understood, but we had to get that interview. When his workout was over, Liston finally allowed Marciano to approach him, but the Rock was so shook he virtually couldn't speak. So I said, "Now, look, Sonny, you're going to be the heavyweight champion of the world and it's not going to take you long. You're going to have to present a whole new image to the American public, 'cause you got a lot to make up for. I don't give a goddamn if you hate me; I don't like you either, and I just met you. But you gotta do this interview."

PLAYBOY: You really said that to him?

COSELL: Yes, I did, but I still don't know why. Liston, though, just gave me a big smile and suddenly I realized that the son of a bitch was really just a big bully. And he finally did quite a pleasant interview. When we left, they were playing *Night Train* again. That was the first time I met Sonny Liston.

PLAYBOY: There are many people who still can't believe that Liston, massive and seemingly invincible, could have been knocked out so quickly—and so mysteriously—by Ali in their second bout. You were there; was the fight fixed?

COSELL: I'm suspicious about that fight. I was then, I am now. I never saw a punch. Certain sportswriters saw a punch, but they see a lot of things. Jimmy Cannon, a fine boxing writer, said he was situated exactly right when the knockout occurred. Cannon said he definitely saw the punch—and that it couldn't have crushed a grape.

PLAYBOY: Were you surprised when Ali beat Liston in their first title fight?

COSELL: I couldn't have been *more* surprised: I thought Liston would kill him. But a strange thing happened in that bout. Rocky Marciano and I were covering the fight, and I believe it was in the third round when Ali landed a right on Liston's left cheek. Sonny had a paunchy, slightly flabby face, and the blow split the whole side of his face wide open, from the corner of his left eye down to the corner of the lip; blood just began pouring out. Ali, if you remember, used to turn his punches at the moment of impact, and they had a damaging, slicing effect. Absolutely devastating; he could really cut a man to ribbons in those days—which is what he did to Liston in that third round.

I'll never forget what Marciano said to me just a few moments after that punch: "Jesus Christ, Howie, Liston's become an old man." And it was true; Sonny stood exposed from that moment on. I don't really have any questions about that first fight, because after Ali opened that wound, Sonny was ready to quit. And I think that under almost any circumstances, Ali would have won the second fight rather easily. But the curious way it ended; I remember students from Bates College running down to ringside and shouting, "Fix! Fix! Fix!" Saint Dominic's Arena in Lewiston, Maine has to be one of the signal sites in boxing history. I still don't know what happened there on the night of May 25, 1965 and I guess I'll never know.

PLAYBOY: Just a few months after the second Liston fight, Ali defended his title against Patterson. Though you've always been a friend and partisan of Ali's, you criticized him severely after that bout. Why?

COSELL: It was clear to me that Ali purposefully tormented an outclassed Floyd Patterson for 12 rounds, at which point referee Harry Krause finally stopped the one-sided fight. Muhammad despised Floyd. He's since grown up and changed, but when they fought, Ali really felt that Floyd was a white man's black man who was a kind of surrogate white hope. Patterson, if you remember, had made a number of deprecating remarks about the Black Muslims and had even had a letter published in several newspapers in which he vowed to bring the heavyweight championship "back to America." That got to Muhammad, as did Patterson's quiet and subdued manner. Ali never took to him and Floyd's attitude about the Muslims really angered him.

PLAYBOY: Isn't it possible that Ali was using the Muslim theme as a prefight strategical ploy in the same way he feigned insanity at the weigh-in for the first Liston bout?

COSELL: That's possible but not probable. I really believe Patterson irritated Muhammad. On the other hand, Ali's attack of insanity on the day of the first Liston match was a great, great act. I, for one, left that weigh-in convinced that Ali had genuinely popped his cork.

PLAYBOY: Since you're a fairly perceptive observer of athletes, don't you think it's possible that he really *did* freak out?

COSELL: No chance at all, and I'll tell you why. When I got to Miami's Convention Hall, where the bout was to take place, I arrived early enough to see Muhammad's brother, Rahaman Ali, fight in a preliminary. As I was walking down to ringside, who the hell do I see standing there but Ali, who clouts me on the shoulder and shouts, "It's my man, Howard Cosell! Howard, stand here and watch my brother take care of this chump!" And I could only think to myself, "Why, that son of a bitch, what an actor! Never saw a man cooler and he's about to go up against the most feared heavyweight in a decade." I realized then he'd put on a show that had taken everyone in.

PLAYBOY: Did Ali ever admit it to you?

COSELL: Indeed he did. I remember asking him about it and Muhammad, with a straight face but twinkling eyes, said, "Oh, I was scared, man, *scared*. I just thought I'd let all those writers see how scared I was. Remember your radio show the afternoon of the fight? From what you said, I was just going to *die* when Liston stared at me in the ring." Ali then paused and said, "Well, *Liston* died when he got in that ring; *he* was the guy who was scared. And I made him scared. I wanted him to know I was crazy, because any man who's not a fool has *got* to be scared of a crazy man."

On the night of the fight, however, no matter how cool I realized he was, I still didn't give him a chance to beat the dreaded Big Black Bear, as he'd come to call Liston. Ali always had nicknames for his opponents; Patterson was the Rabbit, Terrell the Octopus and George Chuvalo the Washerwoman. But after he'd cut and demoralized Liston in that third round, I turned to Marciano and said, "There's no way this guy can lose. We've been completely fooled, Rock. The kid's a fighter." And what a fighter he was. Before they put him into enforced idleness, Muhammad Ali was the greatest fighter I ever saw in my life.

PLAYBOY: Is he less than that now?

COSELL: Unfortunately, yes. He lost so much in the three and a half years he was out of the ring that it's almost indescribable. Muhammad has lost his two basic attributes—the swiftness of his feet and the swiftness of his hands. And when you lose that hand speed, you lose the sharpness of your punches. And Ali has totally lost that punishing ability to turn his punches the way he did against Liston nearly eight years ago. Otherwise, there's no way he could have lost to Joe Frazier. Frazier is a good, tough fighter of the club variety who leads with his head. Ali fought him after all that idleness and you know the damage he did to him. Frazier is not to be even remotely compared with Muhammad.

In their title fight, I agreed completely with referee Arthur Mercante's score card; Ali was leading six rounds to four and he'd almost decked Frazier in the ninth. I'm personally convinced that the Ali of old would have knocked Frazier out within five rounds. And to me it was remarkable that Muhammad was ahead in the fight until that surprising episode in the 11th round, when he lay against the ropes with his gloves at his sides; Frazier then got in a left hook that knocked Ali silly, even though it didn't knock him down. From then on, Frazier dominated the fight and fairly won the decision. But the damage done to Frazier! Good Lord, I was standing right next to his manager, Yancy Durham, and, believe me, they had to carry Joe out. When Muhammad left the ring, he actually gave me a *wink*!

An amazing thing then happened: Within 60 days, Ali had many people believing he had been robbed and that he'd really won the fight—which he didn't. Let's face it, the man is some personality. He's the most famous athlete in the world; there's nobody even close, and that includes Pele, El Cordobés and anyone else you might care to name. In all honesty, I feel sorry for Joe Frazier. He's the heavyweight champion of the world, but a lot of people don't accept him as that. And quite understandably, it's killing him inside. Joe wasn't responsible for Ali being banned. He fought Ali as hard as he could, he beat him, and yet nobody really accepts him. And so he has grown to hate Ali.

PLAYBOY: If Frazier really feels that way, doesn't that portend another severe test for Ali in their rematch?

COSELL: In all honesty, I'm not sure there will *be* a rematch. I'm not sure about Frazier's boxing future, but I don't know enough about the subject right now to talk authoritatively about it. First I want to be satisfied that Joe didn't suffer permanent damage in the Ali fight. While Frazier was in the hospital for three weeks, his doctor talked about blood in the urine, a kidney ailment, and so on. And now it develops that he's got recurring high blood pressure, which they maintain he's had since childhood. Maybe that's true, I don't know. I don't know, either, whether or not he suffered any head injuries. Joe may very well be completely healthy, and I don't mean to imply that there's something wrong with him. I'm just concerned about it because he's a fine young man and I wouldn't want to see him damaged for life.

PLAYBOY: Have you talked to Ali since the *Wide World of Sports* show when you set the "highlights" of his fight with Buster Mathis to music and called the whole thing a farce?

COSELL: No, I haven't. But I talk to Angelo Dundee, Muhammad's trainer, all the time, Angie told me I was absolutely right in my opinion of the fight and he actually thanked me for what we did on the show. He said, "I hope this is gonna wake Muhammad up. He's gotta start training and become a fighter again." If he and Frazier meet in a rematch, by the way, I'm convinced that if Ali gets into reasonable shape, he still has enough left to give him a chance to whip Joe.

PLAYBOY: Supposing he doesn't; is there anyone fighting today who'll be able to keep boxing alive the way Ali has?

COSELL: Do you really think Ali has kept boxing alive? Boxing is a moribund sport, its death inevitable for reasons tied to economics, sociology and electronics. Historically, boxing was the sport of each succeeding wave of underprivileged minorities—the Irish, Italians, Jews, blacks and, most recently, Puerto Ricans. That's because there were never any decent jobs for minority-group members, but equal-opportunity hiring and the growth of the economy has changed all that. The electronic factor was television: Wednesday- and Friday-night fights eventually caused the sport to become oversaturated many years ago. Did Ali keep it alive? Only in the sense of the occasional heavyweight championship fight. Essentially, boxing is dead and has been for a long time.

PLAYBOY: Do you regret its demise?

COSELL: I don't have much feeling about boxing today, but the sport will always have a hold on me because of the men who fight. They are the most interesting of all athletes, for they seem to have the deepest feelings about life; maybe it's because their sport is so naked and brutal and is such a lonely pursuit. You have to get inside a ring to appreciate how small it is; you wonder how men can *ever* escape. There's something special about a boxer and something special about his sport, for it engages our basic emotions like no other athletic activity.

PLAYBOY: Do you still react emotionally to a boxing match?

COSELL: Yes, especially if I'm watching a heavyweight championship bout, a *good* heavyweight title fight, which I believe is the most exciting sports event in the world. It's the *only* event that can totally engulf me emotionally. The tension and anticipation that run through a crowd before the opening bell of a long-awaited heavyweight championship bout is just overwhelming, and I've never seen it reach the pinnacle that it did at the Ali-Frazier fight. The excitement was almost unbearable. On a broader, less emotional scale, the Olympic Games give you a sense of the sweep of civilized society on the planet Earth. You walk into that

Olympic Village and you can't help feeling as if you've stumbled upon a utopia, a society where people love and care about one another. In spite of autocrats like Avery Brundage and the bureaucrats who make up the U.S. Olympic Committee, the overriding memory I'm left with after an Olympiad is one of understanding and friendship among the young people of the world. And then perhaps you get a chance to see a victory in the Olympics that has a very special meaning, such as Bill Toomey's gold-medal performance in the 1968 Olympic decathlon. His was probably the most extraordinary victory I've ever witnessed.

PLAYBOY: Why?

COSELL: When Bill was five years old, he was playing with a piece of ceramics that shattered; the nerves in his right wrist were severed, paralyzing the hand. Doctors said he'd never be able to use the hand again, and to this day his right hand is shriveled. But somehow he made that hand work so that he could put the shot, carry the pole for the vault, throw the discus and heave a javelin. Toomey always dreamed of becoming an Olympic champion and at age 25, he paid his own way to watch the 1964 Tokyo games. He'd dabbled in track and field for some time and because Bill couldn't do anything superbly well, he decided to diversify. Soon after the Tokyo Olympics, we began to read Bill Toomey's name in the decathlon results of international track meets. He seemed to be getting somewhere, but then he caught infectious hepatitis in West Germany. Toomey was hospitalized for six months and close to death, but finally he recovered. Then, almost incredibly, he came down with mononucleosis, and shortly after that, one of his knees got cracked up in a car accident—and what's an athlete without good knees? But Toomey overcame it all, and at 29, this schoolteacher was our country's hope in the 1968 Olympic decathlon—48 hours of the most intense competition in the world.

In Mexico City, I snuck into the athletes' room because I wanted to wish Bill luck before the final decathlon event, the 1500-meter run. If he won that, he'd win the gold medal. But there was no conversation between Bill and me: Toomey lay prostrate on a rubbing table, out cold from utter exhaustion. But an hour later, he was back out on the track. Dusk had descended and Mexico City was cold, wet and windy. They ran the damned race and it was no contest: The man with the finishing kick was Bill Toomey, and as I stood next to the cinder path watching him stride to victory, I just felt exultant for the whole human race. He gave vivid evidence that man can do virtually whatever he wants to do if he wills it, and then lives by that will. Bill Toomey's Olympic victory was an absolute demonstration of the magnificence of the human spirit. And I love him for it.

PLAYBOY: You sound like a man who's fulfilled by his work. Are you?

COSELL: When I'm dealing with compelling events like an Olympiad or an Ali-Frazier heavyweight title fight, yes, I am. But those are rare occasions. To me, the biggest virtue of working in sports are some of the people you meet; you *do* have a brush with greatness. And I've been very lucky that way. I think Vince Lombardi was a great man. I think Bill Toomey is a great man. I think Jackie Robinson is one of the greatest men human society has yet produced. I thought Fred Hutchinson, the baseball manager, was a great man. It's a positive thrill for me to go back through my life and know that these men were my friends. And because they were in the public arena, I think each of them had a beneficial impact on society. The president of a corporation doesn't have that kind of visible impact, nor does the president of a university. Neither does a great scientist, unless he comes up with an electrifying breakthrough like Jonas Salk's. But an athlete can have it because sport has such a peculiar place in our society. But can I really take games seriously? No. Sport is not going to cause a cessation of hostilities in Vietnam. Sports will not assuage the nation's racial inequities. Sport will not rebuild a single ghetto in America. And so the answer for me is, finally, no: My work does not fulfill me.

PLAYBOY: Aside from sport, what are the main passions of your life?

COSELL: I have a deep and abiding interest in politics that has never been fulfilled. I don't regret for a minute leaving my law practice, but would I like to be in the United States Senate? Yes, I would. Would I like to do something about the problems of the world and especially the problems of our great cities? Yes, I certainly would. Politics, incidentally, is not my only private passion. To take you from the significant to the absurd, I don't mind admitting that I like to act.

PLAYBOY: Was that triggered by your appearance in Woody Allen's *Bananas*?

COSELL: I'm afraid so. Actually, I was pleasantly surprised with my work in it, because when I left Puerto Rico after the shooting, I had grave misgivings about having done it.

PLAYBOY: Didn't you think you were the perfect choice to play yourself?

COSELL: Truthfully, I thought I was in over my head. And that's because Woody Allen is a comic genius. Twenty years from now, there may very well be Woody Allen film festivals just as there are now with the movies of W.C. Fields, Charlie Chaplin and the Marx Brothers. I came home to New York worrying if I'd made a fool of myself, but then a few months later, Woody called me and said, "Howard, we've rough-cut the movie and the best thing in it is your opening." When I finally saw the film, I couldn't believe my scenes came over as well as they did. Since *Bananas*, I've done some comedy spots on several TV shows, and I enjoy that kind of thing. But the most satisfying TV work I've done were the times I guest-hosted the Dick Cavett and David Frost shows. Both of those allowed me the chance to let my mental curiosity come out and play.

PLAYBOY: If you finally get weary of sports reporting, would you want to have your own TV talk show?

COSELL: One of the reasons I've been doing all these things is that, to a degree, I *have* gotten weary of sports. You have to if you've got a mind and if you're an educated man. But I wouldn't get into the talk-show field at the expense of leaving sports, because that's a practical matter, not an intellectual one. I've been in sport too long, established too firm a base and make too much money at it to get out now. I wouldn't venture into an entirely new field unless my wife and children were taken care of for the rest of their lives in the event of my death, and that's not the case yet.

PLAYBOY: Is that the only reason you remain in a field you find unfulfilling?

COSELL: Truthfully, no. I've crested at the relatively advanced age of 51 in what is a very young man's industry, and at this stage of my life, even if the finances were right, I don't know if I'd care to risk everything I've worked so damned hard for. I think I have found, or at least created, a role for myself. But in a very real sense, sport has become too important not just in my life but in all our lives; such is the nation's need to escape from itself, a sad commentary, to be sure. If you've ever been around the world of sport, especially with most of my sportscasting colleagues and even with newspaper sportswriters, you know that all they ever talk about is the contest within the arena—who should have been sent up to pinch-hit, what the matchups should have been, who may or may not win the next game, and so on. It's unceasing and all-pervasive, and I find myself thinking, "What's become of me? There's got to be something more to life than isolating a setback on a linebacker."

Within sports journalism, however, there *is* something more, and that's the gut reason I feel a responsibility to stay in it. Let the operators of sport field their teams and let them play their games and let's have the fun that sport provides. But the people who run sport must not feel that they can imperiously rule a make-believe world in which everything they do is to be either applauded or excused. Never let them think for even a minute that there's nobody out there in the real world to expose them when they defy the public interest or reap injustice upon an athlete. The sports establishment has an accountability to the public, which so handsomely rewards them, and to the athlete, whose talents enable them to grow rich. And when they openly defy either, I'll be there to call them on it.

October 1964

CASSIUS CLAY

A candid conversation with the flamboyantly fast-talking, hard-hitting heavyweight champ

It wasn't until 9:55 on a night last February that anyone began to take seriously the extravagant boasts of Cassius Marcellus Clay: That was the moment when the redoubtable Sonny Liston, sitting dazed and disbelieving on a stool in Miami Beach's Convention Hall, resignedly spat out his mouthpiece—and relinquished the world's heavyweight boxing championship to the brash young braggart whom he, along with the nation's sportswriters and nearly everyone else, had dismissed as a loudmouthed pushover.

Leaping around the ring in a frenzy of glee, Clay screamed, "I am the greatest! I am the king!"—the strident rallying cry of a campaign of self-celebration, punctuated with rhyming couplets predicting victory, which had rocketed him from relative obscurity as a 1960 Olympic Gold Medal winner to dubious renown as the "villain" of a title match with the least lovable heavyweight champion in boxing history. Undefeated in 100 amateur fights and all 18 professional bouts, the cocky 22-year-old had become, if not another Joe Louis, at least the world's wealthiest poet (with a purse of $600,000), and one of its most flamboyant public figures.

Within 24 hours of his victory, he also became sports' most controversial cause célèbre when he announced at a press conference that he was henceforth to be billed on fight programs only as Muhammad Ali, his new name as a full-fledged member of the Black Muslims, the militant nationwide Negro religious cult that preaches racial segregation, black supremacy and unconcealed hostility toward whites.

Amidst the brouhaha that ensued—besieged by the world press, berated by more temperate Negro leaders, threatened with the revocation of his title—Cassius preened and prated in the limelight, using his worldwide platform as a pulpit for hymns of self-adulation and sermons on the virtues of Islam. Still full of surprises, he then proceeded to appoint himself as an international goodwill ambassador and departed with an entourage of six cronies on an 8000-mile tour of Africa and the Middle East, where he was received by several heads of state (including Ghana's Nkrumah and Egypt's Nasser), and was accorded, said observers, the warmest reception ever given an American visitor.

We approached the mercurial Muslim with our request for a searching interview about his fame, his heavyweight crown and his faith. Readily consenting, he invited us to join him on his peripatetic social rounds of New York's Harlem, where he rents a three-room suite at the Hotel Theresa (in which another celebrated guest, Fidel Castro, hung his hat and plucked his chickens during a memorable visit to the UN).

For the next two weeks, we walked with him on brisk morning constitutionals, ate with him at immaculate Muslim restaurants (no pork served), sat with him during his daily shoeshine, rode with him in his chauffeured, air-conditioned Cadillac limousine on leisurely drives through Harlem. We interjected our questions as the opportunities presented themselves—between waves and shouts exchanged by the champion and ogling pedestrians, and usually over the din of the limousine's dashboard phonograph, blaring Clay's recording of "I Am the Greatest." We began the conversation on our own blaring note.

PLAYBOY: Are you really the loudmouthed exhibitionist you seem to be, or is it all for the sake of publicity?

CLAY: I been attracting attention ever since I been able to walk and talk. When I was just a little boy in school, I caught onto how nearly everybody likes to watch somebody that acts different. Like, I wouldn't ride the school bus, I would *run* to school alongside it, and all the kids would be waving and hollering at me and calling me nuts. It made me somebody special. Or at recess time, I'd start a fight with somebody to draw a crowd. I always liked drawing crowds. When I started fighting serious, I found out that grown people, the fight fans, acted just like those school kids. Almost from my first fights, I'd bigmouth to anybody who would listen about what I was going to do to whoever I was going to fight, and people would go out of their way to come and see, hoping I would get beat. When I wasn't no more than a kid fighter, they would put me on bills because I was a drawing card, because I run my mouth so much. Other kids could battle and get all bloody and lose or win and didn't hardly nobody care, it seemed like, except maybe their families and their buddies. But the minute I would come in sight, the people would start to hollering "Bash in his nose!" or "Button his fat lip!" or something like that. You would have thought I was some well-known pro 10 years older than I was. But I didn't care what they said, long as they kept coming to see me fight. They paid their money, they was entitled to a little fun.

PLAYBOY: How did your first fight come about?

CLAY: Well, on my 12th birthday, I got a new bicycle as a present from my folks, and I rode it to a fair that was being held at the Columbia Gymnasium, and when I come out, my bike was gone. I was so mad I was crying, and a policeman, Joe Martin, come up and I told him I was going to whip whoever took my bike. He said I ought to take some boxing lessons to learn how to whip the thief better, and I did. That's when I started fighting. Six weeks later, I won my first fight over another boy 12 years old, a white boy. And in a year I was fighting on TV. Joe Martin advised me against trying to just fight my way up in clubs and preliminaries, which could take years and maybe get me all beat up. He said I ought to try the Olympics, and if I won, that would give me automatically a number-10 pro rating. And that's just what I did.

PLAYBOY: When did you hit upon the gimmick of reciting poetry?

CLAY: Somewhere away back in them early fights in Louisville, even before I went to the Olympics, I started thinking about the poetry. I told a newspaperman before a fight, "This guy must be done/I'll stop him in one." It got in the newspaper, but it didn't catch on then. Poetry didn't even catch on with *me* until a lot later, when I was getting ready to fight Archie Moore. I think the reason then was that *he* talked so much, I had to figure up something new to use on him. That was when I told different reporters, "Moore will go in four." When he *did* go down in four, just like I said, and the papers made so much of it, I knew I had stumbled on something good. And something else I found out was how it had bugged

Archie Moore. Before the fight, some people got it to me that he was walking around and around in the Alexandria Hotel in Los Angeles, saying over and over, "He's not going to get me in no four, he's not going to get me in no four"—and the next thing he knew, he was getting up off the floor. I been making up things that rhyme for every fight since.

PLAYBOY: Your poetry has been described by many critics as "horrible." Do you think it is?

CLAY: I bet my poetry gets printed and quoted more than any that's turned out by the poem writers that them critics like. I don't pay no attention to no kind of critics about nothing. If they knew as much as they claim to about what they're criticizing, they ought to be doing that instead of just standing on the sidelines using their mouth.

PLAYBOY: As your own best critic, what do you consider your finest poem?

CLAY: I don't know. The one the newspapers used the most, though, was the time I covered the waterfront with a poem I wrote before my fight with Doug Jones. I said, "Jones likes to mix / So I'll let it go six. / If he talks jive / I'll cut it to five. / And if he talks some more / I'll cut it to four. / And if he talks about me / I'll cut it to three. / And if that don't do / I'll cut it to two. / And if you want some fun / I'll cut it to one. / And if he don't want to fight / He can stay home that night."

PLAYBOY: How often have you been right in predicting the round of a knockout?

CLAY: I ain't missed but twice. If you figure out the man you're up against, and you know what you can do, then you can pretty much do it whenever you get ready. Once I call the round, I plan what I'm going to do in the fight. Like, you take Archie Moore. He's a better fighter than Sonny Liston. He's harder to hit, the way he bobs and weaves, and he's smart. You get careless and he'll drop you. I guess he knows more tricks in the ring than anybody but Sugar Ray. But he was fat and 45, and he had to be looking for a lucky punch before he got tired. I just had to pace myself so as to tire him. I hooked and jabbed him silly the first round, then I coasted the second. Right at the end of the second, he caught me with a good right on the jaw, but it didn't do me no harm. Then I started out the third throwing leather on him, and when I could feel him wearing down, I slowed up, looking for my spots to hit him. And then in the fourth round, when I had said he was going down, I poured it on him again. And he did go down; he was nearly out. But he got up at eight. A few combinations sent him back down, and then the referee stopped it. It was just like I planned.

PLAYBOY: In that fight, you were 20 and Moore was 45. It's often been said that you got to the top by beating a succession of carefully picked setups. What's your response?

CLAY: I didn't beat nobody that wasn't trying to beat me. I don't care who I fought fair and beat, but they said something was wrong. Archie Moore, yeah, they said he was an old man. Doug Jones, he was one of the toughest fights I ever had. He was one of them what-round calls that I missed. I had said just before the fight, "I'll shut the door on Jones in four," but it went the limit, 10 rounds. When the judges and referee gave me the decision, everybody was calling it a fix. Then Henry Cooper in London, after he caught me in the fourth with a right that sent me through the ropes, I took him out in the fifth just like I had said I would; I had said, "It ain't no jive/Henry Cooper will go in five." But sure enough, people said that Cooper hadn't been in shape. I'm surprised they haven't been saying Liston was underage, or something, since I whipped *him* good.

PLAYBOY: To get back to Archie Moore for a moment: Do you give him any credit, as a master of self-promotion, for helping you develop your own ballyhoo technique?

CLAY: I learned a lot from the old man, yeah. He showed me some proof of what I had already figured out myself, that talking is a whole lot easier than fighting, and it was a way to get up fast. It's a shame he wasn't fighting big time when he was in his prime. It would have been like a young Satchel Paige in the big leagues. I picked up quick how the old man would talk up a fight to make a gate, how he'd talk it up that the guy he wanted next didn't want no part of him. But the big difference between the old man and me is I'm bigger and louder and better. He believed in whispering something to reporters for them to print—but I believe in yelling.

PLAYBOY: At what point in your career did you first put this yelling technique into practice?

CLAY: Right after I had won the Olympic Gold Medal. One day, back home in Louisville, I was riding on a bus. I was reading a paper about Patterson and Ingemar Johansson. I didn't have no doubt I could beat either one of them, if I had a chance to fight them. But Machen, Folley, Jones and all of them other bums were standing in the way, and I decided I wasn't just about to stand around like them. I'd won the Olympic title, that was all in the papers, but hadn't nobody really heard of me, though, and they never would as long as I just sat thinking about it. Right there on that bus is where I figured I'd just open up my big mouth and start people listening and paying attention to me. Not just talking, but really screaming, and acting like some kind of a nut. That day was when I started out after getting in the ring with the champion.

PLAYBOY: Even though you never fought him officially, you did have a run-in of sorts with Ingemar Johansson, didn't you?

CLAY: Yeah. Boy, I sure made him mad! He hired me as his sparring partner in Miami, and by the end of the first round I had him pinned against the ropes, all shook up and very mad. And he hadn't put a glove on me at the end of the second round. You talk about somebody upset! He was so mad he wanted me to go to Palm Beach, where we could spar in private. Not me! I wanted the newspapermen to see me if I did anything great and sensational.

PLAYBOY: Do you feel that you could have beaten Johansson?

CLAY: I just finished telling you I did beat him. The only difference between that and a regular fight was that we had on headgear and we didn't have no big fight crowd, and I didn't have no contract.

PLAYBOY: After you had scored victories over Archie Moore, Charley Powell, Doug Jones and Henry Cooper, how did you go about your campaign to get a match with Liston?

CLAY: Well, the big thing I did is that until then, I had just been loud-mouthing mostly for the *public* to hear me, to build up gates for my fights. I hadn't never been messing personally with whoever I was going to fight—and that's what I started when it was time to go after Liston. I had been studying Liston careful, all along, ever since he had come up in the rankings, and Patterson was trying to duck him. You know what Patterson was saying—that Liston had such a bad police record, and prison record and all that. He wouldn't be a good example for boxing like Patterson would—the pure, clean-cut American boy.

PLAYBOY: You were saying you had been studying Liston. . . .

CLAY: Yeah. His fighting style. His strength. His punch. Like that—but that was just part of what I was looking at. Any fighter will study them things about somebody he wants to fight. The big thing for me was observing how Liston acted *out* of the ring. I read everything I could where he had been interviewed. I talked with people who had been around him, or had talked with him. I would lay in bed and put all of the things together and think about them, to try to get a good picture of how his mind worked. And that's how I first got the idea that if I would handle the thing right, I could use psychology on him—you know, needle him and work on his nerves so bad that I would have him beat before he ever got in the ring with me. And that's just what I did!

PLAYBOY: How?

CLAY: I mean I set out to make him think what I wanted him thinking: that all I was was some clown, and that he never would have to give a second thought to me being able to put up any real fight when we got to the ring. The more out of shape and overconfident I could get him to be, the better. The press, everybody—I didn't want nobody thinking nothing except that I was a joke. Listen here, do you realize that of all them ring "experts" on the newspapers, wasn't hardly one that wasn't as carried away with Liston's reputation as Liston was himself? You know what everybody was writing? Saying I had been winning my fights, calling the rounds, because I was fighting "nothing" fighters. Like I told you already, even with people like Moore and Powell and Jones and Cooper, the papers found some excuse; it never was that maybe I could fight. And when it come to Liston, they was all saying it was the end of the line for me. I might even get killed in there; he was going to put his big fist in my big mouth so far they was going to have to get doctors to pull it out, stuff like that. You couldn't read nothing else. That's how come, later on, I made them reporters tell me I was the greatest. They had been so busy looking at Liston's record with Patterson that didn't nobody stop to think about how it was making Liston just about a setup for me.

PLAYBOY: Would you elaborate?

CLAY: I told you. Overconfidence. When Liston finally got to Patterson, he beat him so bad, plus that Patterson *looked* so bad, that Liston quit thinking about keeping himself trained. I don't care who a fighter is, he has got to stay in shape. While I was fighting Jones and Cooper, Liston was up to his neck in all of that rich, fat ritual of the champion. I'd nearly clap my hands every time I read or heard about him at some big function or ceremony, up half the night and drinking and all that. I was looking at Liston's age, too. Wasn't nothing about him helping him to be sharp for me, whenever I got to him. I ain't understood it yet that didn't none of them "experts" ever realize these things.

What made it even better for me was when Liston just half-trained for the Patterson rematch, and Patterson looked worse yet—and Liston signed to fight me, not rating me even as good as he did Patterson. He felt like he was getting ready to start off on some bum-of-the-month club like Joe Louis did. He couldn't see nothing at all to me but mouth. And you know I didn't make no sound that wasn't planned to keep him thinking in that rut. He spent more time at them Las Vegas gambling tables than he did at the punching bag. He was getting fatter and flabbier every day, and I was steady hollering louder to keep him that way: "I'm going to skin the big bear!" . . . "I'm the greatest!" . . . "I'm so pretty I can't hardly stand to look at myself!" Like that. People can't stand a blowhard, but they'll always listen to him. Even people in Europe and Africa and Asia was hearing my big mouth. I didn't miss no radio or television show or newspaper I could get in. And in between them, on the street, I'd walk up to people and they'd tell one another about what "that crazy Cassius Clay" said. And then, on top of this, what the public didn't know was that every chance I got, I was needling Liston *direct*.

PLAYBOY: How?

CLAY: I don't see no harm in telling it now. The first time, it was right after Liston had bought his new home in Denver, and my buddies and me was driving from Los Angeles to New York in my bus. This was Archie Robinson, who takes care of business for me, and Howard Bingham, the photographer, and some more buddies. I had bought this used 30-passenger bus, a 1953 Flexible—you know, the kind you see around airports. We had painted it red and white with World's Most Colorful Fighter across the top. Then I had Liston Must Go In Eight painted across the side right after Liston took the title. We had been driving around Los Angeles, and up and down the freeways in the bus, blowing the horn, *Oink! Oink! Oink!* drawing people's attention to me. When I say I'm colorful, I believe in *being* colorful. Anyway, this time, when we started out for New York, we decided it would be a good time to pay Liston a visit at his new house.

We had the address from the newspapers, and we pulled up in his front yard in the bus about three o'clock in the morning and started blowing: *Oink! Oink! Oink! Oink!* In other houses, lights went on and windows went up. You know how them white people felt about that black man just moved in there anyway, and we sure wasn't helping it none. People was hollering things, and we got out with the headlights blazing and went up to Liston's door, just about as Liston got there. He had on nylon shorty pajamas. And he was mad. He first recognized Howard Bingham, the photographer, whom he had seen in Los Angeles. "What you want, black mother?" he said to Howard. I was standing right behind Howard, flinging my cane back and forth in the headlights, hollering loud enough for everybody in a mile to hear me, "Come on out of there! I'm going to whip you right now! Come on out of there and protect your home! If you don't come out of that door, I'm going to break it down!"

You know that look of Liston's you hear so much about? Well, he sure had it on standing in that door that night. Man, he was tore up! He didn't know what to do. He wanted to come out there after me, but he was already in enough troubles with the police and everything. And you know, if a man figures you're crazy, he'll think twice before he acts, because he figures you're liable to do *anything*. But before he could make up his mind, the police came rushing in with all their sirens going, and they broke it up, telling us we would be arrested for disturbing the peace if we didn't get out of there. So we left. You can bet we laughed all the way to New York.

PLAYBOY: You said this was your first direct needling of Liston. What came next?

CLAY: Every time I got anywhere near him, I'd needle him. Sometimes it was just little things. I had to keep right on him, because I knew he was confused. He had told different people, who got it to me, that he was just going along with my clowning because it would help to build up a gate that would make money for him. So at first I couldn't get him really mad, because he had this idea fixed in his mind. But I kept right on working on him. A man with Liston's kind of mind is very funny. He ain't what you would call a fast thinker. Like I am.

PLAYBOY: What do you mean by the "kind of mind" Liston has?

CLAY: He's got one of them bulldog kind of minds. You understand what I mean. Once he ever starts to thinking something, he won't let hold of it quick.

PLAYBOY: And you feel that your mind is faster?

CLAY: I know it is. What I did to Liston proves it. I'll tell you another way I know. Nobody ever could have conned me the way I did him. If I know a man is going to get in the ring and try to beat me, and take the title, then anything he does outside of regular training, I figure he's got some good reason, and I'd sit down and give his actions careful examination. Liston didn't never even *think* about doing that. Neither did nobody around him, all of his advisors and trainers—didn't even none of them think about it. Even if they had, they sure couldn't have never told him that I represented danger. He was too fixed in his thinking. That's what I mean by his kind of mind.

PLAYBOY: What other direct confrontations did you have with Liston before the fight?

CLAY: Well, another time was just before we signed to fight. It was in Las Vegas. I was there to be on *David Brinkley's Journal*, and it didn't take me no time to find Liston at a gambling table. People was standing around watching him. He was shooting craps, and I walked up behind him and reached and took some of his chips. He turned around, and I said, "Man, you can't shoot dice!" But he was good-humored. Maybe it was because the people were watching, and maybe he was seeing me helping build up a gate for the fight we were about to sign for—or maybe he was *winning* something for a change. I don't know *what* it was that put him in good spirits, but I just kept right on him. I'd snatch up the dice from him. I could see I was beginning to get to him a little, but not enough. Finally, I had to shoot a loaded water pistol on him. That did it. But he still played it cool, trying to show the people he was trying to humor me. Naturally, the word had spread and people were piling around us. But then very suddenly, Liston *froze* me with that look of his. He said real quiet, "Let's go on over here," and he led the way to a table, and the people hung back. I ain't going to lie. This was the only time since I have known Sonny Liston that he really scared me. I just felt the power and the meanness of the man I was messing with. Anybody tell me about how he has fought cops and beat up tough thugs and all of that, I believe it. I saw that streak in him. He told me, "Get the hell out of here or I'll wipe you out."

PLAYBOY: What did you do?

CLAY: I got the hell out of there. I told you, he had really scared me.

PLAYBOY: Did you consider giving up your campaign to rattle him?

CLAY: Oh, no, I never did think about that. Soon as I got time to think about how he had reacted, I saw I had started for the first time to really get under his skin, and I made up my mind right then that by the time we got to Miami in training, I was going to have him so mad that he would forget everything he knew about fighting, just trying to kill me.

PLAYBOY: Was the scene you made at the airport, when Liston arrived in Miami, part of the plan?

CLAY: You know it. They were making such a big thing of his arriving, you would have thought the Cubans was landing. Well, I wasn't just about to miss *that*! Liston came down off the plane, all cool, and the press was ganged around waiting for an interview. That was when I rushed in the scene, hollering, "Chump! Big ugly bear! I'm going to whip you right now!" Stuff like that. Police were grabbing for me and holding me and I was trying to break loose, and finally I did. I could see I was really turning Liston on. I got up close enough to him and he gave me that evil look again, but I wasn't even thinking about him. "Look, this clowning, it's not cute, and I'm not joking," he said. And I nearly threw a fit. "Joking? Why, you big chump, I'll whip you right here!" And people were grabbing me again, and somebody had rushed up one of them little VIP cars they have at airports. They got Liston, his wife and his bodyguard in it. Joe Louis and Jack Nilon were trying to calm things down. I saw the little car taking off down the tunnel. So I broke loose and took out after it. I was waving my cane, and hollering at Liston. In the tunnel, I guess he told the driver to stop, and he hopped off. Was he *mad*! He hollered, "Listen, you little punk, I'll punch you in the mouth—this has gone too far!" Then people was rushing in and hollering at both of us, and I was throwing off my coat and shouting, "Come on chump, right here!" Finally Liston swung at me, and I ducked. He didn't know he'd had his preview of the fight right then.

PLAYBOY: Who won?

CLAY: I bet you it went on two hours before it really got settled. There weren't no more swings, but Joe Louis and Jack Nilon and the cops and bodyguards got Liston in the airport lounge, and they were guarding the doors to keep me out. I was banging my cane on the door, hollering, "Free! I'll fight you free!" I knew everybody inside could hear me. They couldn't hear nothing else *but* me. "Free! You think I'm jiving, chump? I'll fight you free, right here!"

PLAYBOY: And, of course, it was all an act?

CLAY: Completely—and it was also building the gate. At least, if it hadn't been for the reporters, it would have been a better gate. But right then I didn't want nobody in Miami, except at my camp, thinking I wasn't crazy. I didn't want nobody never thinking nothing about I had any fighting ability.

PLAYBOY: Why do you say that if it hadn't been for the reporters, the gate would have been better?

CLAY: They made people think that Liston was so mean and I was so nothing that they would be throwing away money to buy a ticket. There was over 16,000 seats in that Convention Hall, and it was only about half full. I read where the promoter, Bill MacDonald, lost something like $300,000. But he sure can't blame *me* for it. I was the one that let him get seat prices up as high as $250. I was the first fighter who ever talked a fight into being bounced off Telstar to 50 nations. I got more publicity than any fight ever had. I'm colorful when I rumble. But the people listened to the so-called "experts." If they had listened to me, that Convention Hall would have been overflowing even if they had charged twice the prices.

PLAYBOY: But the reporters' attitudes, you have said, were in the best interests of your strategy.

CLAY: It's six of one and half a dozen of the other. They still made me mad. But, lookahere, I wasn't nearly about done with Liston yet. I mean, right up to the fight I was messing with him. Everybody in my camp carried canes and wore jackets with Bear-Hunting across the back. Guys from my camp went into Liston's camp, standing around, watching him training, until Liston quit to personally order them out. We put out the word that we was going to raid Liston's camp. He got so jumpy and under strain that every day, different reporters would come telling me, serious, "Stop angering that man—he will literally kill you!" It was music to my ears. It meant if he was that mad, he had lost all sense of reasoning. If he wasn't thinking nothing but killing me, he wasn't thinking fighting. And you got to think to fight.

PLAYBOY: The press was generally unimpressed with your workouts, and the Liston camp knew it. Was that part of your plan, too?

CLAY: You ain't so stupid. I made sure nobody but my people saw me *really* working out. If anybody else was around, I didn't do no more than go through motions. But look, I'm going to tell you where Liston really lost the fight. Or *when* he lost it. Every day we had been leaking word over there that we were going to pull our raid that day. The Liston people got to the mayor and the police, and we got cautioned that we'd be arrested if we did it. So we made a court case out of it. We requested legal permission to picket Liston's camp, but we were told that a city ordinance prevented carrying signs. We had paid, I remember, $325 for signs like Big Ugly Bear, Bear-Hunting Season, Too Pretty To Be a Fighter, Bear Must Fall, and like that. So we taped the signs all over my bus. It wasn't no ordinance against signs on a bus. And we loaded the bus up with people from my camp, and screaming teenage girls, and we drove over there and caused such a commotion that people left off from watching Liston train, and we heard he nearly had a fit. One of his men—I know his name, but I guess I better not call it—even pulled a knife on Howard Bingham. Joe Louis run and asked the guy what in the world was the matter with him. But that's the day Liston lost. We heard he went to pieces. It wasn't long before the weigh-in, where they said *I* was the one went to pieces.

PLAYBOY: One doctor described your conduct at the weigh-in as "dangerously disturbed." Another said you acted "scared to death." And seasoned sportswriters used such terms as "hysterical" and "schizophrenic" in reporting your tantrum, for which you were fined $2500. What was the real story?

CLAY: I would just say that it sounds like them doctors and sportswriters had been listening to each other. You know what they said and wrote them things for—to match in what they expected was about to happen. That's what I keep on telling you. If all of them had had their way, I wouldn't have been allowed in the ring.

PLAYBOY: Had you worked out a fight plan by this time?

CLAY: I figured out my strategy and announced it *months* before the fight: "Float like a butterfly, sting like a bee," is what I said.

PLAYBOY: We read that. But what specifically did you mean?

CLAY: To start with, I knew that Liston, overconfident as he was, and helped by reading what all of the newspapers were saying, he never was going to train to fight more than two rounds. I don't know if you happened to read it later that some of his handlers admitted, after the fight, that this was exactly what he did. So that was my guide how to train, to pace myself. You know, a fighter can condition his body to go hard certain rounds, then to coast certain rounds. Nobody can *fight* 15 rounds. So I trained to fight the first two rounds, and to protect myself from getting hit by Liston. I knew that with the third, he'd start tiring, then he'd get worse every round. So I trained to coast the third, fourth and fifth rounds. I had two reasons for that. One was that I wanted to prove I had the ability to stand up to Liston. The second reason was that I wanted him to wear himself out and get desperate. He would be throwing wild punches, and missing. If I just did that as long as he lasted on his feet, I couldn't miss winning the fight on points. And so I conditioned myself to fight full steam from the sixth through the ninth round, if it lasted that long. I never did think it would go past nine rounds. That's why I announced I'd take him in eight. I figured I'd be in command by the sixth. I'd be careful—not get hit—and I'd cut him up and shake him up until he would be like a bull, just blind, and missing punches until he was nearly crazy. And I planned that some time in the eighth, when he had thrown some punch and left himself just right, I'd be all set, and I'd drop him.

Listen here, man, I *knew* I was going to upset the world! You know the only thing I was scared of? I was scared that some of them newspaper "experts" was going to quit praising Liston's big fists long enough to wake up and see what was just as clear as day to me and my camp; and if they printed it, that Liston's camp people might be able to get it into his skull. But I was lucky; that didn't happen. Them newspaper people couldn't have been working no better for me if I had been paying them.

PLAYBOY: Then the fight went about as you had planned?

CLAY: Almost. He came in there at 220 pounds, and untrained to go more than two rounds, and as old as he is—too old—against a kid, and I didn't have an ounce of fat on me. And he didn't have *no* respect for me as a fighter. He was figuring on killing me inside of two rounds. He was a perfect setup. If you remember, I didn't throw many punches, but when I did, they made their mark. I have vicious combinations, and just like I had planned, I hurt his body and I closed his eyes.

PLAYBOY: But Liston did do you some damage, too.

CLAY: You don't expect to fight no fighter without getting hit sometime. But you don't want to get hurt bad, and knocked out—that's the point. Yeah, he hit me some damaging punches. With all the talking I been doing, ain't nobody never heard me say Liston can't hit. He got me in the first with a right to the stomach. In the second, I made the mistake of getting maneuvered on the ropes, and he got in some good shots. And in the last of that second round, after I had cut his eye, he really staggered me there for a minute with a long, hard left. In fact, he did me more damage with that than any other punch. In the fifth, when that stuff—rosin, I guess it was—was in my eyes, and I couldn't see, he hit me with a good left hook to the head.

PLAYBOY: Would you be able to give us a round-by-round account of the fight from your viewpoint?

CLAY: Yeah, I guess I could. The first round, I beat him out, dancing, to keep from getting hit. He was shuffling that way he does, giving me that evil eye. Man, he meant to *kill* me, I ain't kidding! He was jabbing his left—but missing. And I was backpedaling, bobbing, weaving, ducking. He missed with a right hook that would have hurt me. I got away from that, but that was when he got me with that right to my stomach. I just kept running, watching his eyes. Liston's eyes tip you when he's about to throw a heavy punch. Some kind of way, they just flicker. He didn't dream that I'd suddenly stop running when I did, if you remember—and I hit him with a good left and then a flurry of lefts and rights. That was good for points, you know. He nearly flipped, and came after me like a bull. I was hitting and ducking at the same time; that's how neither one of us heard the bell, and was still fighting after it. I remember I got to my corner thinking, "He was supposed to kill me. Well, I'm still alive." Angelo Dundee was working over me, talking a mile a minute. I just watched Liston, so mad he didn't even sit down. I thought to myself, "You gonna wish you had rested all you could when we get past this next round." I could hear some radio or television expert, all excited, you know the way they chatter. The big news was that I hadn't been counted out yet.

Then, at the second-round bell, just like I knew he would, Liston come at me throwing everything. He was going to make up for looking so bad that I had lasted *one* round. This was when he got me on the ropes, where everybody had said he was supposed to kill me. He hit me some, but I weaved and ducked away from most of his shots. I remember one time feeling his arm grazing the back of my neck and thinking—it was like I shouted to myself—"All I got to do is keep this up." And I got out from under and I caught him with some lefts and rights. Then I saw that first cut, high up on his cheekbone. When a man's first cut, it usually looks a bright pink. Then I saw the blood, and I knew that eye was my target from then on. It was my concentrating on that cut that let me get caught with the hardest punch I took, that long left. It rocked me back. But he either didn't realize how good I was hit or he was already getting tired, and he didn't press his chance. I sure heard the bell *that* time. I needed to get to my corner to get my head clear.

Starting in the third round, I saw his expression, how shook he was that we were still out there and *he* was the one cut and bleeding. He didn't know what to do. But I wasn't about to get careless, like Conn did that time against Joe Louis. This was supposed to be one of my coasting, resting rounds, but I couldn't waste no time. I needed one more good shot, for some more insurance with that eye. So when the bell rang, I just tested him, to see was he tiring, and he was; and then I got him into the ropes. It didn't take but one good combination. My left was square on his right eye, and a right under his left eye opened a deep gash. I knew it was deep, the way the blood spurted right out. I saw his face up close when he wiped his glove at that cut and saw the blood. At that moment, let me tell you, he looked like he's going to look 20 years from now. Liston was tiring fast in the fourth, and I was coasting. We didn't neither one do very much. But you can bet it wasn't nobody in there complaining they wasn't getting their money's worth.

Then, in the fifth, all of a sudden, after one exchange of shots, there was a feeling in my eyes like some acid was in them. I could see just blurry. When the bell sounded, it felt like fire, and I could just make it back to my corner, telling Angelo, "I can't see!" And he was swabbing at my eyes. I could hear that excited announcer; he was having a fit. "Something seems to be wrong with Clay!" It sure was something wrong. I didn't care if it was a heavyweight title fight I had worked so long for, I wasn't going out there and get murdered because I couldn't see. Every time I blinked it hurt so bad I said, "Cut off my gloves, Angelo—leave me out of here." Then I heard the bell, and the referee, Barney Felix, yelled to me to get out there, and at the same time Angelo was pushing me up, shouting, "This is the big one, daddy. We aren't going to quit now!" And I was out there again, blinking. Angelo was shouting, "Stay away from him! Stay away!" I got my left in Liston's face and kept it there, kind of staving him off, and at the same time I knew where he was. I was praying he wouldn't guess what was the matter. But he had to see me blinking, and then he shook me with that left to the head and a lot of shots to the body. Now, I ain't too sorry it happened, because it proved I could take Liston's punching. He had found some respect for me, see? He wasn't going so much for the knockout; he was trying to hurt my body, then try for a kill. Man, in that round, my plans were *gone*. I was just trying to keep alive, hoping the tears would wash out my eyes. I could open them just enough to get a good glimpse of Liston, and then it hurt so bad I blinked them closed again. Liston was snorting like a horse. He was trying to hit me square, and I was just moving every which way, because I knew if he connected right, it could be all over right there.

But in the corner after that fifth round, the stuff pretty well washed out of my eyes. I could see again, and I was ready to carry the fight to Liston. And I was gaining my second wind now, as I had conditioned myself, to pace the fight, like I was telling you. My corner people knew it, and they were calling to me, "Get mad, baby!" They knew I was ready to go the next three rounds at top steam, and I knew I was going to make Liston look terrible. I hit him with eight punches in a row, until he doubled up. I remember thinking something like, "Yeah, you old sucker! You try to be so big and bad!" He was gone. He knew he couldn't last. It was the first time in the fight that I set myself flat-footed. I missed a right that might have dropped him. But I jabbed and jabbed at that cut under his eye, until it was wide open and bleeding worse than before. I knew he wasn't due to last much longer. Then, right at the end of the round, I rocked back his head with two left hooks.

I got back to my stool, and under me I could hear the press like they was gone wild. I twisted around and hollered down at the reporters right under me, "I'm gonna upset the world!" I never will forget how their faces was looking up at me like they couldn't believe it. I happened to be looking right at Liston when that warning buzzer sounded, and I didn't believe it when he spat out his mouthpiece. I just couldn't believe it—but there it was laying there. And then something just told me he wasn't coming out! I give a whoop and come off that stool like it was red hot. It's a funny thing, but I wasn't even thinking about Liston—I was thinking about nothing but that hypocrite press. All of them down there had wrote so much about me bound to get killed by the big fists. It was even rumors that right after the weigh-in I had been taken to the asylum somewhere, and another rumor that I had caught a plane and run off. I couldn't think about nothing but all that. I went dancing around the ring, hollering down at them reporters, "Eat your words! Eat! Eat!" And I hollered at the people, "I am the *king!*"

PLAYBOY: Despite your victory, the fight ended under a cloud of doubt about the genuineness of Liston's arm injury. What's your own opinion?

CLAY: Eight doctors said his arm was hurt. I ain't going to argue with no eight doctors' opinion. And I don't mean that I think nothing different at all. You take a man punching with the strength and force Liston has in a punch; if all he connects with is air—because wherever he hit, I wasn't there—then, yeah, I think it explains how he could have torn a muscle.

PLAYBOY: There was another controversy about the honesty of your failure to pass the three Army preinduction qualification tests that you took shortly after the fight. Any comment?

CLAY: The truth don't hurt nobody. The fact is I never was too bright in school. I just barely graduated. I had a D-minus average. I ain't ashamed of it, though. I mean, how much do school principals make a month? But when I looked at a lot of the questions they had on them Army tests, I just didn't know the answers. I didn't even know how to *start* after finding the answers. That's all. So I didn't pass. It was the Army's decision that they didn't want me to go in the service. They're the boss. I don't want to say no whole lot about it.

PLAYBOY: Was it embarrassing to be declared mentally unfit?

CLAY: I have said I am the greatest. Ain't nobody ever heard me say I was the smartest.

PLAYBOY: What is your feeling about the fact that your purse was withheld after the fight?

CLAY: I don't understand it. I'm not involved in any tax problems. How can they justify holding up my money? But let me tell you something:

Money and riches don't mean nothing to me. I don't care nothing about being no rich individual. I'm not living for glory or for fame; all this is doomed for destruction. You got it today, tomorrow it's gone. I got bigger things on my mind than that. I got Islam on my mind.

PLAYBOY: Speaking of Islam, the National Boxing Association announced that it was considering the revocation of your heavyweight title because of your membership in the Black Muslims, which you announced just after the fight. Have you heard any official word on their decision?

CLAY: It just fizzled out. But until it did, the NBA was going to condemn me, try me, sentence me and execute me, all by themselves. Ain't this country supposed to be where every man can have the religion he wants, even *no* religion if that's what he wants? It ain't a court in America that would take a man's job, or his title, because of his religious convictions. The Constitution forbids Congress from making any laws involving a man's religion. But the NBA would take it on itself to take away my title—for what? What have I done to hurt boxing? I've *helped* boxing. I don't smoke, I don't drink, I don't bother with nobody. Ain't it funny they never said nothing about Liston? He's been arrested for armed robbery, beating up cops, carrying concealed weapons, and I don't know *what* all. And how come they didn't lift Gene Fullmer's title? He was a Mormon. His religion believes Negroes are inferior; they ban Negroes from membership. But I guess that's all right. The NBA don't have no power noway. They can't stop nobody from fighting. And even if they could, it wouldn't matter, because I don't put that much value on no heavyweight crown anyway. Time was when I did, but that was before I found the religious convictions that I have. When I started getting attacked so bad because I am a Muslim, I had to decide, if it would come to me having to give up one or the other, what was most important to me, my religion or my fighting. I made up my mind that I could give up fighting and never look back. Because it's a whole pile of other ways I could make a living. Me being the world heavyweight champion feels very small and cheap to me when I put that alongside of how millions of my poor black brothers and sisters are having to struggle just to get their human rights here in America. Maybe God got me here for a sacrifice. I don't know. But I do know that God don't want me to go down for standing up.

PLAYBOY: What or who made you decide to join the Muslims?

CLAY: Nobody or nothing *made* me decide. I make up my mind for myself. In 1960, in Miami, I was training for a fight. It wasn't long after—I had won the 1960 Olympic Gold Medal over there in Rome. Herb Liler was the fellow I was going to fight, I remember. I put him on the floor in four. Anyway, one day this Muslim minister came to meet me and he asked me wouldn't I like to come to his mosque and hear about the history of my forefathers. I never had heard no black man talking about no forefathers, except that they were slaves, so I went to a meeting. And this minister started teaching, and the things he said really shook me up. Things like that we 20 million black people in America didn't know our true identities, or even our true family names. And we were the direct descendants of black men and women stolen from a rich black continent and brought here and stripped of all knowledge of themselves and taught to hate themselves and their kind. And that's how us so-called "Negroes" had come to be the only race among mankind that loved its enemies. Now, I'm the kind that catches on quick. I said to myself, listen here, this man's *saying* something! I hope don't nobody never hit me in the ring hard as it did when that brother minister said the Chinese are named after China, Russians after Russia, Cubans after Cuba, Italians after Italy, the English after England, and clear on down the line everybody was named for somewhere he could call home, except us. He said, "What country are we so-called 'Negroes' named for? *No* country! We are just a lost race." Well, *boom!* That really shook me up.

PLAYBOY: Was that when you joined the Muslims?

CLAY: Not right then, no. Before I joined, I attended a lot of mosque meetings in different places I went. I never did come out of a meeting not understanding something I hadn't known or even thought about before. Everywhere I looked, I started seeing things in a new light. Like, I remember right in our house back in Louisville, all the pictures on the walls were white people. Nothing about us black people. A picture of a white Jesus Christ. Now, what painter ever *saw* Jesus? So who says Jesus was white? And all my life, I had been seeing the black man getting his head whipped by the white man, and stuck in the white man's jails, and things like that. And myself, I had to admit that up to then, I had always hated being black, just like other Negroes, hating our kind, instead of loving one another. The more I saw and thought, the more the truth made sense to me. Whatever I'm for, I always have believed in talking it up, and the first thing you know, I was in Muslim meetings calling out just like the rest, "Right, brother! Tell it, brother! Keep it coming!" And today my religion is Islam, and I'm proud of it.

PLAYBOY: How has it changed your life?

CLAY: In every way. It's pulled me up and cleaned me up as a human being.
PLAYBOY: Can you be more explicit?
CLAY: Well, before I became a Muslim, I used to drink. Yes, I did. The truth is the truth. And after I had fought and beat somebody, I didn't hardly go nowhere without two big, pretty women beside me. But my change is one of the things that will mark me as a great man in history. When you can live righteous in the hell of North America—when a man can control his life, his physical needs, his lower self, he elevates himself. The downfall of so many great men is that they haven't been able to control their appetite for women.
PLAYBOY: But you have?
CLAY: We Muslims don't touch a woman unless we're married to her.
PLAYBOY: Are you saying that you don't have affairs with women?
CLAY: I don't even kiss a woman. I'm ashamed of myself, but sometimes I've caught myself wishing I had found Islam about five years from now, maybe—with all the temptations I have to resist. But I don't even kiss none, because you get too close, it's almost impossible to stop. I'm a young man, you know, in the prime of life.
PLAYBOY: You mention temptations. What are they?
CLAY: All types of women—white women, too—make passes at me. Girls find out where I live and knock at the door at one and two in the morning. They send me their pictures and phone numbers, saying please just telephone them, they would like to meet me, do I need a secretary? I've even had girls come up here wearing scarves on their heads, with no makeup and all that, trying to act like young Muslim sisters. But the only catch is a Muslim sister never would do that.
PLAYBOY: Did you have any other religious affiliation before Islam?
CLAY: When I was 12 years old, and didn't know what I was doing, I was baptized in the Centennial Baptist Church in Louisville.
PLAYBOY: Have you given up Christianity, then?
CLAY: The Christian religion has just been used to brainwash the black man here in America. It has just taught him to look for his heaven in the sky, in the hereafter, while the white man enjoys his heaven here on earth.
PLAYBOY: As the owner of four Cadillacs and the recipient of a $600,000 purse earned largely from white patronage of your fight with Liston, do you think that assertion is entirely true in your own case?
CLAY: Have you heard anybody complaining he didn't get his money's worth? No! All of the noise is about my religion, something that has nothing to do with fighting. They didn't mind my being champion until

they found out I was a Muslim. Then they didn't want nothing to do with me. White people, they worry more about Islam than they do about the championship.

PLAYBOY: Don't you feel that whites have some reason for concern that the heavyweight champion belongs to an organization that is alleged to teach hatred of whites?

CLAY: Look, the black man that's trying to integrate, he's getting beat up and bombed and shot. But the black man that says he don't want to integrate, he gets called a "hate teacher." Lookahere, now Chubby Checker is catching hell with a white woman. And I'm catching hell for *not* wanting a white woman. The followers of Mr. Elijah Muhammad, we're not trying to marry no white man's sisters and daughters. We're not trying to force our way into no white neighborhoods. It look like to me that the white people who are so against integrated schools and restaurants and hotels ought to be *glad* about what Mr. Muhammad is teaching his followers. The only way for peace between the races is a separation of the races.

PLAYBOY: Are you against the Civil Rights Act, then?

CLAY: I think that the Civil Rights Act will lead to bloodshed. It already has. It won't change people's hearts. But I don't call it hate. I call it human nature. I don't think that white people hate colored people. You just don't never see a rabbit eating with a lion. I think that all of this "integration" started backfiring when it put the white man on the spot. It ain't going to go on much further. I think that the black man needs to get together with his own kind. He needs to say, "Let's don't go where we're not wanted." You take Sonny Liston. He was the champion of the world, and that's supposed to include America. But when he tried to buy a house in a segregated neighborhood in Miami, he was turned down. The white people don't want integration: I don't believe in forcing it and the Muslims don't either.

PLAYBOY: Is that why you've chosen to live in Harlem?

CLAY: Right. I could be living all exclusive, downtown, in some skyscraper hotel. I could be living right up in the hotel's penthouse, with my friends in rooms all around me. But I don't want none of that. I stay right in the heart of Harlem, in a place that a workingman with a good job could afford. I'm just used to being around my own people. I like being around my own people. It's just human nature to enjoy being around your own kind. I don't want no trouble. I am up here in the heart of blacktown. I can't find nothing wrong with that, but it seems to bother everybody else, it looks like. I been around my own people all of my life. Why would I want to try to leave them now? You have to be all the time putting on an act when you're trying to live and hang around somewhere you're not wanted, or they just put up with you for your money. I'm at ease living among my people. I'm never all tensed up; I don't have to be a sideshow all the time. I'm around unity, rhythm and soul. Our people are warm people. I don't like to be around cold people. I go out every morning early and walk up and down in the streets, and I talk to winos and the working people and everybody. I stand where they go down to the subway, and I say hello. I'm different from when Patterson was the champ. He wasn't anywhere near as popular as I am—not among our people, anyway.

PLAYBOY: What do you have to say about the fact that many Negroes, including several Negro leaders, have said that they have no desire to be identified with a heavyweight champion who is a Black Muslim?

CLAY: It's ridiculous for Negroes to be attacking somebody trying to stand up for their own race. People are always telling me "what a good example I could set for my people" if I just wasn't a Muslim. I've heard over and over how come I couldn't have been like Joe Louis and Sugar Ray. Well, they're gone now, and the black man's condition is just the same, ain't it? We're still catching hell. The fact is that my being a Muslim moved me from the sports pages to the front pages. I'm a whole lot bigger man than I would be if I was just a champion prizefighter. Twenty-four hours a day I get offers—to tour somewhere overseas, to visit colleges, to make speeches. Places like Harvard and Tuskegee, television shows, magazines, recordings. I get letters from all over. They are addressed to me in ways like "The Greatest Boxer in the World, U.S.A." and they come straight to me wherever they're mailed from. People want to write books about me. And I ought to have stock in Western Union and cable companies, I get so many of them. I'm trying to show you how I been elevated from the normal stature of fighters to being a world figure, a leader, a statesman.

PLAYBOY: Statesman?

CLAY: That's what I said. Listen, after I beat Liston, some African diplomats invited me to the United Nations. And because I'm a Muslim, I was welcomed like a king on my tour of Africa and the Middle East. I'm the first world champion that ever toured the world that he is champion of.

PLAYBOY: Is it true that you incensed Nigerians during your tour, by reneging on a promise to fight an exhibition match there, and by making the remark, on departing for Egypt, that "Cairo is more important than Nigeria"?

CLAY: It was a whole lot of confusion going on. We had planned a week in Nigeria, then a week in Ghana. But when we got over there, somehow with all kinds of this and that functions calling for me, our whole schedule got messed up. One Sunday I come back from Ghana to Nigeria to fight that exhibition. It was arranged for us to get to Cairo that Wednesday. Then my exhibition fight date got put forward. I figured it would make us disappoint the Cairo government that had bumped people off planes for us, things like that. So I said how important it was to get to Cairo on time. But when somebody got done quoting it, it wasn't told like I had said it. Any time you hear about me insulting black people, it's a lie. Anyway, wasn't nobody over there mad at me because of my *religion*. Somebody told me over there that I got the biggest welcome ever given to any American.

PLAYBOY: You met both Prime Minister Nkrumah of Ghana and Egypt's President Nasser on the trip. What was your impression of them?

CLAY: Well, I looked at Prime Minister Nkrumah, and it come to me that he looked just like so many Negroes in America—except there he was, the head of a country. And President Nasser, one of the six most powerful men in the world, he welcomed me as a Black Muslim, just as friendly as if he had been knowing me all my life.

PLAYBOY: Apart from influential friends, what do you feel you got out of the trip?

CLAY: Well, it showed me what Mr. Elijah Muhammad's teachings had taught me: that Africa is the home of Original Man, the black man, and that Africa, where the slaves was stolen from, has all kinds of rich history. And it is the richest continent on earth. Everybody knows that the biggest diamond ever found was found in black Africa. And let me tell you something—it wasn't just seeing the new buildings and cars and stuff; it's what you *feel* in Africa. Black people that's free and proud—they don't *feel* like that over here. I never have felt it here except among my Muslim brothers and sisters.

PLAYBOY: Your Muslim activities will soon have to be interrupted long enough to defend your title against Sonny Liston in your upcoming rematch. Now that he's familiar with your strategy and skills, do you think he'll be a tougher opponent?

CLAY: I know one thing: He would have to think he could put up a better fight than he did the last time. Liston has been through quite a bit.

PLAYBOY: Do *you* think he'll put up a better fight?

CLAY: Maybe, but I'll have the edge again. Liston will be fighting a comeback. He'll be in the position of having to *prove* he can beat me.

So he'll come in that ring scared he's going to lose. A lot of people still refuse to accept it, but Liston *knows* he was whipped by a better boxer. Another thing, don't never forget that boxing is for young men. How old is Liston?

PLAYBOY: According to published reports, around 32.

CLAY: Well, I hear he's pushing 40. He ain't physically *capable* of forcing a body that old through four and a half months of the strong training a fighter would need to meet a young, strong fighter like me.

PLAYBOY: Doug Jones has been touted as another possible contender for your title. What's your appraisal of him?

CLAY: He's a good, strong man, a good boxer. He's fast, and he's got determination. He's the possible champ after I quit.

PLAYBOY: How about Patterson? Do you think he has a chance to regain his title a second time?

CLAY: Patterson! Don't make me laugh. I'm a natural heavyweight, and he was never anything but a blown-up light–heavy. He could never take my punches. I could play with him, cut him up and take him out whenever I got ready. And he knows it. That's why he always ducked me when he was champ. He ain't no fool. You know, at the Olympic games in Rome, I told Patterson, "Two, three years from now, I'm going to take your title." He said, "You're a good kid, keep trying, kid." Well, I bet you he has since thought that over many a day.

PLAYBOY: If he knows he couldn't beat you, how do you explain his recent campaign to meet you in a title match?

CLAY: Only reason he's decided to come out of his shell now is to try and make himself a big hero to the white man by saving the heavyweight title from being held by a Muslim. I wish you would print for Patterson to read that if he ever convinces my managers to let him in the same ring with me, it's going to be the first time I ever trained to develop in myself a brutal killer instinct. I've never felt that way about nobody else. Fighting is just a sport, a game, to me. But Patterson I would want to beat to the floor for the way he rushed out of hiding after his last whipping, announcing that he wanted to fight me because no Muslim deserved to be the champ. I never had no concern about his having the Catholic religion. But he was going to jump up to fight me to be the white man's champion. And I don't know no sadder example of nobody making a bigger fool of himself. I don't think three more weeks had passed before it was in the papers about him trying to sell his big, fine home in a so-called "integrated" neighborhood because his white neighbors wouldn't speak to his family, and white children were calling his children "nigger" and a white man next door even had put up a fence to keep from having to even *see* Patterson. I ain't never read nothing no more pitiful than how Patterson told the newspapers, "I tried to integrate—it just didn't work." It's like when he was the champion, the only time he would be caught in Harlem was when he was in the back of a car, waving, in some parade. The big shot didn't have no time for his own kind, he was so busy "integrating." And now he wants to fight me because I stick up for black people. I'll tell him again, he sure better think five or six times before he gets into any ring with me.

PLAYBOY: Are there any other active heavyweights, apart from Doug Jones, whom you rate as title contenders?

CLAY: Not in my class, of course. But below that, after Jones—and Liston—there's Ernie Terrell. He's a tall boy, a good left jab. He moves good, but he tires easy. He doesn't have enough experience to take me on yet. But he's a good kid. And Cleveland Williams. If he even *dreamed* he fought me, he'd apologize. He needs a *lot* more experience. Liston knocked him out twice. Williams, if he's pressured, will quit in a minute. I can't see any more after these. I don't really even watch fighting much, except films of the greatest.

PLAYBOY: Just you?

CLAY: Just me.

PLAYBOY: Are you the greatest now fighting, or the greatest in boxing history?

CLAY: Now, a whole lot of people ain't going to like this, but I'm going to tell you the truth—you asked me. It's too many great old champions to go listing them one by one. But ain't no need to. I think that Joe Louis, in his prime, could have whipped them all—I mean anyone you want to name. And I would have beat Louis. Now, look—people don't like to face the facts. All they can think about is Joe Louis's punch. Well, he did have a deadly punch, just like Liston has a deadly punch. But if Louis didn't hit nothing but air, like Liston didn't with me, then we got to look at other things. Even if Louis did hit me a few times, remember they all said Liston was a tougher one-punch man than even Joe Louis. And I took some of Liston's best shots. Remember that. Then, too, I'm taller than Louis. But I tell you what would decide the fight: I'm *faster* than Louis was. No, Louis and none of the rest of them couldn't whip me. Look—it ain't *never* been another fighter like me. Ain't never been no *nothing* like me.

November 1975

MUHAMMAD ALI
A candid conversation with the greatest—and prettiest—poet in the world

As we go to press, Muhammad Ali is in training for his third match with Joe Frazier, slated for Manila; whether or not he retains his title will be known by the time this issue appears. But whatever the outcome, interviewer Lawrence Linderman feels "they ought to retire the title with Ali, anyway." So, without further ado, we're pleased to introduce a man who needs no introduction.

PLAYBOY: The last time we interviewed you, 11 years ago, you were still Cassius Clay. What would the old Cassius be doing today?

ALI: Cassius Clay would now be training in Paris, France, because French promoters would've offered me—like they've done—free rooms in a hotel on some beach. If not, I'd probably be in Jamaica, training in a plush hotel. When I see a lady now, I do my best to try to teach her about the Honorable Elijah Muhammad so I can help her. Cassius Clay would carry her to some hotel room and use her.

If I was Cassius Clay today, I'd be just like Floyd Patterson. I'd probably have a white wife and I wouldn't represent black people in no way. Or I'd be like Charley Pride, the folk singer. Nothin' bad about him—he's a good fella and I met his black wife, but Charley stays out of controversy. It's not only him, because I could name Wilt Chamberlain and others who just don't get involved in struggle or racial issues—it might jeopardize their position. I'd be that kind of man.

If I was Cassius Clay *tonight*, I'd probably be staying in a big hotel in New York City, and I might say, "Well, I got time to have a little fun. I'm going out to a big discotheque full of white girls and I'll find the prettiest one there and spend the night with her."

PLAYBOY: Is that what Cassius Clay used to do?

ALI: I was on my way to it.

PLAYBOY: You never got there?

ALI: Before I was a Muslim, I had one white girlfriend for two days, that's all. I wasn't no Muslim then, but I just felt it wasn't right. I *knew* it wasn't right, 'cause I had to duck and hide and slip around, and I thought, "Man, it's not *worth* all this trouble." Black men with white women just don't *feel* right. They may think it's all right, and that they're in love, but you see 'em walking on the street and they're ashamed—they be duckin' and they be cold. They're not *proud*. Once you get a knowledge of yourself, you see how stupid that is. I don't even think about nothin' like that, chasing white women. I'm married and in love with a pretty black one. But if I wasn't, I'd run after the next pretty black girl I saw.

PLAYBOY: Since a lot of people are wondering about this, level with us: Do you write all the poetry you pass off as your own?

ALI: Sure I do. Hey, man, I'm so good I got offered a professorship at Oxford. I write late at night, after the phones stop ringin' and it's quiet and nobody's around—all great writers do better at night. I take at least one nap during the day, and then I get up at two in the morning and do my thing. You know, I'm a worldly man who likes people and action and I always like cities, but now when I find myself in a city, I can't wait to get back to my training camp. Neon signs, traffic, noise and people—all that can get you crazy. It's funny, because I was supposed to be torturing myself by building a training camp out in the middle of nowhere in northern Pennsylvania, but this is good livin'—fresh air, well water, quiet and country views. I thought I wouldn't like it at all but that at least I'd work a lot instead of being in the city, where maybe I wouldn't train hard enough. Well, now I like it better than being in *any* city. This is a real good setting for writin' poetry and I write all the time, even when I'm in training. In fact, I wrote one up here that's better than any poem in the world.

PLAYBOY: How do you know that?

ALI: My poem explains truth, so what could be better? That's the name of it, too, *Truth*:

> The face of Truth is open, the eyes
> of Truth are bright
> The lips of Truth are ever closed,
> the head of Truth is upright
> The breast of Truth stands forward,
> the gaze of Truth is straight
> Truth has neither fear nor doubt,

Truth has patience to wait.
The words of Truth are touching,
the voice of Truth is deep
The law of Truth is simple: All you
sow, you reap.
The soul of Truth is flaming, the
heart of Truth is warm
The mind of Truth is clear and
firm through rain and storm.
Facts are only its shadow, Truth
stands above all sin.
Great be the battle of life—Truth
in the end shall win.
The image of Truth is the Honorable
Elijah Muhammad, wisdom's message is his rod
The sign of Truth is the crescent
and the soul of Truth is God.
Life of Truth is eternal
Immortal is its past
Power of Truth shall endure
Truth shall hold to the last.

It's a masterpiece, if I say so myself. But poems aren't the only thing I've been writing. I've also been setting my mind to sayings. You want to hear some?

PLAYBOY: Do we have a choice?

ALI: You listen up and maybe I'll make you as famous as I made Howard Cosell. "Wars on nations are fought to change maps, but wars on poverty are fought to map change." Good, huh? "The man who views the world at 50 the same as he did at 20 has wasted 30 years of his life." These are words of wisdom, so pay attention, Mr. Playboy. "The man who has no imagination stands on the earth—he has no wings, he cannot fly." Catch this: "When we are right, no one remembers, but when we are wrong, no one forgets. Watergate!" I really like the next one: "Where is man's wealth? His wealth is in his knowledge. If his wealth was in the bank and not in his knowledge, then he don't possess it—because it's in the bank!" You got all that?

PLAYBOY: Got it, Muhammad.

ALI: Well, there's more. "The warden of a prison is in a worse condition than the prisoner himself. While the body of the prisoner is in captivity, the mind of the warden is in prison!" Words of wisdom by Muhammad Ali. This is about beauty: "It is those who have touched the inner beauty that appreciate beauty in all its forms." I'm even going to explain that to you. Some people will look at a sister and say, "She sure is ugly." Another man will see the same sister and say, "That's the most beautiful woman I ever did see." How do you like *this* one: "Love is a net where hearts are caught like fish"?

PLAYBOY: Isn't that a little corny?

ALI: I knew you wasn't smart as soon as I laid eyes on you. But I know you're gonna like this one, which is called *Riding on My Horse of Hope*: "Holding in my hands the reins of courage, dressed in the armor of patience, the helmet of endurance on my head, I started on my journey to the land of love." Whew! Muhammad Ali sure goes deeper than *boxing*.

PLAYBOY: That's for sure. But let's talk about boxing anyway. What's the physical sensation of really being nailed by hitters like Foreman and Frazier?

ALI: Take a stiff tree branch in your hand and hit it against the floor and you'll feel your hand go *boingggggg*. Well, getting tagged is the same kind of jar on your whole body, and you need at least 10 or 20 seconds to make that go away. You get hit again before that, you got another *boingggggg*.

PLAYBOY: After you're hit that hard, does your body do what you want it to do?

ALI: No, because your mind controls your body and the moment you're tagged, you can't think. You're just numb and you don't know where you're at. There's no *pain*, just that jarring feeling. But I automatically know what to do when that happens to me, sort of like a sprinkler system going off when a fire starts up. When I get stunned, I'm not really conscious of exactly where I'm at or what's happening, but I always tell myself that I'm to dance, run, tie my man up or hold my head way down. I tell myself all that when I'm conscious, and when I get tagged, I automatically do it. I get hit, but all great fighters get hit—Sugar Ray got hit, Joe Louis got hit and Rocky Marciano got hit. But they had something other fighters didn't have: the ability to hold on until they cleared up. I got that ability, too, and I had to use it once in each of the Frazier fights. That's one reason I'm a great defensive fighter. The other is my rope-a-dope defense—and when I fought Foreman, he was the dope.

PLAYBOY: If you prepared that tactic for your fight with Foreman in Zaire, then why was Angelo Dundee, your trainer, so shocked when you suddenly went to the ropes?

ALI: Well, I didn't really *plan* it. After the first round, I felt myself getting too tired for the pace of that fight, but George wasn't gonna get tired, 'cause he was just cutting the ring off on me. I stayed out of the way, but I figured that after seven or eight rounds of dancing like that, I'd be really tired. Then, when I'd go to the ropes, my resistance would be low and George would get one through to me. So while I was still fresh, I decided to go to the ropes and try to get George tired.

PLAYBOY: What was your original Foreman fight plan?

ALI: To dance every round, I had it in mind to do what I did when I was 22, but I got tired, so I had to change my strategy. George didn't change his strategy, 'cause he can't do nothin' but attack—that's the *only* thing he knows. All he wants to do is get his man in the corner, so in the second round, I gave him what he wanted. He couldn't do *nothin'*!

PLAYBOY: Did Foreman seem puzzled when he had you cornered but couldn't land any punches?

ALI: Nope, he just figured he'd get me in the next round. When he didn't do it in the third, he thought he'd get me in the fourth. Then he thought it would be the fifth, and then the sixth. But in the sixth round, George was so *tired*. All of a sudden, he knew he'd threw everything he had at me and hadn't hurt me at all. And he just lost all his heart.

PLAYBOY: How could you tell?

ALI: He stopped attacking the way he'd been doin'. He had shots to take and didn't take 'em, and then I purposely left him some openings and he wouldn't take *them*. George knew he'd been caught in my trap and there wasn't but one way he could get out of it: by knocking me out. He kept trying with his last hope, but he was too tired, and a man of his age and talent shouldn't get used up that quick. George was *dead* tired; he was throwing wild punches, missing and falling over the ropes. So I started tellin' him how bad he looked: "Lookatcha, you're not a champ, you're a tramp. You're fightin' just like a sissy. C'mon and *show* me somethin', boy."

PLAYBOY: You also called him all kinds of names before the fight. How does that help?

ALI: You mean when I called him The Mummy, 'cause he walks like one? Listen, if a guy loses his temper and gets angry, his judgment's off and he's not thinking as sharp as he should. But George wasn't angry. No, sir. George had this feeling that he was *supreme*. He believed what the press said—that he was unbeatable and that he'd whup me easy. The first three rounds, he still believed it. But when I started throwing punches at him in the fourth, George finally woke up and thought, "Man, I'm in trouble." He was *shocked*.

PLAYBOY: Do you think Foreman was so confident of beating you that he didn't train properly?

ALI: No, George didn't take me lightly. He fought me harder than he fought Frazier or Norton. *Whoever* I fight comes at me harder, because if you beat Muhammad Ali, you'll be the big man, the legend. Beating me is like beating Joe Louis or being the man who shot Jesse James. George just didn't realize how hard I am to hit and how hard I *can* hit. He thought he was greater than me. Well, George is humble now. I did just what I told him I'd do when the ref was giving us instructions. There was George, trying to scare me with his serious look—he got that from his idol, Sonny Liston. And there I was, tellin' him, "Boy, you in *trouble*! You're gonna meet the greatest fighter of all time! We here now and there ain't no way for you to get out of this ring—I *gotcha*! You been readin' about me ever since you were a little boy and now you gonna see me in action. Chump, I'm gonna show you how great I am—I'm gonna eat you up. You don't stand a *chance*! You lose the crown tonight!"

PLAYBOY: Foreman claims he was drugged before the fight. Did you see any evidence of that?

ALI: George is just a sore loser. The day after the fight, he actually said he was the true champion; he beat me. Then, when he got to Paris, he said the ropes had been too loose. Then, after the ropes were too loose, his next excuse was that the count was too fast. Then it was the canvas—he said it was too *soft*. Well, it was soft for me, too. Weeks after the fight, he finds out he was drugged? If he was drugged, he'd have knew it the next day. Somebody oughtta ask him just *how* he was drugged. Did somebody give him a needle? If it was dope, what *kind* of dope? *Excuses*! The truth is that the excuses started comin' as soon as George began to realize he *lost*. He couldn't take losing the championship.

PLAYBOY: Won't it make him that much tougher an opponent when and if you fight him again?

ALI: Next fight is gonna be *easier*. George now knows he can be knocked out, so he'll be more on guard and attackin' less. But his only chance of winning is to charge and corner me and wham away and hope one or two shots get through my defense. But he's gun-shy of that, 'cause he tried it—threw everything he had—and all he got was tired. For him to go into that same old bam-bam-bam thing again will mentally destroy him, because the first thing he's gonna think is, "Uh-oh, I'm going to wear myself out again." So then he'll keep more to the center of the ring and do more boxing.

And that's just where I want him. Poppin' and jabbin' in the center of the ring is *my* thing, so now he's really beat. The only chance he has to whup me is to stay on me and keep me on the ropes—and he knows that's bad, 'cause the odds are he's not gonna hurt me and he's gonna tire himself out. But if he don't do that, he's in *more* trouble, 'cause I'll pop away at him with my left. In other words, Foreman's wrong if he do and wrong if he don't. The second time around, I'll beat him 'cause he has no confidence. The first fight, I beat him 'cause he thought he was a big indestructible lion—but George found out the facts of life when we had our rumble in the jungle.

PLAYBOY: Did you like the idea of Zaire as the fight site?

ALI: I wanted my title back so bad I would've fought George in a telephone booth. World heavyweight champion, that's a big title. When you're the champ, whatever you say or do is news. George would go to Las Vegas and the newspapers are writin' about it. I turn on the television and there's George. It was Foreman this and Foreman that, and I was sitting here in my Pennsylvania training camp, thinkin', "Dadgummit, I really had somethin'. People looked up to *me* that way." That really got me down and made me want to win that title *bad*.

Now that I got it back, every day is a sunshiny day: I wake up and I know I'm the heavyweight champion of the world. Whatever restaurant I walk into, whatever park I go to, whatever school I visit, people are sayin', "The *champ*'s here!" When I get on a plane, a man is always sayin' to his little boy, "Son, there goes the heavyweight champion of the world." Wherever I go, the tab is picked up, people want to see me and the TV wants me for interviews. I can eat all the ice cream, cake, pudding and pie I want to and still get $100,000 for an exhibition. That's what it means to be champ, and as long as I keep winning, it'll keep happenin'. So before I fight, I think, "Whuppin' this man means everything. So many good things are gonna happen if I win I can't even imagine what they'll *be*!"

When I first won the championship from Sonny Liston, I was riding high and I didn't realize what I had. Now, the second time around, I appreciate the title, and I would've gone anywhere in the world to get it back. To be honest, when I first heard the fight would be in Africa, I just hoped it would go off right, being in a country that was supposed to be so undeveloped. Then, when we went down to Zaire, I saw they'd built a new stadium with lights and that everything would be ready, and I started getting used to the idea and liking it. And the more I thought about it, the more it grew on me, and then one day it just hit me how *great* it would be to win back my title in Africa. Being in Zaire opened my eyes.

PLAYBOY: In what way?

ALI: I saw black people running their own country. I saw a black president of a humble black people who have a modern country. There are good roads throughout Zaire, and Kinshasa has a nice downtown section that reminds you of a city in the States. Buildings, restaurants, stores, shopping centers—I could name you 1000 things I saw that made me feel good. When I was in training there before the fight, I'd sit on the riverbank and watch the boats going by and see the 747 jumbo jets flying overhead, and I'd know there were black pilots and black stewardesses in 'em, and it just seemed so nice. In Zaire, *everything* was black—from the train drivers and hotel owners to the teachers in the schools and the pictures on the money. It was just like any other society, except it was all black, and because I'm black oriented and a Muslim, I was *home* there. I'm not home *here*. I'm trying to make it home, but it's not.

PLAYBOY: Why not?

ALI: Because black people in America will never be free so long as they're on the white man's land. Look, birds want to be free, tigers want to be free, everything wants to be free. We can't be free until we get our own land and our own country in North America. When we separate from America and take maybe 10 states, then we'll be free. Free to make our own laws, set our own taxes, have our own courts, our own judges, our own schoolrooms, our own currency, our own passports. And if not here in America, the Honorable Elijah Muhammad said the white man should supply us with the means to let us go back somewhere in Africa and build up our own country. America, rich as it is, was made rich partly through the black man's labor. It can afford to supply us for 25 years with the means to make our own nation work, and we'll build it up, too. We can't be free if we can't control our own land. I own this training camp, but it ain't really *my* land, not when some white lady comes up and gives me a $4000 tax bill to pay if I want to stay here. If I thought the taxes I paid was really going to benefit my people, I wouldn't mind paying up. But that ain't what's happening. Black people need to have their own nation.

PLAYBOY: Since it's unlikely they'll get one carved out of—or paid for by—the U.S., are you pessimistic about America's future race relations?
ALI: America don't *have* no future! America's going to be destroyed! Allah's going to divinely chastise America! Violence, crimes, earthquakes—there's gonna be all *kinds* of trouble. America's going to pay for all its lynchings and killings of slaves and what it's done to black people. America's day is over—and if it doesn't do justice to the black man and separate, it gonna *burn*! I'm not the leader, so I can't tell you how the separation will take place or whether it will happen in my lifetime or not, but I believe there's a divine force that will make it happen. I wish *I* could make it happen, but I can't—Allah will. It took the white men 500 years after they got here to get this country the way they want it, it took a lot of time and work, and it's gonna take *us* time and work. And if it takes 1000 years, well, the world is millions of years old, and 1000 years can be regarded as a day in the history of the world; so according to time, it's just around the corner.

And it'll happen, because it's right that black people should have their own nation. God bless the child that has his own—Christians teach that. Well, we don't have *nothin'* that's our own. If white men decide to close their grocery stores tomorrow, black people will starve to death. We're *tired* of being slaves and never having nothing. We're *tired* of being servants and waiting till we die and go to heaven before we get anything. We want something while we're living. The Honorable Elijah Muhammad has passed on physically, but his message is still with us: Muslims will never be satisfied with integration and all the little jobs and promises black people get. We want our own nation. We're 25 million black people—there's a lot of Negroes in America, you know? Man, there's only about 10 million people in Cuba, and when they tell America to stay out, America *stays* out. They're just a few million, but they got their own nation and can get away with it. Nigerians and Ghanians have *their* own country. When I rode through Zaire and looked at their little flag and watched them doing their little dances, hey, it was *their* own country. But we're a whole nation of slaves still in bondage to white people. We worked 300 years to make this country rich and fought for it in the Japanese war, the German war, the Korean war—in all the wars—and we *still* don't have nothing! So now, since they don't need cotton pickers 'cause machines can do it, and since we're walkin' the streets and multiplying, and there are no jobs for us—why *not* separate? Why *not* say, "OK, slave, we don't need you no more for picking cotton"?

PLAYBOY: Aren't you ignoring the fact that the nation's universities are now turning out black graduates at what would have seemed an unreachable rate as recently as 15 years ago?

ALI: No, 'cause all the white man's sayin' now is, "OK, slave, you're a doctor, you're a lawyer, you're a technician. You can do anything today, slave, and you're the most educated people there is next to white people. Black man, you got your degree."

And there ain't nothin' we can't do. We can build Empire State Buildings, 'cause we got our plumbers, designers, architects, electricians and construction workers. But since we're in your house, we got no jobs. You say we're free and you're not gonna lynch us anymore—but here we are without work, and we're still not getting along with each other. All right, I believe it, 400 years prove we can't get along. Fine, thank you, Master. Now, will you let us go and build *us* a house? What's *wrong* with us having our own house—our own country? If we had our own nation, the courts would become courts of justice. We wouldn't have a bunch of blue-eyed white judges lookin' at us bad and wanting to get us. We wouldn't have policemen laying back on the highway, waiting for us to do something wrong and stopping every black man they see drivin' a new car.

Doesn't all this make sense? Don't it sound good? See, this is why Muslims convert people every day. If they was black, even white people would join. We want to be free. The Honorable Elijah Muhammad *made* us free.

PLAYBOY: Elijah Muhammad preached that all white men are blue-eyed devils. Do you believe that?

ALI: We know that every individual white ain't devil-hearted, and we got *black* people who are devils—the worst devils I've run into can be my own kind. When I think about white people, it's like there's 1000 rattlesnakes outside my door and maybe 100 of them want to help me. But they all look alike, so should I open my door and hope that the 100 who want to help will keep the other 900 off me, when only one bite will kill me? What I'm sayin' is that if there's 1000 rattlesnakes out there and 100 of them mean good—I'm still gonna shut my door. I'm gonna say, "I'm sorry, you nice 100 snakes, but *you don't really matter*."

Yeah, every Negro can say, "Oh, here's a white man who means right." But if that's true, where are the 25 million whites standing next to the 25 million blacks? Why can't you even get 100 of them together who are ready to stand up and fight and maybe even die for black freedom? Hey, we'd *look* if you did that.

PLAYBOY: Didn't white freedom riders of the 1960s—at least four of whom were murdered—demonstrate that many whites were ready to risk their lives for black civil rights?

ALI: Look, we been told there's gonna be whites who help blacks. And we also know there's gonna be whites who'll escape Allah's judgment, who won't be killed when Allah destroys this country—mainly some Jewish people who really mean right and do right. But we look at the situation as a whole. We *have* to. OK, think about a white student who's got long hair and who wants minority people to have something and so he's against the slave white rule. Well, other whites will beat his behind and maybe even kill him, because they don't want him helping us. But that doesn't change what happens to the black man. If white boys get beat up, am I supposed to say, "Oh, some white folks are good. Let's forget our whole movement and integrate and join up in America"?

Yes, a lot of these white students get hurt 'cause they want to help save their country. But listen, your great-granddaddy told my great-granddaddy that when *my* granddaddy got grown, things would be better. Then your granddaddy told my granddaddy that when *my* daddy was born, things would be better. Your daddy told my daddy that when *I* got grown, things would be better. But they ain't. Are you tellin' me that when *my* children get grown, things'll be better for black people in this country?

PLAYBOY: No, we're just trying to find out how you honestly feel about whites.

ALI: White people are good thinkers, man, but they're crazy. Whoever makes the commercials shown on Johnny Carson's TV show and whoever makes all them movies, well, they're smart, they're planners and they can rule the world. Mostly 'cause they always got a story to tell. Is Martin Luther King marching and causing trouble? OK, we'll let the blacks use the public toilets, but let's make 'em fight six months for it, and while they're fighting, we'll make another plan. They wanna come in the supermarket next week? OK, let's make 'em fight two years for that. Meanwhile, we're still trying to get into schools in *Boston*, of all places. I'm telling you, the same men who write movies *must* be writing these plans. It's like, OK, the airlines will give jobs to a few black pilots and black stewardesses—but by the time they're finally hired, white folks are on the moon in *spaceships*.

So black folks stay far behind, *so* far behind that it's a shame. Think of how rich America is: The government spends more than $300 billion a year to run this country and, meanwhile, black people ain't even got money to go to the hospital. For a man who's alive, a man like Muhammad Ali, who's listened to the wisest black man in America, the Honorable Elijah Muhammad, the only thing to want is freedom in our own nation. Ain't *nothing* you can tell me or show me to match what I'm saying. The only thing the white man can offer me is a job in America—he ain't gonna offer me no flag, no hospitals, no land, no freedom. But once a man knows what freedom is, he's not satisfied even being the president of your country. And as Allah is my witness, I'd die today to prove it. If I could be President of the U.S. tomorrow and do what I can to help my people or be in an all-black country of 25 million Negroes and my job would be to put garbage in the truck, I'd be a garbageman. And if that included not just me but also my children and all my seed from now till forever, I'd still rather have the lowest job in a black society than the highest in a white society. If we got our own country, I'd empty trash ahead of being President of the U.S.—or being Muhammad Ali, the champion.

PLAYBOY: You've earned nearly $10 million in fight purses in the past two years alone. Would you really part with all your wealth so easily?

ALI: I'd do it in a minute. Last week, I was out taking a ride and I thought, "I'm driving this Rolls-Royce and I got another one in the garage that I hardly ever use that cost $40,000. I got a Scenicruiser Greyhound bus that sleeps 14 and cost $120,000 and another bus that cost $42,000—$162,000 just in mobile homes. My training camp cost $350,000 and I just spent $300,000 remodeling my house in Chicago. I got all that and a lot more."

Well, I was driving down the street and I saw a little black man wrapped in an old coat standing on a corner with his wife and little boy, waiting for a bus to come along—and there I am in my Rolls-Royce. The little boy had holes in his shoes and I started thinkin' that if he was *my* little boy, I'd break into tears. And I started crying.

Sure, I know I got it made while the masses of black people are catchin' hell, but as long as they ain't free, *I* ain't free. You think I need to hire all the people I do to help me get in shape? Listen, I can go down to Miami Beach with my cook and my sparring partners and get three hotel rooms and live it up—and I'd save money. I spent $850,000 training for George Foreman, most of it employing the few black people I could. In two months of training for Chuck Wepner, I spent $30,000. I wasn't doing it for me. See, once you become a Muslim, you want for your brother what you want for yourself. For instance, Kid Gavilan was a black boxing champion who had trouble in Cuba after he retired and he wound up in Miami working in a park. Newspaper reporters used to write stories about it that would embarrass Kid Gavilan and when I heard what he was doing, I thought, "Kid Gavilan ain't gonna work in no *park*." So I found Kid Gavilan and now he works for me, and I pay him a lot better than what he made in the park. Why should I allow one of the world's greatest black fighters in history to end up workin' in a park? He's representing all of us. The Honorable Elijah Muhammad gave me that.

Man, I think white folks would actually be *frightened* if they could see a Muslim convention. Not frightened from fear of Muslims bothering you, only that you can see the end of white rule coming when you see 50,000 Muslims together, all clean, all orderly, all dedicated. And the reason for that is because being a Muslim wakes you up to all kinds of things.

PLAYBOY: Such as?

ALI: Black people in America never used to know that our religion was Islam or that Jesus was a black man—we always made him white. We never knew we were the original people. We thought black was bad luck. We never thought that Africans would own their own countries again and that they were our brothers. God is white, but we never knew that the proper name of God is Allah—and Allah ain't white. We never even knew our names, because in slavery we were named what our white masters were named. If our master's name was Robinson, we were Robinson's property. If they sold you to Jones, you were Jones's property. And if you were then auctioned off to Mr. Williams, you were Williams's property. So we got identified by our masters' names. Well, today there's no chains on us, yet we still got names like *George Washington*. But as we wake up, we want our own beautiful names back. If a black man and woman have their first son, name him somethin' pretty like Ahad, which means the beginning. A black woman whose name is Constance or Barbara, let her change her name to a black name. Like Rashida or Jamilla, Satina, Alissia. Those are black people's names you find in Africa and Asia.

Black people in America should have those names, too, and lemme show you why. If I say Mr. Chang Chong or Mr. Loo Chin, the name tells you to look for a Chinaman. If I say Mr. Castro or Mr. Gonzales, you look for a Cuban or a Spaniard. If I say Mr. Weinstein or Mr. Goldberg, you look for a Jew. If I say Mr. Morning Star or Mr. Rolling Thunder, you know it's an Indian. If I say Mr. Mobutu or Mr. Kenyatta, you know it's an African. But if I say Mr. Green or Mr. Washington or Mr. Jones, the man could be white or black. See, you can identify everybody else by their names but us. And everybody *should* have their own names, which is what Elijah Muhammad taught us and which is what God taught him. I mean, did you ever hear of a white Englishman named Lumumba? Well, that's how black Americans feel about English names like Robinson. See how our teaching wakes you up? And not only are our names beautiful, they also have beautiful meanings.

PLAYBOY: What does *your* name mean?

ALI: Muhammad means worthy of all praises, Ali means the most high. And a lot of brothers today are doing like me and giving up their old slave name and taking new first and last names, nice-soundin' ones like Hassan Sharif or Kareem Shabazz. Those *were* our names before we were brought over here and named after George Washington. It's important we get them back, too, because if black folks don't know God's name, which is Allah, or their own name, they're starting too far behind. So the first step is to get out of that old slave name and start you a new family name—every time I hear about another black family doin' that, I get happier and happier. And if you know truth when *you* hear it, then you know how joyful I am to be a Muslim.

PLAYBOY: Will you assume a place in the Muslim movement when your boxing career is over?

ALI: Yes, sir. If I'm blessed to and they allow me, I'm gonna be a minister. I'm goin' to work with our new spiritual leader, brother Wallace D. Muhammad, son of Elijah Muhammad.

PLAYBOY: How has Elijah Muhammad's death affected the Black Muslims?

ALI: Naturally, it was saddening, because it's bad to lose him physically, but if we should lose him in ourselves, that's worse. So we just have to keep pushing, and we now follow his son, who's taking up just where his father left off. And we're 100 percent behind him. We were taught by Elijah Muhammad not to fear or grieve, and we don't.

PLAYBOY: What difference did he make in your own life?

ALI: He was *my* Jesus, and I had love for both the man and what he represented. Like Jesus Christ and all of God's prophets, he represented all good things and, having passed on, he is missed. But prophets never die spiritually, for their words and works live on. Elijah Muhammad was my savior, and everything I have came from him—my thoughts, my efforts to help my people, how I eat, how I talk, my *name*.

PLAYBOY: Do you think you could ever lose the faith?

ALI: I pray to Allah it don't happen, but it could. Every day, I say, "Surely I have turned myself to thee, O Allah, trying to be upright to him who has originated the heavens and the earth. Surely my prayers, my sacrifices, my life and my death are all for Allah, the lord of all the world." That's the beginning of a long prayer and I say it daily, and sometimes five times a day, to keep myself strong and on the right path. It's possible that I can lose faith, so I gotta pray, and to keep myself fired up, I gotta talk like I'm talkin' now. It's the kind of talk that keeps us Muslims together. And you can tell a bunch of Muslims: no violence, no hate, no cigarettes, no fightin', no stealin', all happy. It's a *miracle*. Most Negro places you be in, you see folks fussin' and cussin', eatin' pork chops and women runnin' around. You've seen the peace and unity of my training camp—it's all Elijah Muhammad's spirit and his teachings. Black people never acted like this before. If every one of us in camp was just like we were before we heard Elijah Muhammad, you wouldn't be able to see for all the smoke. You'd hear things like, "Hey, man, what's happenin', where's the *ladies*? What we gonna *drink* tonight? Let's get that music on and *party*!" And hey, this isn't an Islamic center. We're *happy* today. And we're better off than if we talked Christianity and said, "Jesus loves you, brother, Jesus died for your sins, accept Jesus Christ."

PLAYBOY: You find something wrong with that?

ALI: Christianity is a good philosophy if you live it, but it's controlled by white people who preach it but don't practice it. They just organize it and use it any which way they want to. If the white man lived Christianity, it would be different; but I tell you, I think it's against *nature* for European people to live Christian lives. Their nations were founded on killing, on wars. France, Germany, the bunch of 'em—it's been one long war ever since they existed. And if they're not killing each other over there, they're shooting Indians over here. And if they're not after the Indians, they're after the reindeer and every other living thing they can kill, even elephants. It's always violence and war for Christians.

Muslims, though, live their religion—*we* ain't hypocrites. We submit entirely to Allah's will. We don't eat ham, bacon or pork. We don't smoke. And everybody knows that we honor our women. You can see our sisters on the street from 10 miles away, their white dresses dragging along the ground. Young women in this society parade their bodies in all them freak clothes—miniskirts and pantsuits—but our women don't wear them. A woman who's got a beautiful body covers it up and humbles herself to Allah and also turns down all the modern conveniences. Nobody else do that but Muslim women. You hear about Catholic sisters—but they do a lot of screwing behind doors. Ain't nobody gonna believe a woman gonna go all her life and say, "I ain't never had a man," and is happy. She be *crazy*. That's against nature. And a priest saying he'd never touch a woman—that's against nature, too. What's he gonna do at night? Call upon the hand of the Lord?

PLAYBOY: Catholic readers will no doubt provide you with an answer, but, meanwhile, perhaps you could tell us why restrictions on Muslim women are far more stringent than upon Muslim men.

ALI: Because they should be. Women are sex symbols.

PLAYBOY: To whom?

ALI: To me.

PLAYBOY: And aren't you a sex symbol to women?

ALI: Still, men don't walk around with their chests out. Anyway, I'd rather see a man with his breasts showing than a woman. Why should she walk around with half her titties out? There gotta be restrictions that way.

PLAYBOY: But why should men formulate those restrictions?

ALI: Because in the Islamic world, the man's the boss and the woman stays in the background. She don't *want* to call the shots.

PLAYBOY: We can almost hear women's liberation leaders saying, "Sisters, you've been brainwashed. You should control your *own* lives."

ALI: Not Muslim women—Christian women. Muslim women don't think like that. See, the reason we so powerful is that we don't let the white man control *our* women. They obey *us*. And when a Muslim girl becomes a woman, she don't *want* to walk around with her behind hanging out. Horses and dogs and mules walk around with their behinds out. Humans hide their behinds.

PLAYBOY: Are Muslim women allowed to have careers or are they supposed to stay in the kitchen?

ALI: A lot of 'em got careers, working for and with their brothers, but you don't find 'em in no white man's office in downtown New York working behind secretarial desks. Too many black women been *used* in offices. And not even in bed—on the floor. We know it because we got office Negroes who've told us this. So we protect our women, 'cause women are the field that produces our nation. And if you can't protect your women, you can't protect your nation. Man, I was in Chicago a couple of months ago and saw a white fella take a black woman into a motel room. He stayed with her two or three hours and then walked out—and a bunch of brothers saw it and didn't even *say* nothin'. They should have thrown rocks at his car or kicked down the door while he was in there screwing her—do *something* to let him know you don't like it. How can you be a man when another man can come get your woman or your daughter or your sister—and take her to a room and screw her—and, nigger, you don't even *protest*?

But nobody touches our women, white *or* black. Put a hand on a Muslim sister and you are to *die*. You may be a white or black man in an elevator with a Muslim sister and if you pat her on the behind, you're supposed to die right there.

PLAYBOY: You're beginning to sound like a carbon copy of a white racist. Let's get it out front: Do you believe that lynching is the answer to interracial sex?

ALI: A black man *should* be killed if he's messing with a white woman. And white men have always done that. They lynched niggers for even looking at a white woman; they'd call it reckless eyeballing and bring out the rope. Raping, patting, mischief, abusing, showing our women disrespect—a man should die for that. And not just white men—black men, too. We will kill you, and the brothers who don't kill you will get their behinds whipped and probably get killed themselves if they let it happen and don't do nothin' about it. Tell it to the president—*he* ain't gonna do nothin' about it. Tell it to the FBI: We'll kill anybody who tries to mess around with our women. Ain't *nobody* gonna bother them.

PLAYBOY: And what if a Muslim woman wants to go out with non-Muslim blacks—or white men, for that matter?

ALI: Then *she* dies. Kill her, too.

PLAYBOY: Are Muslim women your captives?

ALI: Hey, our women don't want no white men, period. Can you picture me, after what I been talking and thinking, wanting a white woman? Muslims think about 300 years of slavery and lynching, and you think we want to *love* our slave masters? No *way* we think about that. And no, our women aren't captives. Muslim women who lose their faith are free to leave. I'm sure that if all the black men and women who started following Elijah Muhammad were still with us, we'd have an easy 10 million followers. That many came through the doors but didn't stay. They free to go if they want to.

PLAYBOY: If all the blacks in America became Muslims by the end of the year, what do you think would happen as a result?

ALI: President Ford would call our leaders to the White House and negotiate about what states he wants to give us or what country we want to be set up in. Can you imagine 25 million Negroes all feeling the way I do? There'd be nothing you could do with them but let 'em go.

PLAYBOY: "Let 'em go" doesn't mean handing over a group of states to Muslim religious leaders.

ALI: Maybe, maybe not. You could rope off Georgia, Alabama, Tennessee, Kentucky, we could go in there and live, and whites could have passports to come in, do business and leave. Or a mass exodus from America. I wish I can see it before I die. Let me ask *you* something.

PLAYBOY: Shoot.

ALI: You think I'm as pretty as I used to be? I was *so* pretty. Somebody took some pictures of me and they're in an envelope here, so let me stop talking for a few seconds, 'cause I want you to take a look at 'em....

Hey, I'm *still* pretty! What a wonderful face! Don't I look *good* in these pictures? I can see I gotta stay in shape if I want to stay pretty, but that's so *hard*. I've been fighting for 21 years and just *thinkin'* about it makes me tired. I ain't 22 anymore—I'm 33 and I can't fight like I did eight or 10 years ago. Maybe for a little while, but I can't keep it up. I used to get in a ring and dance and jump and hop around for the whole 15 rounds. Now I can only do that for five or six, and then I have to slow down and rest for the next two or three rounds. I might jump around again in the 11th and 12th rounds, or I might even go the whole rest of the fight like I used to, but I have to work much more to be able to do it now; weight is harder to get off and it takes more out of me to lose it. That means getting out every day and running a couple of miles, coming into the gym and punching the bags four days a week, and eatin' the right foods. But I like to eat the *wrong* foods. I'll go to a coffee shop and order a stack of pancakes with strawberry preserves, blueberry preserves, whipped cream and butter, and then hit them hot pancakes with that good maple syrup and then drink a cold glass of milk. At dinnertime, I'll pull into a McDonald's and order two big double cheeseburgers and a chocolate milk shake—and the next day I weigh 10 pounds more. Some people can eat and not gain weight, but if I just *look* at food, my belly gets bigger. That's why, when I'm training, about all I eat is broiled steaks, chicken and fish, fresh vegetables and salads. I don't even get to *see* them other things I like.

PLAYBOY: Are there parts of training you enjoy?

ALI: Except for gettin' up at five or six in the morning and runnin' for two miles, it's all work. But I don't train like other boxers. For instance, I let my sparring partners try to beat up on me about 80 percent of the time. I go on the defense and take a couple of hits to the head and the body, which is good: You gotta condition your body and brain to take those shots, 'cause you're gonna get hit hard a couple of times in every fight. Meanwhile, I'm not gonna beat up on my sparring partners, because what's the pleasure in that? Besides, if I kill myself punching at them, it'll take too much out of me. When you're fightin' as much as I have lately, you're supposed to be boxin' and doin' something every day, but I can't dance and move every day like I should, because my body won't let me. So I have to stall my way through.

PLAYBOY: Have you always been so easy on yourself in training?

ALI: That's not being easy, it's being smart. I pace my training the way I do my fights—just enough to let me win. When I boxed tough but unranked fighters like Jurgen Blin, Rudi Lubbers, Mac Foster and Al "Blue" Lewis, I hardly trained, but I was in shape enough to beat them. You got to realize that after I fought Joe Frazier—who took a lot out of me—for the second time, I had had 15 fights. If I had trained for all 15 the way I trained for Frazier, I wouldn't be here today, 'cause I'd have killed myself. So instead of being all worn out for that second fight, I was able to come back and beat Frazier. The second time with Norton, I almost killed myself training, but that turned out to be right, because I had something left at the end of that fight. For George Foreman, I *did* kill myself. But I didn't have to do that for Chuck Wepner, Ron Lyle or Joe Bugner; because they're not the same quality. So nobody should worry about how I train or tell me to train differently, for I'm the master of my craft. The main thing is to watch my performance on fight night, that's the only thing that counts. When the money is on the table and my title is on the line, I always come through.

PLAYBOY: How much longer do you intend to defend your title?

ALI: I'd like to give up the championship and retire today, but there's too many things I've got to do. We're taught that every Muslim has a burden to do as much as he can to help black people. Well, my burden is real big, for I'm the heavyweight champion and the most famous black man on the whole planet, so I got to do a whole lot. That's why I just bought a shopping center in a black part of Cleveland, Ohio, for $500,000. It's got room for 40 stores and we'll rent them out for just enough money to pay the upkeep and taxes—I'm not looking to make a quarter off it. That's gonna create jobs for black people. I'm also buying an A&P supermarket in Atlanta that will employ 150 black people. Then I'm going down to Miami, Florida, which doesn't have one nice, plush restaurant for black people; I'm goin' to get one built. You know, there used to be a sign along Miami Beach that said, No Jews Allowed.

Well, the Jews got mad, united and bought up the whole damn beach. That's what *we* got to start doin'—uniting and pooling our money—and I hope to get black celebrities and millionaires behind me, because the Muslim movement is the onliest one that's really going to get our people together. I may be just one little black man with a talent for fightin', but I'm going to perform miracles: When black people with money see what I can do with my pennies, they'll begin to see what can be done with their millions.

My big contribution is goin' to come after the next Foreman fight. I might get $10 million for fighting George again, and out of that I'll give the government its $5 million in tax, I'll put aside $1 million for myself and spread the other $4 million around. With that kind of money, we can make a lot of this country's black neighborhoods bloom, which will show that Allah is surely with me and my Muslim brothers. For we *can* change things. Look at our restaurants and buildings along Lenox Avenue in Harlem and you know we're not just *jivin'*. The $4 million I'll invest in my people after the Foreman fight will be the start of making every ghetto in America beautiful, and you'll be able to see where *that* money went. The government says it spends billions in the ghettos—but *we* can't see where the money goes.

People might read all this and say it's easy to talk, but I'm not just talkin'. You watch; I'm goin' to spend the next five years of my life takin' my fight money and settin' up businesses for the brothers to operate. That's the *only* reason why I'll hold on to my title.

PLAYBOY: Since you've already told us that age has been steadily eroding your skills, what makes you think you'll still be champion when you're 38?

ALI: Hey, Jersey Joe Walcott *won* his title when he was 37. Sugar Ray Robinson fought till he was in his 40s and Archie Moore went until he was 51.

PLAYBOY: At which point you took him apart with ease. Would you want to wind up your career the same way?

ALI: Archie didn't end up hurt and he's still intelligent—in spite of thinking Foreman could beat me. Going five more years don't mean going till I'm 51, and I can do it just by slowing down my style. You also got to remember I spent three and a half years in exile, when they took away my title because I wouldn't be drafted. That's three and a half years less of tusslin', trainin' and fightin', and if not for all that rest, I don't think I'd be in the same shape I am today. Because of my age, I don't have all of those three and a half years coming to me, but I have *some* of them.

PLAYBOY: Was that period of enforced idleness a bitter part of your life?

ALI: I wasn't bitter at *all*. I had a good time speaking at colleges and meeting the students—whites, blacks and all kinds, but mainly whites, who supported me 100 percent. They were as much against the Vietnam war as I was.

In the meantime, I was enjoying everything I was doin'. As a speaker, I was makin' $1500 and $2500 at every stop, and I was averaging $5000 a week, so I had money in my pocket. I was also puttin' pressure on the boxing authorities. I'd walk into fight arenas where contenders for my title were boxing and I'd interrupt everything, because I wanted to show everybody that I was still The Man. The people would jump up and cheer for me and the word soon got out that the authorities would have to reckon with me. When I won the Supreme Court decision and they had to let me go back to work, a lot of people came around saying, "Why don't you sue the boxing commission for unjustly taking your title away?" Well, they only did what they thought was right and there was no need for me to try to punish them for that. It's just too bad they didn't recognize that I was sincere in doing what *I* thought was right at the time.

PLAYBOY: Did you receive a lot of hate mail during those years?

ALI: Only about one out of every 300 letters. And I kinda liked those, so I put 'em all away in a box. When I'm 90 years old, they'll be something to show my great-grandson. I'll tell him, "Boy, here's a letter your great-granddaddy got when he fought the draft way back when they had wars." Anyway, there's good and bad in every race. People got their own opinions and they free to talk.

PLAYBOY: Considering your feelings about white America, did it surprise you that so many whites agreed with your stand against the draft?

ALI: Yes, it did. I figured it would be worse and that I'd meet with a lot more hostility, but that didn't happen. See, that war wasn't like World War II or like America being attacked. I actually had a lot going for me at the time: The country was halfway against it, the youth was against it and the world was saying to America, "Get out." And there I was, among people who are slaves and who are oppressed by whites. I also had a platform, because the Muslim religion and the Koran preaches against such wars. I would've caught much more hell if America was in a declared war and I didn't go.

PLAYBOY: Would you have served if America had been in a declared war?

ALI: The way I feel, if America was attacked and some foreign force was prowling the streets and shooting, naturally I'd fight. I'm on the side of America, not them, because I'm fighting for myself, my children and my people. Whatever foreigners would come in, if they saw some black people with rifles, I'm sure they'd start shooting. So, yeah, I'd fight if America was attacked.

PLAYBOY: When you returned to the ring in 1970, most boxing observers felt you'd lost a good deal of your speed and timing. Did you think so?

ALI: Nope, I thought I was about the same, maybe even better. My first bout when I came back was with Jerry Quarry, who I'd fought before. It was the strangest thing, but when I watched films of the first Quarry fight, I looked fast; yet when I looked at the second Quarry fight I was *superfast*. Then, after I lost to Frazier, I studied the films and even though I wasn't in great shape and clowned a lot, look at how *sharp* I was, how much I *hit* Joe. Anyway, you saw what Foreman did to Frazier and then what I did to Foreman, so what could I have lost by resting for three and a half years? Couldn't be much, could it? That's why I can stay champ for a long time, and if I fight just twice a year, my title can't be taken away. And those'll be big, big fights worth at least $5 million apiece. That's $10 million a year for five years, which means I'll split $50 million with the government. I'll wind up with $25 million after taxes. Whew!

PLAYBOY: That kind of money wasn't around when you began boxing professionally. Are you ever astonished by the fact that you can make $5 million in the course of an hour?

ALI: No, and when I leave boxing, there will never be that kind of money for fighters again. I can get $5 million or $7.5 million a fight because I got a world audience. The people who are puttin' up that money are the richest people in the world—black oilmen. It was a rich black man who paid me and George Foreman, and he did it because he wanted some publicity for his little country, and he got it. For 15 years after the white Belgians had to get out of there, no one—including me—ever heard of Zaire. No one knew it was a country of more than 22 million people, but now we do.

I just got offered $7.5 million to fight Foreman in Djakarta, Indonesia, by a black oilman who wants to promote *his* country. How to do it? Call Muhammad Ali over and have him fight for the title and the *world* will read about where he's fighting. But after I'm out of boxing and the title goes back to a fighter like a George Foreman or any good American, title fights won't travel no further than America and England. And that'll be the end of the big, big money.

PLAYBOY: Do you think you'll miss boxing when you finally retire?

ALI: No, because I realize you got to get old. Buildings get old, people get old and we're all goin' to die. See the fat I have around my stomach?

10 years ago, it would come off in two weeks, but not anymore. I can't exactly *feel* myself getting old, but I ain't like I was 10 years ago; so time equips me to face the facts of life. When I get to be 50, I won't really miss boxing at all, because I'll know I can't do it anymore.

But when I quit, I sure ain't goin' out like the old-time fighters. You ain't gonna hear it said about me that when I was champ I bought me a Cadillac, had me a couple of white girls on my arm, and that when I retired I went broke. You'll *never* read articles about me that say, "Poor Muhammad Ali, he made so much money and now he's working in a car wash." No, sir.

PLAYBOY: Will you continue to associate yourself with boxing after you retire?

ALI: I don't think so. I'm the champion right now and I can't even find time for training because of other things. I talk to senators like John Tunney of California, and black bourgeois congressmen who like to act so *big*, and black doctors and lawyers who have white friends and who no longer want to be black—and who act like they're too good for any of the brothers. I can always say to them, "Why do you all act like this? I don't act like that, and *you* can't get no bigger than Muhammad Ali."

That's the truth, too. I was over in Ireland and had dinner with Jack Lynch, the prime minister. I was in Cairo and stayed at Sadat's palace for two days. I wined and dined with King Faisal of Saudi Arabia. I might not've been that happy around all of those leaders, but people who look up to them see *them* looking up to *me*. Now when I bring my program down, they'll listen. See, you got to have something going in front for you. A smart fella might go down the street, but if people look at him and think, "Oh, just an ordinary fella," he won't get things done. But when a guy in a Rolls-Royce drives up and says, "Hey, I want to make a deal," people will talk money with him. Same thing with me: My money and my title give me influence.

And I also have something to say. You notice that when we talk, 85 percent of our conversation is away from boxing? Interview some other fighters and see what *they* can talk about: nothing. We couldn't talk this long—you couldn't *listen* this long—if we just talked boxing.

PLAYBOY: Agreed; but let's stick with that 15 percent a bit longer. Many people believe that after you retire, boxing will disappear in America. Do you believe that?

ALI: Boxing will never die. There will always be boxing in schools and clubs, and the fight crowd will always follow the pros. And every once in a while, a sensational fighter will come through.

PLAYBOY: As sensational as yourself?

ALI: Physically, maybe, but not in the way I'm known worldwide. I just don't think another fighter will ever be followed by people in every country on the planet. You can go to Japan, China, all the European, African, Arab and South American countries and, man, they know me. I can't name a country where they *don't* know me. If another fighter's goin' to be that big, he's goin' to have to be a Muslim, or else he won't get to nations like Indonesia, Lebanon, Iran, Saudi Arabia, Pakistan, Syria, Egypt and Turkey—those are all countries that don't usually follow boxing. He might even have to be named Muhammad, because Muhammad is the most common name in the world. There are more Muhammads than there are Williamses, Joneses, Ecksteins, Smiths or anything else on earth. And he's also gonna have to say the name Allah a lot, can't say God. I know that God is the Supreme Being, but Allah is the name used most on the planet. More people pray to Allah than to Jehovah, Jesus or just plain Lord, 'cause there are about 11 Muslims in the world to every non-Muslim.

But he's got to have the personality, too, because just being a Muslim champ won't make it. My corn, the gimmicks, the acting I do—it'll take a whole lot for another fighter to ever be as popular as Muhammad Ali.

PLAYBOY: You once said that you act all the time. Where does your act begin and where does it end?

ALI: The acting begins when I'm working. Before a fight, I'll try to have something funny to say every day and I'll talk 10 miles a minute. Like before the Chuck Wepner fight, I was tellin' reporters all *kinds* of things.

PLAYBOY: Care to give us a small sampling?

ALI: All right: "If Chuck Wepner becomes the only white man ever to beat the arrogant Muhammad Ali, he will be America's greatest hero! He will make White Tornado commercials and go on *Gunsmoke*, but for him this fight is really *Mission: Impossible*! Wepner has a strong will—and if the will is great, the will can overpower the skill! I understand Wepner had a meeting with the Ku Klux Klan and they told him to *whup* this nigger!"

That's acting, and it ends when I get into the ring. There are no pleasures in a fight, but some of my fights have been a pleasure to win—especially the second Norton and Frazier fights and the Foreman fight. I was left for dead before the second Norton fight, because my jaw had been broken the first time out. One loss to Frazier and *Sports Illustrated* ran a headline on its cover saying "End of the Ali Legend." And I was also left for dead against Foreman, who was supposed to be the toughest champ of all time. You know, I once read something that said, "He who is not courageous enough to take risks will accomplish nothing in life." Well, boxing is a risk and life is a gamble, and I got to take both.

PLAYBOY: People close to you say that in the past year you've grown visibly weary of boxing. Is that true?

ALI: Well, I started fighting in 1954, when I was just 12, so it's been a long time for me. But there's always a new fight to look forward to, a new publicity stunt, a new *reason* to fight. Now I'm fighting for this charities thing, and it helps me get ready. When I think of all the money and the jobs winning means, I'll run those two miles on mornings when I'd rather sleep.

PLAYBOY: With the possible exceptions of a few of our politicians, you're probably the most publicized American of this century. What kinds of problems does fame on such a grand scale create?

ALI: None. It's a blessing if you use publicity for the right thing, and I use it to help my brothers and to promote truth around the world. It's still an honor for me to talk to TV reporters who come all the way from Germany and Australia just to interview me. And when we're talking, I don't see a man from Germany, I see millions of Germans. The reporter will go back home and show his film to his entire nation, which keeps me popular and sells fight tickets, which is how I earn my living—and also how I can keep buying up buildings for my people. That's why talkin' so much don't bother me, but I'll be bothered when the reporters quit coming around, because on that day I'll realize I'm not newsworthy anymore, and that's when it all ends. So I enjoy it while it's happening.

PLAYBOY: Do you enjoy being mobbed by autograph seekers as well?

ALI: Most of the time, it's OK with me, because service to others is the rent I pay for my room on earth. See, when you become spiritual and religious, you realize that you're not big and great, only Allah is. You can't hurt people's feelings just because you're up there. When I was younger, Sugar Ray Robinson did that to me, and I didn't like it at all.

PLAYBOY: What happened?

ALI: I was on my way to fight in the Rome Olympics, and I stopped by a nightclub in Harlem, because Sugar Ray—my idol, *everybody's* idol—was there. I'd watched all his fight films and I just wanted to see him and touch him. I waited outside for him to leave that club and I was hoping he'd talk to me and maybe give me his autograph. But he didn't do it and I was so *hurt*. If Sugar Ray only knew how much I loved him and how long I'd been following him, maybe he wouldn't have done that.

Man, I'll *never* forget how bad I felt when he turned me down. Sugar Ray said, "Hello kid, how ya' doin'? I ain't got time," and then got into his car and took off. I said to myself right then, "If I ever get great and famous and people want my autograph enough to wait all day to see me, I'm sure goin' to treat 'em different."

PLAYBOY: Still, aren't there times when living in the public eye becomes slightly unbearable?

ALI: Yeah, and when that happens, I get into my bus, stock up on food and take my wife and four children and drive somewhere near the ocean and just rest for four or five days.

My real pleasure is having no appointments, but that hardly ever happens. There's always people I gotta talk to, business deals I gotta think about, telephones that are always ringing and road work and time in the gym that I gotta take care of. There's always *something* I have to do, but I guess we're all busy in our own ways. I'm sure President Ford has a bigger job than all of us. Like any big man—a spiritual leader like Wallace D. Muhammad, a politician, a president of a college—he's in prison. Same thing with me, because I'm a heavyweight champion who represents not only boxing but many, many other things that boxers can't even speak of. Therefore, I always have a deskful of stuff, piles and piles of letters and projects that no other boxer would be literate enough to even imagine handling. The times when it all gets me down, I just want to get away—from the commercials and TV and college appearances and airline flights and friends asking for loans and people begging for money that they need. I don't like to do it, but I wind up ducking: "When the phone rings, tell 'em I'm not here." It never lets up, so if I can just get away for a day every once in a while, I'm happy. Yet I don't let that stuff get me *too* bothered, because I have only one cause—the Islamic cause—and my mission is to spread the works and faith that Elijah Muhammad taught me.

PLAYBOY: For a man who's become more and more of a missionary, boxing must occasionally seem like a particularly brutal and inappropriate way to make a living. Did you ever consider a career in any other sport?

ALI: About the onliest other sport I ever thought about was football, but I didn't like it, because there was no personal publicity in it; you have to wear too much equipment and people can't see you. Folks sitting back in the bleachers can't hardly pick you out of a field of 22 men and a bunch of other guys shufflin' in and out, but in a boxing ring there's only two men. I made my decision about sports when I was a 12-year-old kid, and

I went with boxing because fighters can make more money than other athletes and the sport isn't cut off by a season, like football. And I've never regretted that decision, 'cause when you're the greatest at what you're doing, how can you question it?

PLAYBOY: Does your claim of being the greatest mean that you think you could have beaten every heavyweight champion in modern ring history?

ALI: I can't really say. Rocky Marciano, Jack Johnson, Joe Louis, Jack Dempsey, Joe Walcott, Ezzard Charles—they *all* would have given me trouble. I can't know if I would've beaten them all, but I do know this: I'm the most talked about, the most publicized, the most famous and the most colorful fighter in history. And I'm the fastest heavyweight—with feet and hands—who ever lived. Besides all that, I'm the onliest poet laureate boxing's ever had. One other thing, too: If you look at pictures of all the former champions, you know in a flash that I'm the best-looking champion in history. It all adds up to being the greatest, don't it?

PLAYBOY: Do you think you'll be remembered that way?

ALI: I don't know, but I'll tell you how I'd *like* to be remembered: as a black man who won the heavyweight title and who was humorous and who treated everyone right. As a man who never looked down on those who looked up to him and who helped as many of his people as he could—financially and also in their fight for freedom, justice and equality. As a man who wouldn't hurt his people's dignity by doing anything that would embarrass them. As a man who tried to unite his people through the faith of Islam that he found when he listened to the Honorable Elijah Muhammad. And if all that's asking too much, then I guess I'd settle for being remembered only as a great boxing champion who became a preacher and a champion of his people.

And I wouldn't even mind if folks forgot how pretty I was.

December 1973

BOB HOPE

A candid conversation with the fast-talking Daddy Warbucks of comedy

No one—not even John Wayne and certainly not Richard Nixon—can lay a better claim to the title of Mr. America than a fast-talking, swoop-nosed comedian who wasn't even born in this country. And yet during the past 20 years, he has unquestionably become a national monument, instantly recognizable and beloved by Americans everywhere and, more significantly, a symbol to the outside world (and to some in this country) of the traditional American spirit—optimistic, energetic, pragmatic and generous to a fault, but also proselytizingly patriotic, tiresomely wisecracking and dangerously simplistic, especially in the sensitive area of politics.

What foreigners may think of Bob Hope, however, doesn't concern most Americans, especially that segment of the population that deeply mistrusts not only foreigners abroad but ethnic minorities at home. To that America, Bob Hope speaks most eloquently; in fact, though he says he has never aspired to be anything but what he is—a gifted and supremely disciplined entertainer—he could conceivably run for president and win. After all, it's been pointed out, his colleagues George Murphy and Ronald Reagan made it from showbiz to high elective office on far less talent than his.

To bolster any possible political aspirations he might have, the story of Hope's early life is right out of *Horatio Alger*. Born Leslie Townes Hope on May 29, 1903 in Eltham, a working-class suburb of London, he was the son of a stonemason, a hard-drinking, hard-gambling man who immigrated with his family to America in 1906 and settled down in Cleveland in search of a better life. He never found it, and it was his wife, Avis, the tough-minded daughter of a Welsh sea captain, who kept the family together by taking in boarders and sending Leslie and his four brothers out into the world as soon as they were old enough to walk. Young Leslie did time as a newspaper boy, a caddie, a butcher's helper, a shoe salesman and a stockboy; he also became proficient with a pool cue and by the age of 12 was hustling successfully. In between jobs, hustling and school, he sang on amateur nights at the local vaudeville houses, where his mother invariably led the claque and helped him win prizes. It seemed only natural to him that, after a brief and not too successful stint as a boxer, he'd wind up in show business.

He began in vaudeville, working with male and female partners, first as a softshoe dancer, then as a blackface comedian. Along the way, he changed his name and soon graduated to tabs—miniature musicals and variety revues that toured the various theater circuits—playing several shows a day. The pay was low and the life grueling, but the experience, Hope has always claimed, was invaluable. It was also during this period, while he was working a tiny theater in New Castle, Pennsylvania that he stumbled onto his extraordinary talents as a monologist and ad-libber. Asked on short notice by the manager of the theater to introduce the other acts on the bill, Hope began lacing his improvised spiel with remarks that, to his gratification, made the often dangerously bored local audiences rock with laughter.

By the time Broadway beckoned and Hope went into his first full-scale musical, *Ballyhoo of 1932*, as a solo performer, he was a seasoned veteran who had mastered all the basics of his profession and needed only a lucky break in the form of the right part in the right show to become a star. This came along in the fall of 1933, when he was cast as Huckleberry Haines, the fast-talking best friend of the leading man (Ray Middleton) in *Roberta*, a hit musical with a score by Jerome Kern. Despite an unfavorable personal notice from the prestigious critic of *The New York Times*, Hope all but stole the show from Middleton and such other seasoned male troupers in the cast as George Murphy, Fred MacMurray and Sydney Greenstreet; his career was launched. He soon branched out into radio and films and began, with the help of a stable of top comedy writers, to produce the slick, lightning-fast standup monologs that became his trademark and made him a star.

The Bob Hope style, or what others have called his formula, was most fully developed and established on radio's *Pepsodent Show*, which for over a decade, from 1938 on, kept the comedian among the top four laugh getters in the nation's living rooms. His chief rivals were Jack Benny, Fred Allen and Edgar Bergen; the critics generally considered him inferior to them, but he usually topped them in the ratings. While the other airwave comedians went to great pains to establish characters for themselves and to create the atmosphere of entire milieus, Hope ignored characterization, revealed little about himself or others on his show and created no small worlds for the imagination of his listeners to roam in. What made him unique was simply the monolog that opened every show, in which he peppered his listening audience with a barrage of quips that one of his writers once likened to "casting with a fly rod—flicking in and out." Neither his technique nor his material has ever pleased the intellectuals much, and such critics as John Lahr, whose father, Bert, was one of the great clowns of the American stage, have complained that he never displayed in his comedy "the kind of inner wound that makes an artist." Hope's comedy has always been considered in these circles to be artificial, the machine-made product of a team of gag writers, and Hope himself merely a slick-talking, glorified nightclub emcee.

Apart from the fact that such criticism ignores the finely tuned sense of timing that it takes to deliver such monologs successfully—building and piling laughs on one another to a climax that enables the comic to exit deftly on the crest of a wave of applause—there's no denying that these machine-gun monologs have made him a multimillionaire. According to J. Anthony Lukas, writing a few years ago in *The New York Times*, Hope's image is one of "the guy in front of the drugstore, the fastest tongue in town. And his lines are brisk, flip wisecracks delivered with a mixture of breezy self-confidence and pouting frustration."

The image grew and flowered not only in radio but in most of Hope's 71 films. It was first used to perfection in *The Big Broadcast of 1938* (in which Hope also sang his theme song, "Thanks for the Memory," for the first time) and was most fully exploited in the famous series of *Road* pictures that co-starred him with Bing Crosby and Dorothy Lamour. In these movies, Hope was more often than not the loser; Crosby usually got the girl and almost all of the songs. But it was Hope—as the falsely cocky, girl-crazy, basically cowardly fast-talker, always ready to cut corners, always on the lookout for the main chance and never able to resist a joke, even when about to be dismembered by a gorilla—who got most of the laughs and with whom the American audience immediately identified. "In movies, Bob is sort of the American Falstaff," one of his PR men said recently. "He always survives because he never stops trying, he never gives up, no matter how badly things may be going for him, no matter how long the odds against him. He really believes the cavalry is going to come charging to his rescue any minute."

When Hope went into TV, he had to try a new approach. "I honestly think that the secret of TV is being relaxed, casual and easy," he once observed. He slowed down what he called his "bang, bang, bang" delivery and concentrated more on putting across his personality, which remained basically what it had become back in the 1930s in radio and movies. He also wisely limited his TV appearances to a series of specials every year, so that, alone of all the major comedians, he has remained in consistent public demand year after year for over two decades. The only other exposure he received on the tube was his annual stint as emcee for the Academy Awards, a task that—until it ended, at least temporarily, a couple of years ago—presented vintage Hope to an estimated 60 million viewers. His two Christmas shows, filmed at U.S. military bases in Vietnam in 1970 and 1971, drew the largest viewing audiences for specials in the history of the medium.

Though these two shows suggest the esteem and affection in which the comedian is held, they are also at the heart of the considerable criticism he has received over the past few years for his hawklike stance on Vietnam and his open identification as a leading spokesman for the political right. His detractors say that, though it's perfectly true that Hope has been entertaining regularly at American military bases at home and abroad for 31 years, ever since World War II, he has exploited his most recent trips to Vietnam by making highly successful and commercially lucrative network television specials out of them. He is an outspoken admirer and close friend of Vice President Agnew, as well as a crony of most of the other major conservative figures in American life, from Westmoreland to Wallace, and he seems totally unsympathetic to ethnic minorities and young people, with all of whom, it is said, he is painfully out of touch. Even in his comedy routines, he pays only lip service to objectivity, favors his own side and puts down everyone else, while never digging at all below the surface into the more painful areas of life probed by social commentators such as Mort Sahl and the late Lenny Bruce.

Though Hope's friends say that he donates about $1 million a year to various charities, his so-called humanitarianism, for which he has received an honorary Oscar and dozens of other awards, has also been questioned. Hope is supposed to be one of the richest men in the world (worth, according to one published estimate, at least half a billion dollars) and, though generous enough with his time, he is reputedly a notorious tightwad who would never dream of putting his money where his mouth is. Even his personal life has come under attack: Though he has been married for 39 years to Dolores Reade, a former nightclub singer, and together they have raised four adopted children, it's no secret that he is almost never home and that his wife, a devout Roman Catholic, is most often seen in the company of aged Jesuit priests.

To quiz him on the above and related matters, *Playboy* assigned William Murray to interview the 70-year-old star. Murray reports: "Getting to sit down with Bob Hope is a lot harder than getting an audience with the Pope. It's not that he doesn't want to see you; it's only that the man is hardly ever in one place for more than a day or two, and then he's always surrounded by people—his friends, his writers, his personal staff, his agents and managers and flacks and the boys from the network. It took me three months and the efforts of his son Tony and his two PR firms to get me to him. When a meeting was finally arranged, I was told by someone on his staff that I could have a total of one hour at lunch with him, between rehearsals for his first TV special of the season. I explained I'd need at least two taping sessions of a minimum of several hours each and the poor guy recoiled in horror. 'If I tell Bob that,' he said, 'he won't see you at all.' I decided to take my chances and rely on my famous charm.

"I needn't have worried. Hope is, first and foremost, an entertainer. Get him talking about showbiz and you can take it from there. I also came away, after several long sessions with him over a period of three weeks, liking the man a lot. We talked mostly in what he calls his game room, a bright, airy place in the big house sprawled over seven acres of North Hollywood land that he bought for practically nothing more than 20 years ago. Out the window I could see the fairway of his private one-hole golf course and a corner of a huge swimming pool. Hope bounces as he walks, hums little tunes to himself, seems to vibrate quietly in his chair, as if he's consciously, like a trained athlete, working all the time at keeping himself loose. For a man his age, he's in superb condition, the jowls of his famous profile firm and his flesh tone that of a man in his early 50s. His tongue is still in great shape, too; in the 10 hours we talked, he proved time and again—entertainingly—that he doesn't need his writers around to sound like a comedian, and a great one."

PLAYBOY: You've been involved in every facet of show business for so long that a lot of people now think of you as an American institution. Do you think of yourself as one?
HOPE: Hardly—although I have a few jokes I'm leaving to the Smithsonian. Then I think maybe if they went up on Mount Rushmore and retouched Lincoln a little bit and gave him a ski nose, I could sneak in there. You know, I can't take a question like that seriously. I'm just worried about my next show.
PLAYBOY: Do you have any political ambitions?
HOPE: No way.
PLAYBOY: And yet you've been linked very closely in recent years with men like Nixon and Agnew, whose views presumably you share.
HOPE: From FDR on, I've been very friendly with all the presidents and the men around them, and I've found that they're really all great Americans. Every time I went to Washington, I used to drop in on JFK and swap jokes with him. He was a great audience for comedy; he spent a lot of time in Congress. But I'm also an Agnew man and a Nixon man. And a Reagan man and a Rockefeller man and a Connally man, so during the next election I'm moving to South America. That's how chicken I am.
PLAYBOY: You didn't say you were a Kennedy or a McGovern man. All the politicians you say you support are conservatives.
HOPE: Look, I don't want to get into that. Every article about me recently has been spouting the same bullshit about my politics. They hook me into it on account of Agnew and the Vietnam War. The only reason I was for Nixon and this administration was because I knew that's who would end this war and get those kids back home. None of those jerks walking around with those signs was ever going to end the war. I knew Nixon was the only person who could do it, and it should have been done eight years ago. As for my politics and all that, I vote for the man and only for the man. I'm an American above everything, and that's another reason

I've hated to see this political garbage going on that's been breaking up our country, this political soap opera we've been sitting through.

PLAYBOY: You mean Watergate?

HOPE: Yes. I've been watching The Washington Squares. Every time I see Sam Ervin, I get the feeling that Gomer Pyle has aged. I love to watch him dust off the furniture with his eyebrows. And that Senator Baker, he's a very personable guy. The two of them will do great if minstrel shows ever come back. Ervin's taught me a lot about how to be a chairman. You have to wait for your laugh before you hit the gavel. They're all beauties, though. Some days you take a look at that group up there and you feel the whole mob should have Snow White in front of them.

PLAYBOY: What kind of impression did the witnesses make on you?

HOPE: I thought Ehrlichman was marvelous. And Peterson was great. I love people who aren't awed by that committee. They go in there and stand up and tell their story. Like Peterson said, if the politicians had kept their hands off of it, the Justice Department would have handled it just fine. This is like the McCarthy era. I did a joke about Joe McCarthy one time and a judge in Appleton, Wisconsin, which was McCarthy's home state, wrote in the local paper, which he owned, that I was a Communist. So I wrote him back and told him simply that telling jokes was my racket. After that, he wrote in his paper that Bob Hope was a pretty good American and we became friends. I send him Christmas cards and he sends me cheese.

PLAYBOY: Then you agree with President Nixon that the matter should be handled in the courts?

HOPE: Sure. I think dragging this thing on for years and years is giving dirty politics a bad name. Every administration has been plagued by some kind of scandal or other. The whole thing has had a Mack Sennett feel to it. Actually, I don't know whether they ought to get them into court or Central Casting. I understand Screen Gems wants Ulasewicz for a series. Why would anybody want to bug Democratic headquarters to steal McGovern's campaign plans? That's petty larceny at most.

PLAYBOY: Don't you think the Watergate committee has served a legitimate function?

HOPE: Hell, yes, but it's been dragging on and on and it's not good for the country. I know that the committee is stuck with a lot of television makeup, but I think they ought to sell it to somebody and get on with the real business at hand.

PLAYBOY: How about your *own* television makeup? Have you made your last trip overseas to entertain at our military bases?

HOPE: As far as any kind of formal trip is concerned, yes. I can't say absolutely that I've made my last trip, because, if anything happened and they asked me to go, I would. But on a regular basis, I'm through. In fact, I'm doing a book called *The Last Christmas Show*, which tells the story of the last trip.

PLAYBOY: How many trips have you made?

HOPE: Well, I went overseas six times during World War II and 23 or 24 times between 1948 and 1972, maybe 30 trips in all. My golfing buddy, Stuart Symington, started the whole thing about the Christmas trips by inviting us to go to the Berlin airlift in '48 and then took us to Alaska the next year. From then on, we were locked in by the Defense Department. In fact, we got hooked on the box lunches ourselves. A different kind of trip, one that stands out in my memory, was the Victory Caravan in 1942, which was our own private train that began in Washington and went all over the country for about three weeks, playing everywhere to standing-room-only crowds; the idea was to get people to buy Victory Bonds. We had 25 stars on board. Cary Grant and I were the double emcees and we had Pat O'Brien, Laurel and Hardy, Crosby, Merle Oberon, Claudette Colbert, Jimmy Cagney, Charles Boyer—25 stars; you never saw anything like it in your life. And Groucho used to run around the train and needle everybody. I remember we had a guy named Charley Feldman on board, who was known as "the good-looking agent"—he looked a little like Gable—and Groucho came down the aisle one morning, saying, "The cars got so mixed up last night Charley Feldman found himself back in his own bed." God, it was fun! After that I began going overseas for the troops.

PLAYBOY: You've been getting some mixed reactions to your more recent tours, both here and abroad, and there were reports that, in a couple of places at least, you were actually booed.

HOPE: Well, that's all from politics. It bugs me to think that we have American kids over there fighting, kids who've been asked to go over there and fight for their country, and for some reason it's wrong to go over and entertain them. That's all we've ever done. In World War II they cheered, and I've been lucky enough to have received every medal that's ever been given out by the government. Take a look at the people who criticize; look at their records. An awful lot of great Hollywood people have been on those trips.

Five years ago I took the Golddiggers, and one of the biggest thrills was introducing them in Danang and watching the expressions on those kids' faces. It's an exciting thing to be overseas and see a show that has Ziegfeld Follies proportions, with great big beautiful girls. Last year I took along 12 of the most gorgeous girls, called the American Beauties. For these kids there is nothing you can do better than that. They fight to get into the shows. And we went everywhere, even up to one small base in Alaska where they'd written us, begging us to come. We had trouble landing there. The ground was so cold the plane refused to put its tail down. What a bleak outpost! The big thrill there was to wake up in the morning, count your toes and get up to 10. The guys screamed when we played there; they had to keep warm. Anyway you feel lucky that you're able to do it, and anyone who says anything about any of these trips, well, in my book he's a petty jerk.

PLAYBOY: Don't you think that most of the criticism was motivated by sincere opposition to the Vietnam War?

HOPE: Sure. They linked me with the war. But I *hate* war. I wouldn't get near any kind of conflict if I could help it, and I've had a couple of rough scrapes; but this has been the greatest part of my life and anybody who has ever gone with me knows what it's all about. The emotion and the gratification are fantastic. From the time you get on the plane to the time you get back, you feel you're a sacred cow. They just give you everything and they love you for coming. Look, I didn't go to Vietnam because it was Vietnam. I go to the camps where our guys are and because they're screaming for us. We get requests all the time. But we've had it now, unless there's a new crisis somewhere and we're really needed.

PLAYBOY: But how do you feel about the war itself at this point?

HOPE: I'm concerned about Cambodia now. I guess nobody else is, so I don't know why I should worry. I'm concerned that if we lose Cambodia, the Commies will get a foothold there and maybe start the whole thing over again. I hope not and pray not.

PLAYBOY: Is it any business of ours what form of government other countries choose to live under?

HOPE: Let me explain one thing about South Vietnam. When you get guys like Eisenhower and his staff, Kennedy and his staff, Johnson and his staff, all of whom thought it was important enough to save this little nation from communism or enslavement, then you have to think maybe they know something. When we were in Thailand, the king would invite us into the palace and he'd say, "Thank God the U.S. troops are here, because otherwise the Communists would take over." The same people who didn't like what happened in Hungary and Czechoslovakia don't think about this. Unless it's happened to you, you don't think much about it. But that's why our presidents sent the troops in there. They're brilliant enough to know what they're doing and why. They did it to save this country and all of Southeast Asia and I'm concerned now that, if we run into problems elsewhere, we'll have to go back in. We're patriotic enough in this country that if somebody hurts us in some way, sinks a ship or something, we'll go back in and it'll start all over.

PLAYBOY: Do you think the president has the constitutional right to wage war without the consent of Congress?

HOPE: When you say the president, you're not speaking about one man. The president has a fantastic group around him. And he invites the leaders of both parties and the joint chiefs and everybody has his say. Eisenhower was a great military leader, but he didn't wage war on his own. Neither did Kennedy, and neither did Johnson, and it was Johnson who sent in most of the troops. They have great staffs, and they call on everybody for advice. Of course, the president is the commander in chief, so he's got to issue the order. But he doesn't sit alone in a room and say, "I want to wage war."

PLAYBOY: But doesn't the Constitution specify that Congress must declare war before American troops can be committed to large-scale action abroad?

HOPE: It's true that we haven't declared war. The Korean War was a police action and so was this one. That was the problem. If we had declared war, this thing would have been over in a year, because the military would have taken over. We'd have gone all out and—bang, bang, bang—it would have been over. We wouldn't have lost any international prestige and we'd have saved about half a million lives, as well as a lot of our international prestige.

PLAYBOY: That's debatable. But what do you think we ought to do now in Indochina?

HOPE: As I said, I'm very concerned about the Cambodian situation. I have a lot of friends in Washington—a couple of very big ones, and I don't mean the president, but a couple of guys I play golf with—and I'm going in there next week and I'm going to sit down and ask them, just for my own understanding, what's going to happen. I heard one of these big guys say the other day that Cambodia is going down the drain. Well, if Cambodia goes down the drain, then you tell me what the hell is going to happen with Thailand. They're worried as hell about it. I don't think we have to worry too much, but what about our kids? I'd like to see us never have another war. That would be great, just great. If we handle things right now, especially this situation, then I don't think we'll ever have another war.

PLAYBOY: One of the pledges Nixon made when he was elected in 1968 was to bring the country together. The most recent polls would suggest that he hasn't, because a majority of the public isn't satisfied with the job he's doing and doesn't believe he's telling the truth about Watergate. How do *you* feel about his performance?

HOPE: I think he has a tremendous record, I really do. What he's done with the Russians and the Chinese has taken a lot of the heat off. It was a great job. That and the fact that he brought back 500,000 of our men from Vietnam are enough to make me like him very much. The fact that the polls show that a lot of people don't believe him doesn't mean a hell of a lot. For one thing, the polls are often wrong. It's like the Nielsen ratings. They call up eight people and ask them what they liked on television last night. Three of them were out seeing *The Devil in Miss Jones*, four of them were taking a nap so they could wake up later and watch Johnny Carson and the other one doesn't have a television set. The only time to believe any kind of rating is when it shows you at the top. They should get off Nixon's back and let him be president, because he's a damn good one. He's also got a great-looking nose.

PLAYBOY: What do you think should be done with the young people who refused to have anything to do with the war?

HOPE: I do feel they should serve their country in some way, because it's not fair to the people who did go over there and serve. I've got compassion for everybody, but I've been in places where you see American fighting boys who've been badly hurt. It shakes you up.

PLAYBOY: You seem to get most of your ideas on public issues from conversations with high-ranking politicians and military men. Do you feel you might be out of touch with ordinary people and especially the young?

HOPE: Oh, no. First off, I catch a lot of flack from my own kids, who tell me we ought to just slap the Reds on the wrist and run, and see what happens. It's hard for me to win an argument in my family, because two of my kids are lawyers and another one is married to a lawyer and they have two little briefs. But they're all fans of my trips, because they've all been along on them. They've been with me in the burn wards and intensive-care wards and seen the kids suffering and dying. We argue about a lot of things but not about the trips.

PLAYBOY: Aside from the young men you've played to in army camps, do you think you're popular with young people? Do you feel close to them?

HOPE: NBC took a poll recently and found that, because of my pictures' being on TV, even little kids of eight and nine buy me. The other night, when we taped our first special for the new season, I looked out into the front rows and there were all these kids screaming. I grab all of them. I go and I play the colleges and afterward we have a kind of forum and talk about everything. They ask me about everything, including the war and the killing, and so on, and it gives you a great chance to talk to them. If you talk to young people in a big group, you also find that the sense of fairness in them will come out. They won't let any one guy try to ride over you. And I take my own polls, you know. I ask for votes on whether the kids thought we were doing the right thing in Vietnam or wherever and, you know, the majority of those kids have said we were doing the best thing possible. I love to talk to the kids. I get a great kick out of that, the rapport you reach with them and feeling them out and finding out what they're thinking about. It really gives me a charge.

PLAYBOY: What about some of the things young people are into—such as open marriage and women's lib and the gay liberation front? Can you relate to all that?

HOPE: I'm an excited spectator, and they're all great monolog subjects. Like: I haven't known any open marriages, though quite a few have been ajar. And: When those women throw away their brassieres and then ask for support—I love it. But I think people can get too carried away with this sort of thing. I can't understand why Raquel Welch would want equality with Don Knotts. And I haven't noticed any big changes in Dolores yet. She still hasn't burned her credit cards.

PLAYBOY: What about the trend among the young to turn back to Jesus?

HOPE: Anything that gets them into a straight line helps kids like that, as long as they don't overdo it. About three years ago, Dolores and I—Dolores is so religious, you know, she's something else; we couldn't get fire insurance for a long time because she had so many candles burning—well, anyway, we're getting off this plane and this kid comes up to us and he says, "Get with Jesus!" When we get outside, he comes up to us again and says, "You gotta get with Jesus, because that's where it's at!" I call him over and I say, "Look, you got with Jesus and it's a great thing and we know all about it. But don't sell people off it. Play it cool!"

Because, you know, this guy is yelling. Anyway, he hasn't heard the good news and the bad news. The good news is that Jesus is coming back, but the bad news is that he's really pissed off.

PLAYBOY: You've always been a quick man with a quip, but it's been said that you rely heavily on your writers. How many do you have working for you?

HOPE: Seven right now. If I do a picture, I might add three or four more. I've had a lot of good writers working for me and two or three of them have been with me for years—one guy, Les White, since 1932, off and on. At one Writers Guild show, they asked all the writers who had ever worked for Bob Hope to stand up and about 100 guys came up on stage. I've had fabulous writers. I put them to work in teams and then they bring it in and we put it all together and rewrite whatever we want to do and rehearse and see if it plays and then rewrite again. We can come up with jokes in 15 minutes just talking in my dressing room and save a situation.

PLAYBOY: What's the secret of your comedy? The material?

HOPE: The material has a lot to do with it, but the real secret is in timing, not just of comedy but of life. It starts with life. Think of sports, even sex. Timing is the essence of life, and definitely of comedy. There's a chemistry of timing between the comedian and his audience. If the chemistry is great, it's developed through the handling of the material and the timing of it, how you get into the audience's head. The other night I was at some big dinner here and the guy who was introducing the acts had this very high voice. Well, when I got on I said, "I'm glad I was introduced before his voice changed. He sounds like Wayne Newton on his wedding night." Well, you can't get a better start than that. Here was something that was in the minds of all those people sitting there and when you deliver it to them with the right timing and the right delivery, the light goes on in their heads and you're coming down the stretch. All the good comedians have great timing.

PLAYBOY: But you couldn't get along without your writers.

HOPE: Every comedian needs writers, because to stay on top you always need new material. It's like getting elected to office. You're going to get elected if you say the right things—but only if you say them *right*. The great ad-libbers are the guys with the best timing, like Don Rickles. I showed up in the audience one night at NBC, where he was cutting everybody up on the *Dean Martin Show*. I walked in after the show had started and the people in the back saw me and began applauding and then the audience in front turned around and they applauded and I was taking it big. Rickles backed away to the piano and when everything quieted down, he walked up to the mike and said, "Well, the war must be over." It was just magnificent timing and it hit very large. Timing shows more in ad libs than in anything else.

Back in 1952, I was doing a 15-minute daily show and I had a question-and-answer period with the audience. Most people ask how old you are and all the usual stuff, which is all fun, because I have stock lines for a lot of it, but one night this guy got up and waved his hand and he said, "Which way does a pig's tail turn, clockwise or counterclockwise?" It was such a wild question that the audience laughed like hell, and when they finished laughing I said, "We'll find out when you leave." And the theater rocked, it just rocked. It was so good that after that, I put a plant in the audience in some of those shows to get that laugh again.

PLAYBOY: You've been attacked from time to time for telling ethnic jokes, most recently for one in which your central character was called a Jap. Do you think ethnic humor can be demeaning?

HOPE: It can be, but mostly it has to do with who's telling the joke. I get into trouble when I do it, because I'm supposed to be one of the top guys. The other night in Jersey, I heard some guy do 15 minutes of Polack jokes and nobody said a word. I did two or three Polack jokes at the Garden State Art Center and the guy who owns the local newspaper rushed up and demanded an apology. Everybody in the country tells these jokes, but if I do them, somebody jumps. Usually, I try to even them up. Like I say, "Do you know how a Polack lubricates his car? He runs over an Italian." But then you have the Italians against you and that's not good if you want to eat in New York. I once did a joke about the Mafia joining forces with the gay lib group in New York, so that now with the kiss of death you get dinner and an evening of dancing. I did that joke in Madison Square Garden and immediately I heard from two groups of gay activists. They were going to come around and beat me with their purses. But a lot of it depends on where you do these jokes. You can do a lot of things in a place like Vegas that you can't do on TV.

PLAYBOY: Wouldn't you like to have more freedom on your own TV shows?

HOPE: No, you've got to think about the Bible Belt. They've got a hot finger and they can click you into oblivion faster than the NBC censor. But one of the really great things about TV is that the kids have rediscovered a whole lost era of comedy by seeing all these old films on TV.

For them, it must be like the first time I saw Charlie Chaplin. I waited an hour and a half in a doorway once just to see Chaplin walk out of a building in New York. I couldn't believe he was really human. That's what television does today and everybody thought it was such a bad deal that our pictures were being shown on the *Late Show* and we weren't getting any money for it. But it was the greatest public-relations thing we ever had. I'd like to see a special comedy channel created on TV, where all these great clowns like Jackie Gleason and Red Skelton and Sid Caesar, who have been sitting around for a couple of years, could do their stuff. I think the government should subsidize them, instead of some of this garbage you see on the educational channel. We spend so much money on stupid things, why not entertain the public?

PLAYBOY: Governments aren't noted for having a sense of humor.

HOPE: Maybe not, but I can hear a lot of laughing in the background around tax time. Laughter is important for the country because laughter is therapy—it makes you forget meat. If you can laugh once or twice a day, it relieves a hell of a lot of tension.

PLAYBOY: You were in one movie with W.C. Fields, probably the most iconoclastic comedian we've ever had. Was he your kind of comic?

HOPE: That was my first picture, *The Big Broadcast of 1938*, and I got to know Fields a little bit. He didn't ordinarily talk to many people, you know. He was a strange cat and had his own little group. I was in his dressing room one day when a nice little man from the Community Fund, a charity we all used to give money to, came by and he said, "Mr. Fields, we haven't received your donation." And Fields said, "Well, I only believe in the SEBF Association," and the nice little man from the fund office said, "What is that?" And Fields said, "Screw Everybody But Fields." I think he liked me because he'd heard some of my one-liners. He liked my joke about the drunk who came down to the bar in the morning and asked for a scotch and the bartender said, "With soda?" and the guy said, "I couldn't stand the noise."

PLAYBOY: Who makes you laugh today?

HOPE: Oh, I laugh at a lot of people, I really do. We have one writer named Charley Lee—we call him Grumpy; he makes me laugh. A lot of my writers make me laugh. They have great senses of humor. Shecky Greene and Don Rickles and Benny and Jessel, they all make me laugh. When Jessel rattles his medals, I fall down. Jimmy Durante doubles me up; he's one of the greatest guys around. I used to laugh a lot at Groucho when we hung around together. He'd come to my parties half an hour early. I'd say, "What are you doing?" and he'd say, "I want to break in the room." Funny, really funny.

PLAYBOY: Do any of the younger comics make you laugh?

HOPE: God, yes. Mort Sahl and Woody Allen, they're great. But my favorite was Lenny Bruce. The first time I ever saw him was about 14 years ago. I was working at Paramount in a picture and he was playing in a little Hollywood club, sort of a converted grocery store. I went over there for the first show and the place was about half filled and we had a great time. He did one routine where he called the Pope on the phone and told him he could get him on the *Ed Sullivan Show* if he wore the big ring and would send him some eight-by-10 glossies, and two or three people got up from the audience and walked out. Of course, today that seems so tame.

I saw Lenny several times after that. The last time I saw him was at El Patio in Florida. I'd seen everybody else on the Beach and I just saw a little ad saying, "Lenny Bruce at El Patio," and I said, "We've got to go." We went out there and I sat way in the back. In those days, planes were falling going from New York to Miami, for some reason or other, so he walked to the mike and he said, "A plane left New York today for Miami and made it." That was his opening, not "Hello" or anything. And then he told the audience I was there and he shouted, "Hey, Bob, where are you?" And I said, "Right here, Lenny." And he said, "Tonight I'm going to knock you right on your ass." And he did. Funny material, this cat! He did an impression of Jack Paar on the toilet, looking around the curtain, talking, you know? Then he did a comic dying at the Palladium. Damn, he was funny! He was hilarious! Very sophisticated material, but he had something. He had so much greasepaint in his blood, it came out in his act. That's what I loved about him. He talked our language.

PLAYBOY: You've made a lot of movies over the years, but your biggest hits were in the 1940s and 1950s. Do you think Hollywood has been going downhill since then?

HOPE: No question about it. The movie audience has shrunk from 80 million to about 14 million. Partly it was television, but also it's the dirty pictures. They're doing things on the screen today I wouldn't do on my honeymoon. I can't believe what they're showing on the screen. I remember the days when Hollywood was looking for new *faces*. Parents aren't going to send their kids to see stag material, so they tie them down in front of the television set and tell them to look at those two old guys dancing on their way to utopia.

PLAYBOY: What do you mean by stag material? Would you consider *Last Tango in Paris* a stag movie?

HOPE: I want to see it, but I can't get a note from my doctor. Look, I don't object to dirty material. I love dirty jokes. I tell more dirty jokes than anybody. I tell them at the golf club, and when I get brave I'll tell one to my wife, if I have my track shoes on. But to expose this kind of stuff to kids I think is a shame. I also think our business has lost so much prestige overseas, because we used to send such fabulous pictures all over the world, and the pictures we make represent our country and the morals of our country. I think they should have special theaters just for that stuff—X-rated theaters.

PLAYBOY: They do. That's where movies like *Deep Throat* are shown to adults only.

HOPE: *Deep Throat*—I thought that was an animal picture. I thought it was about a giraffe. I haven't seen it, but I've heard about it and I don't believe it. But my point is that mothers take their children to see a clean picture and they'll have a preview for next week showing people in bed doing all the acts. That's what I object to. People come up to me when I'm traveling around the country and they squawk like hell about it. Our business used to be a glamorous business. Now you don't see any big openings anymore. You know why? It's because a lot of people don't want to be seen going into the theater.

PLAYBOY: Do you think the recent Supreme Court decisions against hard-core pornography are on the right track?

HOPE: Oh, definitely. The hard-core stuff could harm kids. Pictures like *Deep Throat* and *The Devil in Miss Jones* are dangerous pictures. I hear a lot of young couples are going to see these movies now, but we don't even know if they're married or not. It has to affect their lives in some way.

PLAYBOY: Isn't it possible that people might learn something constructive by going to see a pornographic movie?

HOPE: I don't see how any public exhibition of this kind can do any good. I think it could lead to disaster in many cases. Today the sort of people who need help can go and buy a sex book. They don't have to go out in public and see that kind of thing on the screen. We now have sex books and sex counselors. For a few dollars, Masters and Johnson will come to your house and sit on your piano and do it.

PLAYBOY: Much of what you say about America today seems to express a longing many people feel for a time when things were presumably better. Do you remember such a time? Do you think the mood of the country was better when you were young?

HOPE: Not to me. I wasn't that well known. I remember a time I was playing Evansville, Indiana. It was about my third date on the road after opening in Chicago. I rehearsed and then I went into the restaurant and bought a paper to check my billing. It said, "The Golden Bird," which was an act that had a bird that answered questions or something, and underneath that it said, "and Ben Hope." I threw up right at the table, and then I walked into the manager's office and I said, "What's the idea spelling my name Ben Hope?" And he said, "Well, what's your name?" I said, "Bob Hope." He said, "Who knows but you?"

Times have changed for me since then, thank God. Last summer I played the Arlington Park Fair near Chicago and the theater is outdoors and it's raining. It's a pretty strong rain and Joey Heatherton is dancing in the rain, with 40,000 people sitting there and nobody's moving. They sat there and cheered. When I came out, I said, "Joey Heatherton dancing in the rain reminds me of Danang," and they all went "Ye-e-a-ay!" I guess they all remembered that. They are such a great audience today. I played a lot of different dates this summer and everywhere I went I felt things really couldn't be better. Naturally, a lot of things upset them, like Watergate, but basically they're great.

PLAYBOY: What frightens you most about the country today?

HOPE: That I'll run out of tax money.

PLAYBOY: Nothing about the state of our society today worries you?

HOPE: Let me tell you something. This country is so strong, our people are so strong, that nothing's going to happen to this system. They've enjoyed this system too much, and I think that when it gets down to the short licks, everybody's going to think the same. Now, the Democrats I know, they were saying it just the other day, we've got to stop making a public exhibition of the country's politics and get back to taking care of the nation's business. I think the people feel the same way, because I get around with a lot of the people and I talk to them and boy, they're strong. You should travel with me around this country and get into some of these cities and talk to these people and dig the way they feel. It's delightful to go into a residential section of Minneapolis or Oklahoma City or anywhere, I don't care where it is, San Francisco and Seattle, and see wonderful families living the good life, with two or three cars. They aren't going to let this stuff slip away from them. They're well established and they like this system we have, because we have the greatest system in the world. There's nothing like it and, though we may have our problems here and there, we're not going to let it get away from us. I know that. I meet these wonderful people and I get the feeling of them and what they are thinking about. Americans are a great people and they live great lives. You come away very proud of them.

PLAYBOY: You're talking about the white middle class. How about the 25 million poor whites, blacks, Chicanos and Indians who don't feel they're part of the system—and might not even *want* to be part of it?

HOPE: Maybe the best thing about our system is the opportunity it gives people to make something of their lives. I think most people want the good life; they want to live in nice houses and eat well and have some of the material things. And if you don't want them, nobody's forcing you to have them, right? All our system offers anybody is a chance to make good and live well. It's not perfect, but it's the best there is. Let's face it, Bing was from a very poor Catholic family. And Frank Sinatra was from a very poor Italian family. In what other country in the world could a meatball and a piece of spaghetti command so much bread?

PLAYBOY: If you couldn't be a comedian, what would you rather do with your life?

HOPE: I'd probably have a chain of restaurants or hotels, something like that, where I could appeal to the tastes of people. I've always thought about that, because I dig food and I've always noticed how different restaurants and hotels attract people. That's one thing I did in vaudeville. When the other guys were eating in the Greek restaurants, I would always find a tearoom and get the dainty food, because I loved that. I used to go up to the stagehands and say, "Hey, where's a tearoom around here?" They'd look at me like I was a fag, but today I've got the best stomach in town just from being careful.

PLAYBOY: Is it true that you've given a lot of money to universities and schools?

HOPE: Yes, but the only thing I'll tell you about that is that they named an elementary school in San Antonio after me. The kids voted to name the school and I went down there and I got up and said, "I'm flattered because the kids themselves selected me. It just goes to prove how they'll always go for a person who is good-looking and talented, and whose name is easy to spell."

PLAYBOY: Is it true that you're one of the richest men in the world?

HOPE: That's what they say. I wish somebody would tell me where all the money is. Some guy in a magazine article said I was the richest man in America after J. Paul Getty. Listen, Getty sends me a CARE package every year. This money talk about me is silly. I started working in vaudeville for five dollars a day and I have my house paid for and I'm a millionaire, OK, but this stuff they've been writing in the magazines is absolutely ridiculous. One guy said I was worth $500 million. It's become like some of the movie magazines you read. You know, "Does John Wayne sleep with a night light?" They just put this stuff in. It's a provocative style of reporting and it sells magazines. It's just like the dirty movies; it's all for the money. Say, you don't want me to pose for the centerfold, do you?

PLAYBOY: It hadn't occurred to us.

HOPE: A couple of interviewers have asked me to. I told them I wouldn't do it unless I could carry a catcher's mitt. I saw that one with Burt Reynolds. It didn't prove anything except that he's left-handed.

PLAYBOY: So you're not worth half a billion, but you're doing all right. There was an item in a Los Angeles paper a while back saying that you had turned down $40 million or so for 327 acres of prime Malibu land with ocean frontage. Is that true?

HOPE: When you're through with *Playboy*, would you like to be a real-estate agent? It's true, I do own some property in Malibu, but it's not exactly ocean frontage, except in case of a very high tide. Right now we can't do anything with the property because of the ecological restrictions. Not that I have anything against ecology. I'm looking forward to breathing again.

PLAYBOY: When did you buy all that real estate?

HOPE: Oh, I've been buying since 1949. Crosby and I struck oil down in Texas back in the 1940s. It was a big strike; we had a lot of wells and we made a good capital gain on it. To Crosby, it wouldn't have made any difference if he'd struck orange juice. He's been living on *White Christmas* for 20 years. I put the money I made in oil into property. That's where I got whatever I've got. All the rest of my money went to the government, all the money I ever made from pictures and radio. The taxes grabbed me.

PLAYBOY: What are your aspirations now?

HOPE: To keep working. I'm going to do a movie based on the life of Walter Winchell, either a movie or a two-episode television thing. I'm in love with the idea. I knew Winchell, I went through that whole era. I'll really enjoy that.

PLAYBOY: You seem to be always involved in something and constantly on the move. Why?

HOPE: I've always lived that way. There's always so much to do. I've been in town a whole week this time and I don't remember ever being home this much. I'm always working on something—movies, specials, benefits, fairs, running out to wave at the tour bus. A star's work is never done.

PLAYBOY: What about sex? Is there sex after 60?

HOPE: You bet. And awfully good, too. Especially the one in the fall.

May 1971

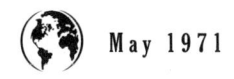

JOHN WAYNE

A candid conversation with the straight-shooting superstar/superpatriot

For more than 41 years, the barrel-chested physique and laconic derring-do of John Wayne have been prototypical of gung-ho virility, Hollywood style. In more than 200 films—from *The Big Trail* in 1930 to the soon-to-be-released *Million Dollar Kidnapping*—Wayne has charged the beaches at Iwo Jima, beaten back the Indians at Fort Apache and bloodied his fists in the name of frontier justice so often—and with nary a defeat—that he has come to occupy a unique niche in American folklore. The older generation still remembers him as Singing Sandy, one of the screen's first crooning cowpokes; the McLuhan generation has grown up with him on *The Late Show*. With Cooper and Gable and Tracy gone, the last of the legendary stars survives and flourishes as never before.

His milieu is still the action Western, in which Wayne's simplistic plotlines and easily discernible good and bad guys attest to a romantic way of life long gone from the American scene—if indeed it ever really existed. Even his screen name—changed from Marion Michael Morrison—conveys the man's plain, rugged cinematic personality. Fittingly, he was the first of the Western movie heroes to poke a villain in the jaw. Wearing the symbolic white Stetson—which never seemed to fall off, even in the wildest combat—he made scores of three-and-a-half-day formula oaters such as *Pals of the Saddle* in the 1930s before being tapped by director John Ford to star in *Stagecoach*—the 1939 classic that paved the way for his subsequent success in such milestone Westerns as *Red River*, the ultimate epic of the cattle drive, and *The Alamo*, a patriotic paean financed by Wayne with $1.5 million of his own money.

By 1969, having made the list of top 10 box-office attractions for 19 consecutive years, Wayne had grossed more than $400 million for his studios—more than any other star in motion-picture history. But because of his uncompromising squareness—and his archconservative politics—he was still largely a profit without honor in Hollywood. That oversight was belatedly rectified when his peers voted the tearful star a 1970 Oscar for his portrayal of Rooster Cogburn, the tobacco-chewing, hard-drinking, straight-shooting, patch-eyed marshal in *True Grit*—a possibly unwitting exercise in self-parody that good-naturedly spoofed dozens of his past characterizations. President Nixon remarked several months later at a press conference that he and his family had recently enjoyed a screening of *Chisum*, adding: "I think that John Wayne is a very fine actor."

Long active in Republican politics, Wayne has vigorously campaigned and helped raise funds for Nixon, Ronald Reagan, George Murphy, Barry Goldwater and Los Angeles's maverick Democratic mayor Sam Yorty. Before the 1968 campaign, a right-wing Texas billionaire had urged Wayne to serve as vice presidential running mate to George Wallace, an overture he rejected. Not least among the Texan's reasons for wanting to draft Wayne was the actor's obdurately hawkish support of the Indochina war—as glorified in his production of *The Green Berets*, which had the dubious distinction of being probably the only pro-war movie made in Hollywood during the 1960s.

Last fall, Wayne's first television special—a 90-minute quasi-historical pageant dripping with God-home-and-country hyperbole—racked up such a hefty Nielsen rating that it was rebroadcast in April. At year's end, Wayne was named one of the nation's most admired entertainers in a Gallup Poll. Assigned by *Playboy* shortly afterward to interview the superstar, Contributing Editor Richard Warren Lewis journeyed to Wayne's sprawling (11-room, seven-bath) $175,000 bayfront residence on the Gold Coast of Newport Beach, California, where he lives with his third Latin wife—Peruvian-born Pilar Pallete—and three of his seven children. Of his subject, Lewis writes:

"Wayne greeted me on a manicured lawn against a backdrop of sailboats, motor cruisers and yachts plying Newport harbor. Wearing a realistic toupee, Wayne at first appeared considerably younger than he is; only the liver spots on both hands and the lines in his jut-jawed face told of his 63 years. But at 6'4" and 244 pounds, it still almost seems as if he *could* have single-handedly mopped up all those bad guys from the Panhandle to Guadalcanal. His sky-blue eyes, though somewhat rheumy from the previous night's late hours, reinforced the image.

"Adjourning to the breakfast room, we spoke for several hours while Wayne enjoyed the first Dungeness crabs of the season, drank black coffee and fielded phone calls. One of the calls settled details of an imminent visit from the Congolese ambassador. (Wayne and several associates own lucrative mineral rights in the Congo.) Another call confirmed a $100 bet on the Santa Anita Handicap, to be contested later that day. (Wayne lost.)

"'Christ, we better get going,' he said shortly before one o'clock. 'They're holding lunch for us.' He led the way past a den and trophy room stacked with such memorabilia as photos of his 18 grandchildren and the largest collection of Hopi Indian kachina dolls west of Barry Goldwater. Outside the house, past jacaranda and palm trees and a kidney-shaped swimming pool, we reached a seven-foot-high concrete wall at the entryway and boarded Wayne's dark-green Bonneville station wagon, a production model with only two modifications—a sunroof raised six inches to accommodate the driver's 10-gallon hat, and two telephone channels at the console beside him.

"At Newport harbor, we boarded Wayne's awesome *Wild Goose II*, a converted U.S. Navy mine sweeper that saw service during the last six months of World War II and has been refitted as a pleasure cruiser. After a quick tour of the 136-foot vessel—which included a look at the twin 500-horsepower engines, clattering teletype machines (AP, UPI, Reuters, Tass) on the bridge disgorging wire dispatches, and the lavishly appointed bedroom and dressing suites—we were seated at a polished-walnut table in the main saloon.

"Over a high-protein diet lunch of charbroiled steak, lettuce and cottage cheese, Wayne reminisced about the early days of Hollywood, when he was making two-reelers for $500 each. Later that afternoon, he produced a bottle of his favorite tequila. One of the eight crew members anointed our glasses with a dash of fresh lemon juice, coarse salt and heaping ice shards that, Wayne said, had been chopped from a 1000-year-old glacier on a recent *Wild Goose* visit to Alaska. Sustained by these potent drinks, our conversation—ranging from Wayne's early days in filmmaking to the current state of the industry—continued until dusk, and resumed a week later in the offices of Wayne's Batjac Productions, on the grounds of Paramount Pictures—one of the last of Hollywood's rapidly dwindling contingent of major studios."

PLAYBOY: How do you feel about the state of the motion-picture business today?

WAYNE: I'm glad I won't be around much longer to see what they do with it. The men who control the big studios today are stock manipulators and bankers. They know nothing about our business. They're in it for the buck. The only thing they can do is say, "Jeez, that picture with what's-her-name running around the park naked made money, so let's make another one. If that's what they want, let's give it to them." Some of these guys remind me of high-class whores. Look at 20th Century Fox, where they're making movies like *Myra Breckinridge*. Why doesn't that son of a bitch Darryl Zanuck get himself a striped silk shirt and learn how to play the piano? Then he could work in any room in the house. As much as I couldn't stand some of the old-time moguls—especially Harry Cohn—these men took an interest in the future of their business. They had integrity. There was a stretch when they realized that they'd made a hero out of the goddamn gangster heavy in crime movies, that they were doing a discredit to our country. So the moguls voluntarily took it upon themselves to stop making gangster pictures. No censorship from the outside. They were responsible to the public. But today's executives don't give a damn. In their efforts to grab the box office that these sex pictures are attracting, they're producing garbage. They're taking advantage of the fact that nobody wants to be called a bluenose. But they're going to reach the point where the American people will say, "The hell with this!" And once they do, we'll have censorship in every state, in every city, and there'll be no way you can make even a worthwhile picture for adults and have it acceptable for national release.

PLAYBOY: Won't the present rating system prevent that from happening?

WAYNE: No. Every time they rate a picture, they let a little more go. Ratings are ridiculous to begin with. There was no need for rated pictures when the major studios were in control. Movies were once made for the whole family. Now, with the kind of junk the studios are cranking out—and the jacked-up prices they're charging for the privilege of seeing it—the average family is staying home and watching television. I'm quite sure that within two or three years, Americans will be completely fed up with these perverted films.

PLAYBOY: What kind of films do you consider perverted?

WAYNE: Oh, *Easy Rider, Midnight Cowboy*—that kind of thing. Wouldn't you say that the wonderful love of those two men in *Midnight Cowboy*, a story about two fags, qualifies? But don't get me wrong. As far as a man and a woman is concerned, I'm awfully happy there's a thing called sex. It's an extra something God gave us. I see no reason why it shouldn't be in pictures. Healthy, lusty sex is wonderful.

PLAYBOY: How graphically do you think it should be depicted on the screen?

WAYNE: When you get hairy, sweaty bodies in the foreground, it becomes distasteful, unless you use a pretty heavy gauze. I can remember seeing pictures that Ernst Lubitsch made in the 1930s that were beautifully risqué—and you'd certainly send your children to see them. They were done with *intimation*. They got over everything these other pictures do without showing the hair and the sweat. When you think of the wonderful picture fare we've had through the years and realize we've come to this shit, it's disgusting. If they want to continue making those pictures, fine. But my career will have ended. I've already reached a pretty good height right now in a business that I feel is going to fade out from its own vulgarity.

PLAYBOY: Don't gory films like *The Wild Bunch* also contribute to that vulgarity?

WAYNE: Certainly. To me, *The Wild Bunch* was distasteful. It would have been a good picture without the gore. Pictures go too far when they use that kind of realism, when they have shots of blood spurting out and teeth flying, and when they throw liver out to make it look like people's insides. *The Wild Bunch* was one of the first to go that far in realism, and the curious went to see it. That may make the bankers and the stock promoters think this is a necessary ingredient for successful motion pictures. They seem to forget the one basic principle of our business—illusion. We're in the business of magic. I don't think it hurts a child to see anything that has the *illusion* of violence in it. All our fairy tales have some kind of violence—the good knight riding to kill the dragon, etc. Why do we have to show the knight spreading the serpent's guts all over the candy mountain?

PLAYBOY: Proponents of screen realism say that a public inured to bloody war—news footage on television isn't going to accept the mere illusion of violence in movies.

WAYNE: Perhaps we *have* run out of imagination on how to effect illusion because of the satiating realism of a real war on television. But haven't we got *enough* of that in real life? Why can't the same point be made just as effectively in a drama without all the gore? The violence in my pictures, for example, is lusty and a little bit humorous, because I believe humor nullifies violence. Like in one picture, directed by Henry Hathaway, this heavy was sticking a guy's head in a barrel of water. I'm watching this and I don't like it one bit, so I pick up this pick handle and I yell, "Hey!" and cock him across the head. Down he went—with no spurting blood. Well, that got a hell of a laugh because of the way I did it. That's my kind of violence.

PLAYBOY: Audiences may like your kind of violence on the screen, but they'd never heard profanity in a John Wayne movie until *True Grit*. Why did you finally decide to use such earthy language in a film?

WAYNE: In my other pictures, we've had an explosion or something go off when a bad word was said. This time we didn't. It's profanity, all right, but I doubt if there's anybody in the United States who hasn't heard the expression son of a bitch or bastard. We felt it was acceptable in this instance. At the emotional high point in that particular picture, I felt it was OK to use it. It would have been pretty hard to say "you illegitimate sons of so-and-so!"

PLAYBOY: In the past, you've often said that if the critics liked one of your films, you must be doing something wrong. But *True Grit* was almost unanimously praised by the critics. Were you doing something wrong? Or were they right for a change?

WAYNE: Well, I knew that *True Grit* was going to go—even with the critics. Once in a while, you come onto a story that has such great humor. The author caught the flavor of Mark Twain, to my way of thinking.

PLAYBOY: The reviewers thought you set out to poke fun at your own image in *True Grit*.

WAYNE: It wasn't really a parody. Rooster Cogburn's attitude toward life was maybe a little different, but he was basically the same character I've always played.

PLAYBOY: Do you think *True Grit* is the best film you've ever made?

WAYNE: No, I don't. Two classic Westerns were better—*Stagecoach* and *Red River*—and a third, *The Searchers*, which I thought deserved more praise than it got, and *The Quiet Man* was certainly one of the best. Also the one that all the college cinematography students run all the time—*The Long Voyage Home*.

PLAYBOY: Which was the worst?

WAYNE: Well, there's about 50 of them that are tied. I can't even remember the names of some of the leading ladies in those first ones, let alone the names of the pictures.

PLAYBOY: At what point in your career were you nicknamed Duke?

WAYNE: That goes back to my childhood. I was called Duke after a dog—a very good Airedale out of the Baldwin Kennels. Republic Pictures gave me a screen credit on one of the early pictures and called me Michael Burn. On another one, they called me Duke Morrison. Then they decided Duke Morrison didn't have enough prestige. My real name, Marion Michael Morrison, didn't sound American enough for them. So they came up with John Wayne, I didn't have any say in it, but I think it's a great name. It's short and strong and to the point. It took me a long time to get used to it, though. I still don't recognize it when somebody calls me John.

PLAYBOY: After giving you a new name, did the studio decide on any particular screen image for you?

WAYNE: They made me a singing cowboy. The fact that I couldn't sing—or play the guitar—became terribly embarrassing to me, especially on personal appearances. Every time I made a public appearance, the kids insisted that I sing *The Desert Song* or something. But I couldn't take along the fella who played the guitar out on one side of the camera and the fella who sang on the other side of the camera. So finally I went to the head of the studio and said. "Screw this, I can't handle it." And I quit doing those kind of pictures. They went out and brought the best hillbilly recording artist in the country to Hollywood to take my place. For the first couple of pictures, they had a hard time selling him, but he finally caught on. His name was Gene Autry. It was 1939 before I made *Stagecoach*—the picture that really made me a star.

PLAYBOY: Like *Stagecoach,* most of the 204 pictures you've made—including your latest, *Rio Lobo*—have been Westerns. Don't the plots all start to seem the same?

WAYNE: *Rio Lobo* certainly wasn't any different from most of my Westerns. Nor was *Chisum*, the one before that. But there still seems to be a very hearty public appetite for this kind of film—what some writers call a typical John Wayne Western. That's a label they use disparagingly.

PLAYBOY: Does that bother you?

WAYNE: Nope. If I depended on the critics' judgment and recognition, I'd never have gone into the motion-picture business.

PLAYBOY: Did last year's Academy Award for *True Grit* mean a lot to you?

WAYNE: Sure it did—even if it took the industry 40 years to get around to it. But I think both of my two previous Oscar nominations—for *She Wore a Yellow Ribbon* and *Sands of Iwo Jima*—were worthy of the honor. I know the Marines and all the American Armed Forces were quite proud of my portrayal of Stryker, the Marine sergeant in *Iwo*. At an American Legion convention in Florida, General MacArthur told me, "You represent the American serviceman better than the American serviceman himself." And, at 42, in *She Wore a Yellow Ribbon*, I played the same character that I played in *True Grit* at 62. But I really didn't need an Oscar. I'm a box-office champion with a record they're going to have to run to catch. And they won't.

PLAYBOY: A number of critics claim that your record rests on your appeal to adolescents. Do you think that's true?

WAYNE: Let's say I hope that I appeal to the more carefree times in a person's life rather than to his reasoning adulthood. I'd just like to be an image that reminds someone of joy rather than of the problems of the world.

PLAYBOY: Do you think young people still feel strongly about you?

WAYNE: Luckily so far, it seems they kind of consider me an older friend, somebody believable and down-to-earth. I've avoided being mean or petty, but I've never avoided being rough or tough. I've only played one cautious part in my life, in *Allegheny Uprising*. My parts have ranged from that rather dull character to Ralls in *Wake of the Red Witch*, who was a nice enough fella sober, but bestial when he was drunk, and certainly a rebel. I was also a rebel in *Reap the Wild Wind* with DeMille. I've played many parts in which I've rebelled against something in society. I was never much of a joiner. Kids do join things, but they also like to consider themselves individuals capable of thinking for themselves. So do I.

PLAYBOY: But isn't your kind of screen rebellion very different from that of today's young people?

WAYNE: Sure. Mine is a personal rebellion against the monotony of life, against the status quo. The rebellion in these kids—especially in the SDSers and those groups—seems to be a kind of dissension by rote.

PLAYBOY: Meaning what?

WAYNE: Just this: The articulate liberal group has caused certain things in our country, and I wonder how long the young people who read *Playboy* are going to allow these things to go on. George Putnam, the Los Angeles news analyst, put it quite succinctly when he said, "What kind of a nation is it that fails to understand that freedom of speech and assembly are one thing, and anarchy and treason are quite another, that allows known Communists to serve as teachers to pervert the natural loyalties and ideals of our kids, filling them with fear and doubt and hate and down-grading patriotism and all our heroes of the past?"

PLAYBOY: You blame all this on liberals?

WAYNE: Well, the liberals seem to be quite willing to have Communists teach their kids in school. The Communists realized that they couldn't start a workers' revolution in the United States, since the workers were too affluent and too progressive. So the Commies decided on the next-best thing, and that's to start on the schools, start on the kids. And they've managed to do it. They're already in colleges; now they're getting into high schools. I wouldn't mind if they taught my children the basic philosophy of communism, in theory and how it works in actuality. But I don't want somebody like Angela Davis inculcating an enemy doctrine in my kids' minds.

PLAYBOY: Angela Davis claims that those who would revoke her teaching credentials on ideological grounds are actually discriminating against her because she's black. Do you think there's any truth in that?

WAYNE: With a lot of blacks, there's quite a bit of resentment along with their dissent, and possibly rightfully so. But we can't all of a sudden get down on our knees and turn everything over to the leadership of the blacks. I believe in white supremacy until the blacks are educated to a point of responsibility. I don't believe in giving authority and positions of leadership and judgment to irresponsible people.

PLAYBOY: Are you equipped to judge which blacks are irresponsible and which of their leaders inexperienced?

WAYNE: It's not my judgment. The academic community has developed certain tests that determine whether the blacks are sufficiently equipped scholastically. But some blacks have tried to force the issue and enter college when they haven't passed the tests and don't have the requisite background.

PLAYBOY: How do they get that background?

WAYNE: By going to school. I don't know why people insist that blacks have been forbidden their right to go to school. They were allowed in public schools wherever I've been. Even if they don't have the proper credentials for college, there are courses to help them become eligible. But if they aren't academically ready for that step, I don't think they should be allowed in. Otherwise, the academic society is brought down to the lowest common denominator.

PLAYBOY: But isn't it true that we're never likely to rectify the inequities in our educational system until some sort of remedial education is given to disadvantaged minority groups?

WAYNE: What good would it do to register anybody in a class of higher algebra or calculus if they haven't learned to count? There has to be a standard. I don't feel guilty about the fact that five or 10 generations ago these people were slaves. Now, I'm not condoning slavery. It's just a fact of life, like the kid who gets infantile paralysis and has to wear braces so he can't play football with the rest of us. I will say this, though: I think any black who can compete with a white today can get a better break than a white man. I wish they'd tell me where in the world they have it better than right here in America.

PLAYBOY: Many militant blacks would argue that they have it better almost *anywhere* else. Even in Hollywood, they feel that the color barrier is still up for many kinds of jobs. Do you limit the number of blacks you use in your pictures?

WAYNE: Oh, Christ no. I've directed two pictures and I gave the blacks their proper position. I had a black slave in The Alamo, and I had a correct number of blacks in The Green Berets. If it's supposed to be a black character, naturally I use a black actor. But I don't go so far as hunting for positions for them. I think the Hollywood studios are carrying their tokenism a little too far. There's no doubt that 10 percent of the population is black, or colored, or whatever they want to call themselves; they certainly aren't Caucasian. Anyway, I suppose there should be the same percentage of the colored race in films as in society. But it can't always be that way. There isn't necessarily going to be 10 percent of the grips or sound men who are black, because more than likely, 10 percent haven't trained themselves for that type of work.

PLAYBOY: Can blacks be integrated into the film industry if they are denied training and education?

WAYNE: It's just as hard for a white man to get a card in the Hollywood craft unions.

PLAYBOY: That's hardly the point, but let's change the subject. For years American Indians have played an important—if subordinate—role in your Westerns. Do you feel any empathy with them?

WAYNE: I don't feel we did wrong in taking this great country away from them, if that's what you're asking. Our so-called stealing of this country from them was just a matter of survival. There were great numbers of people who needed new land, and the Indians were selfishly trying to keep it for themselves.

PLAYBOY: Weren't the Indians—by virtue of prior possession—the rightful owners of the land?

WAYNE: Look, I'm sure there have been inequalities. If those inequalities are presently affecting any of the Indians now alive, they have a right to a court hearing. But what happened 100 years ago in our country can't be blamed on us today.

PLAYBOY: Indians today are still being dehumanized on reservations.

WAYNE: I'm quite sure that the concept of a government-run reservation would have an ill effect on anyone. But that seems to be what the socialists are working for now—to have *everyone* cared for from cradle to grave.

PLAYBOY: Indians on reservations are more neglected than cared for. Even if you accept the principle of expropriation, don't you think a more humane solution to the Indian problem could have been devised?

WAYNE: This may come as a surprise to you, but I wasn't alive when reservations were created—even if I *do* look that old. I have no idea what the best method of dealing with the Indians in the 1800s would have been. Our forefathers evidently thought they were doing the right thing.

PLAYBOY: Do you think the Indians encamped on Alcatraz have a right to that land?

WAYNE: Well, I don't know of anybody else who wants it. The fellas who were taken off it sure don't want to go back there, including the guards. So as far as I'm concerned, I think we ought to make a deal with the Indians. They should pay as much for Alcatraz as we paid them for Manhattan. I hope they haven't been careless with their wampum.

PLAYBOY: How do you feel about the government grant for a university and cultural center that these Indians have demanded as "reparations"?

WAYNE: What happened between their forefathers and our forefathers is so far back—right, wrong or indifferent—that I don't see why we owe them anything. I don't know why the government should give them something that it wouldn't give me.

PLAYBOY: Do you think they've had the same advantages and opportunities that you've had?

WAYNE: I'm not gonna give you one of those I-was-a-poor-boy-and-I-pulled-myself-up-by-my-bootstraps stories, but I've gone without a meal or two in my life, and I still don't expect the government to turn over any of its territory to me. Hard times aren't something I can blame my fellow citizens for. Years ago, I didn't have all the opportunities, either. But you can't whine and bellyache 'cause somebody else got a good break and you didn't, like these Indians are. We'll *all* be on a reservation soon if the socialists keep subsidizing groups like them with our tax money.

PLAYBOY: In your distaste for socialism, aren't you overlooking the fact that many worthwhile and necessary government services—such as Social Security and Medicare—derived from essentially socialistic programs evolved during the 1930s?

WAYNE: I know all about that. In the late 1920s, when I was a sophomore at USC, I was a socialist myself—but not when I left. The average college kid idealistically wishes everybody could have ice cream and cake for every meal. But as he gets older and gives more thought to his and his fellow man's responsibilities, he finds that it can't work out that way—that some people just won't carry their load.

PLAYBOY: What about welfare recipients?

WAYNE: I believe in welfare—a welfare *work* program. I don't think a fella should be able to sit on his backside and receive welfare. I'd like to know why well-educated idiots keep apologizing for lazy and complaining people who think the world owes them a living. I'd like to know why they make excuses for cowards who spit in the faces of the police and then run behind the judicial sob sisters. I can't understand these people who carry placards to save the life of some criminal, yet have no thought for the innocent victim.

PLAYBOY: Who are "these people" you're talking about?

WAYNE: Entertainers like Steve Allen and his cronies who went up to Northern California and held placards to save the life of that guy Caryl Chessman. I just don't understand these things. I can't understand why our national leadership isn't willing to take the responsibility of leadership instead of checking polls and listening to the few that scream. Why are we allowing ourselves to become a mobocracy instead of a democracy? When you allow unlawful acts to go unpunished, you're moving toward a government of men rather than a government of law; you're moving toward anarchy. And that's exactly what we're doing. We allow dirty loudmouths to publicly call policemen pigs; we let a fella like William Kunstler make a speech to the Black Panthers saying that the ghetto is theirs, and that if police come into it, they have a right to shoot them. Why is that dirty, no-good son of a bitch allowed to practice law?

PLAYBOY: What's your source for that statement you attribute to Kunstler?

WAYNE: It appeared in a Christian Anti-Communism Crusade letter written by Fred Schwarz on August 1, 1969. Here, I'll read it to you: "The notorious left-wing attorney, Bill Kunstler, spoke on political prisoners and political freedom at the National Conference for a United Front Against Fascism, which was held in Oakland, California, July 18, 19 and 20, 1969. He urged blacks to kill white policemen when they entered the black ghetto. He told the story of how a white policeman, John Gleason, was stomped to death in Plainfield, New Jersey. The crowd broke into prolonged applause. Kunstler proceeded to state that, in his opinion, Gleason deserved that death. . . . Kunstler pointed out that no white policeman has set foot in the black ghetto of Plainfield, New Jersey, since July 1967." That could turn out to be a terrible thing he said. Pretty soon there'll be a bunch of whites who'll say, "Well, if that's their land, then this is ours. They'd better not trespass on it." It can work two ways.

PLAYBOY: What's your opinion of the stated goals of the Black Panthers?

WAYNE: Quite obviously, they represent a danger to society. They're a violent group of young men and women—adventurous, opinionated and dedicated—and they throw their disdain in our face. Now, I hear some of these liberals saying they'd like to be held as white hostages in the Black Panther offices and stay there so that they could see what happens on these early-morning police raids. It might be a better idea for these good citizens to go *with* the police on a raid. When they search a Panther hideout for firearms, let these do-gooders knock and say, "Open the door in the name of the law" and get shot at.

PLAYBOY: Why do you think many young people—black and white—support the Panthers?

WAYNE: They're standing up for what they *feel* is right, not for what they *think* is right—'cause they don't think. As a kid, the Panther ideas probably would have intrigued me. When I was a little kid, you could be adventurous like that without hurting anybody. There were periods when you could blow the valve and let off some steam. Like Halloween. You'd talk about it for three months ahead of time, and then that night you'd go out and stick the hose in the lawn, turn it on and start singing "Old Black Joe" or something. And when people came out from their Halloween party, you'd lift the hose and wet them down. And while you were running, the other kids would be stealing the ice cream from the party. All kinds of rebellious actions like that were accepted for that one day. Then you could talk about it for three months afterward. That took care of about six months of the year. There was another day called the Fourth of July, when you could go out and shoot firecrackers and burn down two or three buildings. So there were two days a year. Now those days are gone. You can't have firecrackers, you can't have explosives, you can't have this—don't do this, don't do that. Don't . . . don't . . . don't. A continual *don't* until the kids are ready to do almost anything rebellious. The government makes the rules, so now the running of our government is the thing they're rebelling against. For a lot of those kids, that's just being adventurous. They're not deliberately setting out to undermine the foundations of our great country.

PLAYBOY: Is that what you think they're doing?

WAYNE: They're doing their level worst—without knowing it. How 'bout all the kids that were at the Chicago Democratic Convention? They were conned into doing hysterical things by a bunch of activists.

PLAYBOY: What sort of activists?

WAYNE: A lot of Communist-activated people. I know communism's a horrible word to some people. They laugh and say, "He'll be finding them under his bed tomorrow." But perhaps that's because their kid hasn't been inculcated yet. Dr. Herbert Marcuse, the political philosopher at the University of California at San Diego, who is quite obviously a Marxist, put it very succinctly when he said, "We will use the anarchists."

PLAYBOY: Why do you think leftist ideologues such as Marcuse have become heroes on so many of the nation's campuses?

WAYNE: Marcuse has become a hero only for an articulate clique. The men that give me faith in my country are fellas like Spiro Agnew, not the Marcuses. They've attempted in every way to humiliate Agnew. They've tried the old Rooseveltian thing of trying to laugh him out of political value of his party. Every comedian's taken a crack at him. But I bet if you took a poll today, he'd probably be one of the most popular men in the United States. Nobody likes Spiro Agnew but the people. Yet he and other responsible government leaders are booed and pelted when they speak on college campuses.

PLAYBOY: Beyond the anti-administration demonstrations on campuses, do you think there's any justification for such tactics as student occupation of college administrative offices?

WAYNE: One or two percent of the kids is involved in things like that. But they get away with it because 10 percent of the teaching community is behind them. I see on TV how, when the police are trying to keep the kids in line, like up at the University of California at Berkeley, all of a sudden there's a bunch of martyr-professors trying to egg the police into violent action.

PLAYBOY: If you were faced with such a confrontation, how would you handle it?

WAYNE: Well, when I went to USC, if anybody had gone into the president's office and shit in his wastepaper basket and used the dirt to write vulgar words on the wall, not only the football team but the average kid on campus would have gone to work on the guy. There doesn't seem to be respect for authority anymore; these student dissenters act like children who have to have their own way on everything. They're immature and living in a little world all their own. Just like hippie dropouts, they're afraid to face the real competitive world.

PLAYBOY: What makes you, at the age of 63, feel qualified to comment on the fears and motivations of the younger generation?

WAYNE: I've experienced a lot of the same things that kids today are going through, and I think many of them admire me because I haven't been afraid to say that I drink a little whiskey, that I've done a lot of things wrong in my life, that I'm as imperfect as they all are. Christ, I don't claim to have the answers, but I feel compelled to bring up the fact that under the guise of doing good, these kids are causing a hell of a lot of irreparable damage, and they're starting something they're not gonna be able to finish. Every bit of rampant anarchy has provoked a little more from somebody else. And when they start shooting policemen, the time has come to start knocking them off, as far as I'm concerned.

PLAYBOY: What do you mean by "knocking them off"?

WAYNE: I'd throw 'em in the can if I could. But if they try to kill you, I'd sure as hell shoot back. I think we should break up those organizations or make 'em illegal. The American public is getting sick and tired of what these young people are doing. But it's really partly the public's own fault for allowing the permissiveness that's been going on for the past 15 or 20 years. By permissiveness, I mean simply following Dr. Spock's system of raising children. But that kind of permissiveness isn't unique to young people. Our entire society has promoted an "anything goes" attitude in every area of life and in every American institution. Look at the completely irresponsible editorship of our country's newspapers. By looking for provocative things to put on their front pages, they're encouraging these kids to act the way they're acting. I wonder even more about the responsibility of the press when I read about events like the so-called My Lai massacre in Vietnam. The press and the communications system jumped way ahead of the trials. At the time, they made accusations that I doubted they could back up; frankly. I hoped they couldn't. Well, it turns out there may have been something to it. But I could show you pictures of what the North Vietnamese and the Viet Cong are doing to our people over there. I was at a place called Dak Song, where the children were all burned to death by the V.C., and that's not an unusual thing. But for some reason, our newspapers have never printed pictures or stories about it. With all the terrible things that are being done throughout the world, it has to be one little incident in the United States army—and the use of the word massacre—that causes the uproar.

PLAYBOY: Don't you deplore what happened at My Lai?

WAYNE: Not only do I deplore it, but so does the army—which conducted an extensive investigation and charged everyone connected with the alleged crime.

PLAYBOY: Does the fact that the Viet Cong have systematically engaged in atrocities excuse our forces for resorting to the same thing?

WAYNE: No, absolutely not. But if your men go to a supposedly peaceful village and the occupants start shooting at them, they're going to have to shoot back to defend their own lives.

PLAYBOY: The reports say our GIs slaughtered unarmed civilians and babies at My Lai; no one was shooting at them.

WAYNE: If, after going into the town, they brutally killed these people, that's one thing. If they were getting shot at from that town and then they fired back, that's a completely different situation. But you're bringing up the stuff that's being debated in the trials. What I resent is that even before the trials, this stuff was even less of a proven fact, yet the newspapers printed it anyway.

PLAYBOY: Do you think there's a credibility gap between the way the war has been reported and the way it's actually being fought—on both sides?

WAYNE: It's obvious to me, because I've been there. And you'll find that the young veterans who come back from Vietnam have a lot to say that the media haven't told us—even about our allies. These young men know what they're talking about, because they own a piece of that war, and you should ask the man who owns one.

PLAYBOY: Many of those young men who "own a piece of that war" never wanted to go to Vietnam in the first place. Do you think our government is justified in sending them off to fight in an undeclared war?

WAYNE: Well, I sure don't know why we send them over to fight and then stop the bombing so they can get shot that much more. We could easily stop the enemy from getting guns and ammunition that we know are being sent by Chinese and Soviet Communists. But we won't do anything to stop it because we're afraid of world opinion. Why in hell should we worry about world opinion when we're trying to help out a country that's asked for our aid? Of course, Senator Fulbright says the South Vietnamese government doesn't represent the people—even though it's been duly elected by those people. How can a man be so swayed to the opposite side? If he were finding fault with the *administration* of our help over there, that I could understand. What I can't understand is this "pull out, pull out, pull out" attitude he's taken. And what makes it worse is that a lot of people accept anything he says without thinking, simply because the Fulbright scholarships have established an intellectual aura around him.

PLAYBOY: The majority of the American people, according to every poll, agree with Fulbright that we ought to pull out, and many think we never should have intervened in the first place. Many Southeast Asian experts, including Fulbright, believe that if Ho Chi Minh had been allowed to run Vietnam as he saw fit after the Geneva Accords of 1954, he would have established an accommodation with Peking that would have given us perhaps a nominally Communist nation, but essentially a nationalist, independent government.

WAYNE: How? By what example in history can people like Fulbright come to such wishful thinking?

PLAYBOY: The example of Tito's Yugoslavia comes immediately to mind. In any case, what gives us the right to decide for the Vietnamese what kind of government they should have?

WAYNE: I don't want the U.S. to decide what kind of government they have. But I don't want the Communists to decide, either. And if we didn't help the South Vietnamese government, that's just what they'd do.

PLAYBOY: Why couldn't a general election, supervised by some neutral power, be held in both the North and the South to determine what kind of government the people of Vietnam desire?

WAYNE: That would be no more practical than if France, after coming to help us in the Revolution, suggested having an election to decide what we wanted to do. It would be an exact parallel. The majority of those living in the Colonies didn't want war at that time. If there had been a general election then, we probably wouldn't be here today. As far as Vietnam is concerned, we've made mistakes. I know of no country that's perfect. But I honestly believe that there's as much need for us to help the Vietnamese as there was to help the Jews in Germany. The only difference is that we haven't had any leadership in this war. All the liberal senators have stuck their noses in this, and it's out of their bailiwick. They've already put far too many barriers in the way of the military. Our lack of leadership has gone so far that now no one man can come in, face the issue and tell people that we ought to be in an all-out war.

PLAYBOY: Why do you favor an all-out war?

WAYNE: I figure if we're going to send even one man to die, we ought to be in an all-out conflict. If you fight, you fight to win. And the domino theory is something to be reckoned with, too, both in Europe and in Asia. Look at what happened in Czechoslovakia and what's happened all through the Balkans. At some point we have to stop communism. So we might as well stop it right now in Vietnam.

PLAYBOY: You're aware, of course, that most military experts, including two recent Secretaries of State, concede that it would be an unwinnable war except at a cost too incalculable to contemplate.

WAYNE: I think you're making a mistatement. Their fear is that Russia would go to war with us if we stopped the Vietnamese. Well, I don't think Russia wants war any more than we do.

PLAYBOY: Three presidents seem to have agreed that it would be unwise to gamble millions of lives on that assumption. Since you find their leadership lacking, who would you have preferred in the highest office?

WAYNE: Barry Goldwater would at least have been decisive. I know for a fact that he's a truthful man. Before the '64 election, he told me that he said to the Texan, "I don't think we ought to make an issue out of Vietnam because we both know that we're going to probably end up having to send a half a million men over there." Johnson said, "Yeah, that's probably true, Barry, but I've got an election to win." So Barry told the truth and Johnson got elected on a "peace" platform—and then began to ease them in, a few thousand at a time. I wish our friend Fulbright would bring out those points.

If Douglas MacArthur were alive, he also would have handled the Vietnam situation with dispatch. He was a proven administrator, certainly a proven leader. And MacArthur understood what Americans were and what Americans stood for. Had he been elected president, something significant would have happened during his administration. He would have taken a stand for the United States in world affairs, and he would have stood by it, and we would have been respected for it. I also admired the tie salesman, President Truman. He was a wonderful, feisty guy who'll go down in history as quite an individual. It's a cinch he had great guts when he decided to straighten things out in Korea; it's just too bad that the State Department was able to frighten him out of doing a complete job. Seems to me, politics have entered too much into the decisions of our leadership. I can't understand politicians. They're either yellowing out from taking a stand or using outside pressure to improve their position.

PLAYBOY: Is that why you've refused to run for public office yourself?

WAYNE: Exactly.

PLAYBOY: Is that what you told George Wallace when you were asked to be his running mate on the 1968 American Independent ticket?

WAYNE: No, I explained that I was working for the other Wallis—Hal Wallis—the producer of *True Grit*, and that I'd been a Nixon man.

PLAYBOY: What do you think of Nixon's performance since then?

WAYNE: I think Mr. Nixon is proving himself his own man. I knew he would. I knew him and stuck with him when he was a loser, and I'm sticking with him now that he's a winner. A lot of extreme rightists are saying that he isn't doing enough, but I think he's gradually wading in and getting control of the reins of government.

PLAYBOY: What impressed you about him when you first met him?

WAYNE: His reasonableness. When he came into office, there was such a hue and cry over Vietnam, for instance, that it didn't seem possible for a man to take a stand that would quiet down the extreme leftists. He came on the air and explained the situation as it was from the beginning, and then he told the American people—in a logical, reasoning way—what he was going to do. And then he began to do it.

PLAYBOY: What he began to do, of course, was "Vietnamize" the war and withdraw American troops. How can you approve of these policies and also advocate all-out war?

WAYNE: Well, I don't advocate an all-out war if it isn't necessary. All I know is that we as a country should be backing up whatever the proposition is that we sent one man to die for.

PLAYBOY: If that view is shared by as many Americans as you seem to think, then why was *The Green Berets*—which has been labeled as your personal statement on the Vietnam war—so universally panned?

WAYNE: Because the critics don't like my politics, and they were condemning the war, not the picture. I don't mean the critics as a group. I mean the irrationally liberal ones. Renata Adler of *The New York Times* almost foamed at the mouth because I showed a few massacres on the screen. She went into convulsions. She and other critics wouldn't believe that the Viet Cong are treacherous—that the dirty sons of bitches are raping, torturing gorillas. In the picture, I repeated the story General Stilwell told me about this South Vietnamese mayor. The V.C. tied him up and brought his wife out and about 40 men raped her; and then they brought out his two teenage daughters, hung them upside down and gutted them in front of him. And then they took an iron rod and beat on his wife until every bone in her goddamn body was broken. That's torture, I'd say. So I mentioned this in the picture, and the critics were up in arms about that.

PLAYBOY: Did their comments jeopardize the financial success of the film?

WAYNE: Oh, God, no—they ensured it. Luckily for me, they overkilled it. *The Green Berets* would have been successful regardless of what the critics did, but it might have taken the public longer to find out about the picture if they hadn't made so much noise about it.

PLAYBOY: Did you resent the critics who labeled it a shameless propaganda film?

WAYNE: I agreed with them. It was an American film about American boys who were heroes over there. In that sense, it *was* propaganda.

PLAYBOY: Did you have any difficulties getting *The Green Berets* produced by a major studio?

WAYNE: A lot of them. Universal said they wanted to make the picture and we made a deal. Then the boys went to work on the head of Universal.

PLAYBOY: What boys?

WAYNE: The liberals. I don't know their names. But all of a sudden Universal changed its mind. They said, "This is an unpopular war." And I said, "What war was ever popular? You've already made the deal." Then they started saying, "Well, we don't want you to direct"—trying to use that as an excuse. So I said, "Well, screw this." So I let them renege and I just walked out. In an hour, I'd made another deal with Warner Bros., which was in the process of being sold to Seven Arts. Meanwhile, the guy at Universal couldn't keep his mouth shut. I let him off the hook, but he started blasting in the *Hollywood Reporter* that the picture couldn't make any money. I didn't go to the press and say these bastards backed out of a deal, but later—after Warner Bros.–Seven Arts released it—I was very happy to inform Universal of the picture's success.

PLAYBOY: *The Alamo* was another of your patriotic films. What statement did this picture make?

WAYNE: I thought it would be a tremendous epic picture that would say "America."

PLAYBOY: Borden Chase, the screenwriter, has been quoted as saying: "When *The Alamo* was coming out, the word of mouth on it was that it was a dog. This was created by the Communists to get at Wayne. Then there were some bad reviews inspired by the Communists. . . . It's a typical Communist technique and they were using it against Duke for what he did in the early 1950s at the Motion Picture Alliance for the Preservation of American Ideals." Is that true?

WAYNE: Well, there's always a little truth in everything you hear. The Alliance thing was used pretty strongly against me in those days.

PLAYBOY: Was the Motion Picture Alliance formed to blacklist Communists and Communist sympathizers?

WAYNE: Our organization was just a group of motion-picture people on the right side, not leftists and not Commies. I was the president for a couple of years. There was no blacklist at that time, as some people said. That was a lot of horseshit. Later on, when Congress passed some laws making it possible to take a stand against these people, we were asked about Communists in the industry. So we gave them the facts as we knew them. That's all. The only thing our side did that was anywhere near blacklisting was just running a lot of people out of the business.

PLAYBOY: That sounds a good deal worse than blacklisting. Why couldn't you permit all points of view to be expressed freely on the screen?

WAYNE: Because it's been proven that communism is foreign to the American way of life. If you'd read the official Communist doctrine and then listened to the arguments of these people we were opposing, you'd find they were reciting propaganda by rote. Besides, these Communist sympathizers ran a lot of *our* people out of the business. One of them was a Pulitzer Prize winner who's now a columnist—Morrie Ryskind. They just never used him again at MGM after Dore Schary took charge of the studio, even though he was under contract.

PLAYBOY: What was the mood in Hollywood that made it so fashionable to take such a vigorous stand against communism?

WAYNE: Many of us were being invited to supposed social functions or house parties—usually at well-known Hollywood writers' homes—that turned out to be Communist recruitment meetings. Suddenly, everybody from makeup men to stagehands found themselves in seminars on Marxism. Take this colonel I knew, the last man to leave the Philippines on a submarine in 1942. He came back here and went to work sending food and gifts to U.S. prisoners on Bataan. He'd already gotten a Dutch ship that was going to take all this stuff over. The State Department pulled him off of it and sent the poor bastard out to be the technical director on my picture *Back to Bataan*, which was being made by Eddie Dmytryk. I knew that he and a whole group of actors in the picture were pro-Reds, and when I wasn't there, these pro-Reds went to work on the colonel. He was a Catholic, so they kidded him about his religion: They even sang the "Internationale" at lunchtime. He finally came to me and said, "Mr. Wayne, I haven't anybody to turn to. These people are doing everything in their power to belittle me." So I went to Dmytryk and said, "Hey, are you a Commie?" He said, "No, I'm not a Commie. My father was a Russian. I was born in Canada. But if the masses of the American people want communism, I think it'd be good for our country." When he used the word "masses," he exposed himself. That word is not a part of Western terminology. So I knew he was a Commie. Well, it later came out that he was.

I also knew two other fellas who really did things that were detrimental to our way of life. One of them was Carl Foreman, the guy who wrote the screenplay for *High Noon*, and the other was Robert Rossen, the one who made the picture about Huey Long, *All the King's Men*. In Rossen's version of *All the King's Men*, which he sent me to read for a part, every character who had any responsibility at all was guilty of some offense against society. To make Huey Long a wonderful, rough pirate was great; but, according to this picture, everybody was a shit except for this weakling intern doctor who was trying to find a place in the world. I sent the script back to Charlie Feldman, my agent, and said, "If you ever send me a script like this again, I'll fire you." Ironically, it won the Academy Award.

High Noon was even worse. Everybody says *High Noon* is a great picture because Tiomkin wrote some great music for it and because Gary Cooper and Grace Kelly were in it. So it's got everything going for it. In that picture, four guys come in to gun down the sheriff. He goes to the church and asks for help and the guys go, "Oh well, oh gee." And the women stand up and say, "You're rats. You're rats. You're rats." So Cooper goes out alone. It's the most un-American thing I've ever seen in my whole life. The last thing in the picture is ole Coop putting the United States marshal's badge under his foot and stepping on it. I'll never regret having helped run Foreman out of this country.

PLAYBOY: What gave you the right?

WAYNE: Running him out of the country is just a figure of speech. But I did tell him that I thought he'd hurt Gary Cooper's reputation a great deal. Foreman said, "Well, what if I went to England?" I said, "Well, that's your business." He said, "Well, that's where I'm going." And he did.

PLAYBOY: You seem to have a very blunt way of dealing with people. Why?

WAYNE: I've always followed my father's advice: He told me, first, to always keep my word and, second, to never insult anybody unintentionally. If I insult you, you can be goddamn sure I intend to. And, third, he told me not to go around looking for trouble.

PLAYBOY: Don't you sometimes stray from these three tenets—particularly from the third one?

WAYNE: Well, I guess I have had some problems sticking to that third rule, but I'd say I've done pretty damn well with the first and second. I try to have good enough taste to insult only those I wish to insult. I've worked in a business where it's almost a requirement to break your word if you want to survive, but whenever I signed a contract for five years or for a certain amount of money, I've always lived up to it. I figured that if I was silly enough to sign it, or if I thought it was worthwhile at the time, that's the way she goes. I'm not saying that I won't drive as hard a bargain as I can. In fact, I think more about that end of the business than I did before, ever since 1959, when I found that my business manager was playing more than he was working. I didn't know how bad my financial condition was until my lawyer and everybody else said, "Let's all have a meeting and figure out exactly where you stand." At the conclusion of that meeting, it was quite obvious that I wasn't in anywhere near the shape that I thought I was or ought to be after 25 years of hard work. If they'd given me the time to sell everything without taking a quick loss, I would have come out about even.

PLAYBOY: Were you involved in money-losing deals?

WAYNE: Yeah. Oil and everything else. Not enough constructive thinking had been done. Then there was the shrimp fiasco. One of my dearest friends was Robert Arias, who was married to the ballerina Dame Margot Fonteyn. While his brother Tony was alive, we had control of about 70 percent of the shrimp in Panama. We were also buying some island property near the Panama Canal. We were going to put in a ship-repair place. There were tugs standing down there at $150 a day to drag ships back up to the United States, because repair prices in the Canal Zone were so high. But our plans fell through when Tony was killed in an airplane accident. Around a half a million dollars was lost.

PLAYBOY: Has your financial condition improved since then?

WAYNE: If anything happened to me now, I have the right amount of insurance, I hope and pray, for my estate. I'm about as big a rancher as there is in Arizona, so I have outside interests other than my motion-picture work. The turning point was the moment I decided to watch what was being done with my money.

PLAYBOY: Another—and certainly more dramatic—turning point for you was your cancer operation in 1964. At the time, were you optimistic about the outcome of the surgery?

WAYNE: Well, I had two operations six days apart—one for a cancer that was as big as a baby's fist, and then one for edema. I wasn't so uptight when I was told about the cancer. My biggest fear came when they twisted my windpipe and had to sew me back together a second time. When my family came in to see me and I saw the looks on their faces, I figured, "Well, Jeez, I must be just about all through."

PLAYBOY: How did you keep your spirits up?

WAYNE: By thinking about God and my family and my friends and telling myself, "Everything will be all right." And it was. I licked the big C. I know the man upstairs will pull the plug when he wants to, but I don't want to end up my life being sick. I want to go out on two feet—in action.

PLAYBOY: Does the loss of one lung restrict you from doing those rough-house movie stunts?

WAYNE: The operation hasn't impeded anything except that I get short of breath quickly. Particularly in the higher altitudes, that slows me down. I still do my own fights and all that stuff. I'd probably do a little bit more if I had more wind, but I still do more than my share. Nobody else does anything any more than I do, whether they're young or old.

PLAYBOY: Is it a matter of machismo for you to continue fighting your own fights?

WAYNE: I don't have to assert my virility. I think my career has shown that I'm not exactly a pantywaist. But I do take pride in my work, even to the point of being the first one on the set in the morning. I'm a professional.

PLAYBOY: In recent years, you've fallen off horses rather unprofessionally on a couple of occasions—once dislocating a shoulder during the production of *The Undefeated*. Wasn't that embarrassing?

WAYNE: What the hell, in my racket I've fallen off a lot of horses. I even fell off on purpose in *True Grit*. But that fall in *The Undefeated* was irritating because I tore some ligaments in my shoulder. I don't have good use of one arm anymore, and it makes me look like an idiot when I'm getting on a horse.

PLAYBOY: Is that an unfamiliar experience?

WAYNE: Getting on a horse?

PLAYBOY: Looking like an idiot.

WAYNE: Not hardly. One of the times I really felt like a fool was when I was working on my first important film, *The Big Trail,* in Yuma, Arizona. I was three weeks flat on my back with *turistas*—or Montezuma's revenge, or the Aztec two-step, whatever you want to call it. You know, you get a little grease and soap on the inside of a fork and you've got it. Anyway, that was the worst case I ever had in my life. I'd been sick for so long that they finally said. "Jeez, Duke, if you can't get up now, we've got to get somebody else to take your place." So, with a loss of 18 pounds, I returned to work. My first scene was carrying in an actor named Tully Marshall, who was known to booze it up quite a bit. He had a big jug in his hand in this scene, and I set him down and we have a drink with another guy. They passed the jug to me first, and I dug back into it; it was straight rotgut bootleg whiskey. I'd been puking and crapping blood for a week and now I just poured that raw stuff right down my throat. After the scene, you can bet I called him every kind of an old bastard.

PLAYBOY: You've long been known for your robust drinking habits, whether it's rotgut bootleg or imported scotch. How great is your capacity?

WAYNE: Well, I'm full grown, you know. I'm pretty big and got enough fat on me, so I guess I can drink a fair amount.

PLAYBOY: What kind of liquor has provided your most memorable hangovers?

WAYNE: *Conmemorativo* tequila. That's as fine a liquor as there is in the world. Christ, I tell you it's better than any whiskey; it's better than any schnapps; it's better than any drink I ever had in my life. You hear about tequila and think about a cheap cactus drink, but this is something extraordinary.

PLAYBOY: Many people argue that alcohol may be a more dangerous health hazard than marijuana. Would you agree?

WAYNE: There's been no top authority saying what marijuana does to you. I really don't know that much about it. I tried it once, but it didn't do anything to me. The kids say it makes them think they're going 30 miles an hour when they're going 80. If that's true, marijuana use should definitely be stopped.

PLAYBOY: Have you had any other experience with illegal drugs?

WAYNE: When I went to Hong Kong, I tried opium once, as a clinical thing. I heard it didn't make you sick the first time, and Jesus, it just didn't affect me one way or the other, either. So I'm not a very good judge of how debasing it is.

PLAYBOY: Do you think such drugs are debasing?

WAYNE: It's like water against a cliff. Each wave deteriorates it a little more. I'm quite sure that's the same thing that happens to human beings when they get hooked on drugs. What bothers me more is society's attitude toward drugs. We allowed all the hippies to stay together in Haight-Ashbury and turn it into a dirty, filthy, unattractive place. We allow the glorifying of drugs in our business—like in *Easy Rider*, where the guy says, "Jesus, don't you smoke pot?"—as if smoking pot is the same as chewing Bull Durham.

PLAYBOY: You chew tobacco, don't you?

WAYNE: I learned to do that in college. During football season, when we couldn't smoke, we always used to chew. When I was a kid, if you wore a new pair of shoes, everybody would spit on them. I haven't practiced spitting lately, so don't wear your new shoes and expect me to hit them with any accuracy. I'm not the marksman I used to be.

PLAYBOY: You chew, but you don't use drugs. Do you still have as much drink, food and sex as you used to?

WAYNE: I drink as much as I ever did. I eat more than I should. And my sex life is none of your goddamn business.

PLAYBOY: Sexuality, however, seems a large part of your magnetism. According to one Hollywood writer, "Wayne has a sexual authority so strong that even a child could perceive it." Do you feel you still convey that onscreen?

WAYNE: Well, at one time in my career, I guess sexuality was part of my appeal. But God, I'm 63 years old now. How the hell do I know whether I still convey that? Jeez. It's pretty hard to answer a question like, "Are you attractive to broads?" All that crap comes from the way I walk, I guess. There's evidently a virility in it. Otherwise, why do they keep mentioning it? But I'm certainly not conscious of any particular walk. I guess I must walk different than other people, but I haven't gone to any school to learn how.

PLAYBOY: Another integral ingredient of your image is a rugged manliness, a readiness to mix it up with anyone who gets in your way. Have you ever run into situations in a restaurant or a bar in which someone tried to pick a fight with you?

WAYNE: It never happens to me anymore. Whatever my image is, it's friendly. But there was one time, a number of years ago, that I did get a little irritated. I was wearing long hair—the exception then, not the rule—and I was, if I say so myself, a fairly handsome kid. Anyway, I'm dancing with my wife-to-be and I'm saying to her, quietly, "You're beautiful enough to marry." Some punk alongside pipes up, "Forget about him, lady; not with that hair." So I sat her down and went over and explained very gently to him that if he would step outside, I'd kick his fuckin' teeth down his throat. That ended that.

PLAYBOY: Having once worn long hair yourself, how do you feel about long-haired young people?

WAYNE: They don't bother me. If a guy wants to wear his hair down to his ass, I'm not revolted by it. But I don't look at him and say, "Now there's a fella I'd like to spend next winter with."

PLAYBOY: Who *would* you like to spend time with?

WAYNE: That's easy. Winston Churchill. He's the most terrific fella of our century. If I had to make a speech on the subject of communism, I could think of nobody that had a better insight or that said things concerning the future that have proven out so well. Let me read to you from a book of his quotes. While Roosevelt was giving the world communism, Churchill said, "I tell you—it's no use arguing with a Communist. It's no good trying to convert a Communist, or persuade him. You can only deal with them on the following basis . . . you can only do it by having superior force on your side on the matter in question—and they must also be convinced that you will use—you will not hesitate to use—these forces if necessary, in the most ruthless manner.

"You have not only to convince the Soviet government that you have superior force—but that you are not restrained by any moral consideration if the case arose from using that force with complete material ruthlessness. And that is the greatest chance of peace, the surest road to peace." Churchill was unparalleled. Above all, he took a nearly beaten nation and kept their dignity for them.

PLAYBOY: Many pessimists insist that our nation has lost its dignity and is headed toward self-destruction. Some, in fact, compare the condition of our society to the decline and fall of the Roman Empire and the last days of Sodom and Gomorrah. Are you that gloomy about the future of America?

WAYNE: Absolutely not. I think that the loud roar of irresponsible liberalism, which in the old days we called radicalism, is being quieted down by a reasoning public. I think the pendulum's swinging back. We're remembering that the past can't be so bad. We built a nation on it. We must also look always to the future. Tomorrow—the time that gives a man or a country just one more chance—is just one of many things that I feel are wonderful in life. So's a good horse under you. Or the only campfire for miles around. Or a quiet night and a nice soft hunk of ground to sleep on. Or church bells sending out their invitations. A mother meeting her first-born. The sound of a kid calling you Dad for the first time. There's a lot of things great about life. But I think tomorrow is the most important thing. Comes in to us at midnight very clean, ya know. It's perfect when it arrives and it puts itself in our hands. It hopes we've learned something from yesterday. As a country, our yesterdays tell us that we have to win not only at war but at peace. So far we haven't done that. Sadly, it looks like we'll have to win another war to win a peace. All I can hope is that in our anxiety to have peace, we remember our clear and present dangers and beware the futility of compromise; only if we keep sight of both will we have a chance of stumbling forward into a day when there won't be guns fired anymore in anger.

PLAYBOY: Contrasting the America you grew up in and the America of today, is it the same kind of country, or has it changed?

WAYNE: The only difference I can see is that we now have an enemy within our borders fighting with propaganda and coloring events in a manner that belittles our great country. But all in all, it's practically the same.

PLAYBOY: In retrospect, would you have wanted your life to have been any different?

WAYNE: If I had it to do over again, I'd probably do everything I did. But that's not necessarily the right thing to do.

PLAYBOY: What legacy do you hope to leave behind?

WAYNE: Well, you're going to think I'm being corny, but this is how I really feel: I hope my family and my friends will be able to say that I was an honest, kind and fairly decent man.

INDEX

Abourezk, Jim, 81
Academy Awards:
   Brando, Marlon, 49, 72, 73
   Davis, Bette, 105, 106, 107, 109, 114, 115-116, 119
   Hope, Bob, 342, 343
   Oscar, origin of nickname, 116
   Price Waterhouse, 116
   Wayne, John, 362, 367, 368, 382
   West, Mae, performer at, 199
Academy of Motion Picture Arts and Sciences (AMPAS), 115-116
Adler, Jacob P., 68
Adler, Stella, 48, 49, 68, 97
African Queen, The, 114
Agnew, Spiro, 217, 222, 231, 263-264, 342, 344, 374
Alamo, The, 361, 370, 380, 381
Aldrich, Robert, 134,
Alexian Brothers, 86
Ali vs. Foreman, Zaire, 315-318
Ali, Muhammad, 256, 257-259, 277-281, 287-338:
   acting, 335
   aging, 329-331, 333-334
   Army, failure to qualify for, 303
   beginnings, 289
   black community, investment in, 330-331
   black names, 324
   blacks, employment of, 323-324
   childhood, 288-289
   as conscientious objector, 258-259, 331-332
   country living, 313
   fame, 289, 333, 334, 335, 336-338
   integration, 310-311
   interracial relationships, 312-313, 327-328
   Islam, 304-306, 310, 319, 321, 324, 325-328, 330, 332, 335, 337, 338
      discovery of, 304-305
   Jews, 322, 330-331
   lynching, 328
   money, 306, 323, 330-331, 332, 333
   name change, 287, 325
   Olympic Gold Medal, 287, 291, 305
   poetry of, 289-290, 313-314
   press relations, 297-298, 299-300, 303

   race, 294, 305-308, 310, 312-313, 319-325, 334
   religion, 304, 306-307
   retirement, thoughts on, 333-334
   salary, 331, 332, 333
   sayings of, 314-315
   segregation, 307
   training routine, 329-330
   "Truth," 313-314
   women, 306, 326-328
   World Heavyweight Champion title, 318
      See also Liston, Charles "Sonny" *and* Foreman, George
All About Eve, 105, 116, 117, 118, 121-122
All The King's Men, 382
Allah, 320, 322, 324, 325-326, 331, 335, 336
Allen, Fred, 341
Allen, George, 270, 272
Allen, Reggie, 204
Allen, Woody, 72, 283-284, 354
Ameche, Don, 212
America, 80
American Indians. *See* Indians
Anderson, Jack, 91, 227, 232
Annie Hall, 72
Apocalypse Now, 50
Applause, 122
Arledge, Roone, 260, 261-262, 265
Arliss, George, 124
Ashley, April, 28

Bacall, Lauren, 122
Bach, Johann Sebastian, 61
Baez, Joan, 23, 144, 155, 156, 163, 166, 176-182
Baker, Senator Howard, 345
Ballyhoo of 1932, 340
Bancroft, Anne, 116
Bankhead, Tallulah, 106, 117-118
Banks, Dennis, 86, 91
Bara, Theda, 207
Basie, Count, 44
Battle of Algiers, The, 71, 91
Beatles, 11-33, 57, 61, 146, 169, 171, 175:
   America, 27, 31

Americans, 18-19, 20-21
Beatle people, 17, 18, 23, 28
beginnings, 14-15
dolls, 31-32
fame, 12-13, 15, 19-21
fans, 17, 18, 20, 23, 28
friendship between, 21-22
Hitler, comparison to, 23
homosexuality, 22, 27-28
money, 13, 16-17
press relations, 24
religion, 27
riots, 24-25
royalty, 26
salary, 16
Bedtime Story, 70
Bennett, Tony, 96-97, 152
Benny, Jack, 341, 353
Bergen, Edgar, 341
Bergman, Ingmar, 177
Bernini, Gian Lorenzo, 60
Berra, Yogi, 32
Bertolucci, Bernardo, 66-67
"Bette Davis Eyes," 142
Bible Belt, the, 352
Big Broadcast of 1938, The, 341, 353
Bigart, Homer, 247-248
Biggs, Verlon, 271
Bimstein, Whitey, 275
Bingham, Howard, 295, 298
Black Muslims, 287, 304
black separatism, 319-321, 323, 328-329
Black, Hugo, 244
Blonde on Blonde, 170
Blood on the Tracks, 184
"Blowin' in the Wind," 144, 186
Bogart, Humphrey, 114, 125
Bow, Clara, 207
Boyer, Charles, 125
Boys in the Band, The, 206
Brando, Marlon, 47-103, 132-133:
 acting, 58-59, 60, 61, 63, 64-70
 arrests of, 50, 85
 art, 59-60, 61-62
 awards, 49, 72-73
 big business, 77-78
 childhood, 48, 51-52, 100
 as director, 69
 disarmament, 98
 drugs, 100-101
 fame, 56, 57

God, 101
guns, 78, 90-91
heroes, 57
Indians, 50, 51, 52, 53-54, 56, 72, 80-89, 90, 91, 92, 97
Jews, 76, 83, 87-88
marriages, 50
money, 54, 55, 58-59, 62, 69, 78, 96, 100
paparazzi, 95-96
press relations, 52-53, 73, 76-77, 94-95, 99
repulsions of, 102-103
rivalries, 98-99
rock 'n' roll, 61
salary, 63
Shakespeare, 57, 59, 63, 102
social activism of, 50, 53. *See also* Indians
terrorism, 77
war, 99-100
women, 50, 73, 74-75
Brent, George, 125, 129
Bringing It All Back Home, 170
Brooks, Mel, 70
Brown, Jerry, 81, 86
Bruce, Lenny, 342, 354
Buckley, William F., 99
Buñuel, Luis, 177
Burger, Chief Justice Warren, 244
Burn!, 50, 91-93, 94
Butz, Earl, 227

Caan, James, 62
Caesar, Sid, 70
Cambodia, 347, 348
Candy, 50
Cannon, Jimmy, 277
Capitol Records, 16
Capote, Truman, 55
Carnegie, Dale, 59
Carney, Art, 70
Carter, President Jimmy, 80-81, 190-191
Castro, Fidel, 78, 288
Catcher in the Rye, The, 175
Catherine Was Great, 198
Cavett, Dick, 52, 95, 96, 127, 284
CBS Evening News with Walter Cronkite, The, 219, 233
CBS News, 218, 227, 239, 240, 248
CBS, 144, 222, 228, 239, 240
 business interests of, 225
Chamberlain, Wilt, 312
Chaplin, Charles, 50, 68-69, 117, 207, 353
Chaplin, Sydney, 68

Charles, Ezzard, 338
Charlie McCarthy Show, The, 212
Checker, Chubby, 61, 307
Chekhov, Anton, 175
Cheyenne Autumn, 88
"Chimes of Freedom," 189
Christianity, 193, 305, 306, 324, 325, 326-327, 350-351
Churchill, Winston, 26, 68, 387, 391
CIA, 78
Civil Rights Act, 307
Civilization, 60
Clark, Kenneth, 60
Clay, Cassius. *See* Ali, Muhammad
Clayburgh, Jill, 131
Clift, Montgomery, 98
Clurman, Harold, 49
Colbert, Claudette, 122
Cold War, the. *See* Communism
Collingwood, Charles, 212
Columbia Records, 144
Communism, 42-44, 78
Conformist, The, 67
Conn, Billy, 301
Connally, John, 344
Cooper, Gary, 132
Cooper, Henry, 291, 292
Coppola, Francis Ford, 63, 134
Corporation for Public Broadcasting (CPB), 227
Cosell, Howard, 253-285, 314:
    ABC's *Wide World of Sports*, 255
    acting ambitions of, 283-284
    Ali, Muhammad, 256, 257-259, 277-281
    baseball, 259, 274
    boxing, 275, 281
    childhood, 254
    coaches, 269
    college sports, 267-268
    Gifford, Frank, 260, 262-263
    Jackson, Keith, 261, 262-263, 265
    Liston, Charles "Sonny," 276-279
    Lombardi, Vince 255, 269-270, 271, 274, 283
    Meredith, "Dandy" Don, 255, 260-262, 264-266
    Emmy award of, 264-266
    Monday Night Football, NFL, 255
    myths of sports, 257
    Namath, Joe, 253, 259, 271, 272, 273
    national anthem, 266-267
    Olympic Games, 281-282
    Patterson, Floyd, 275-276, 278, 279

    political ambitions of, 283
    race, 264, 276, 281
    Toomey, Bill, 282-283
Countess From Hong Kong, A, 50, 68
Cox, Wally, 48, 72
Crawford, Christina, 119
Crawford, Joan, 108, 109, 118-119
Cronkite, Walter, 217-252:
    beginnings, 218, 219, 247
    boating, 220, 242
    censorship, 225
    childhood, 246
    desegregation, 237, 245
    Emmy awards of, 218
    fame, 241-242
    freedom of press, 224-227, 250-251
    freedom of speech, 229
    interviewees of, 219
    journalistic sources, 232
    labels, 230-231
    liberal, definition of, 230
    local-station license-renewal bill, 222-227
    network news, purpose of, 233
    political ambitions of, 249
    press, bias of, 230-231
    press, effect on events, 233-234
    press, Nixon administration hostility toward, 217-218, 220-229, 250-251
    race, 245-246
    secret ambition of, 242
    surveillance, 243-244
    Vietnam war, editorials on, 237-238
    Vietnam war, press coverage of, 234-236, 250
    war, 248
Crosby, Bing, 341, 357
Cukor, George, 106, 113, 207
Curtiz, Michael, 115

Dangerous, 106
Davis, Bette, 105-142:
    abortion, 120
    abuse of, 128
    aging, 140-141
    censorship, 135
    childhood, 106, 112-113
    children of, 107, 119-120, 121, 142
    directing, 114-115. *See also* Wyler, William, and Arliss, George
    drugs, 130
    famous lines of, 122
    films, favorite, 121, 134, 142

films, least favorite, 134
gay fans of, 138
marriage, 125-126
marriages, 106-107, 120
men, 125-127, 129
men, leading, 124-125
money, 128, 133
musicals, 122-123
nudity, 136-137
pranks of, 134-135
religion, 140
roles, almost played, 114, 123-124
roles, favorite, 121
roles, least favorite, 124
sex, 126, 127-128, 130
superstitions of, 139-140
Davis, Sammy, Jr., 72
Dean Martin Show, The, 351
Dean, James, 174
Deep Throat, 355
Defense Department, 346
Democratic National Convention, 1964 (Atlantic City), 218
Democratic National Convention, 1968 (Chicago), 219, 226, 234, 239, 374
Dempsey, Jack, 338
Desire, 184
Devil in Miss Jones, The, 355
Diamond Lil, 198, 204
Ditka, Mike, 268-269
Don't Look Back, 175-176
Dooley, Edwin, 258
Douglas, Justice William O., 97
Drag, The, 205, 206
Dundee, Angelo, 281, 300, 301, 302, 315
Durante, Jimmy, 353
Dylan, Bob, 61, 67, 143-195:
　albums of, 162, 170-171, 184
　art, 146, 181, 185, 194-195
　as filmmaker, 163, 175-183. See also *Renaldo & Clara*
　childhood, 143, 158, 167
　civil rights, 162
　college, 156-157
　drugs, 157-158, 169
　fame, 159, 160
　fans, 148-149
　folk, 148, 167
　hair of, 153
　inspirations of, 165, 166-167, 174-175, 181, 183
　jazz, 147
　marriage of, 162
　money, 159, 194-195
　motorcycle accident of, 164, 168, 176, 194
　name of, 168
　politics, 189-190
　psychics, 161-162, 183
　rock 'n' roll, 146
　salary, 145
　sex, 157
　songs of, 150-151, 162, 184, 185-187
　sound of, 169-172, 183
　women, 187-188
Dylan, Sara, 162, 163, 178, 179, 180, 181, 182, 188

Ehrlichman, John, 345
Eisenhower, President Dwight D., 347-348
Ekberg, Anita, 32
Elizabeth II, Queen, 26
Ellsberg, Daniel, 236-237
Epstein, Brian, 16
Ervin, Sam, 345
Everly Brothers, The, 31
"Everybody Loves You for Your Black Eye," 147
Ewbank, Weeb, 269, 271

fairness doctrine, 225
Federal Bureau of Investigation (FBI), 78-79, 86, 91, 94
Feldman, Charley, 346
Felix, Barney, 302
Female Eunuch, The, 126
Fields, W. C., 208, 353
First American, The, 89
Fisher, Eddie, 44
Fisher, Liz, 44
Fisher, Murray, viii
Fitzgerald, Ella, 44
Flag is Born, A, 49
Flynn, Errol, 114, 121, 124-125, 129-130
Folley, Zora, 291
Fonda, Henry, 113, 125
Fonda, Jane, 96, 131
football, as inferior to boxing, 337-338
Ford, John, 88
Ford, President Gerald R., 328, 337
Foreman, George, 315-318, 330, 331, 333, 335
Fraley, Oscar, 276-277
Frazier, Joe, 279-280, 281, 315, 317, 330, 333, 335
Freed, Alan, 61
Fullmer, Gene, 304

Gable, Clark, 132
Gabor, Zsa Zsa, 125
Galella, Ron, 95, 96
Garbo, Greta, 207
Garland, Judy, 65, 138
Gavilan, Kid, 323-324
Giancana, Sam, 78
Gifford, Frank, 260, 262-263
Ginsberg, Allen, 165, 175
Gleason, Jackie, 70, 353
God, 154, 193-194
Godfather, The, 49, 62-63, 72, 77
Goldwater, Barry, 362, 363, 378
Goldwyn, Samuel, 117
Golson, Barry, viii
Gone with the Wind, 114
Gowdy, Curt, 261
Grant, Cary, 346
Green Berets, The, 362, 370, 379, 380
Greene, Shecky, 353
Greenstreet, Sydney, 340
Greer, Germaine, 126
Grobel, Lawrence, 50-103
Groppi, Father James, 85
Guinness, Alec, 125
Guthrie, Woody, 143, 144, 167

Hampton, Fred, 78
Hardy, Oliver, 70, 346
Harlem, 307-308, 311
Harlow, Jean, 207
Harrison, George, 11-33, 175:
    description of, 13
    family of, 17
Heat's On, The, 197
Heatherton, Joey, 356
Hefner, Hugh, 56
Heifetz, Jascha, 61
Hello, Dolly!, 204
Henreid, Paul, 125
Hentoff, Nat, 143-161
Hepburn, Katharine, 131
Herman's Hermits, 145
Hersh, Seymour, 236
High Anxiety, 70
High Noon, 382
Highway 61 Revisited, 170, 171
Hitler, Adolf, 23, 26, 254
Hoffman, Dustin, 89
Holly, Buddy, 174
Hollywood, demise of, 354-355
Holocaust, 89-90

Honeymooners, The, 70
Hoover, J. Edgar, 78-79
Hope, Bob, 71-72, 339-359:
    beginnings, 340
    Cambodia, 347, 348
    capitalism, virtues of, 356-357
    charity, 357
    childhood, 339-340
    children of, 343, 349
    ethnic humor of, 352
    Hollywood, demise of, 354-355
    investments of, 358
    marriage of, 343
    money, 341, 343, 357-358
    monologs of, 341
    politics of, 342, 344-350
    porn, 355
    Reade, Dolores, 343, 350
    Road, pictures of, 341
    sex, 359
    television, 342
    Thailand, 347, 348
    USO shows of, 346-347, 349
    Vietnam war, 342, 344, 348, 349, 350
    Vietnam, 346-347, 356
    Watergate, 345, 349, 356
    writers of, 340, 341, 351
Hope, Leslie Townes. *See* Hope, Bob
Hope, Tony, 343
Hopkins, Miriam, 118
Hotel Theresa, 288
Houston, Texas, 246
How to Win Friends and Influence People, 59
Howard, Leslie, 125, 130
Howard, Willie, 71
Hughes, Howard, 129
Huston, John, 66
Hutchinson, Fred, 283

I Am the Greatest, 288
Indians:
    Alexian Brothers and, 86
    Brando, Marlon, 50, 51, 52, 53-54, 56,
        72, 80-89, 90, 91, 92, 97
    Bureau of Indian Affairs, 81
    Cheyenne Autumn, 88
    church and, 84
    Collier, John, 81
    McNickle, D'Arcy, 81
    First American, The, 89
    Ford, John, 88
    Groppi, Father James, 85

Hollywood portrayal of, 87-89
John Wayne, 87, 90
Little Big Man, 88, 89
Menominee Tribe, 85-86
National Indian Youth Council, 81
sense of humor of, 81
separatist movement, 83
Soldier Blue, 88
Wayne, John and, 87, 370-372
I Remember Mama, 48
I Want You, 170
I'm No Angel, 207, 211
Ikiru, 71
Ireland, Dr. Richard, 213
Italian-American Civil Rights Organization, 62

Jackson, Keith, 261, 262-263, 265
Jazz, 44
Jennings, C. Robert, 200-215
Jessel, George, 353
Jezebel, 107, 113, 114, 116, 121
Johansson, Ingemar, 275, 291, 292
Johnson, Jack (heavyweight champion), 338
Johnson, President Lyndon B., 219, 238-239, 347-348
Jones, Doug, 290, 291, 292, 310, 311
Juarez, 107
Jurgensen, Sonny, 265, 269

Kael, Pauline, 49, 61, 67
Kafka, Franz, 57
Kalthoum, Om, 174
Kashfi, Anna, 50
Kazan, Elia, 61, 66, 69, 97
Keeler, Christine, 28
Kelly, Reverend Jack, 212, 213
Kennedy, President John F., 41, 43, 78, 79, 219, 344, 347-348
Kennedy, Robert, 78, 79
Kern, Jerome, 340
Kerouac, Jack, 165, 175
Kheel, Theodore, 254
Khrushchev, Nikita, 41, 43
Kierkegaard, Søren, 57
King, Martin Luther, Jr., 78, 79, 153, 237, 322
Klosterman, Don, 263, 264
Korean War, 348
Kubrick, Stanley, 69, 134

Lahr, Bert, 341
Lahr, John, 341
Lamour, Dorothy, 341

Landry, Tom, 253, 262
Last Christmas Show The, 46
Last Tango in Paris, 66-67, 355
Laurel and Hardy, 70, 346
Laurel, Stan, 70, 346
"Lay, Lady, Lay," 186
Lee, Charley, 353
Lennon, John, 11-33, 175:
    description of, 13
    family of, 18
Leonard, Sugar Ray, 290, 315
Letter, The, 107
Life, 16, 217
"Like a Rolling Stone," 147, 186
Liler, Herb, 305
Linderman, Lawrence, 255-285, 312-338
Liston, Charles "Sonny," 276-279, 287, 290, 291, 292-303, 304, 307, 309, 310, 317
Little Big Man, 88, 89
Little Foxes, The, 107, 117
Little League, 254
Lombardi, Vince 255, 269-270, 271, 274, 283
Louis, Joe, 293, 297, 298, 301, 311, 315, 338
Lumet, Sidney, 69

MacDonald, Bill, 297
Machen, Eddie, 291
MacMurray, Fred, 340
Mafia, the, 78
Magnani, Anna, 131
Malden, Karl, 69
Mankiewicz, Joseph, 112, 121
Mann, Abby, 91
Mansfield, Jayne, 23, 32
Mansfield, Judge Walter, 258
Mao Tse-tung, 41, 61
Marciano, Rocky, 276-277, 315, 338
Marijuana, 169, 385
Marlon Brando Film Festival, 62
Martin, Dean, 29
Martin, Joe, 289
Marx Brothers, 70
Marx, Groucho, 70, 346, 353-354
Mason, Marsha, 131
Mathis, Buster, 280
Matte, Tom, 263
McCartney, Paul, 11-33:
    description of, 13
    family of, 18
McCarthy, Joseph, 345
McGovern, George, 230, 249, 345
McQueen, Steve, 132

Means, Russell, 56, 86, 91
Men, The, 49
Meredith, "Dandy" Don, 255, 260-262, 264-266
Merrick, David, 204
Merrill, Gary, 107, 128-129, 140
Method acting, 49, 101, 132
Michelangelo, 60
Middleton, Ray, 340
Miller, Henry, 175, 185
Minnesota, 164-165, 172
Miracle Worker, The, 116
Moiseyev Dancers, 44
Mommie Dearest, 119
Mondale, Walter, 80
Monday Night Football, NFL, 255
Monroe, Bill, 167
Monroe, Marilyn, 32, 54-55, 207-208
Moore, Archie, 289-291, 292, 331
Morris, Maynard, 48
Morrison, Marion Michael. *See* Wayne, John
Motion Picture Alliance for the Preservation of American Ideals, 381
Movita, 50
Muhammad, Honorable Elijah, 307, 312, 314, 319, 320, 321, 323, 324-325, 338
Muhammad, Wallace D., 325, 337
Muni, Paul, 49, 107
Murphy, George, 339, 340
Murray, William, 343-359
Mutiny on the Bounty, 50, 94
My Grandmother Called it Carnal, 112
My Lai massacre, 235-236, 375-376
My Little Chickadee, 208
Myra Breckinridge, 199-200, 201-203, 213

Namath, Joe, 253, 259, 271, 272, 273
NASA, 218, 239-240
Nasser, Gamal Abdel, 309
National Boxing Association (NBA), 304
National Geographic, 52
Native Americans. *See* Indians
NBC, 76, 212
Nelson, "Ham," 106
New School for Social Research, The, 48
New York City, 165-166, 172-173
New Yorker, The, 55
Newman, Paul, 98, 132
Newport Folk Festival, 144, 148-149
Newsweek, 16
NFL vs. AFL, 272-273
Nicholson, Jack, 132
Night After Night, 211

Night of the Iguana, The, 108, 117
Nightcomers, The, 50, 63
Nilon, Jack, 297
Nixon, President Richard M.: *See also* Watergate
    administration's hostility to the press. *See under* Cronkite, Walter
    China trip, 219, 240, 349
    friendship with Hope, Bob, 344, 345
    job qualifications of, 250-251
    labeling of, 230
    Russia trip, 219, 240, 349
    Supreme Court appointees, 244
    and Vietnam, 344, 349, 379
    on Wayne, John, 362
Niven, David, 70
Nkurmah, Kwame, 309
Norton, Ken, 317, 330, 335
Now, Voyager, 107, 115, 121

Odetta, 166-167
Of Human Bondage, 106, 116
oil crisis, 77
Olivier, Laurence, 67-68, 121
Olympic Games, 1960 (Rome), 291, 287, 305, 310
Olympics, the, 281-282, 289. *See also* Toomey, Bill
On The Waterfront, 49, 65, 66, 132-133, 181
One-Eyed Jacks, 69
Oscars. *See* Academy Awards
"Over the Rainbow," 65

Pacino, Al, 61
Paramount Pictures, 197
Patterson, Floyd, 275-276, 278, 279, 291, 292, 293, 308, 310, 312
Payment on Demand, 121
Pentagon papers, 236-237
Pepsodent Show, 340-341
Perry Mason, 139
Person to Person, 212
Peterson, Peter, 345
Picasso, Pablo, 62
Piscator, Erwin, 48
Playboy, 23:
    All-Star Jazz Poll, 30, 35
    clubs, 29-30
    magazine, 30
Pontecorvo, Gillo, 91-93
Powell, Charley, 292
Powers, Ron, 219-252
Presley, Elvis, 31, 32, 57, 174, 211

Price Waterhouse, 116
Pride, Charley, 312
Prince Phillip, 26
Princess Margaret, 26
Private Lives of Elizabeth and Essex, The, 115
Profumo, John, 28

Quarry, Jerry, 333
Queimada. See *Burn!*

Radner, Gilda, 70
Rains, Claude, 125, 132
Rand, Tamara, 162-163, 183
Randall, Stephen, vii-viii
Rather, Dan, 239
Ray, Johnnie, 57
Ray, Satyajit, 76
Reade, Dolores, 343, 350
Reader's Digest, 99
Reagan, Ronald, 57, 139, 339, 344
Redford, Robert, 96, 132
Reed, Carol, 94
Reed, Rex, 206, 213
Reflections in a Golden Eye, 66
Reiner, Carl, 70
Renaldo & Clara, 163, 175, 178-183, 184, 188
Reynolds, Burt, 62-63, 93, 132
Rickles, Don, 71, 351-352, 353
Rilke, Rainer Maria, 175
Roberta, 340
Robinson, Archie, 294
Robinson, Jackie, 283
Robinson, Sugar Ray, 331, 336-337
rock 'n' roll, 30-31, 61, 146
Rockefeller, Nelson, 344
Rockwell, George Lincoln, 90
Roland, Gilbert, 111
Rolling Stones, 61, 145
Romanoff, Prince Michael, 41
Roots, 90
Rosenbaum, Ron, 161-195
Rosenbloom, Carroll, 263-264
Ross, Lillian, 55
Rozelle, Alvin Pete, 260
Run to Daylight, 255

Sahl, Mort, 354
Sarne, Michael, 200
Saturday Evening Post, 94
Saturday Night Live, 70
Schecter, Leonard, 270
Scott, Ray, 260

Seale, Bobby, 56
Selling of the Pentagon, The, 228-229
Selznick, David, 114
Sergeant, The, 205
Sermon on the Mount, 38
Sex, 205-206, 211
Shakespeare, William, 57, 59, 60-62, 63, 64, 102
Shane, 181
She Done Him Wrong, 211
Shepard, Jean, 11-33
Shields, Brooke, 136
Shula, Don, 269, 270, 272
Sinatra, Frank, 32, 35-45, 98, 133, 357:
    China, 41, 43, 44
    Communism, preventing spread of, 41-44
    desegregation, 38
    disarmament, 39-41
    money, 35
    poverty, 42
    press relations, 39
    race, 38
    religion, 37-39
    Russia, 40, 42, 43, 44
    singing, 36-37
    women, 44
Sing Out, 167
Sirhan, Sirhan, 78
60 Minutes, 229
Smith, Jerry, 269
Soldier Blue, 88
Space program, United States, 218, 239-240
Spielberg, Steven, 134
Sports Focus, 255
Stanislavsky, Constantin, 48
Starr, Ringo, 11-33, 169:
    description of, 13, 14
    family of, 18
Star, The, 118-119
Steiger, Rod, 66
Stengel, Casey, 273-274
Stram, Hank, 269, 270, 272
Strategy of Peace, 43
Streetcar Named Desire, A, 49, 60-61, 101
Streisand, Barbra, 51, 61, 131, 204
Student Nonviolent Coordinating Committee (SNCC), 153
Sunset Boulevard, 117
Superman, 50, 52, 64
Supreme Court, United States, 244-245, 332, 355
Swanson, Gloria, 117
Symington, Stuart, 346

Taco Pronto, 145
Tahiti, 50, 51, 86
Tarantula, 168, 175
Tarita, 50, 95
Tarkenton, Fran, 256, 272, 273
Taylor, Elizabeth. *See* Fisher, Liz
Tell-Tale Heart, The, 163, 194
Terrell, Ernie, 311
Tet offensive, 238
Tetiaroa. *See* Tahiti
Thailand, 347, 348
"Thanks for the Memory," 341
Thomas, Duane, 253
Thomas, Dylan, 67, 168
Time, 16
"The Times They Are A-Changin'", 144, 176
Tomlin, Lily, 71
Toomey, Bill, 282-283
Tracy, Spencer, 125, 132
Truckline Café, 49
Truman, Harry, 160, 191, 259, 378
Turner, Lana, 207

U. S.-Soviet wheat deal, 219
Ugetsu, 71
Ulasewicz, Anthony, 345
Unicef, 54, 75-76
Unitas, John, 263, 271-272
United Jewish Appeal, 76
United Nations, 40, 41, 43, 81
United Press (U.P.), 218, 248, 249
Universal Studios, 110-111
USO shows of Bob Hope, 72, 342, 346-347, 349, 350

Valenti, Jack, 76
Van Cleve, Edith, 49
Vietnam War:
   American involvement in, 83, 238, 344, 347, 377-378
   American policy on, 59, 219, 237, 347, 350, 376, 377, 379
   editorials on, 237-238
   jokes about, 203
   and King, Martin Luther, Jr., 79
   My Lai massacre, 235-236, 375-376
   and Nixon, President Richard M., 344, 349, 379
   opposition to, 79, 154, 155, 219, 237, 238, 283, 332
   performances during, 72, 342, 346-347, 349, 350, 356
   press coverage of, 219, 234, 237, 238, 375-376
   support of, 342, 347, 350, 375-379
   Tet offensive, 238
Viva Zapata!, 49

Walcott, Jersey Joe, 331, 338
Wallace, Mike, 55
Wallis, Hal, 124
Warner Bros., 106, 107, 124:
   contract dispute with Bette Davis, 107, 113-114
Warner, Jack L., 107
Warren, Chief Justice Earl, 244, 245
Washington Square, 166
Watergate:
   reporting on, 219
   public reaction to, 56, 229
   jokes about, 345
   mentions of, 76, 314, 349, 356
Waterproof, 66
Wayne, John, 87, 90, 361-388:
   Academy Award, 362, 367, 368, 382
   alcohol, 363, 375, 385, 386
   blacks, employment of, 370
   cancer of, 384
   communism, 369, 374, 381, 387
   Communists, 369, 374, 377, 381
   critics, 366, 379-380
   drugs, 385-386
   films of, 361
   hair, long on men, 387
   homosexuality, 365
   investments of, 383-384
   marriages, 362
   money, 364, 383-384
   political fundraising of, 362
   press, responsibility of, 375
   profanity in movies, 366
   race, 369-370
   sex, 364-365, 386
   as singing cowboy, 367
   slavery, 370
   tobacco, 386
   Vietnam war, support of, 362, 376-378
   violence in movies, 365-366
   welfare, 372-373
   white supremacy, 369
   youth, 368, 373-375
Welch, Raquel, 199-200, 203-204, 350
Wepner, Chuck, 323, 330, 335
West, Mae, 197-215
   aging, 214
   breasts, 198, 214

    camp, 206
    censorship, 201, 202, 205, 212
    Diamond Lil, 198, 204
    Hello, Dolly!, 204
    homosexuality, 204-205
    I'm No Angel, 207, 211
    impersonators of, 204-205
    Ireland, Dr. Richard, 213
    Jennings, C. Robert, 200-215
    Kelly, Reverend Jack, 212, 213
    lovers of, 208, 209
    marriage, 208, 211
    money, 200
    motherhood, 211
    My Little Chickadee, 208
    Myra Breckinridge, 199-200, 201-203, 213
    nudity, 203
    regime of, 214
    religion, 212-213
    sex, 197, 202-203, 205, 206, 208-210, 214
    tributes to, 197, 198, 199
Welch, Raquel, 199-200, 203-204
What Ever Happened to Baby Jane?, 108, 116, 118, 134, 135
White, Les, 351
Whitehead, Clay T., 222-227
Wiesel, Elie, 89
Wild Bunch, The, 365
Wild One, The, 49
Williams, Cleveland, 311
Williams, Tennessee, 49, 60-61, 63, 64, 97, 108. See also *A Streetcar Named Desire* and *Night of the Iguana*
Williamson, Bruce, 108-142
Willingham, Calder, 69
Winchell, Walter, 358
Woodstock, 172
Wounded Knee, 52, 86, 91
Wyler, William, 107, 114, 115, 118, 124, 129, 142

X, Malcolm, 79-80

Young Lions, The, 50
Young, Dick, 259
Young, Loretta, 89
Your Show of Shows, 70

Zaire, 318-319, 333
Zanuck, Darryl, 115, 116, 129
Zanuck, Richard, 204
Zimmerman, Robert. *See* Dylan, Bob

WITHDRAWN FROM
Greenville (SC) Co. Library System